WITHDRAWN

WHAT DOESN'T KILL HER

Available from
Christina Dodd
and HQN Books

Cape Charade

Hard to Kill (ebook novella)
Dead Girl Running
Families and Other Enemies (ebook novella)
What Doesn't Kill Her

WHAT DOESN'T KILL HER

CHRISTINA DODD

Mount Laurel Library
100 Walt Whitman Avenue
Mount Laurel, NJ 08054-9539
856-234-7319
www.mountlaurellibrary.org

Recycling programs
for this product may
not exist in your area.

ISBN-13: 978-1-335-00578-6

What Doesn't Kill Her

Copyright © 2019 by Christina Dodd

All rights reserved. Except for use in any review, the reproduction or utilization of this work in whole or in part in any form by any electronic, mechanical or other means, now known or hereafter invented, including xerography, photocopying and recording, or in any information storage or retrieval system, is forbidden without the written permission of the publisher, HQN Books, 22 Adelaide St. West, 40th Floor, Toronto, Ontario M5H 4E3, Canada.

This is a work of fiction. Names, characters, places and incidents are either the product of the author's imagination or are used fictitiously, and any resemblance to actual persons, living or dead, business establishments, events or locales is entirely coincidental.

This edition published by arrangement with Harlequin Books S.A.

For questions and comments about the quality of this book, please contact us at CustomerService@Harlequin.com.

® and TM are trademarks of Harlequin Enterprises Limited or its corporate affiliates. Trademarks indicated with ® are registered in the United States Patent and Trademark Office, the Canadian Intellectual Property Office and in other countries.

www.HQNBooks.com

Printed in U.S.A.

Last year, an organization called Quilts of Honor created, personalized and donated a quilt to be given to my ninety-three-year-old father-in-law, a WWII veteran, in a touching ceremony at the local high school in Emmett, Idaho. The work that went into the quilt and the kindness behind the "Quilted Hugs of Gratitude" gave my father-in-law (and his family) and the other honored veterans a great deal of pleasure. Thank you to the people who created the quilts, to the high school students who showed such respect to the men and women who have served in the military, and of course to the veterans themselves.

If you'd like to request a quilt for a veteran or volunteer to make them, you can contact Quilts of Honor at www.quiltsofhonor.org.

WHAT DOESN'T KILL HER

What doesn't kill her...had better start running.

1

Sleeping Beauty was such a sucker.

You can say stuff in her defense. She was young and unwary. She didn't know much about wicked men and cruel women. No one warned her not to touch sharp objects. But ultimately, everything that happened—the kingdom taking a hundred-year nap, her prince having to hack back thorns and fight a dragon, him having to run up a gazillion stairs, wheezing and gasping, to revive her with true love's kiss—that was all her fault. Everything melts down around her and all she does is lie there, snoozing away.

As I said, a sucker.

Why am I bringing up corny, politically incorrect, completely unfeminist Sleeping Beauty?

Because I am that sucker/loser/fool.

When I was eighteen, I was Cecilia Adams. I met and married the handsome wealthy prince of my dreams, Gregory Lykke, a charming guy twice my age with buckets of money.

You guessed it—he was a wicked man, a monster. When after two years he tried to perform the classic husband/wife murder/suicide, he instead killed himself and my successful, brave and loving cousin.

Her name was Kellen Adams. Remember that.

Did I do the right thing, admit what had happened, start a

campaign to raise social awareness about dragons and abusive husbands?

Nooo. Like the coward I was, I stole my cousin's identity and ran away to the big city. I called myself Kellen Adams, but I was still gullible little Ceecee, easily wounded, unprepared to face the world, falling into homelessness, helplessness and fear.

One day, as I wandered through Philadelphia smelling like garbage and reeking of paranoia, I saw a wicked man dragging a terrified little girl toward his car.

Points to me for recognizing wicked. Getting smarter is a great thing.

Points to me for having all my terror transformed into rage. I saw myself in that helpless child. I attacked the man, helped Annabella Di Luca escape and won the eternal gratitude of the little girl's family.

The Di Lucas were an Italian-American clan, successful, close and loving. Maximilian Di Luca was the girl's uncle. He liked me, despite the garbage smell. He didn't know about the Sleeping Beauty dumb stuff or the cowardice or that I was impersonating my dead cousin. I told him my name was Ceecee, no last name. He apparently saw something in me that he admired, because he didn't ask questions, and he courted me.

Turns out, I *really* liked him. I slept with him. I *loved* him. I dreamed that somehow this romance would be different than my marriage, with some happily-ever-afters and no thorns or dragons. For a few months, it seemed as if I would have my heart's desire.

But lies and omissions have a way of catching up with a person.

I still had Kellen's papers. Without telling me, Max looked through them. He thought I was Kellen Adams, with all her degrees and her credentials. I guess I don't blame him, but when I found out, I panicked and ran away. The wicked man who had tried to kidnap Annabella took his revenge; he tracked me down and shot me in the head.

Here comes the real Sleeping Beauty part.

I didn't die. Instead, I lay in a coma.

The seasons passed. I didn't know.

The world changed. I didn't know.

None of that was important. What mattered was, I didn't realize the changes my body was going through.

Pay attention. That's significant.

After thirteen months, I woke in a hospital. I didn't know where I was or why, and I didn't remember anything about the Di Luca family or Max. I only knew I was afraid. I rose from my bed and fled.

Using Kellen's papers, I joined the US Army.

In the military, in war and peace, I changed from the timid, fragile young woman I had been. I became strong, competent and fierce, a warrior for good.

Yay, me.

Six years later, I was given a medical discharge.

Pay attention again. That's significant, too. The Army liked me, my degrees, my efficiency. They didn't want to discharge me, and I didn't want to go. But the news they gave me wasn't good, so I was out of the service and in need of employment.

I got a job at a Di Luca resort and met Max once more.

He might have been true love's prince, but I didn't remember him. I didn't remember anything about that year when I was lost in the coma's gray fog.

But Max could not let me go, for he knew more about me than I did…

And neither of us knew all the truths.

Hello. I'm Sleeping Beauty.

Not really, though.

★ ★ ★

One secret, one nightmare, one lie. You guess which is which.

—I'm the new mother of a seven-year-old girl.

—I've got the scar of a bullet on my forehead and a medical discharge from the US Army.

—I've misrepresented my identity to the US government.

My name is Kellen Adams…and that's half a lie.

2

Willamette Valley in Oregon
Di Luca Winery

Bark mulch pressed splinters into her bare knees and the palms of her hands. Evergreen azaleas scratched at her face and caught at her hair, and the white blossoms smelled musky as they dropped petals on the ground around her. Spiderwebs brushed her skin and stuck. She could feel the scurry of tiny segmented feet down her back.

Or could she? The feet might be an interesting figment of her imagination, but whether they were or not, she still crawled close to the back wall of the Tuscan-style winery building, under the hedge, and constantly scanned the sunlit lawn beyond.

Retired Army Captain Kellen Adams did not intend to be caught. Not now. Not when she was so close to her goal—that small locked side door that led down the stairs and into the cool quiet wine cellar.

A sudden notion brought her to a halt. Had she brought the key? She groped at her button-up shirt pocket. Yes! The key was there. She breathed a sigh of relief—and her phone whistled, alerting her she had a text.

It was Birdie.

BIRDIE HAYNES:
FEMALE, 5'10", 130 LBS. AMERICAN OF COLOR: HISPANIC, AFRICAN AND FAR EASTERN. MILITARY VETERAN. RECENT WIDOW. LEAD MECHANIC. BIG RAW HANDS, LONG FINGERS. BEAUTIFUL SMILE IN A NOT-BEAUTIFUL FACE. **BEST FRIEND.**

She had sent a photo of her and the film star, Carson Lennex, leaning against a beautiful old car. Birdie had thoughtfully labeled it *1931 Bugatti Royale Berline de Voyager.*

Beautiful! Kellen texted back. Like she cared about the car. It was the smile on Birdie's face that warmed her, and Carson Lennex had put it there. God bless the man. After the death of Birdie's husband, Kellen had feared she would never smile again.

Putting her phone back in her pocket, she started forward again. One meter remaining until she broke into the open. She knew from previous missions this was the tricky part; moving from the relative cover provided by the shrubs and into the open. She made a last reconnaissance, started forward—and a scattering of dirt, moss and debris landed on the last shrub in the line, then tumbled to the ground directly in front of her. In a split second, her brain registered the source.

From three stories straight up, something was falling off the roof of the Italian-style villa.

Kellen flung herself backward, away from the onslaught of baked terra-cotta roof tile that slammed to the ground and shattered like shrapnel. A jagged shard bounced and hit her, pierced her jeans and her hip.

Son of a bitch.

She grabbed the jagged shard and pressed, holding it in place—if she pulled it out, blood would gush—and rolled in agony.

Three stories above, someone screamed.

More debris followed, and more screams.

Still holding the shard, she scrambled out from the shrubbery, backed away from the building and looked up.

A stout man dangled off the roof, feet kicking, screaming

wildly. She'd seen him two days ago, and earlier today, in the tasting room. Thank God for the Rolodex in her brain; she remembered all she had observed about him.

RODERICK BLAKE:
MALE, WHITE, 30-40 YO, BLOND HAIR, OVERWEIGHT, TOURIST GARB WORN BADLY. BRITISH ACCENT. GRIPED ABOUT PAYING THE TASTING FEE. PAID AND OVER-TASTED, PRIMARILY PINOT NOIR. LEERED AT HER AND THE FEMALE TOURIST, WHO HASTILY DEPARTED. LEFT IN A LEXUS, LOUDLY PROCLAIMING HIS INTENTION TO GO TO A GOOD WINERY.

Now he was hanging off the roof.

Guess he didn't find a *good* winery.

She dialed the winery's emergency number. As soon as Rita Grapplee picked up, Kellen said, "I've got a man dangling off the winery roof, back side of the building close to the cellar door." *The cellar door which I almost reached and thank God I stopped to check for the key or I would have been in the wrong place at the wrong time.* A broken piece of terra-cotta tile piercing her hip was better than a six-pound roof tile slamming down on her cranium. She had enough trouble with her head... "I'm going to try to bring him down safely, but get the EMTs here ASAP."

Rita gave a squawk that sounded like, "Whatnotrooffall?"

Kellen guessed they didn't get emergencies like this very often. "Send help!" She hung up.

From above, she heard Roderick yell again. How much had he imbibed that he'd climbed onto the roof of a three-story building and almost fallen to his death?

The original estate on this site had been orchards surrounding an early twentieth-century farmhouse. A few towering cherry trees surrounded the now remodeled farmhouse and provided gracious shade for the well-tended yard. The trees still bore fruit, and workers now picked the fruit and loaded it into buckets strapped to their belts.

She ran into the trees, each step more and more crooked as

the pain in her hip blossomed into agony. A twenty-foot spike ladder leaned against a tree; the picker was all the way up in the top branches. She grabbed the ladder and lifted it. Every muscle in her poor abused hip told her that was a mistake.

In the tree, the picker cursed at her.

"Thank you!" she yelled and headed back to the winery, dragging the long heavy wooden ladder behind her.

The winery building was three stories of classic Tuscan architecture, a jewel that glowed like ancient amber in the setting of Oregon's long lush Willamette Valley. The front of the building faced west toward I-5 and welcomed wine tasters with a long winding drive bordered by tall thin evergreens, rows of grapes growing in purple clumps and a walled garden. On the first floor, in addition to the tasting room, was a special events center, a kitchen tended by an impatient chef and wine storage.

Guests fought to stay in the exorbitantly priced second-and third-story suites, lounge on the balconies, enjoy the cuisine and if they wished, take part in bicycling tours and unique-to-them wine tastings.

Things like a guy falling off the roof did not happen here—or at least, never had before.

Kellen took a second look at the splinter of tile protruding about an inch from her hip. It hurt like a dirty bitch and blood oozed around it, staining the shredded thread of her jeans. The sharp tip had hit bone and backed out a little, so it wasn't scraping her with every movement. *Folks, that's all the good news for tonight.*

Taking a fortifying breath, she lifted the end of the ladder and slammed it against the building close to one of the third-story balconies. The spike sank into the golden-colored stucco, knocking flakes and chunks down on her.

Max was not going to be happy about that.

He wasn't going to be happy about *any* of this.

She hit the rungs hard, climbing fast.

She had to, right? She didn't have forever to save this guy.

She had a chunk of roof tile protruding from her hip, wiggling with every movement. Sooner or later, she was going to faint, and she didn't fancy falling off the ladder eighteen feet up. She made it to the balcony and over the wide Italianate railing.

That was when the situation got hairy. The dumbass on the roof was five feet too far to the left to drop *onto* the balcony. He hung over nothing but thirty feet of air and if he let go, he faced a backbreaking splat landing onto Mother Earth.

Inside the exclusive guest bedroom behind the balcony and through the open screen door, she heard a woman shriek and a man shout. They'd seen her, and she knew whatever else happened, two unhappy guests would be making their complaints known.

Yeah. Bummer. She spoke through the screen. "Throw your pillows and comforter out on the balcony. We're going to save a life here." Looking up, she shouted, "Hey! Roderick! Move to your right!"

A moan of terror answered her.

"One hand at a time. You can do it." Actually, she didn't know if he could. He had a lot of body mass and didn't look as if he had much upper strength. "Hand over hand," she instructed in a calm, encouraging voice.

The idiot wailed and kicked his feet.

She put her hand to her hip and moaned—and climbed up on the top of the concrete railing. It was a foot wide; wide enough for her to stand with no problem—as long as she avoided looking down the three stories to the ground. That got her close enough to grab at him. She didn't, though. She didn't want to startle him. "Roderick, can you look at me? See how close I am to you? Come on, Roderick, a quick glance."

Roderick glanced, his face a combination of blistering red effort and green-white terror.

"Hand over hand," she said. "It's Oregon. We have a lot of

rain. That gutter will hold you. All you have to do is move a little bit."

He looked up at the sky and hung, gasping. Then he shuffled his hands to the right in three quick movements.

"That's great," she said. He'd hardly moved at all. "When you get closer, I can guide you down to the balcony."

"I'll break my legs," he yelled.

"The people inside the room are bringing out pillows and blankets. Aren't you?" She blared the question toward the screen door in her Captain-Adams-in-command voice.

The screen door snapped open and a man in a white terry bathrobe stood there, looking annoyed. "Look," he said.

"You look!" She pointed up.

Had he thought she was kidding? Apparently so, because as soon as he saw Roderick dangling there, he ran inside and came back hauling pillows, sheets, the comforter.

She switched her attention back to Roderick. "Rod, listen."

"Roderick," he snapped.

For a guy hanging by his fingertips, he was pain-in-the-ass arrogant.

"Roderick, we've got you a soft place to land. Come on, shuffle over a little more." Because hand over hand was apparently too much to ask.

He shuffled.

She made approving sounds.

The bathrobe-clad woman in the room stepped out, looked up and shrieked, "He's going to plunge to his death!"

Little Mary Sunshine, that one.

From below, Kellen became aware of a growing mutter, like the rumble of thunder from a faraway storm. "You've got an audience, Roderick," she said. "You've got something to prove. You can do it." She measured with her gaze. "You've got about three feet before you can drop onto the balcony."

He shuffled a little more. "I'll break my legs."

"Maybe." She figured this was the time to be blunt. "But it beats dying of a broken neck. That's a three-story drop below you. Come on! Move it!" She'd moved from Captain Adams to Army drill sergeant, balancing on the top of the broad balcony railing, braying out orders at an unseasoned recruit.

Roderick moved on her command. He shuffled, hung, shuffled, hung. Sweat stained his armpits.

She moved back to allow his flailing legs to get past her.

He got about a foot past her, and his hand slipped.

"He's coming down, get out of the way," she shouted at the people on the balcony.

They leaped back against the building.

He swung his legs.

His foot hit her outstretched hand.

Already overbalanced, she fell sideways onto the balcony. She landed on the comforter; agony slashed at her hip, and she blacked out. Somewhere in the depths of her mind, she had heard a sickening crunch.

He'd made it to the balcony—barely.

Seconds later, she woke to Roderick's screams. He had missed the pillows and the padding. When she looked, she saw blood and shattered white bone sticking out of one leg.

The man on the balcony, the one in the robe, leaned over the edge and heaved.

EMTs burst through the screen door and knelt beside Roderick.

Another man came out behind them.

MAXIMILIAN DI LUCA:
TALL, DARK, HANDSOME, ITALIAN-AMERICAN, BROAD-SHOULDERED FORMER FOOTBALL PLAYER WITH A SCOWL, WINERY OWNER. FORMER (PERHAPS FUTURE?) LOVER. SCOWLING, CLEARLY FURIOUS.

Max knelt beside her, grasped her hand, looked into her eyes. "Tell me the truth—how badly are you hurt?"

"I'm not dying," she hastily assured him.

He closed his eyes, cradled her fingers against his chest, then opened his eyes and roared, "You couldn't have called me directly? You called Rita instead? You couldn't have waited for me to assist?"

Wow. For a moment, he looked as if he cared. "He was going to fall!"

"You're bloody and you've got something sticking out of your hip. What the hell have you done?" Apparently it was a rhetorical question, because he yelled over the railing, "I need more EMTs up here!"

"I'm okay," she said.

"So's he, except for the compound fractures of his tibia!" Max put his hand toward the shard of roof tile sticking out of her side.

She flinched away. "Don't! If you pull it out—"

"You'll bleed to death. Yeah, I understand."

Roderick must have gotten enough morphine in his system, because his screams quieted to the whining of the world's largest mosquito.

Max gestured at the EMTs attending Roderick, and one rose, ready to attend Kellen.

Then, from the top of the spike ladder, at the outside edge of the balcony, a chirpy sunny childish voice said, "Mommy, that was awesome. You're like Warrior Woman. That makes me Warrior Girl. I'm going to be Warrior Girl for Halloween. What are you going to be?"

RAE DI LUCA:
FEMALE, 7 YO, MIXED ITALIAN/NATIVE AMERICAN/ANGLO ANCESTRY. BLONDE, BROWN-EYED, TALL FOR HER AGE, FRONT TEETH TOO BIG FOR HER FACE, INTELLIGENT, RELENTLESSLY CHEERFUL, TALKS LOUDLY AND CONSTANTLY. PREFERRED APPAREL: PINK TUTUS, PINK TIGHTS, PINK T-SHIRTS WITH GLITTERY EMBOSSED WIDE-EYED OWLS, ANKLE-HIGH PINK FUZZY BOOTS. PREFERRED MENU: PEANUT BUTTER, CHEESE STICKS, YOGURT, ANYTHING COVERED IN BALSAMIC VINEGAR. HATES GOLDFISH CRACKERS.

Max stood and swiftly, efficiently grabbed their daughter off the top of the ladder. In his fierce father voice, he asked, "What have I told you about climbing trees and tall ladders? Haven't I told you no?"

"Mommy did it!" Rae said.

Kellen intercepted a livid glare from Max and judged it a good time to pass out cold.

So she did.

3

By some accident of nature, probably that she had needed less triage than Roderick, Kellen's ambulance got to the hospital first. Some cute young guys wheeled her through the ER entrance—they probably weren't any younger than her, but really, they were cute, for all the good that did her—and down the hall to a room occupied by tall female in a white coat:

DR. CHERYL BRUNDAGE:
FEMALE, INDIAN ANCESTRY, 45, 6', 160 LBS. BROWN EYES, HEAVY BAGS BENEATH, BROWN SKIN, BROWN HAIR WITH GRAY STRANDS. SITTING ON A TALL STOOL, FEET PROPPED ON ONE ANOTHER, LEANING AGAINST THE WALL. WEARY.

Dr. Brundage took one look at the roof tile protruding from Kellen's hip. Her eyes lit up, she stood, and in a booming voice, she said, "We don't usually get good stuff like this in here. Usually it's car wrecks and home canning accidents. Now this—this is something interesting."

"Thanks," Kellen muttered. "I do my best."

With an air of efficient competence, Dr. Brundage helped transfer Kellen off the stretcher and onto the table beneath the overhead light. She cut the jeans off Kellen's hip. "How'd you do it?"

The adrenaline that had kept Kellen going through the rescue attempt had faded, and she couldn't come close to meeting the doctor's enthusiasm. "Tile fell off the roof. Broke. Got me."

"I'll say!" The doctor glanced up. "Max, this happen at your place?"

"Yes." He stood in the door, looking visibly displeased.

"You taking care of the insurance?"

"Yes."

"Great. Don't worry about it. Shouldn't cost you too much. Unless she decides to sue." Dr. Brundage peered at Kellen. "She doesn't look like the type."

"I won't sue," Kellen said.

"There you go, Max. Now go fill out the forms so I can work on my patient."

"Right," Max snapped back and headed toward the waiting room.

He didn't even ask Kellen how she was feeling. She guessed right now he considered her more trouble than she was worth. "Maybe that's true, but I did save the guy's life." She blinked at the doctor's face. "Know what I mean?"

"Not really, but I am glad you saved someone's life." Dr. Brundage's voice changed. "Hi, Rae, how are you? Any more trouble with shutting your finger in the car door?"

Rae's high piping seven-year-old voice said, "I only shut my finger in once. It hurt. I won't do it again."

"Max needs to take her with him," Kellen said.

"She's fine," Dr. Brundage assured her. "We're good friends. Aren't we, Rae?"

Kellen heard the sound of a stool scraping across the linoleum toward her.

"I like you except when you stick me with needles." Rae's voice got closer. She was the stool scraper. "Know what? I climbed the ladder all the way to the top, just like my mommy."

In a normal voice, Dr. Brundage said to Kellen, "This is

going to hurt a little," and plunged a hypodermic needle about the size of a Craftsman screwdriver into her hip. In a return to that cajoling kid-talk voice, Dr. Brundage asked Rae, "Who's your mommy?"

"She is!"

Kellen didn't have to look to know Rae was pointing at the examining table.

Dr. Brundage's voice changed to sharply inquisitive. "This is your mommy?"

"It's a long story," Kellen said. "Not interesting at all."

"I beg to differ!" Kellen suspected Dr. Brundage always said what she thought.

Out in the corridor, they heard a scuffle: shouting and swearing. "What's going on out there?" Dr. Brundage asked.

"Roderick Blake has arrived," Kellen said.

"My mommy saved that man's life," Rae confided.

"Did she? Sounds like he didn't appreciate it," Dr. Brundage said.

Impatient voices murmured around Roderick's wildly abusive language.

"We love getting those kinds of guys into Emergency." Dr. Brundage looked closely at Kellen. "How's your pain on a level from one to ten?"

"About eight. Seven. Six..." Kellen's voice slurred as her grip on reality slipped. "What did you give me?"

"The good stuff." Dr. Brundage yelled, "Brenda, I need you! We've got some irrigation and sewing to do in here."

The sound of Roderick's yelling faded, followed by an indistinct swell of indignation from the hospital staff as those who could hurried away.

In her cajole-a-kid voice, Dr. Brundage said, "Honey, we're going to fix your mommy now, so you need to go find your daddy."

"I want to stay! My mommy is ThunderBoomer."

"ThunderBoomer?" Kellen and Dr. Brundage said at the same time.

"What happened to Warrior Woman?" Kellen asked.

"No, you can't be Warrior Woman, because I'm Lightning-Blast."

"ThunderBoomer sounds like I have a flatulence problem," Kellen complained.

Dr. Brundage snorted and laughed—and snorted. Then she sobered and with a grim intensity, said, "Rae, your mommy's going to spout a lot of blood."

"Oo. No. Gross." Without hesitation, Rae abandoned ThunderBoomer. The stool scraped away. From the door, her piping voice admonished, "Mommy, you be good and don't cry too much."

"More likely I'll dance." Kellen wasn't sure the words came out right, she was slurring so much.

"Brenda's my nurse," Dr. Brundage said. "Once she gets in here, we'll have you cleaned up in no time. This is going to hurt a little. I'm removing the tile."

She wasn't finished speaking before she'd done it.

Bright pain spots on a black humming background. How was it possible to hurt so much coming out when it hurt so much being in there?

"You going to toss your cookies?" Dr. Brundage asked.

Kellen folded her lips tightly over her nausea and shook her head.

"That's official doctor talk," Dr. Brundage informed her. "This is more official doctor talk. I'm going to irrigate the wound now. With saline. It's going to sting."

In the hallway outside the room, Kellen heard a woman say, "Hi, honey, how are you? Have you fallen out of a tree and scared your daddy again?"

"Hi, Nurse Brenda. No way, I haven't fallen out, and Daddy doesn't know about the walnut tree, so it's okay."

"The walnut tree?" Brenda asked.

"I made a tree house."

Kellen squeezed her eyes shut, then opened them wide. A tree house? Rae had made a tree house? The kid was seven. How could she make a tree house?

"How did you make a tree house?" Brenda must be channeling Kellen.

"I got the boards from the, um, place where Daddy's new shed is getting built."

"You stole the boards?" Brenda sounded surprised and maybe a little admiring.

"No! Stealing is against the law. I took boards from the scrap pile." In a confidential tone, Rae said, "That's another way of saying the garbage dump."

"Daddy doesn't know you confiscated those boards, does he?" Brenda asked.

"No way." Rae sounded absolutely unrepentant. "You know what? My mommy's in there *bleeding.*"

"Is she?" Brenda sounded interested and a little skeptical. "Who's your mommy?"

"My mommy is a superhero. She's secretly ThunderBoomer. See, she got shot in the head by a bad man."

Kellen felt Dr. Brundage brush the bangs off her forehead.

Dr. Brundage made a "hmm" sound as she revealed the round red scar. She didn't call Brenda in, either, but started irrigating.

"Mommy was in comma."

"A comma?" Brenda sounded as if she was torn between amusement and a vast captivated interest.

"She couldn't wake up," Rae explained.

"That's not good."

"It was bad." Rae sounded like she was telling a horror story. "Because she was pregnant with me and she didn't know it."

"That's really not good," Brenda agreed.

"She had me early." Rae's voice got gloomy. "My daddy and

my grandma took care of me, and they were sad. Then one day, my mommy woke from her comma."

"Coma… Never mind. What happened?" Brenda sounded eager.

Dr. Brundage was clearly riveted, too, because she pulled up a stool, said in a quick low voice, "I'm stitching now," and went to work.

Lucky for them both Rae had such a piercing voice.

"She woke up and…?" Brenda's voice trailed off invitingly.

"She didn't remember she had a little baby girl. She didn't remember my daddy. She didn't know where she was. So she got up and got dressed and left the hospital, and we didn't know where she was!"

"Wow. That's quite a story." Brenda sounded as if she wasn't sure she believed it. Sensible woman.

"Don't you want to know where she was?" Rae asked.

"Sure!"

"She joined the Army. She got to be a captain. She got shot and blown up and stuff. That's how she got to be ThunderFlash."

"I thought she was ThunderBoomer," Brenda said.

"I haven't decided."

"Makes total sense."

Rae continued, "One day she came back from the war and she still didn't remember."

The stitches pulled and tugged at Kellen's hip. She could hear Rae's voice grow uncertain.

"She went to work at Yearning Sands Resort for Annie and Leo—they're my great-great-aunt and uncle, because I like them a lot and they're great. Mommy met my daddy and she saved people's lives and she kind of remembered and she almost got killed and then I told her she was my mommy." Rae's voice wavered more and more.

"And then?"

"I *think* she believed me."

Oh, God. Kellen was such a bad mother. Maybe a bad person. She had a daughter, a daughter she hadn't known, and sure, she was trying to be a mother now. But it was tough. She didn't know much, but she knew she wasn't supposed to make Rae uncertain and scared. Mothers were supposed to be smart. She was supposed to be right. She was supposed to know what she was doing—and she didn't know anything!

She had no instincts.

She was a bad mother.

"Stop worrying about it. No mother knows what she's doing." Dr. Brundage was reading her mind.

Or maybe Kellen was thinking out loud.

Dr. Brundage continued, "I had my daughter when I was in high school, I wouldn't give her up to a good family, and I did everything wrong. But she's a good kid, and she's in premed. Rae's a good kid, too. She'll be okay."

Out in the corridor, Max's voice, wry and amused. "Honey, are you telling the whole hospital our family secrets?"

"No, Daddy, only about Mommy and me and you."

"That'll do it," Max said. "Hi, Brenda."

His tone must have made the elusive Brenda nervous, because she suddenly appeared at Kellen's bedside. "I'm here, Doctor."

Outside the door, Max said, "Grandma has arrived. She's in the waiting room, and she's going to the cafeteria."

Kellen heard the steady thump-thump of Rae's heels against the linoleum. "I want ice cream!"

"You'll have to talk to Grandma about that," Max said.

"Ice cream!"

"*Don't* tell her I said you could." Max could get quite a stern tone to his voice. "That would be lying!"

"Okay..." Rae's enthusiasm audibly waned, and the sound of her boots faded in the distance.

Max stepped through the door.

Dr. Brundage finished her sutures, pulled off her gloves and stepped back to let Brenda cover the wound. "Who's your next of kin?" she asked Kellen.

"I guess… Max. Why?" Kellen asked warily.

"You're going to need care. Are you going home with him?"

"Yes," Max said.

Dr. Brundage looked at Kellen for confirmation.

"Yes," Kellen said.

"Good. Listen up, you two." Dr. Brundage stared into Kellen's eyes. "Although with the drugs I put into you, I don't think you'll remember. I'm keeping you here overnight. I'm not happy about the look of this puncture. We never want any kind of puncture with an unsterile object. I think we can safely say the roof tile was not sterile. We're going to do a course of intravenous antibiotics. Then we'll send you home with instructions and pain pills and—"

"I want to see the bitch!" In the corridor, Roderick's belligerent voice got louder again. "Let me see the bitch. I want to see her now!"

Dr. Brundage looked up in annoyance. "Shut that door," she said to Max.

But a harried-looking intern stuck his head in. "Dr. Brundage, I'm sorry. We're transporting this guy to Portland for surgery, and he's throwing a fit. He wants to speak to your patient."

Max clearly didn't give a damn. "Drug him!"

"We can't give him any more drugs. He's had the limit and he's still yelling." The intern turned his head back toward the continued shouting, then looked at Kellen. "Is it possible…?"

"No, it is not possible!" Dr. Brundage said.

The synapses in Kellen's brain flashed her an urgent dispatch. "I'll see him. I want to see him." Because what message was so important to a guy with a compound fracture that he stayed conscious to say it?

Dr. Brundage sighed. "All right. Is she ready to be transported to a room?"

"Yes, doctor." Brenda removed the brakes from the bed and Dr. Brundage helped her wheeled it toward the door. They maneuvered Kellen into the corridor and placed her so her head was even with Roderick's.

What few strands of hair the guy had were stuck together with blood and perspiration. His skin was sweaty pale green. Both legs were wrapped and elevated. Clearly, despite whatever drugs they had given him, he was in agony. Yet his bulging blue eyes narrowed on Kellen. He rolled onto his shoulder toward her. His hand shot out and grabbed her neck, and he spoke.

Max struck his fingers away.

Dr. Brundage shouted, "Get him out!"

The staff shoved him toward the door.

But Kellen had heard him loud and clear. As he stared into her eyes and squeezed her throat, he had clearly said, "Run, bitch."

4

The resulting infection kept Kellen in the hospital for an extra two days and by the time Max came to get her, she had read the first four books in the Mercy Thompson series, laughed herself silly with her three best Army friends—Birdie and Temo and Adrian, who drove down from Yearning Sands Resort to visit—listened every afternoon to Rae's description of the enthralling happenings at day camp and was locked in a battle of wills with Dr. Brundage, who wanted her to stay another day.

When Kellen finally won, Dr. Brundage turned to Max and said, "You make sure she stays in bed for another three days at the least." She turned back to Kellen. "Do *not* work out."

She lectured as if Kellen liked to exercise, when in fact Kellen's goal was to be in shape to defend herself. Against what, she didn't know, but having some guy grab her by the throat and say, "Run, bitch," sent a chill down her spine.

Yes, Roderick was probably drunk and crazy. He'd climbed onto the winery roof, for the love of God. When he grabbed her, he had been on enough drugs to send a normal person to paradise. Telling her to run made no sense, and being so hostile made no sense, either. It was as if he was warning her of some impending doom, when in fact her life had never been so boring. Or peaceful. Whatever.

Dr. Brundage finished her lecture with, "A few days off won't kill you."

"Probably not," Kellen muttered.

"Don't let her do anything," Dr. Brundage ordered Max and handed him a page of instructions.

He read through the list. "I have no control over any of the women in my life, including you, Brundage."

"Fair enough." Dr. Brundage helped Kellen into a wheelchair. "Kellen, Brenda will be in to push you to the doors. Try not to do anything stupid at least before you leave the hospital grounds."

"I haven't done anything stupid at all," Kellen said.

Max and Dr. Brundage snorted in unison.

Kellen wanted to smack them both, but getting in the wheelchair had exhausted her, and she slept until Max pulled to a stop in front of the sprawling two-story farmhouse.

Max's home had been built in 1913 for a large family, added onto throughout the past century and now blended architectural styles with a relaxed comfort. In 1971, the Di Luca family had recognized the wine-producing potential of the Willamette Valley and acquired the land with the intention of growing primarily pinot noir. Grapes replaced orchards. Their venture had been successful, their wines expanded to include traditional Italian varietals, and when Max had needed a place to bring his baby and forget his lost love, he had brought Rae and his mother, Verona, to a home that had been, according to her, a wreck dedicated to the survival of the fittest.

Being a woman of exceptional character, Verona had not only taken care of Max and the child, she had also refurbished the home. The kitchen was modern, the plumbing and electricity were all new and worked reliably, the wooden floors had been refinished, the furniture invited a person to lounge and enjoy; all that, and it retained hints of its farmhouse roots.

Now Verona stood on the steps of the wide porch, smiling coolly, as Max helped Kellen out of the passenger seat.

Rae, on the other hand, was thrilled to have her mother back and hopped around so much she put exhausted pleased tears in Kellen's eyes.

Max fended off their daughter, sent her away and put Kellen to bed in the main floor master bedroom—Max's bedroom.

She was trembling with weakness. Max handed her a pain pill and a glass of water; her hands shook so much she dropped the pill and the glass rattled against her teeth.

He sat down on the bed and helped her swallow the pill and drink the water.

That was embarrassing. Yes, they'd once been lovers. Yes, they'd created a child. But she remembered only bits and pieces of her time with him, and she didn't remember anything about the thirteen months in a coma. For her, everything about living in Max's house was awkward, and even more awkward was her relationship with Max. Were they supposed to become lovers again? Could they be friends with a child? Did Max even want her anymore? Sometimes she knew he did, but sometimes he looked at her as if she was a stranger he didn't quite like.

"I'm not the person I used to be," she blurted. "Before."

"No, you're not. You're not the Ceecee I knew in Pennsylvania who was frail and fragile and needed someone to care for her. You're tough."

It sounded like a critique. "I like being tough." *No one can hurt me when I'm tough.*

"You're a good role model for our daughter."

There. He hadn't said he liked her the way she was now. Which meant he didn't, and she guessed that answered the question about them becoming lovers.

That was fine. She didn't want to be lovers, either. Look at the mess she'd made of everyone's lives last time she slept with him: a shot to the cranium, a baby her body sheltered, nurtured and produced while she hovered between life and death, a year forgotten. Better to stay cool and distant, be friends, like civil divorced parents of the same child.

Yes. That was perfect.

Too bad she remembered…things. Warm hands, gentle caresses. Brown eyes, heated glances. A man's body and her body, and nights without end… For the first time since she'd moved into his home, Kellen allowed herself that deep rare upsweep of sexual arousal Max could so easily create.

Not the time to remember all that! Not here, not now! Focus!

She didn't sound breathless *at all* as she said, "I don't know that you approve of our daughter wanting to be like me."

"It would be *good* if you could explain to her *in a way she understands* why she needs training before she behaves like LightningBlast." His emphasis echoed with sarcasm.

"Me explain it to her?" Kellen laughed, then grabbed her stitches and waited for the pain to subside. "She never listens."

"You'd be surprised. She hears everything and that little mind is quick and nimble." He leaned forward and looked into Kellen's eyes, not like a lover, but like a medical professional accessing her condition. "This possibly isn't the time, but we have to talk and the pain pills are cracking that clamshell you keep so tightly closed."

"Talk? About personal stuff?" *Oh, no.*

"You sound like me when my sisters want to discuss emotions and feelings. I wonder if I'm as annoying as you are?"

She supposed she should be crushed instead of wanting to smack him. "What can be so important that it can't wait?"

"Why were you crawling through the shrubs?"

"Um." Busted! "What?"

"That day you rescued Roderick Blake, why were you crawling through the azalea hedge?"

She wet her lips. Obviously, a good plan, waiting until the pain pill took effect to interrogate her, and one she had been trained by the Army to circumvent.

She could lie or pretend not to understand.

But two things—they might not be lovers, but they were in a relationship; they were the parents of a child, and deceit wasn't a good option. If he asked why she'd been crawling in the shrubs, he probably had unassailable evidence that she had. "Obviously, my skulking skills aren't all I hoped."

"My mother saw you." He gestured out the window.

Yes, the back of the winery was clearly visible from the house, and his mother did not like Kellen. "Of course she did."

"Three days in a row."

Kellen took a long breath.

He didn't wait. "You were hiding from Rae."

She let out the breath with a whoosh.

"She comes home from school, excited to tell her new mommy about her day, you listen for a half hour, send her for a snack and you sneak away."

"She's a lovely child." Kellen meant it.

He spoke softly, "But she's not your child."

"I know she is!" Really, she did.

"You know it in your mind. You don't know it in your heart."

What kind of man said this stuff? "She's a nice little girl."

"She *is* a nice little girl." He leaned back, away from her, and wrapped his hands around one knee, and his dark eyes shone with anger.

Kellen suspected at least some of it was directed at her.

He looked at her. "What I'm trying to say is—you don't love Rae."

"I like her."

"You're her mother, but to you, she's merely someone's nice child."

Kellen hadn't understood before. Now she began to glimpse the depth of the tragedy being played out in this home.

Max hadn't dreamed it was possible for her to return, and

when he saw her again, he thought, or hoped, the two of them could once again fall in love.

But Rae stood between them.

They couldn't create a family because Kellen didn't feel the depth of emotion for Rae a mother would feel. Maybe if she hadn't been in the military... Maybe if she hadn't been so careful to do no more than form friendships... "I don't know what to say. I wish—"

"I wish, too. I had hoped that time and exposure would begin to form a love between you, but if you're crawling through bushes to get away from her, that's not working."

Kellen leaked tears. She wiped them off on her sleeves. In a tiny voice, she asked, "Do you want me to go?"

"No! No, I'm not saying that."

"What *do* you want? I am trying. I have been trying. I simply don't know how to form that kind of bond with her. With any child." When she looked at Rae, when she felt twinges of affection, she was transported to that terrible moment in Afghanistan when—

The smell of charred wood and burned flesh. A metal coil melted in the dirt and the knowledge of young lives ended too soon.

He sensed nothing of her terrible memories; instead, he smiled as if bitterly amused. "That's part of the problem. If you'd hidden in a day care instead of the Army, we'd have somewhere to start. But when Rae hugs you, you flinch."

There weren't enough pain relievers in the world to get Kellen through this conversation without anguish. "It's not that I don't want to be part of Rae's life. I do. But I have never loved anyone without grief." *God. Had she really said that?*

He focused on her so sharply she would have scampered backward if she could move. As it was, she could only stare back and wish she could pass out.

No such luck.

He leaned forward, put his hands on either side of her hips

and spoke right into her face. "I'd tell you not to worry about the pain, but that would be lying. Being a father is the most excruciating torture I've ever endured, and that includes losing you. Being a parent is worrying every time Rae leaves my sight. I want to wrap her in Bubble Wrap, and instead, when she falls out of a tree and splits her chin open, I have to tell her to shake it off and admire her stitches. When she gets bullied, I hurt for her, and I want to step up and tell that little girl to knock it off or give her and her mother a good thump on the head. Instead, I have to read up on techniques to handle bullies and discuss them with Rae. I worry about her math skills, her reading skills. When she's five minutes late, I remember how kind she is and hope to God some pervert doesn't tell her he needs help, because no matter how clearly I tell her she has to be careful with strangers, I know she would go to help a stranger with a good story and I'll never see her again."

"Dear God." Kellen pressed her knuckles to her stomach.

Max continued, "She's going to get older, she's going to go through adolescence and be miserable, because that's what adolescence is. She'll have pimples and braces. She'll date the wrong guy. She'll be hurt every day and she won't admit it to me. I'll do the wrong thing. Say the wrong thing. I know these are the good times. I know it's going to get worse."

Kellen was horrified. "Why does anybody want to be a parent?"

He thought about it, grinned. "Well. When I was sleeping with you, becoming a parent was the last thing on my mind."

Kellen remembered only fragments of the times she'd spent with him, but somehow the moments in his bed were imprinted on her mind; the hours when he lingered over body, the deep kisses that tasted of wine and passion, the weight of his body covering hers, the way he taught her to pleasure him. She hadn't brought out those memories, but now, here they were, dusky with sunset and bright with sunrise. "Right," she whispered.

He seemed unaware, sounded matter-of-fact. "But I did always want to be a father. Didn't you ever want to be a mother?"

"Yes, but I thought it was impossible and..."

"And?"

She rocked back and forth, caught herself and stopped the betraying gesture. "I didn't think I was fit."

"Why not?"

"I did such a lousy job of...of becoming an adult. Of picking a partner." She was skittering around a truth she didn't want to discuss, not with Max. Not with anybody. She had a victim's mentality. Somehow, even now, she felt guilty about her husband's abuse. "While I was living on the streets, I almost got killed and raped. I was such a disaster." She didn't remember over a year of her life. Why did she have to remember all the bad stuff?

"While you were in a coma, I kept your papers in a locker close to you, in your hospital room. You had been so protective of those papers. They'd seemed to give you a sense of safety. That turned out to be not so smart, since when you woke, you got dressed, took them and joined the Army." He was getting to the meat of the matter. "But in the meantime, I used them to research you and your family."

Just like that, everything got complicated. "You did? Of course you would. That's fair."

"Your cousin was Cecilia, married to Gregory Lykke, and they were involved in an infamous murder/suicide."

Kellen breathed slowly, trying to slow the spinning of her head. "That's right."

"You're Kellen, Cecilia's cousin, and you witnessed the deaths. The police wanted you for questioning." Max spoke slowly, as if trying to find the right path through a minefield of personal information.

"That's right, too."

"When I met you, you told me your name was Ceecee."

She wet her lips. Ceecee, her childhood name, short for Cecilia.

He tapped his blunt fingers on the blankets and watched them. "I suppose you didn't want to talk to the police? You were keeping a low profile?"

"Yes." That made sense. It was even true.

He nodded, but he stared up at her as if he didn't believe or didn't understand or something equally uncomfortable. "You look very much like your cousin Cecilia."

"We were like sisters. When we were kids, sometimes people couldn't tell Kellen and Cecilia apart." There! That was completely true.

"Okay. Thanks for clearing that up." Still, he tapped his fingers. "You were telling me why you didn't think you were fit to have a child."

"All those things I said!" This felt like an interrogation with too many questions and not enough answers. "And, and, I wasn't ready to have a child."

"My mother says no one's ever ready to have a child." He stopped tapping. "I can't argue with that."

"Maybe not, but you're an awfully good father." Kellen meant it, too. He was so giving of his time, so patient, so openly affectionate.

"Thank you. I make terrible mistakes all the time. If you could love Rae, you'd understand what real guilt is. Children make you guilty for every mistake, every cross word—and they don't even try. Rae loves me no matter what." He leaned back, shoved his hands through his hair. "She loves you, too."

"Even though I don't deserve it."

He sighed. "*Deserve* is not in her vocabulary. You're her mother. Her whole life, I've told her about you, and to find you at last! She's thrilled. Yes, she loves you."

"But I haven't bonded with her."

"No." He sounded sad. "It's not your fault."

"What's the solution?" she asked.

"When…if we're convinced this isn't going to work, we can do things differently. She can live with me. You can visit."

Kellen wanted to whimper so badly it almost seemed as if she heard a whimper.

Max continued, "She knows, of course, most mommies and daddies don't live this way, but the divorced ones do, and it's not until she's older that she will realize that you, perhaps, are not ThunderBoomer." He walked toward the door.

Tears leaked from beneath Kellen's closed lids. She turned on her side, pressed her face into the pillow and thought out loud. "It's not so much that I'm stifled by Rae, or by domesticity. I need a task, a focus, to help me sort out my new role." She took a quivering breath. "I need a job."

Behind her, she heard the door open. A pause. Then it shut.

He was gone, along with any hope she had of ever having a family. She wanted to cry, she wanted to be awash in tears, but she couldn't keep awake. She slept.

And came awake on the sound of her door closing again. Her eyes were wide, her ears strained to hear. But there was no further sound, and as she drifted to sleep once more, she decided she must have been mistaken before.

That second time must have been Max leaving the room.

When Kellen woke the next morning, on the foot of her bed she found a drawing of Daddy, ThunderBoomer and Lightning-Blast. It was signed by Rae. Kellen held it and smiled. Max really had raised a cute, kind kid. Good for him.

5

The doctors and nurses had an attitude that grated on Roderick. They were nothing but glorified servants, but the way they behaved, they thought they were his masters. He told them he was in pain, and they told him he had had as much morphine as he was allowed. He couldn't have more for another half hour. No matter how he yelled and cursed, they allowed him no more.

After the first day, they put him in a soundproof room and left him alone. The nurses only answered his call button once an hour. Every half hour, he got a nurse's aide. The biggest outrage—he got a doctor once a goddamn day, and half the time it was a female and sometimes not even white. If he could, he would kick their asses, but the fall had shattered his legs and after the surgeries, he was in traction. He couldn't move, he was ignored, and he was in pain.

He wanted drugs. *Now.* If he couldn't have morphine, then a pain patch, and Oxycontin.

He twisted the self-medication button, trying to break it open and bring the rest of the morphine into his system, then punched the nurse's call button once, twice, three times, four times, five...

Persistence finally produced results. A male nurse came in, one Roderick didn't recognize. He wore a surgical mask. Everybody who came in wore a mask; the hospital was terrified

Roderick's compound fracture would result in infection and he assured them he would sue if it did.

The nurse stopped by the bed. "What can I do for you, Mr. Blake?"

"I want pain reliever. I want more morphine. I want Oxy-contin. I want it all. I'm in pain here and no one in this god-damn place cares."

"That's true. No one does care. You've made yourself so obnoxious everyone will be glad to see you die." The nurse fiddled with the morphine drip.

Roderick had put up with a lot of insolence since he'd come to this godforsaken country, but this was the worst. "You impertinent nobody. I'm not going to die! I'm going get out of here and sue the hospital and you—"

The nurse released a stream of morphine into his system. "No, you're definitely going to die." He pulled his mask down.

Roderick was in such a froth of rage, he didn't notice the man's features. He screamed, "Cover your face. You're worthless. You're incompetent!" Then the morphine hit. The pain was suddenly a minor annoyance, something to be contemplated from a distance. "That's better," he grunted and looked up at the nurse.

Recognition dawned.

"I expected better of you," the nurse said. "You assured me you could watch her and kill her and make it look like an accident. You assured me you were the best."

Roderick was aware his senses were rolling away on a tide of morphine, that he should be alarmed. But he wasn't. "Don't kill me."

"You should have thought about that before you failed."

"I never failed before." Roderick slurred his words.

"Once was all it took."

Roderick saw the nurse's cold implacability. His hand moved in slow motion to push the call button.

The male nurse watched with coldly cynical encouragement. "Push it all you want. You've used up their goodwill. Not that they ever had any toward you."

Roderick was dying. He knew he was dying. He thrashed. He tried to scream, but a huge weight rested on his chest. Morphine. Morphine depressed the respiratory system. He knew this. He'd killed with it before.

The nurse watched the life fade and blink out from Roderick's eyes. "It would have been so much easier if you'd done your job. Now—it's on to plan B." He pulled up the mask and left.

6

Three weeks later, Kellen kicked at the boxing bag in the gym. One side kick, two side kicks, slow and easy. These movements were half balance and half making sure she warmed up the muscles in her hip and tore nothing loose in the healing tendons and veins. They were nothing like her usual rigorous workout and ferocious fighting attitude. She believed Dr. Brundage and her warnings; this healing would take time.

Next to her, Rae kicked at the bag, too, imitating Kellen's reach and her speed, if not her strength.

Kellen grinned at the intensity of the child's concentration. Rae so badly wanted to be Kellen. Flattering as hell—and worrisome. After Max's lecture, Kellen was very, very worried.

The door opened.

Max stepped in. "Rae, your grandma's looking for you. It's time to get ready to go to day camp."

Kellen stopped kicking and made conversation with the child. Her child. "What are you doing at camp today?"

"We practice our play. We have Bible study. We swim in the lake. The water's cold. We have lunch in the tree house. We go down on the zip line. We get to buy one snack candy… I'm getting coffee brownie bites."

"Coffee brownie bites?" Kellen was horrified.

"They make my lips vibrate." Rae's eyes got wide with awe.

"What are you going to do now, Mommy?" Unlike Kellen, there was real interest behind her question.

"When I finish kicking the bag, I'm going to do a yoga routine. It's good for stretching and balance, it includes meditation, and it will help me heal."

"I like yoga! Can we do yoga now?"

Verona Di Luca stuck her head in. "Rae, come on. You'll be late!"

"We can't do yoga if you're going to camp." Kellen could not imagine Rae sitting still long enough to meditate.

"We can do it later!" Rae flung her arms around Kellen and kissed her.

Kellen patted her head.

Rae flung her arms around Max and kissed him.

He picked her up and smooched her neck, gave her a big hug and a pat on the behind as she ran from the room.

That was the problem in a nutshell. Kellen didn't feel compelled to hug and love on Rae, and she didn't meet Max's gaze while he judged her. "Coffee brownie bites?" Kellen asked. "Does that kid need more energy?"

He could, and did, ignore her. "I've found you a job."

She blinked. "You did?"

"You said you wanted one."

So he had heard her sleepy murmur. "Great. Here at the winery?" Because as she'd learned when she worked at Yearning Sands Resort, a career in the Army had not prepared her to work well with the public.

"No. I called Uncle Leo and Aunt Annie—"

Kellen's heart jumped. For her, in the months she had lived at Yearning Sands, the place had become her home. She had brought her military friends to be employed there, and rejoiced when they found their homes there, also. She had enjoyed supervising the huge resort, and more important, there was something about the wild rugged coast that appealed to her in a way that the tamed land of the Willamette Valley could not match.

But Max continued, "Aunt Annie said Brooks called. He was searching for you."

"Nils Brooks?"

"He is the only Brooks we know, isn't he?"

"Yes."

"Good. One is more than enough."

Awkward.

Nils Brooks was the top dog at the newly re-formed government agency Monuments, Fine Arts and Archives. In World War II, the MFAA had been formed to rescue and restore the art stolen by the Nazis. Art historians and experts had saved towering cathedrals, priceless paintings, irreplaceable books… but so much more had been lost when, in their retreat, the Nazis burned everything in their possession.

After the war, the MFAA had been disbanded, and only recently through Nils's efforts been revived to halt the flow of contraband antiquities that were financing the world's terrorists.

Nils Brooks was understaffed, underpaid and a sneaky lying bastard who the previous winter had almost got himself—and Kellen—killed tracking down the notorious serial killer and smuggler Mara Philippi, aka the Librarian. Kellen had saved Nils, Max had saved Kellen, and Max cordially hated Nils for dragging Kellen into her near encounter with death, and for leading Max to believe Kellen was romantically and passionately involved with Nils.

Max might not be sleeping with her, but he didn't want someone else to, either.

So having Max drop Nils's name was both unexpected and required delicate handling. "What's up with Nils?"

"He's got a problem with a shipment."

Patiently, she asked, "What kind of problem? What kind of shipment?"

"There's some kind of head coming this way."

"A head?"

"A mummy's head. Or something. There's something about an authentication and a recluse and protection. But the upshot is, somehow the head made it to the airport, got put on the conveyer and is in baggage on the airplane."

"The head is boxed up?"

"It's in a suitcase. Nils suspects someone intends to lift the head—as it were—and he wants security for it when it lands in Portland."

"Let me see if I'm following this. The head is currently on an airplane flying to Portland. It needs to go to a restorer who is…where?"

"Somewhere in the Olympic Mountains. He's the recluse. He's going to authenticate the head. Or not."

She wasn't confused, exactly, but she still wanted clarification. "Nils wants me to go and get the head and deliver it to this guy?"

"That's about the sum of it."

"Did you tell Nils I was recently injured?"

"Yes. He said, 'What? Again?'"

"God forbid he should inquire what happened or if I was all right!"

"That's what I told him, but he said if you were dead I would have led with that."

"What a prick." She wasn't sure she was talking about Nils.

Max didn't seem worried. "I've thought so all along. Nils wears a tie to keep the foreskin from flipping over his head."

She gave a gasp of laughter, then put her hand to her hip. Apparently she could do kicks, but laughter was out.

Max continued, "Not the point, though. You're merely backup. He has a specialized moving firm coming to get the head from baggage claim. Apparently, these guys move precious objects all the time for wealthy patrons and are experienced in protecting the goods. Nils says they're the best, they've got a reputation to maintain, and they're on their way here now to pick you up."

"What? *Now?*"

"The mummy's head, or whatever this precious thing is, is landing in Portland at 1:23." Max tapped his watch. "That's two hours and forty-three minutes from now."

She gaped at him, then snapped, "Thanks for finding me employment," and stalked away. Sure, she felt 300 percent better, but to take on a security job with no briefing and no time to prepare—what the hell?

Right before she made her grand exit, Max said, "Kellen."

She turned to face him.

"Brooks asked if you could hike. I said I thought you were good for a couple of hours, and I think… I think some time away might do you good. Take your hiking boots—it sounds as if the recluse is back in the woods somewhere."

"Right. Thank you." She hustled out of the gym and toward Max's house. In a fury, she texted Birdie, Men are asses.

I know, honey. Any particular one?

If he wanted to get rid of me that badly, he could have simply told me to go. Which he wouldn't do, because she was the mother of his daughter. Maybe he wanted her eliminated without any trouble to him.

Immediately, she felt ashamed.

Max is getting rid of you? Birdie ended with a shocked face emoji.

No. Never mind. Later. Maybe he hadn't found an ideal job for someone who wasn't yet recovered from an injury and infection, but why should he have to? She should have found her own job, but she'd been trying to stay close to Rae.

Okay. Try not to do anything stupid. Birdie had a way of being wise about people. Thank God, because for all Kellen's smart

Rolodex cataloging of personalities, she got it wrong an amazingly large part of the time.

Turning on her heel, she marched back toward the gym. She stepped in, intending to confront Max, ask the name of the restorer guy, how long this job was supposed to last and if Max expected her to come back when it was done.

Max stood in the middle of the gym, punching the bag with blinding speed and terrifying force.

Left, right, face the mirror, kick the inflatable stability ball.

Ball slams the wall.

Left, right, face the mirror, kick!

Ball slams the wall.

Left, right, face the mirror, kick!

He scowled every time he punched. Smiled when he kicked and the ball slammed into the mirror. Left, right, kick…

This time he was too slow. The ball smacked him. He staggered backward. Kicked again. Left, right…

His knuckles left a red smudge on the punching bag. Blood. He'd torn his knuckles open. Clearly, he was a man in the throes of vivid brilliant Technicolor frustration.

Kellen backed out the door, shut it softly behind her and tiptoed away.

She wasn't exactly sure what had angered Max—her, her inability to bond with Rae, her way of leading Rae into danger by encouraging her to climb to ridiculous heights? Or it was nothing to do with her, maybe his mother's tendency to burn oatmeal butterscotch cookies until the bottom was black and he had to scrape them off with a bread knife?

Maybe he didn't care what happened to Kellen. But probably he did, and maybe he was angry the way everything was falling out. And not that she didn't feel the same way, but—damn.

She didn't know how to make this work. As far as she knew, there wasn't a manual that explained how, while in a coma, to push a baby out of her loins and seven years later bond with it.

She felt so stupid. *Cows* produced *calves* and bonded with them. She had unknowingly produced a child and couldn't bond. Was she less than a notoriously dumb barnyard animal?

Maybe.

No wonder Max was kicking and punching.

Across the miles, Birdie must have sensed the tangle of Kellen's emotions. She texted, Everything okay?

I've got a job. So yes. Everything's okay. It's good to be busy.

What kind of job?

Security.

A pause.

Last time you worked security, you almost got killed.

Shouldn't happen this time.

Make sure it doesn't!

Kellen headed back to her bedroom in the old farmhouse and pulled her duffel bag out of the depths of the closet. She stared into the dark interior.

The clothing basics: underwear, toiletries, poncho, three pairs of socks—a change of socks made every day better—and a change of clothes for rugged terrain. Her hiking boots. A cap.

Emergency basics: compass, flashlight, waterproof matches, nylon rope, knife, nylon zip ties.

Those items were always in there.

She needed more. She added ammunition, her sleeping bag and an all-weather blanket. She assumed this would be at most two nights, but one thing the military had taught her—things go wrong, people lie, and a mission schedule wavers according to those two things.

Okay, that was three things the military had taught her.

She unlocked her weapons safe, the tall thin steel safe that kept her firearms out of the way of small curious hands. She stashed a thin sharp knife in a nylon holster up her sleeve. She removed her favorite pistol, a Glock 21 SF, and placed it in a nifty little holster that hid inside her pants below her belt. Tug on the loop, the holster slid up and placed the grip into her hand. She'd found that tricky little devil while she was recovering in the hospital, cruising the internet out of sheer boredom. She hadn't expected to try it out so soon, though.

She showered and dressed in layers, tough clothes that would hold up against trouble. Not that she expected trouble. But. She thought it was General MacArthur, or maybe Jimmy Kimmel, who said, "Shit happens, especially when a mummy's head is involved."

She was as ready as she'd ever be, so she went out and sat on the front porch step like a kid waiting for the school bus.

In less than a minute, she saw Rita Grapplee hurrying out of the tasting room and toward her.

RITA GRAPPLEE:
FEMALE, RUSSIAN ANCESTRY, MIDDLE-AGED, BROWN HAIR, PALE SKIN, PALE EYES, 5'10". EXUBERANT, INTELLIGENT, TOO ENTHUSIASTIC. WORKED FOR MAX FOR THREE MONTHS AFTER RELEASE FROM DRUG REHAB; ANSWERS PHONE, STOCKS SHELVES.

As soon as Rita got in earshot, she asked, "Kellen, I saw you sitting there—are you all right?"

Funny. The men and women who had served with Kellen frequently called her "Captain." She never asked them to; they were welcome to call her by her first name. Bank tellers, waitstaff, all kinds of service people called her "Kellen"; she thought nothing of it. But the familiar way Rita said her name made her want to snap out an order to stand at attention and salute. Rita was one of *those*; the people who got by doing as little as possible while wanting everything. The other employees hated her, and Kellen had been through too much in her twenty-eight years to admire that lack of initiative.

Yet today, Rita had done nothing except express concern, so Kellen took a patient breath. "I'm fine, why?"

"You were hurt just a few weeks ago, and you called *me*, remember?"

"I didn't call you in particular, I called the winery's emergency number, and you were on duty. In any case, I'm simply waiting for a ride."

Rita smirked. "How nice. Is Max coming to take you for a drive?"

Kellen didn't understand how one woman, a near stranger, could be so presumptuous. "No."

"Another suitor?" Rita sounded shocked.

It was on the tip of Kellen's tongue to tell Rita to mind her own business. But she knew that Max and Rae and Kellen and their situation was the source of rampant speculation among the employees and she didn't want to cause Max more grief, or imagine Rae being pulled aside and pestered with vulgar questions. So Kellen contained her impatience. "No, Max found me a job. I'll probably be gone for a day or two."

A white Ford van with dark tinted windows turned up the drive. It veered toward the winery, so she stood and waved. The driver waved back and headed toward the farmhouse. "There's my ride now." As the van pulled to a stop, Kellen saw the discreet monogram, RM, on the door.

"RM? What does that stand for?" Rita didn't wait for an answer. She pulled out her phone and looked it up. "Richart Movers? You're going to work for a moving company?"

"Apparently."

Rita continued to read from her phone. "Ohhh. They move fancy art stuff. Rich. Art. Get it?"

"Yes. I get it."

"That's a weird job for you. Where are you going?"

A man slid out of the driver's seat, came around and offered his hand.

Ignoring Rita, Kellen moved to meet him.

He said, "Hey, I'm Horst Teagarten. Horst isn't a family name, my folks just had a weird sense of humor, giving that to a kid from Florida."

Kellen filled out her mental file with speed and precision; he checked all the boxes as a cliché.

HORST TEAGARTEN:
MALE, NORTHERN EUROPEAN, 6'2", SHAVED HEAD (BALDING), BLUE EYES, UNIDENTIFIED ACCENT. TIGHT T-SHIRT, JEANS. MUSCLED SHOULDERS, TIGHT BUTT, FATTY BULGE AROUND THE WAIST. SMILING, CHARMING. IMAGINES WOMEN ARE IMPRESSED WITH HIM.

She shook. He had a good grip, didn't try to crush her fingers like guys so often did. "I'm Kellen Adams, glad to work with you."

His gaze shifted to Rita.

She leaped forward and in that overly loud voice of hers, she said, "Hi, I'm Rita Grapplee. I work here at the winery with Kellen. Good to meet you. So you move art?"

"Yes. Um..." He glanced at Kellen.

Kellen shook her head slightly.

He got the hint. "Come on. You can put your bag in the back."

She followed him around, watched him open the van's cargo doors and slung her duffel bag onto the floor behind the last row of seats.

Rita did not get the hint. She followed, too. "Where are you two off to?"

"We're picking up an important antique at the Portland Airport, and we need to get going." Horst was polite, but apparently Rita grated on him, too, for he was terse.

Kellen heard a shout and turned toward the tasting room. "Look, Rita. They're calling you back to work."

Rita barely glanced at the temporary manager. "Yeah, yeah. I'm on break."

"Not according to him," Horst said.

Rita sighed loudly. She lifted her phone, clicked a photo of the van and trudged back to work, her big feet slapping across the lawn.

Horst watched her. "She's weird."

"She's got...problems."

"Don't we all?" Horst turned back to Kellen. "My boss briefed me about you. He told me you're Army honorable discharge."

"That's right."

"Good news, that. I wasn't sure if you were someone's girlfriend looking for adventure or actually in security. What rank?"

She bumped herself down to an enlisted man. "Spec-4."

"Hey, I outranked you. E-6." He looked incredibly pleased, as if he hadn't had the chance to be in charge very often. "Did you bring your weapons?"

No, no. She wasn't giving up her secrets so soon. "Richart Movers doesn't supply weapons and ammunition?"

"What security person doesn't have weapons he prefers?"

"My body is my weapon."

He laughed.

She didn't crack a smile. Her drill instructor said her hand-to-hand attacks were organized, focused and deadly in a way he had seldom seen in a woman.

No reason to bring that up.

Horst said, "You *are* kidding."

She allowed her solemn face to break and she laughed back at him. "You caught me." She flipped the knife out of her sleeve. "What do you have on you?"

He showed her a side holster under his jacket.

"If this mission is dangerous," she said, "we'd better have more than that."

"We do." He pointed toward the ceiling. "Shotgun up there." He walked her around to the driver's side. "More shotguns in the door holsters, one for you, one for me. Ammunition above."

"Slick." The holsters had been constructed to look like part of the vehicle, unobtrusive yet easily reached.

He pulled one of the shotguns out, a Browning A-5 semiautomatic, handed it to her and watched her check it over.

"Looks good." She relaxed a little. This operation looked legitimate and well armed. Horst was Army. She felt comfortable with him and his easygoing personality. But she didn't tell him the truth about her weapons and her background; she had the scars to prove she'd been wrong before.

Horst went around to the back and shut the doors. He didn't ask which one of them should drive. He assumed he would, because he was the man or because he was of higher rank, and Kellen didn't tell him that she'd been a transportation coordinator in Afghanistan and Kuwait. She knew vehicles, she knew repairs, and yes, she knew how to drive.

But in her experience, at this point in any mission, it paid to sit back and observe. As she climbed into the passenger seat, she asked, "Will we make it to the airport in time?"

"If we're lucky and the cops don't stop us." Horst put the van into gear.

Kellen looked in the rearview mirror.

Max stood in the driveway, watching her leave, and he looked…lonely.

Was that good news? Did she want him to miss her even before she left? She should have said goodbye to him and—

She sat up straight. "Damn."

"Forget something?" Horst asked.

"I did."

"Hope it wasn't anything important. We haven't got time to go back." Horst turned onto the highway.

Max disappeared from view.

"It was important." She hadn't said goodbye to Rae. She hadn't even thought about it. "But it is too late."

7

Kellen's phone rang. She unbuttoned her pants pocket and pulled it out, hoping it was Max and Rae, calling to say the goodbye she had forgotten.

But no, it was a Washington, DC, number, and that meant only one person—Nils Brooks, head of the MFAA, dedicated to halting the flow of purloined artifacts into the US and always willing to put her life on the line to do it. She answered, "Adams here."

Nils didn't take the hint. "Kellen, it's Nils. I have a text that you've been picked up and are on your way to the airport."

"That's right."

"Did Max tell you anything about the job?"

"That me and Horst from Richart Movers are picking up a mummy's head at the airport and transporting it to some guy who's going to restore it, he's somewhere in the Olympics, and there's going to be a hike."

Horst shot her an inquiring look.

She smiled at Horst and shrugged.

Nils said, "Sort of. This piece is rare, one of those artifacts that's going settle fights among the experts and start fights among thieves."

"Valuable."

"Priceless."

Priceless. She never liked to hear that word.

Nils continued, "My courier was supposed to take it on the plane with him, never let it out of his sight."

She could almost hear the drumbeat of doom. "And?"

"He died. In the airport. The official report said he was knocked down as he was checking in at the machine. He hit his head. Current medical diagnosis is that it was a brain hemorrhage."

Kellen closed her eyes and rubbed her forehead. "Probably not, huh?"

"Probably not, since he went against orders and checked the bag through to Portland, knowing full well it couldn't easily be retrieved from the hold of the plane." Nils waited for a response.

She thought through all the possible scenarios. "So Horst and I could face some…challenges?"

"Possible challenges. Yes."

"Nils."

"Probable. I don't believe in coincidence."

"No kidding." She ladled on the sarcasm. "What does this restorer guy have to say?"

"Not much. He's only got a wireless up there—"

"What? Is he living in World War II?"

"And he didn't respond when I called."

She took a moment to let that soak in. She and Horst were taking a priceless antique head into the Olympic Mountains and hiking it up to a weird recluse expert…and the guy didn't know they were coming? "Nils…"

"How well do you trust Horst?" Nils asked.

"Good question."

"You don't want to say too much."

"Not now!" Not with Horst sitting next to her.

"I told the boss at Richart Movers we needed someone trustworthy, and he said he'd do the best he could on such short notice."

"Oh, dear." The short notice thing was not promising.

Horst glanced at her as if trying to follow the conversation, but he seemed uncertain.

That worked for her. "Why the late update?"

"If I'd told Max all this, he wouldn't have passed the message on."

"So you men fixed things up between the two of you, and this is the result?" She hadn't packed everything she would need, like her body armor and her extra weapons. She rode in a van with firearms that looked good but which she had not tested, with some guy she hoped had had proper security training. She was acquiring a head that Nils Brooks called *priceless*. Great. Just great.

And…her adrenaline kicked up to enjoyable levels.

Yes, she had missed this.

"It's not that bad," Nils said. "I've dealt with Richart Movers before. They're a young company, but the owner is reputable and—"

Kellen hung up on the pompous self-satisfied chauvinist asshole, smiled tightly at Horst and said, "Just getting the details of the operation."

"Anything I should know?"

"Men are jerks."

"Yes, ma'am."

Smart guy, this Horst. He didn't argue with her. He might be okay; just because Max and Nils were jerks, that was no use thinking Horst was going to grab the mummy's head and run with it.

"What challenges are we going to face?" he asked.

"Hmm?"

"You said, 'So Horst and I could face some…challenges?'"

"How much do you know about this operation?" Kellen asked.

He shrugged. "We have to retrieve the head from the airport because it's an important artifact that needs to be studied.

Somebody dropped it off at the airport back east. We pick it up from baggage claim and head toward the mountains to deliver this thing to, um, this guy."

"The Restorer? Is that his name? His title?"

"I dunno. I think he's this eccentric guy who lives in the boonies and is the go-to for figuring out if an artifact is real. No one told me he had a name."

"So he's...the Restorer."

"Whatever."

"That's all?"

"Pretty much. I've worked for Richart Movers for almost a year, and we've moved some pretty important expensive stuff for some pretty important expensive people. When I signed on, I was hoping for a little action, but so far, nothing's happened. It's been all driving and carrying and thanking people for the tips. Don't worry." He patted her knee.

She didn't knock his block off, but only because he was driving and she was thinking. Apparently, he didn't know about the courier's death, or even that there had been a courier charged with bringing the head to the Restorer. Why hadn't Horst been told? It seemed that kind of information should have been passed on to heighten preparedness. Unless Nils had kept the information to himself and only passed it on to her. Nils was paranoid and suspicious, and she *was* the one person on this assignment he knew without a doubt he could trust.

She asked Horst, "When did this call come in?"

"A couple of hours ago. I happened to come in after a few days off, so the boss grabbed me and told me we had an emergency job. He sent me to pick you up and go to the airport." The van reached the freeway entrance; Horst put his foot on the accelerator and they merged to the honking of furious drivers. "Lucky for me. Mostly I work with guys, and they aren't pretty like you."

Yeah, he was full of bullshit and ill-deserved confidence.

He pegged the van at ninety miles per hour and wove in and out of traffic, inciting honks and well-deserved hand gestures. In a way, that was good—while she was terrified for her life, she had no time to worry about her lousy parenting skills or the future of their mission.

Horst chatted as he drove, about the military, his parents' home in Florida, speculation about the mummy's head and gossip about the Restorer who he said was some weird whacked-out hermit.

So he did know *some* things about this mission.

Luckily for her, she didn't have to lie any more about her military and security experience. He never, not once, indicated by query or comment, that he was interested in anything she had to say. Instead, she made engrossed noises, agreement noises. Or possibly they were exclamations of muffled terror as he changed lanes with inches to spare.

Her sounds encouraged him to tell her that he'd joined the military when he was nineteen because he had been caught picking pockets at Disney World. His father had blown a gasket and threatened to cut off his funds unless he joined up.

That captured her interest, and she looked Horst over again. Nothing about him shouted urban pickpocket. Mostly he seemed like a well-built guy who liked to impress women one way or another, and maybe since she'd been in the Army he was playing the bad-boy card to impress her.

When they pulled into a parking place at Portland Airport, she sagged in the seat and hoped her high blood pressure hadn't ripped opened the still red scar on her hip.

Horst unsnapped his seat belt and checked his phone. "Let's go. Luggage is arriving *now*." He hoofed it for baggage claim so fast, Kellen ran to keep up with him, and she rejoiced as he kept up a monologue about how this head was an antiquity of great importance and if he didn't manage to grab it on its first swing around the carousel, someone would confiscate it and it would disappear into some rich guy's collection of illegal goods, and the archeological world would never have the time to study its origins and legends.

Kellen admired the sentiments and wondered if she should put Horst back on the good-guy list. In her mind, he was changing from bad to good to bad pretty quickly.

"Also, my boss would kill me."

That sounded more like it. "What kind of bag is it in?"

"Small black rolling bag."

She moaned.

He laughed. "Yeah. But it has a lime-green yarn puffball attached to the handle."

"I guess…that's a good idea. Who would think a mummy's head would be marked like that?"

"The bad guys," he said. "If there really are any, and if they're on this end of the continent. Personally, I'll bet this is all a lot of hooey about nothing. I'm telling you, these jobs are never exciting."

"Hope you're right."

They arrived at baggage carousel eight as the first bags were tumbling down the chute. Kellen was pleased to note that Horst was out of breath, and she was not. A few weeks off for injury and she was still in good shape.

They both watched, poised to leap at the first black bag with an attached lime-green yarn fuzz ball. As time wore on, the waiting grew tense and worried, and Kellen scanned the crowd, looking for someone who fit the physical profile of a thief and killer. Foolish, that; last winter she had learned the hard way that killers hid in plain sight. Still, she watched for suspicious behavior.

She saw a large family having a rambunctious reunion…how easy to steal a bag and pass it from one person to another.

She saw a businessman standing right in front of the chute and staring hard, intent on grabbing his bag even before it slammed against the carousel's bumper.

She saw a woman watching her and smiling, as if they were acquaintances. With a shock, Kellen realized they were; last December, that woman had vacationed at Yearning Sands Resort with her girlfriend and their children. That was the trouble with having worked for a well-known Washington resort—a lot of people knew Kellen Adams.

Kellen waved, and Horst elbowed her. "She your special friend?" He had that smarmy tone people get when asking personal questions that are none of their business.

"No."

"You have a special friend?"

Kellen didn't want him to develop any ideas, so she said, "Yes. Max Di Luca. He found me this job."

"Sounds like your *special friend* wants you to scram."

Kellen smiled with chilling precision. "Maybe. But mostly, he knows I can take care of myself."

"There it is!" Horst dived for the small black bag with the fluorescent green yarn fuzzy.

Kellen stood back and observed, ready to spring after him if he ran with the bag.

He didn't. He pulled the handle out full-length, walked it over to her and handed it over. "You take it. That yarn poof makes me feel like an idiot."

Leaning down, she unwound the yarn ball and tossed it in the garbage. "Let's go." She headed for the exit.

"Wait a minute." He started toward the men's room. "I need to take a leak."

She kept walking. "You should have thought of that before."

"I wasn't allowed to leave you alone to pick up the bag by yourself!"

"You're not supposed to leave me alone with the bag at all."

"I'm going to pee." He took more steps toward the men's room, as if that would make her halt.

"Meet you at the van," she said.

He stopped and said, "I've got the keys!"

She stopped and viewed the spoiled, frustrated man. "Do you really imagine I can't break into that van and start it?" She turned and headed out of the terminal.

He joined her on the sidewalk, puffing like a steam engine. "What am I supposed to do? Hold it all the way into the mountains?"

"When we get to a rest stop, you can visit the little boys' room. In the meantime, we're a sitting target at the airport." The parking garage was dark and cool, and she observed every person who passed, listened to every footstep behind them.

"Let's go back to the airport so I can pee. Who's going to grab the bag with all these people around?"

"Someone who has the proper ID to match the bag. Which we don't." She reached the back of the van.

He unlocked the doors.

She flung the bag into the back. It was heavy, forty or fifty pounds.

Mummy's head, indeed. No mummy's head would weigh so much.

"Here!" Horst tossed something at her.

She snapped to attention and caught it. The keys.

"You drive," he said.

Hmm. Unusual behavior for a macho man, allowing the female to control speed, route, stops. Really unusual behavior for a man who claimed he had a pressing bladder situation. That, combined with his determination to stop in the airport and leave her alone with the bag, gave her reasonable grounds for doubt. Horst Teagarten was now officially on her List of Suspicious Characters.

"Sure." She stuck the keys in her pocket and pulled off her

jacket. Her T-shirt fit snugly, showing off her toned arms and clearly proving she had no pistol or holster hidden around her narrow waist.

His eyes widened and she would swear she saw his brain empty.

Yep. Distraction of the female form plus reaffirmation of her vulnerability. Maybe he was going to try to steal the mummy's head, maybe he wasn't, but she had nailed him right in the stupidity.

She slammed the back doors closed. "Where am I driving?"

"The map's inside."

She walked around to the driver's side, and as she slid into the seat, she smoothly pulled the loop at her waistband, bringing the nylon holster up and putting the pistol grip high on her left hip, where she could reach it...just in case. "Let's see the map," she said.

8

The route took them north on I-5 out of Portland, across the state line into Washington, then cut west on Highway 12 toward the Olympic Peninsula. Yearning Sands Resort was on the Peninsula; during her time there, Kellen had studied the terrain, learned the flora and fauna, read the maps. For her, who had fought in a war zone, knowing your environment made good tactical sense.

What she had learned filled her with awe; the isolated peninsula was like no place else on earth. The Pacific Ocean battered the wild coast with storms. The earth moved with the roiling fiery hell beneath; earthquakes were always a threat, and for as long as the ocean had existed, cold blue tsunamis had swept the beaches clean and white. The mountains grew with every earthquake; every violent storm fought to bring them down with torrents of rain and wind and snow.

Wildlife—bunnies, bears, wolves, birds—thrived. Tourists passed through to gape and wonder. And of course, a few hearty, marvelous, eccentric souls lived there through warm summer days and long dark winter nights.

Kellen stopped along a lonely stretch of coastal road and let Horst out to take his leak. He'd been complaining ever since she took the "wrong" turn onto a highway small enough to barely be a mere scratch on the map. But she knew where she was going, and her sense of wrongness increased every time Horst picked up his phone to text. He cursed furiously when he discovered this region was so isolated cell service was sporadic and cheered when they drove through a tiny town and he was able to send his barrage of texts.

Now she watched him in the rearview mirror, and yes, he did take a leak, but as soon as he was done, he had his cell in his hand again, and when he glanced guiltily at her, she used her finger and pretended to be applying lipstick. When he glanced away, she adjusted the pistol on her left hip so she could grab it with her right hand, aim and shoot. Maybe she wouldn't have to. But that sensation of *odd* continued building, and she had learned to trust her instincts or die.

Horst climbed back in. "Whew! I feel better. You need to go?"

"I'm fine, thank you."

"You've got the bladder of a camel."

"You're not the first guy to notice." What was it with some men that even urination was a contest? "Ready?"

"Let's go." He didn't fasten his seat belt. He wanted to be ready for action.

They reached the junction of Highway 101 and Kellen turned onto the Olympic Mountains.

"You seem to know where you're going." He sounded annoyed.

"You showed me the map."

"If you remember so good, how come you took the wrong road back there?"

"There aren't very many roads out here, so a little diversion in case we're being followed is a good idea." She gave him time to digest that, then, "How much do you think that head is worth on the illegal market?"

"I don't know." His hand inched toward his pistol. "Maybe not so much."

"Enough to kill for."

"The courier could have died by accident."

Earlier, he had pretended not to know about the courier or his death. Horst had just officially become one of the bad guys. In a calm voice meant to soothe and explain, she said, "The trouble with trouble is, if you get mercenaries involved, and they kill one person, they're not going to stop. You were in the Army. You know what mercenaries are like. They'll keep coming. They'll betray the people who work for them to keep an extra dollar." She felt like she had to give him warning before this went any further.

"What do you know about it?"

"I've got experience. Why do you think I got called on this job?"

He stared as if he couldn't decide whether to believe her or not.

She added, "No honor among thieves and all that."

For one moment, his hand stopped inching. But he'd already proved he wasn't the brightest guy, and now he moved more quickly, as if he wanted to handle the matter before she talked him out of it.

He pulled his pistol.

She heard him release the safety.

He turned toward her, pistol leveled at her, arm outstretched to grab the wheel.

She slammed hard on the brakes.

His head thumped the windshield hard enough to send a spiderweb of cracks across the safety glass. The pistol flew out of his hand. Didn't go off. Thank God.

She goosed the van.

He slapped back into the seat hard enough (she hoped) for whiplash. But no—he recovered fast, proving he had great reflexes and not much in the cranium. He lunged at her.

She leveled her pistol and shot him in the chest.

The impact drove him against the passenger-side door. He looked surprised—but not dead.

Figured. He was a professional. He wore body armor.

He gasped in agony. Taking a shot from that close, he probably had a couple of broken ribs.

Good.

She slammed on the brakes again, released her seat belt and kicked him against the passenger side, a good solid blow to the chest, then leaned past him, opened the door and shoved him on to the road.

She drove off, door swinging, moving as fast as she could along the narrow rutted road. Dust boiled in the still-open door, and she watched the rearview mirror for a cloud created by a following vehicle. She saw nothing.

This road headed toward a trailhead that led to Lake Rannoch and the falls. Pure wilderness, and no chance of help.

She turned onto President Roosevelt Road. If the map was right, President Roosevelt Road would wind up and down and around the mountains, cross into the Olympic National Forest and eventually end in a paid parking area. Hikers and mountain bikers took off from there on their jaunts to lakes and peaks, and if she was lucky, there would be a national park ranger around. The rangers *were* the law enforcement up here, and she needed help.

If she was unlucky, there would be an unmanned payment box.

In the last year, luck had been scarce, and victories hard-fought and won with a lot of pain.

She drove unhurriedly, making sure she raised no betraying dust.

What with crazy Roderick on the roof sending a tile down to pierce her hip and then telling her, "Run, bitch!"... Well, no one could call the last month *lucky*. She'd played enough cards in the Army to know when luck had deserted you, you should throw it in and walk away. She intended to do just that...but!

She'd taken this job in good faith. She couldn't abandon the head. At best, it would disappear into a private collection, never to be seen again. At worst, it would be sold to finance terrorist operations around the world.

Run, bitch.

When she had gone several miles and seen the National Forest sign, she came to a halt and allowed herself one despairing moment with her head on the steering wheel.

She was in trouble. She needed help, and she didn't know who to call. Max? Nils? Birdie and her Army buddies? None of them would get here fast enough to help her. The park rangers? Yes, maybe, but there was money behind this operation and a uniform would be easy to rent and wear.

She had to help herself and save that head, and she didn't know how her situation could get any more dire.

She groped for her phone to text Birdie, give her a heads-up that she needed help, ask her to call Max, give her the general route she was traveling.

Something rustled behind her.

Her pistol leaped into her hand. She turned and pointed it, straight-armed, into the back seat.

Rae sat there, a bruise on her cheek, eyes wide, trying to smile through trembling lips. "Mommy, I came to bond with you."

9

Arthur Waldberg sat across the polished table from Max in the tasting room's private dining room and sipped from each of five glasses. "Do you mind if I take notes?"

"Please do."

Arthur pulled a small leather notebook out of his shirt pocket, removed the miniature stainless steel pen from the loop that held it closed and meticulously marked 1, 2, 3, 4, 5 on the sheet.

Max watched in amusement and some relief. If this man had the slightest knowledge of wines, and his résumé claimed that he did, he was their new wine room manager. They needed someone who was organized, precise and who understood how to hire and supervise the personnel necessary to run a busy and successful winery tasting room. Max had been handling everything since their last manager had been lured away by the rival Whistling Winds Winery, and it had eaten into the time Max needed to be spending with Kellen and Rae.

If he could somehow figure out how to bring those two together, he knew they would relate as mother and daughter. He saw the similarities between them every day and saw, too, that fear Kellen so carefully hid; to fall in love with a man, with him, would leave her vulnerable, but to fall in love with her own child... Nothing could hurt so much.

Arthur tasted again, clearing his palate between each sip with a sliver of bread, finished his notes and said, "This glass—" he pointed "—is a classic Italian blend. Sangiovese, cabernet sauvignon and cabernet franc. This glass is, not surprisingly, pinot noir. This wine has cork taint." He pushed it away. "The white is Arneis, a wine I haven't tasted since my last visit to Northern Italy. And this last is a quite insipid rosé."

Max met his eyes steadily, sternly. "What if I told you I blended the rosé?"

"Then I would tell you to keep to the organizational part of the winery."

"That's what my vintner says, too." Max sighed. It took a special knack to blend wines, and he had proved time and again that he didn't have it. For a man who was used to being good at everything, it was a lowering experience. "Your references are impeccable—" for a relative unknown in the wine world "—but at this moment, I can safely say I'd like to discuss the conditions of your employment."

"I'm not worried about salary. You have a reputation for being openhanded with your employees. Insurance is important, of course. But my only real condition is that as the positions open, I'd like the opportunity to bring in some of my people."

Max was taken aback. "Are you saying you'd run off the current employees to bring in your friends?"

"Not at all! I have the greatest empathy for those who are gainfully employed and are willing to work to stay that way. But inevitably in this business, there is a turnover. Young people go back to school, better job offers come along, the chance to travel becomes irresistible."

"Is that why you're here? You wished to travel beyond European wineries?"

"I wish to take a good winery to a great winery. I wish to grow a label from regional renown to world dominance. It takes the right wine for that kind of success, and the Oregon Di Luca wines are capable of making the transition." Arthur preached like an old-fashioned evangelist who had found his audience. "Are you interested, Mr. Di Luca, in that opportunity?"

"Hmm. Sure." Max scratched his cheek. "How?"

"You'll see. You'll be the person interviewing my friends, so of course the final decision to hire permanently or not would be yours. But I can safely promise that if you're on board with the idea of expanding Di Luca wines into a greater market, you will be satisfied with my suggestions."

Max stared at the prissy, exacting man across the table. Max knew he was good—anyone employed by top-end wineries in Germany, Spain and France had to be good. He'd proved his expertise with the wine tasting. But the man was frankly odd and something struck him as not quite right...

The door opened, and his mother stuck her head in the door. In an impatient voice, she asked, "Max, where is Rae? I've been waiting in the car. She's going to be late for camp."

Max looked up without surprise.

Arthur got to his feet and bowed formally from the waist.

"Mother, this is Arthur Waldberg. He's interviewing as winery manager."

Verona looked at Arthur in disbelief. "Are you?"

Max knew why she was surprised. Most wine room managers were younger, disheveled in a trendy way and very aware of themselves. Arthur Waldberg looked as if he was sixty, thin, clean-shaven, wore an expensive tailored black suit, white shirt and discreet blue tie with a diamond tie pin. To Max, he was as fussy with his dress as he was with his tasting, totally uncaring of what was trendy, and those were more points in his favor.

Verona came forward to shake Arthur's hand. "Where have you previously worked?"

"Mostly Europe." He cradled her hand.

"Dove sei vissuto in Europa?" A test; she spoke Italian fluently.

"In Francia, Germania, Spagna. Ovunque creano vino." His dark eyes glinted as he answered just as fluently.

"Bene." She looked at her hand, smiled, then disengaged from his grip. "Max? About Rae?"

"Did you check her room? She probably got distracted sneaking Princess Gigi into her new princess bag."

"I did, and her room is a mess. Max, you've got to get tough on that girl or she's going to spend her life thinking everyone else is going to pick up after her." Verona's voice dropped into ominous disapproval mode. "You can't say you feel bad because she hasn't got a mother. She has one now."

Verona was a handsome woman, tall, spare, stern and protective of her family, and when Rae was born, she had been their savior. She had showed him how to care for an infant, tended Rae when he went to the hospital to visit Kellen or to work at the office and never made him feel guilty for intruding on what should have been her retirement from teaching. When Kellen disappeared, Verona had been his support, had moved with him from Pennsylvania to Oregon, understanding his need to go someplace away from the trauma of his tortured romance. She hadn't exactly intruded on his relationship with Rae; he would never say that. But she had been the final word on scheduling and discipline.

So while he loved his mother, Kellen's return had not gone well, and it was mostly Verona's fault. Verona could not quite believe Kellen had forgotten Max, couldn't conceive that a woman didn't remember giving birth and resented Kellen's invasion into the smooth tenor of their lives.

Yet Kellen hadn't really attempted to intrude; Max wished she cared enough about Rae to do so. But every time Rae observed Kellen's actions and mannerisms, then imitated her behavior, Verona bristled.

Arthur Waldberg cleared his throat. "Should I...go out and wait?"

Max made his decision. "No. Stay." He scribbled a salary on his sheet, inserted it into the employment package folder, and pushed it across the table. "If that amount and the conditions of employment are agreeable to you, go out to the tasting room and take up the management reins."

"And?" Arthur raised his brows.

"Sure. Expand the operation as you see fit. Bring in your people as needed; I won't interfere unless I see a problem. I'll check in occasionally to see how it's going." Max wasn't too worried; he kept pretty close tabs on all operations. "The old manager took three of my best employees with him. Bring in your friends for an interview."

Arthur smiled, an amused crooked smile. "Eventually, when you trust me, I'll be allowed to hire my own employees?"

"Yes. When I know and trust you. Now excuse me, I have to go find my daughter." Max held the door for his mother to precede him.

"Maybe she turned into LightningBug and flew away," Verona said.

"LightningBug?" Max headed out the back door toward the house.

"That superhero name she made up for herself."

"LightningBlast."

"No, it's definitely morphed into LightningBug."

Max laughed shortly and ran up the stairs to Rae's room. He half expected to find her there, dressing her princess dolls in superheroine clothes, oblivious to the time. But she didn't respond to his calls, and the floor was suspiciously clean of dolls or clothes or tiny high heels, and her pink princess bag was nowhere to be found.

That wasn't right.

In fact, that was very wrong.

He toured the second floor, calling Rae's name.

His mother yelled, "Max!"

He ran down to the main level.

"Max!" Verona's broken voice lured him into the master bedroom. Verona stood by the bedside, holding a crinkled page of lined notebook paper in her shaking hands.

His heartbeat picked up, going from slightly concerned to something-is-really-wrong in a second. He took the paper, saw the drawing of two caped females, one big and one little, and read Rae's childish scrawl:

Daddy, I'm with Mommy on ad vencher...

He gave a roar of horror and grabbed for his phone.

10

"Rae!" Kellen sat unmoving, staring at her daughter.

Her daughter, who wore a pink leotard, a pink glittery tutu, a gold plastic necklace with matching bracelets and black rain boots with big-eyed pink owls on them. She held her big brown stuffed dog, Patrick, in one arm. On one side of her head, she wore her hair in a French braid. On the other, her flyaway blond shoulder-length hair looked as if it had been combed by a chicken. She was pale. She looked scared. But by God, she didn't stop smiling.

"Mommy?" Rae's brown eyes were fixed on the gun pointed in her face.

Kellen lowered the pistol, set the safety and slid it with shaking hands into her holster. "Sweetheart...you shouldn't have... You don't understand what you..." Kellen sucked in a breath, tried to focus. "Bond?"

"I heard Daddy. He said you hadn't bonded with me and I've been making our comic book ThunderFlash and LightningBug, and when they go on an adventure together, we bond." Rae started bouncing up and down and grinning.

Kellen felt physically ill. Light-headed. She wanted to faint, to froth, to cry. She said the first thing that came to her mind. "Your father's going to kill me."

"No, it's okay," Rae said smugly. "I wrote him a note."

Wrote him a note. Kellen mouthed the words, and with that, sense returned. And fear. Even more fear than before. She glanced behind them.

She'd left Horst on the road, but clearly he was working with someone. That someone wanted the mummy's head, or at least wanted the money they would get for it. There might be, was probably, a tracking device on the van or in the head's travel bag or both. She already knew these guys would kill to obtain the head. She needed to get going, get away, save the head… save Rae.

"Get up here on the seat, sit down, strap in." Kellen fumbled for her phone. "We have to go."

"Okay, Mommy, let me get my blankie." Rae knelt beside the back seat and dragged out her Ocean Princesses backpack.

Now Kellen remembered that flash of pink. If only she'd followed up, she would have found Rae, called Max, and she and Rae would be on their way home now. Horst could have stolen the head without trying to kill her, and he'd be dead because whoever wanted that head wouldn't share the profits. But Kellen wouldn't be involved, and her child would be safe. "We don't have time for your blankie." She ran her hands over herself, searching. *Where is my phone?*

The look Rae shot at her was nothing less than incredulous. "I have to have my blankie!"

From somewhere, Kellen heard those very words echoing down the years. Who, time and again, had said that?

Oh, no. That was her voice. "Right. I'm going to start driving." She put the van in First and eased forward. She felt in her lower pants pockets, then her shirt pockets, then back into the pants pocket where her phone should be. That pocket was unbuttoned.

She hadn't unbuttoned it. How had it come to be—?

She caught her breath and stared up the slope of the road.

Horst. His claim to be a Disney World pickpocket. All that

bragging she had put down to nothing but words from that big silly man-boy—and he'd lifted her phone slick as a whistle.

When had he done it?

When she was loading the head into the van. When she was removing her jacket. When she was distracted by that glimpse of pink.

"Mommy, I have to be in the seat belt!" Rae's indignation practically fogged the van. "If I'm not in the seat belt and you stopped suddenly, I could be hurt or even killed."

Kellen kept driving up the narrow road, picking up speed, keeping one eye on the rearview mirror. "Did your grandma tell you that?"

"Yes, and my daddy."

"They're right. Did they tell you you're a big girl and you can strap yourself in?"

"No..."

"Give it a try."

In a slow and disorganized operation, Rae dragged Patrick, her ragged stained yellow yarn blankie and a bunch of ragged pieces of paper stapled together between the front seats, then looked at the passenger side. "Where's my car seat?"

Kellen squeezed the steering wheel and for the first time, realized she was on the fine edge of hysteria. She wanted to shout, *How should I know where your car seat is?* She wanted to grab Rae by the shoulders, to shake her and insist she admit she'd done a terrible, dangerous, reckless thing. She wanted to explain that they would probably both die.

No matter what Kellen did or said, or what Rae agreed to, they would probably die.

Oh, God. Kellen was a terrible mother. She wanted to rattle her own child, and they were going to die. She had to try, but if she couldn't save them...

She glanced at her daughter, at the dirty bruised bewildered face, and knew Rae didn't have a clue. Kellen took a breath and got control of her temper. "We don't have your car seat. If I'd known you were coming, I would have brought it, but since you surprised me, you should slide up there and buckle your seat belt."

"I need my car seat. If I can't see out the window, I'll vomit."

Of course you will. In a soft coaxing voice that hid an overflow of worry and irritation, Kellen said, "Sit on your friend Patrick. He won't mind."

"Okay!" Rae put Patrick on the seat, hopped up on him, turned to Kellen. "Buckle me in."

I'm driving. Kellen bit back her response. Bad mother or not, she could see that a seven-year-old couldn't—

"Or I can do it!" Rae got on her knees to reach the seat belt, dragged it over her and clicked it tight. She stuffed her blankie between the high end of the belt and her neck, leaned against it and sighed. "I hurt my face when you killed that man."

"I didn't kill him…! That bruise on your cheek?"

"You shot him." Rae touched her bruise. "Yes, there."

"He wore body armor. That protected him from the bullet so he didn't die. I did throw him out on the road, and he's after us with his bad friends." Kellen groped at the side of her door, found the first aid kit, dug around and got a chemical ice bag. She snapped it and when it got cold, she passed it to Rae. "Put that on your cheek."

"Okay!" Rae did for maybe five seconds, then held tattered pages out at arm's length. "Look at our book!"

The road was gravel and cluttered with washboards. Every curve turned in on itself and climbed straight up the side of a mountain. Occasionally the road dipped into a creek bed. The wheels clattered over rounded stones and through trickling waters that, despite the summer months, would be still bracing. Or icy. Depending how long your feet were in them. Kellen maintained a speed that kept the roil of dust at a minimum, and all the time, she wanted to give way to her panic and put her foot flat on the accelerator. "I can't look at it right now. What does our book say?"

"We're ThunderFlash and LightningBug."

"Wait. I thought I was ThunderBoomer?"

"No. I've decided we are ThunderFlash and LightningBug, and we have adventures and save everybody."

"Yay, us." Kellen was still trying to grapple with the reality of her child here, with her at the crossroads of disaster and death. "Rae, if you're supposed to always be in a seat belt, why did you crawl in the back and hide?"

"I told you. To bond!"

"Do you think that was the right thing to do?"

"You're my mommy, and I don't want you to go away."

Kellen guessed that was a good answer. "Do you know what it means to bond?"

"It's like glue, only stickier."

Kellen opened her mouth and shut it. Actually, that described bonding pretty well.

Rae said, "Monster MegaBond! Bonds metal, plastic, paper, silk, porcelain! Not even two monsters can pull it apart." She grunted deeply and made a gorilla face.

An infomercial. The kid got her bonding smarts from an infomercial. Kellen couldn't believe how stupid this was, and at the same time—damn. Funny and clever.

"When are you going to call Daddy?"

"I can't. Horst stole my phone." And didn't Kellen feel stupid admitting that to a child.

"If I had my own phone, we could call Daddy right now."

"Your own phone? You're seven!"

"Martin has his own phone. Amelia has her own phone. Scarlett has her own phone. Jackson has his own phone." Rae recited their names with solemn certainty.

"Your friends have cell phones? That's appalling."

Rae sagged in the seat. "I need a phone!"

"Why?"

"So we could call Daddy!"

"Why else?"

"So I could text!"

"Why else?"

"So I could play the game where you pop the Bubble Wrap."

"I'm not helping you with this one, Rae. I agree with your daddy and your grandma. You're too young for a phone."

Rae crossed her arms over her chest, hunched down in the seat and pouted mightily. Then she pointed at the floor. "Look, your man left *his* phone."

Kellen glanced down and there it was—Horst's phone, big as life. She must have knocked it out of his pocket when she kicked him. "Can you pick it up for me?"

"I'm not supposed to—"

"I know, you're not supposed to get out of your seat belt, but this is a special occasion."

"Like when Grandma wants to smoke a secret cigarette but she can't reach her Marlboros?"

Kellen grinned in evil delight. That explained that occasional whiff of forbidden tobacco floating around Verona. "Exactly like that, except *I'm* not doing anything naughty."

Rae unclicked, squatted on the floor, picked up the phone and handed it over, then sat on Patrick, pulled up her blankie and belted herself in.

Kellen slowed to a crawl. "Let me see if I can call 9-1-1." She checked for service. None. Damn it. Absolutely no cell, no satellite. They were too far into the mountains for any kind of signal. "I'm sorry, honey, I can't call Daddy *or* 9-1-1."

"That's okay. This is fun!" Rae beamed.

"Right." Kellen poked at Horst's phone, trying to get around the lock screen, and the last text message slid past.

How many miles until the van blows?

11

The text disappeared.

"What?" Kellen said to the phone. "What?"

Predictably, the phone didn't answer, but a quick glance at the gauges told her everything she needed to know. The engine was overheating, the arrow rising steadily. "You treacherous bastard." What had Horst done? Cut a line? No, there should have been trouble before now, and anyway, the worst that could happen was an engine fire.

The text said, Blow. As in a bomb. As in…as in the explosion that had killed her cousin.

For what purpose? Horst didn't think she was going to get away in the van, so he and his friends wanted to retrieve the head and destroy the evidence.

Smoke curled out from under the hood.

At best, this was going to mark the place she and Rae started walking. At worst—

Kellen pulled as far over toward the edge of the road as possible, unfastened her seat belt, Rae's seat belt, opened Rae's door and said, "Jump out and go stand—" she scanned the area "—over by the creek and behind that hemlock."

"Okay." Rae gathered her blankie and Patrick and lowered herself to the ground. "What did the treacherous bastard do now?"

"Run!" Later they would talk about repeating what Mommy said and what the treacherous bastard had done. Now, Kellen climbed in the back and started throwing weapons, ammunition, her bag and the mummy's head out onto the road. Rae's bag went last; it was open and junk flew everywhere in the van and on the road.

Kellen knew there would be hell to pay, but the van started trembling like a volcano about to erupt. She jumped out and grabbed the head and her bag and sprinted toward Rae.

Toward Rae, who was running toward her, yelling, "My princesses!"

"Shit!' Kellen dropped everything, grabbed Rae and bodily carried her, kicking and screaming, back to the protection of the creek bed.

The van went up like a lighter in a whoosh of flame and heat that Kellen felt singe the hair on the back of her head. Kellen clutched Rae, hugged her, held her back.

My God. They'd almost died. Rae had almost died.

Rae struggled and sobbed, "My princesses! My nail polish! My glitter shoes!"

Kellen held her tighter and tried to calm the thunderous beating of her heart. In a voice that trembled, she said, "Honey, we need to have a serious discussion about what to pack next time you stow away for a bonding adventure."

Kellen looked back at the van. Flames reached up into the Douglas fir. This was Western Washington, the Teflon forest on the Olympic Peninsula, one of the rainiest places on earth.

But it was high summer, the dry season, and the heat of the fire made the cedars and Douglas fir around the van smolder. If their luck turned bad, if the fire caught and spread, they could roast sitting beside a trickling mountain creek.

If their luck was good, they might somehow find their way to a ranger station.

Unfortunately, Horst's map didn't show anything but the torturous path to the Restorer.

Kellen looked around. Which way to go?

The Olympic National Forest and the adjoining park were isolated, deeply forested, slashed by freezing rivers, divided by windswept mountain peaks. Narrow paths served the hikers and bikers, but dare to veer off the track into trackless wilderness, and it could be years before anyone found your body. Kellen had a child to care for, and she needed her bag, which was scorched, and she couldn't leave Rae's bag. Whatever was inside, they might need it. More than that, no one knew Rae was with her, not even Horst. Whoever he was working with would take her, use her, kill her.

Sure, Kellen's feelings for her daughter were a confused tangle, but one thing she knew—no one was taking the kid.

Rae won't burn. She won't die. I won't be responsible for another innocent death.

Kellen took Rae's face between both her hands and turned it to hers. "If you promise you'll stay here, I'll see what I can retrieve."

Rae's damp brown eyes peered at Kellen. "You'll save my princesses?"

"I will try." Kellen peeked at the open pink bag, its contents spilled all over the road. She was pretty sure the fate of at least one doll was grim.

Kellen grabbed the suitcase with the head, her backpack and the pink bag, in that order. She paused only long enough to scoop up one doll with a dishcloth cape—somehow it seemed that Supercotton Dishcloth Princess deserved to be saved—and fling a bunch of other random stuff into the bag. She ran back to Rae, who was standing at the edge of the road and crying.

"It's okay. We saved almost everything. Look. You've got Patrick. You've got your blankie, here's your superhero princess."

Kellen risked a glance at the van and the trees. "And the flames are dying down."

"I want my daddy!" Rae sobbed.

Of course she did. "Him we don't have." Driven by the intense need to hide, to hurry, to run, Kellen pushed Rae up the rocky banks of the creek and away from the road. "But we're superheroes, aren't we? We'll be fine on our own. Won't we?"

Rae caught her breath, shuddering as she tried to stop crying. "Y…yes."

"Who are we? ThunderBoomer and LightningBug?"

"ThunderFlash and LightningBug," Rae corrected.

Kellen offered her fist to bump.

Rae stared, then bumped it.

"Wipe your nose."

Rae looked around for something to wipe it on.

"On your sleeve."

"Grandma says I'm not supposed to—"

"Out here, we're superheroes and we don't have grandma rules. When we get home—then we'll put on our disguises and keep the grandma rules."

Rae wiped her nose on her sleeve.

Kellen was getting pretty good at handling the kid. But she was dragging under the weight of the pink bag, her own backpack and the weight of the suitcase with the head. She looked around. They stood in a grove of tall hemlocks and fir, out of sight of the road. "We have to consolidate our belongings in my backpack."

"What do you mean?" Rae asked suspiciously; the kid was no fool.

"I mean we have to put all the necessary stuff from your bag into mine so I can carry it."

"I can carry my bag."

"You can't. You need to put all your effort into hiking."

"You can carry my bag."

"Can't. It's pink."

"I like pink!"

"It's bright and we're superheroes…in hiding."

"I want my bag!"

"We'll stash your bag."

"I have to have all my princesses!"

"Then you'll have to leave Patrick."

"But I have to have Patrick!"

"I won't be able to carry it all."

"I can carry it."

And…they were back at the beginning. Kellen had lost track of the issues. The kid had her wound up in knots.

Rae took a long breath, ready to fight or cry or—

Kellen reached into Rae's bag, grabbed the crumpled brown bag and pulled out the first thing she found. "Here. Eat this!" She shoved a muffin studded with cranberries into Rae's hand.

Rae debated for a moment, crying or eating, and eating won. She gobbled the muffin.

Thank God. The rule was that an Army always traveled on its stomach. Kellen needed to remember—so did Rae.

She stared at her child and for one painful moment she remembered Afghanistan and…

A burned-out house. A melted coil of metal. The stench of desperation and death.

God. God. Kellen had tried so hard not to get involved with Rae, to care so much she hurt herself…and the child. More than anything in the world, she didn't want to hurt her own child.

Rae stared at her. "Mommy, are you sad?"

Was she crying? Kellen put her hand to her face. No. Her cheeks were dry. But somehow, Rae saw too much. "I'm okay. I'm just concerned about what we do next."

From down the road, they heard the sound of an approaching vehicle.

"It's Daddy!" Rae leaped to her feet.

"Or it's the bad guys." Kellen grabbed her arm, pulled her down and tucked her close.

"No, Daddy!"

Wishful thinking, kid. "If it's Daddy, we'll see and come out of hiding. If it's the bad guys, we won't. Okay?"

Rae struggled to answer.

Kellen put her finger on Rae's lips. "Let's climb a tree. Do you know how to climb a tree?"

"Daddy and Grandma won't let me climb trees. Not since I fell out and hurt myself."

"We're superheroes, and the tree-climbing is one more thing we're not going to tell Grandma or Daddy."

Verona stood in the door of Max's room, watching him pack. "What's happening?"

"I can't get Kellen. Her phone goes directly to voice mail. I called that bastard who set her up with the job and told him to bring her back. Brooks said he had no way to reach her, and when I told him Rae was with Kellen, he finally admitted it wasn't the straightforward job he told me. The first courier is dead, Kellen and the guy she was with have disappeared into the mountains in a van and—" Max choked.

"Why doesn't he send in his team?"

"He hasn't got a team! He hasn't got a staff! The MFAA is underfunded, barely hanging on as a federal department. I don't even know if the guy who was killed was a part of the operation or somebody Nils hired!"

Verona moved swiftly into the room and put her hand on his arm. "Max." She shook him. "Max, listen to me. Kellen is a lousy excuse for a mother. But she had experience in the mountains. Right? In Afghanistan?"

"Right."

"She's loyal to her people, and I know without a doubt she

would lay down her life before she allowed anything to happen to Rae."

He stopped packing and looked at Verona. "You're right. But what if it doesn't matter if she lays down her life? What if that's not enough to save Rae? If the worst happens—how can I live?"

Verona stared back at her son and saw anguish and a loneliness she had hoped was vanquished forever. Time to do more than offer words of support. "What can I do to help you get ready?"

"I need food I can easily carry on an on-foot search. Toilet paper. Water filter. Headlamp."

"I'll round up the camping gear." She went to the door and paused. "Rae and I made banana bread yesterday. I'll send a loaf. You can share it with Kellen and Rae when you find them."

12

Mercenaries were like deer. They never looked up.

Kellen sat on a tree branch, one arm wrapped around the tree trunk, one holding Rae with her hand over her mouth, and using all her powers of observation to figure out who they were and what they wanted. Thank God for her Rolodex brain. *Thank God!*

There were two groups:

GROUP 1: THE GREEDY BASTARDS
THREE MEN WITH GUNS AND KNIVES HELD CASUALLY, AS IF THEY KNEW EXACTLY WHAT TO DO WITH THEM. FROM THE CONVERSATION, THEY WERE VERY SERIOUS ABOUT WANTING THE MUMMY'S HEAD AT ANY COST, AND THEY WOULD KILL KELLEN AND RAE IN AN INSTANT FOR THEIR CUT OF THE REWARD FOR THE HEAD. NO ONE BELIEVED SHE HAD DIED IN THE VAN FIRE (TOO BAD), AND EVERYONE BELIEVED THEY COULD CATCH HER, KILL HER AND RETRIEVE THE HEAD.

GROUP 2: THE COLD-EYED MERCENARIES
FOUR MEN AND ONE WOMAN, IN JEANS, DENIM BUTTON-UP SHIRTS AND JACKETS, NO WEAPONS IN VIEW, EXAMINING THE GROUND FOR TRACKS AND SPEAKING BRIEFLY AND SHARPLY TO GROUP 1 FOR RUINING THE TRACKS. THEY HAD A CLEAR HIERARCHY AND AN AGENDA THAT DIDN'T INCLUDE THE MUMMY'S HEAD. THEY WERE HUNTING A PERSON. THEY WOULD BE PAID FOR ACQUIRING OR KILLING... A PERSON.

Observations:

GROUP 1 DIDN'T BELONG OUT HERE; THEY WORE SHINY SHOES AND CITY GARB, AND A FEW HOURS ON THE FOREST TREK WOULD PUT BLISTERS ON THEIR HEELS, AND A NIGHT SPENT IN THOSE SUITS WOULD TEACH THEM HOW DIRT AND COLD WOULD STRIP A MAN OF AVARICE AND REPLACE IT WITH A NEED FOR COMFORT.

GROUP 2 WERE PROFESSIONALS, USED TO DISCOMFORT, PREPARED FOR THE TERRAIN, READY TO KILL.

It was Group 2 she feared, and as she watched, she remembered Roderick Blake's lunge at her and his hoarse command, *Run, bitch.*

Fine. Maybe she had made an enemy she didn't know about. But Rae didn't deserve this.

Kellen watched them, hoped they would all die of a sudden terrible rash and knew they wouldn't. Bad guys never conveniently perished. But eventually they divided up into two teams, four people in each team, both teams directed by one of the Cold-Eyed Mercenaries. Together they would go to meet their leader, whoever that might be, and get their next instructions. Then they would go on the hunt for the head, one team going one way, one team the other. Kellen's job would be to evade them both.

Kellen only relaxed when they left the clearing and Kellen and Rae were alone in the tree.

Rae wanted to climb down right away.

Kellen decided they should sit for another thirty minutes... and at minute twenty-six, she was rewarded with Horst, eyes fixed to the ground, wandering toward their tree.

He looked as if he had been picked up and shoveled into the bad-guy vehicle without respect or ceremony. He walked hunched over, protecting his midsection, and Kellen reflected with some pride she must have broken a few ribs. But he wasn't feeling quite as sure about her escape as his compatriots; he'd already dealt with her once and been outsmarted. So as he moved, he kept his gaze to the ground, watching for footprints and… damn it. He was circling the tree, and in a minute he would look up.

Kellen had hung Rae's pink bag on a short branch. Her own backpack was tucked between a branch and the trunk. She had opened the roller suitcase and pulled out the mummy's head.

But it wasn't a mummy's head. Not even close. It was heavy, a marble stone with its features obscured by Bubble Wrap and tape. The base was square; in the far distant past when it had been made, it had been meant to sit in a position of honor on a fireplace or a family's hearthstone. Kellen knew it deserved to be handled with respect and consideration for its great age.

But when Horst looked up, she flung it at him.

He ducked and shouted.

It hit his shoulder.

From twenty feet up, Kellen leaped out of the tree and smacked him with her feet. She landed in a sprawl on top of him and to the side.

He gave an abbreviated bleat and clutched at his belly. His body went limp.

She leaped aside, stumbled, turned to observe him. Was he faking it, preparing to lunge at her and drag her down?

No. He was lying on his back, his face up, his eyes rolled back. He didn't twitch. She'd knocked him unconscious and if she was lucky, one of his broken ribs had pierced some vital organ. Not that she was feeling vindictive…

"Mommy! Are you all right?" Rae's whisper pierced the quiet of the forest.

Kellen gave her the thumbs-up, hoped Rae knew what that meant, spent a few moments clutching her hip where the roof tile had pierced, then gathered herself and went over to Horst's prone body. She kept her pistol pointed at his head as she rifled through his pockets and found a carefully folded paper, printed from a hand-drawn map, that showed the real route to the Restorer. "You two-faced son of a bitch," she said quietly.

"What did the two-faced son of a bitch do?" Rae had slipped down the tree and sat on the branches six feet up.

Kellen debated whether she was supposed to give Rae the no-profanity speech, and decided she needed to give it to herself. "He lied about where we were going." The map showed nothing but the actual path up the mountain to the Restorer when what Kellen actually needed was a ranger station.

"He's a bad man," Rae observed.

"Yes. He sold us out. That's the worst kind of traitor. But now I know the right way to go." Surely on the way, they'd see a sign for a ranger station. Maybe they'd even run into a ranger.

Maybe hope springs eternal.

Kellen lock-clicked the safety on her pistol, grabbed Horst under the arms and dragged him toward a tree, smaller than the rest, and sat him against the trunk. "Rae, toss me down my bag."

Rae clambered back up the branches and got Kellen's backpack. She tottered under the weight, then dropped it from twenty feet up.

Kellen leaped aside as it smashed to the ground. "Right. Thank you." The breakfast cookies had just disintegrated into cookie dust. She pulled a couple of long nylon zip ties off the side of the bag, and with a few quick yanks, she secured Horst's wrists behind the tree trunk. He wasn't getting away anytime soon.

But when he had looked up into the tree, he had paused for a mere second in absolute astonishment. He had seen Rae. He knew she had a child with her. When his team found him, he was going to blab.

Yet Kellen couldn't kill him, not in cold blood and certainly not in front of Rae. She would simply have to hope no one stumbled onto him for a couple of days. Once she reached the Restorer whose name, if this map was to be believed, was

Zone—sure, Zone—she would send someone to free Horst from the tree and arrest him for attempted theft and murder.

She stepped away, watched Horst's head loll on his chest and went back into his pockets. She still didn't find her phone, and somewhere along the line he'd lost his pistol, but he had a short push-button-operated stiletto strapped to his belt and she secured that. She supposed a normal mother wouldn't consider the possibility of training Rae to use it, but if she could teach Rae enough knife work to survive…well. Childhood innocence was all well and good, and Kellen would do everything in her power to preserve it, but mostly, she wanted to give Rae a chance to live.

Rae had to live.

Kellen gathered the dirty Bubble-Wrapped mummy's head. She secured it to her bag with more long zip ties, then looked up at her bespangled daughter. "Toss Mommy down your bag. We've got to get moving."

The pink bag thumped to the ground, and Rae jumped into Kellen's arms. Kellen put her on her feet, and they set off into the woods.

Two hours later, Horst heard the sound of a vehicle on the road. It slowed to a stop, probably to examine the burned-out van. As soon as the door opened, he shouted for help. He kept shouting until he heard footsteps crunch across the pine needles toward him, and he started talking as soon as the man came into sight.

"I'm a bounty hunter. There's a woman loose in the woods, she's a criminal, she jumped me and tied me up here. She's armed and dangerous. You need to cut me free so I can go after her."

The guy nodded. Weird guy, dressed in pressed khakis, a long-sleeved golf shirt, hiking boots and a felt fedora.

Horst realized this guy must be a Californian and probably

wouldn't be carrying anything as practical as scissors or a knife.
"Are you lost?" Horst asked him.

"I'm exactly where I belong." In the shadowy woods, Mr. Fedora was not exactly easy to see. He was white, with a healthy tan, but Horst couldn't see the color of his eyes, only that they glittered beneath the brim of his hat. "Which way did this dangerous criminal go?"

"I don't know." Depended on whether she had found the real map. He'd figure that out as soon as he got his hands free. "I was unconscious when she left. But I can track her."

"If she jumped you, healthy specimen of a man that you are, she's in good shape." He had a pleasant voice, modulated, easy to listen to and without a discernable accent. "What makes you think you can catch her?"

For the first time, Horst felt a niggle of worry. This guy was observing him too closely, asking too many questions and smiling ever so slightly. "Come on. Cut me loose. I need to get going." He waited to hear the guy say he didn't carry anything sharp.

But the guy pulled out a pocketknife from his khakis and flipped out a blade, about two inches long and honed often and well if the curve of the steel was anything to go by.

"Thanks, man." Horst watched him walk around behind the tree. "I've gotta tell you, I've been worried no one would find me until it was too late and I was just a skeleton tied to a tree." Horst laughed, a little giddy at the idea of freedom.

"Can you move back firmly against the trunk?" the guy asked.

"Sure." Horst scooted so his spine was flat against the tree, then held his hands up behind him to make them easy to reach. "Feels like she used nylon handcuffs. Is that it?"

The guy mashed his knee on top of Horst's bound hands, driving them into the dirt and making Horst's head slam against the wood.

Ouch! "What are you doing?"

Two strong hands reached around the trunk. One grabbed Horst's chin and jerked it up and back. Horst had one moment of clarity, one moment to yelp in terror and struggle, before the guy's other hand, the one with the knife, slid firmly across his throat, slitting him from jugular to jugular.

The killer pulled his hands back. But not soon enough. Blood sprayed his wrists.

He grimaced at the mess on his sleeves, and without a backward glance at the incompetent fool, he returned to his car, a silver Lexus NX Hybrid, and changed to a clean short-sleeved golf shirt. Getting behind the wheel, he drove up the steep and narrow gravel road to meet his new team—and give them their new directive.

13

After they left Horst unconscious against the tree, Kellen led, pushed and assisted Rae below the road, and along a parallel track for over two hours. Then Rae sighed so pitifully that Kellen listened for the sounds of pursuit, then called a halt in a grove near a cold babbling stream. The jump out of the tree had not done her hip any good. She hurt, and she was tired, too; from the heaviness of Rae's bright pink bag, Kellen assumed Rae brought a brick wall. The marble head was no lightweight, either.

She dropped everything off her shoulders into a heap. "We'll stop and rest and eat. What else is in your lunch sack?"

"String cheese!" Rae shouted.

"Shhh."

Rae said, "Shhh," back.

"No, really, Rae. We don't want the bad guys to hear us."

"They left! And we tied the traitor up." To Rae, the matter was settled.

Kellen put her hand on the mummy's head. "As long as we have this, they're looking for us. They want it." At least Group 1 did. Group 2 had a different agenda, but Rae would be able to understand about the head, an object, better than she could understand about hunting a person.

"Why?" Rae asked.

"Because it's very old and worth a lot of money."

Dramatically, Rae thumped her forehead with her palm. "Why?"

Kellen took a breath and did her best to explain the whole situation to Rae, what had happened, where they were going. She spoke slowly and clearly and hopefully used words the child understood. When she was done, she asked, "Now do you understand what's going on with those men and the guy I tied to the tree and the mummy's head?"

"We're going to get whacked," Rae said.

Whacked. *Killed?* Kellen didn't ask whether Rae knew what that meant. "Not if I have anything to do with it. But we are in trouble. So let's talk quietly while we eat, and move out quickly." She opened Rae's pink bag. "Let's see what you brought to eat."

The good news: Rae's bag included Rae's lunch for camp. Carrot sticks! A turkey and Havarti sandwich! A baggie of mushed cherry tomatoes! An assortment of loose citrus Jelly Bellies with little bits of fuzz attached! And yes, string cheese! The food was a lifesaver.

The bad news: this was lunch for one little girl for one day. Every time Kellen put food in Rae's hand, she conveyed it to her mouth and it was gone. The kid was a bottomless pit, absorbing calories as if by osmosis.

When Kellen scowled, Rae offered her half the sandwich. "Here, Mommy, you're hangry."

Hungry-angry. Yes, she probably was. Kellen bit into the whole wheat bread full of mayonnaise, slices of organic turkey, creamy Havarti cheese, lettuce and tomato. She wanted to moan as the flavors hit her tongue. "This is so good. Thank you, Rae. I guess we have something in common."

"We're ThunderFlash and LightningBug!" From somewhere in her tutu, Rae pulled the tattered stapled notebook with drawings of the two of them.

"We are!" With every bite, Kellen was feeling more like

ThunderFlash. She pulled a peanut butter raisin celery stick out of the bag and bit into it. "That's a funny tasting raisin," she said.

"I don't like raisins. Neither does Daddy. We use prunes."

Kellen didn't spit it out. But it was close. "Prunes?"

"I like prunes. I like the orange-flavored ones best. Oo! And the chocolate-covered prunes."

"Right." Kellen had fallen into an alternate universe. "Here. Let me put sunscreen on your face."

"Grandma already put it on me. She thought I was going to camp." Rae sounded triumphant.

"I thought so, too." Kellen applied sunscreen on her own neck, face and hands, pulled her hair back and stuck it under her cap. "Do you have a hat?"

"My duck hat."

"Does it have a bill?" Rae gave Kellen a look that made her feel stupid. "I guess it does if it's a duck hat." Kellen opened the bag. "I don't suppose you remember where you put it?"

"Grandma put it away for the winter."

"You didn't bring your duck hat?"

"No!"

Kellen reviewed the conversation in her mind. She had asked if Rae had a hat; not if Rae had a hat with her. Taking her own hat off her head, she adjusted the back strap and fit it to Rae's head. "Do you have crayons?"

"Are we going to color?"

"Maybe." Kellen was trying to figure out what in Rae's bag they could possibly use for weapons and survival. Red crayons could be melted to look like blood and fake someone out.

She looked at Rae. The whole assortment of crayons also could be used to entertain her daughter during the times they were resting. She put them, the ThunderFlash and Lightning-Bug book, and some crumped pieces of plain paper in her bag. "We don't need this." Kellen held up the computer tablet.

"My tablet!"

"We can't use your tablet out here. There's no electricity and you didn't bring a charger anyway."

"It's okay. It doesn't work."

"If it doesn't work, why do you have it?"

"It's my tablet!"

Kellen found herself wanting to say, "That makes no sense." But somehow, it did make sense—to Rae. "What's wrong with it?"

"The battery catches on fire."

"Really?" Kellen switched it on. It was charged.

"Daddy said not to turn it on because the battery catches on fire."

Kellen held it while the temperature began to climb, then switched it off. "I heard about this. Wasn't there a recall?" She looked to Rae for an answer.

Rae peeled a cheese stick and held it out. "I guess. Can I have peanut butter?"

Rae clearly knew nothing about a recall, but if this thing caught on fire, it was like owning a time bomb and that was no end of useful. Kellen stuck the tablet in her bag. "There's no more peanut butter."

"I brought a jar of peanut butter!"

"I... Really?" Kellen delved into Rae's bag and found an entire unopened jar of all-natural organic peanut butter rolling around at the bottom. She laughed in delight. "Dear Lord." Was that swearing? "Heavens, this is the best news ever. Do you realize how much protein and energy is in a jar of peanut butter?"

Rae examined her as if she was slightly mad.

"I don't suppose you brought a loaf of bread or some graham crackers, did you?"

"Why? Can I have a banana?"

Kellen almost said no. Then she remembered the battered banana she had packed, pulled it out, divided it in half and passed it to Rae. They ate it piled with peanut butter. Then Kellen loaded the broken computer tablet, Rae's yellow blankie, Patrick and the cotton-caped princess into her backpack. "Did you bring any extra socks?"

Rae tilted her head and viewed Kellen as if she was crazy.

"Underwear? Clothes? Toothbrush?"

"My Halloween costume!" Rae leaped to her feet. "I'm going as Luna Lovegood!"

That explained the great mop of blond hair in the bag. Rae hadn't scalped someone. She was channeling her inner Harry Potter.

Kellen noticed parenthood had suddenly created an odd conglomeration of thoughts in her brain, now, at a time when she needed to be thinking clearly. "Let me see your feet."

Rae pulled off her rain boots and stuck her feet out. Somehow, by the grace of God and Grandma Verona, she wore sturdy athletic shoes and tall socks. "How do your feet feel?"

"Fine." Rae looked bored.

"Did you bring any other shoes?"

"Yes! My Dorothy magic red sparkly shoes. There's no place like home. There's no place like home!"

"You said it, kiddo." That explained the red sequins tangled in the blond hair. "We're going to hide your bag. We'll hang your bag in a safe tree." Kellen looked up from trying to pack Rae's blankie into her backpack in time to see tears well up into Rae's eyes. Rae opened her mouth to sob and Kellen said quickly, "We'll come back for it."

"Really?" Rae's voice quavered.

"Really." Kellen prepared to climb. "When I was a little girl, my father and mother died, and my uncle and aunt took me in. They were wonderful people, but I was little and they had to clean out my parents' home. Some of the stuff they got rid of was… I missed it. My ugly baby doll with the hair I had chewed on. She was missing an eye, but I loved her. My comic book collection, and… I had my mother's records from when she was little. They threw those away. I'm not trying to get rid of your precious things."

Rae had fixated on one thing. "Your mother and father died? Oh, Mommy, I'm so sorry!" She reached out, all sticky fingers and peanut butter–smeared face, and hugged Kellen.

"It's okay. It was a long time ago. I'm better now." Rae looked so distressed, Kellen found her own voice shook. She was okay. She had been for a long time. But looking back, she knew the loss of her parents' love and support left her so hungry for someone of her own, she'd fallen prey to an older man, a Prince Charming who dramatically transformed into a monster.

She looked down at Rae, at her child, and imagined Rae falling prey to someone like Gregory. Suddenly, fiercely, she hugged her back. "I won't let anyone hurt you," she promised.

"I know," Rae said matter-of-factly. "I won't let anyone hurt you, either."

A childish promise made in all sincerity. Kellen quickly kissed the top of Rae's head, embarrassed now at the display of affection, and yet...inside she felt warm and mushy. "I've got to..." She freed herself from Rae's gummy embrace and hoisted herself into the lower branches of the Douglas fir. "See how this tree leans out over the bend of the creek? I can find it again."

From below, she heard the crinkle of plastic and Rae's voice saying, "That's astonishing."

"What's astonishing?" Kellen looked down.

Rae had unwrapped the mummy's head from its Bubble Wrap and was walking around it, looking at it from every side. "It's the Triple Goddess!"

"Why did you—?" Kellen sighed. "Never mind." She perched Rae's bag in the fork of a branch and slid back onto the ground. She didn't know whether she should react to Rae describing an ancient artifact as "astonishing," which seemed a huge word for a seven-year-old, or ask why Rae recognized the Triple Goddess, whatever that was. She settled on the easy one. "I don't know if you're right, but I do know it's definitely not a mummy's head. It's white marble, maybe Phoenician or Greco-Roman."

"Uh-huh." Rae squatted beside the head. "If you rub a statue of the Triple Goddess, it will bring you good luck." She rubbed it gently with her palm.

"I sure hope so." Kellen squatted down and rubbed, too. It couldn't do any harm. "What's a triple goddess?"

In an incredibly patient and patronizing manner, her child said, "*The* Triple Goddess is Mother, Maiden, Goddess."

Kellen turned the head around to view both sides. Yes, one side portrayed a young female on the verge of womanhood with a riot of curly hair around her youthful, hopeful face. On the opposite side, was a matron, an unsmiling woman with mature features. "Where's the goddess?" she asked.

Rae pointed at the top of her own head.

Kellen turned the head and jumped. There was a face peering out from the curls and stylings of the mother and daughter, a cruel face that protected, warned and intimidated. "Wow, kid, you really know what you're talking about. Where did you learn about this Triple Goddess?"

"Comics." Rae had lost interest. "Can I go wade in the creek?"

"Okay." Rae was halfway to the water when Kellen suddenly realized she was the parent, Rae was a child and Kellen would have to deal with any wet clothes. "Take off your shoes and socks first and roll up your pants!"

Rae waved at her as if she was being annoying. Which Kellen supposed, to a seven-year-old, she was.

She picked up the Triple Goddess head and strapped a zip tie around the base, not bothering with the Bubble Wrap. The damned thing weighed a ton, and the idea of toting it around the mountains trying to get Rae back to civilization made her—

"Miss Adams, give that to me."

She looked. A man stood in the shadows on the edge of the

clearing. He was tall, young, athletic and definitely one of Group 2. He'd tracked them. He'd found them. He was demanding the head, and he had a rifle pointed at her chest.

"Of course," she said. "I'm not willing to die for this." She slung her bag over one shoulder, walked toward him, plastic tie looped to the head's base in hand, and when she was close, she swirled, swung the head and knocked him in the skull with forty pounds of carved marble.

The element of surprise always worked—once.

He went down, bleeding from the forehead, sprawled across the pine-needle-strewn ground like a broken doll.

She pulled her pistol and pointed it at him.

He didn't move.

With her foot, she pushed his rifle out of his reach.

Still he didn't move.

Picking it up, she slammed the barrel against a tree trunk, bending the barrel, rendering the rifle unusable. She gave him a quick search, pulled his phone out of his pocket and used the butt of the rifle to smash the screen to smithereens. She picked it up and slipped it into her bag. Behind her she heard, "Mommy, who's that man with the gun?"

Arms outstretched, pistol ready to shoot, Kellen turned.

Rae was back from the stream. Water soaked her clothes and matted her hair; she'd fallen in.

Ten feet away from her, a second mercenary pointing a pistol at Kellen's back swung toward Rae.

Instantly, Kellen shot.

She was good with a pistol, but the distance across the clearing was forty feet. She tried for his chest; the bullet struck his shoulder. It should have blasted his arm away. Instead, it hit, slapped him sideways, blew his weapon out of his suddenly limp hand, knocked him down. He screamed like guys do when in combat and they're wearing body armor but the impact breaks the joint underneath. So she was a pretty good shot after all.

Kellen swung back to the guy she'd hit with the head. He was still out, his eyes rolled back in his head. She ran toward the guy writhing on the ground, picked up his weapon, set the safety and tucked it into her belt. She pointed her pistol in his face.

Abruptly, he stopped screaming and stared.

"How many more?" she asked. "Where are they?"

"Twenty!" His dark eyes were furious and fixed on the head dangling from the tie at her wrist. "They're all around you."

This guy was Group 1, overdressed and under-convincing. "You're not even a good liar," she said and used her foot to shove him on his face.

That made him scream, too.

Shoulders are so delicate.

She looped the zip tie around the handle of her duffel bag, securing the head. Grabbing his wrist on the broken side, she twisted it behind him. While he screamed, she used a plastic tie to bind his hands behind him. He was secure.

She glanced across the clearing. The guy with the rifle was out for the count.

She frisked the guy in the suit and found his phone. No signal—but she pressed his thumb to the keypad and changed the lock setting anyway.

He moaned, "Yeah, baby, you love it!"

She kicked his shoulder.

He screamed again.

Rae watched, eyes wide with amazement and horror. Of course. The child had never seen this kind of violence.

Kellen pocketed the phone. "Who do you work for?"

"Depends on whether I'm hunting the head or hunting the woman."

"What?" She dropped to one knee, pulled his pistol, released the safety with a loud satisfying click and pointed it at the side of his head. When the cold metal touched his temple, she asked, "What do you mean, hunting the woman?"

His eyes swiveled as far to the side as he could make them go, and when he caught a glimpse of the pistol, he got serious. "The first boss dropped out of the chase. I don't know why, got a case of decency or got eliminated."

"Killed?"

"This is a rough game. Lots of money at stake."

"I know that." If rival thieves were vying for the Triple Goddess, that explained the two bands who were chasing Rae and Kellen.

"I wanted to drop out, too. I don't run around in the mountains like a goddamn hillbilly. I'm not dressed for this. We don't have the right communication. But the new guy—once you're in, he doesn't let you go. His directions are to get the woman."

That set her back on her heels. "Get *me*?"

"Don't flatter yourself. You're not priceless. It's the head we're after. As long as you've got the head, you're the target." He laughed and turned his head into the dirt. "If you're going to shoot me, do it. My life's not worth spit now anyway."

Kellen wasn't going to shoot him in cold blood, she really wasn't going to shoot him in front of her little girl and she needed to get that little girl out of here in a hurry. So she set the safety, put the pistol in her belt again and in a voice she kept steady and understated, she asked, "Rae, honey, are your feet all wet?"

Rae stomped her boots up and down, and even from this distance, Kellen could hear sloshing inside. "Yes, Mommy."

"Then come on." Kellen walked toward her, projecting so much calm she was positively Zen. "I'll carry you on my back."

"I'm too big!"

"I can't carry you very far, but we need to get away from here and fast." Kellen pulled her bag off her back, pushed her arms through the straps, settled the weight on her chest and squatted down in front of Rae. "Let's go."

Rae hesitated.

Kellen waited, tense with fear. Had the violence scared her child so much she didn't want to touch Kellen?

Rae's arms wrapped around Kellen's neck, Kellen took her legs and wrapped them around her waist, and Kellen started running. Right now, it didn't exactly matter where they ran, only that they got away from here.

Because maybe the guy was telling the truth; maybe the new boss had called in more searchers. Even if he hadn't, the other three guys were in the area. The shot would bring them running, and she didn't have much time to get Rae and the Triple Goddess away from here. Once the other men talked to the guys on the ground and discovered Kellen was on the move with a child, that child became a weapon in their hands. Kellen couldn't allow that. She didn't know how long she could hold out, running full tilt with a backpack, the Triple Goddess and a forty-five pound child. Yet she had to save Rae and the marble head.

As they jumped the stream, Kellen dropped the first phone, the broken one, into the water. That should disable the GPS, and hopefully the two guys she'd left behind would remain undiscovered long enough for Kellen and Rae to escape.

"Mommy?" Rae's voice wobbled pathetically.

Kellen wanted to moan. But she had to save her breath. Rae was going to ask about Kellen's ruthless treatment of those men. "Rae?"

"I gotta go potty."

Now Kellen did moan. She took a path that led downhill. "I do, too. Can you hold it for a while?"

"Yes. Is it bad that I just heard thunder?"

14

The rain was brief and violent, a downpour of thunder and lightning that had Rae hiding her face in Kellen's neck and Kellen squishing through puddles. "This is good," she told Rae. "The rain will hide our tracks."

"The rain… I really got to go potty."

Kellen let her down under a heavy-branched old pine, which protected them from the worst of the downpour. She helped her hang her skinny little bottom over a log, and reflected that she hadn't changed diapers like Max had, but somehow hearing Rae complain about one sheet of toilet paper made things feel a little more even. Rae's horror that they had to put the used toilet paper into a baggie to carry out made Kellen waver between laughter and the environmental lecture about *carry in, carry out.*

The child was shivering in her wet clothes, so Kellen gave the lecture while she dried her with one of her own extra T-shirts, and dressed her in a pair of Rae's pink tights—

"Mommy, I need panties!"

"Did you bring them?"

—and Kellen's sweatshirt hoodie. Kellen used the log facilities, shared the last of the water from her canteen and said, "We're almost out."

"We can drink some out of a stream."

"And get giardia." *Shut up, Kellen.* "We'll do that." She pulled the second phone out of her pocket and in hope and desperation, used her thumb to open it. If she could make one call for help…

But no. Here, now, there was no service and she didn't dare carry it because she didn't want these guys, whoever they were, to use it to track her. So she placed it on a rock, slammed her heel into the screen and buried it in a mud puddle.

Rae watched, wide-eyed, and said solemnly, "When I get a phone, I'm not going to let you near it."

Kellen didn't think she could laugh. But she did, softly. "That's probably a smart decision."

"Where are we going?" Rae asked.

Good question. Kellen had been running without a destination in mind, her sole aim to misdirect anyone who followed. Now she had a decision to make—go down the mountain and try to find a ranger station or head up the mountain and to the Restorer.

Either way, the Mercenaries would try to take a stand between her and her destination, and if that last guy was telling the truth, their orders were to *get the woman.* That meant the Triple Goddess—and whoever was carrying her. "Maybe we ought to dump the head." She was merely thinking out loud; she'd taken the job in good faith and she had faith in her ability to survive and deliver the Triple Goddess and keep her daughter from harm.

Until Rae said in an ever-louder voice, "Dump the Triple Goddess? What is wrong with you, Mother? The Goddess deserves our care—"

"Okay, shhh!"

"The Goddess represents us. She is Woman, hear me roar!"

Rae sounded like Kellen herself in a long-ago snit, and if she didn't shut up, she would announce them to the whole forest.

Kellen wrestled the poncho over the two of them. "Who did you hear that from?"

"After-school cartoons! Rowr!"

Kellen picked Rae up again. "I didn't know your grandmother let you watch cartoons after school."

"Um..." Rae squirmed. "Sometimes I go visit my friend Chloe. Her babysitter lets us watch."

"What else does she let you do?" Kellen ran.

"Eat Fruit Roll-Ups!" Rae shouted right in Kellen's ear.

"Okay. That was loud. If you promise not to shout again—" at least for the next ten minutes "—I promise I won't tell Grandma about the cartoons and the Fruit Roll-Ups."

Rae kept her voice polite and sedate. "Thank you, Mommy."

Kellen avoided the paths, using the sun as guidance, heading deeper and higher into the wilderness to put some space between her and the guys in the slick suits and the city shoes.

Rae drooped and slept, then roused and in an excited voice said, "Mommy, stop. Stop!"

Kellen was glad to. Her back was creaking, Rae was squirming, and surely they had put any search parties behind. She pulled off the poncho. "Do you need to go potty again?"

"No. No! Huckleberries. We found huckleberries!" Rae hopped around the six-foot-tall sprawling dark green hedge, collecting the dark purplish fruit with wild abandon.

Kellen followed in alarm. "Are you sure these are edible?"

Rae looked a question.

"Not poisonous. If we eat them, will we die?"

"No! They're *huckleberries*!" Rae acted as if Kellen was an idiot.

Not in a mean way, Kellen realized, but in total surprise, as if she expected Kellen to know everything.

Kellen took another look at Rae. Oh, no. She *did* expect Kellen to know everything.

Rae popped the handful of berries in her mouth.

Kellen lunged to stop her, but it was too late. Was Rae going to die from eating poisoned berries? Should Kellen stick her finger down Rae's throat?

She couldn't. She just couldn't. Rae seemed so sure, and Kellen didn't know a thing about Pacific Northwest berries, and she couldn't traumatize the child any further on a vague fear. After all, it wasn't as if she'd eaten poisoned mushrooms…

There was only one thing to do. Kellen ate a handful of berries, too.

They were fabulous. If they were going to die, they were going to die together and die happy, too. "How do you know about huckleberries?" she asked as she picked more and ate them.

"Mrs. Maniscaldo lived down the road from the winery. She was old." Rae's shaking voice dramatically indicated Mrs. Maniscaldo's age. "Grandma and me used to go down to her house to help her pick her raspberries and blueberries. Grandma would make jam, and we'd keep some, and she'd give the rest to Mrs. Maniscaldo, who gave it out as Christmas presents. I'd go down there and eat it with her on fried bread. Last summer, me and Daddy and Grandma took Mrs. Maniscaldo up in the mountains. Because she's from the mountains, but she was so old she couldn't live up there anymore. She showed us huckleberries and how to pick them, and she yelled at Daddy on the other side of the thicket to start picking the berries and stop eating them, and when we walked around so she could yell at him again, it wasn't Daddy."

"Who was it?"

"It was a *bear.* I saw it. It was big and black!"

Fascinated, Kellen kept popping berries in her mouth. "What happened?"

"She yelled at the bear and waved her arms and it ran off. She laughed and laughed, and sat down, and Daddy had to help her get up. She said she was scared the bear would get us, but I didn't know it. She yelled right at him!"

"Mrs. Maniscaldo sounds like quite a woman."

"She was nice. She died."

Whoa. Kellen hadn't seen that coming. She stopped eating. "I'm sorry."

"It's okay. Grandma didn't want me to go to the funeral, but I wanted to see her again, so Daddy took me."

To Kellen's relief, Rae didn't look sad. She looked, well, philosophical. For a kid, that was quite an expression. Kellen asked, "What did you think?"

"She wasn't there."

"Mrs. Maniscaldo?"

"She was gone. Grandma said she went to heaven. I think she went to the mountains."

Kellen didn't know whether to grin or console.

"When I get new crayons, I'm going to draw LightningBug riding Patrick, because I sat on Patrick in the van. Grandma's not going to be happy because I wasn't in my car seat."

"Maybe we shouldn't tell her?"

Rae mulled that over. "That's lying."

"It's not telling all the truth. Rae, I promise when your grandmother finds out about this trip, we're going to have a lot to tell her and we'll want to make it so she isn't too scared. In the big scheme of things—" like knocking people out with an ancient marble head and shooting them "—it won't hurt her not to know."

"So it doesn't matter whether I sit in my car seat or not?"

"I *didn't* say that. I'm saying we had no choice and it turned out well, so we'll keep it between ourselves. Okay?"

"Okay! In my drawing, Patrick's going to wear my pink tutu and I'm going to have a pink cape with jewels and flowers."

"You bet. Let's pick more berries and save them for later." Kellen looked around.

The sun was going down and with the mountains surrounding them, the light would disappear quickly. Temperatures would drop to near freezing. They needed a place to stop for the night, a spot she could protect, someplace they'd be safe.

"Mommy, can you find me?" Rae's voice was muffled.

Alarm sent a trill up Kellen's spine. She looked around. "No. Where are you?"

Rae's head popped out from under the bushes. "Here!"

"Is there room under there?" Kellen pushed her way into the hedge. The densely leafed branches grew low to the ground, and in here, no one could see them… "This is a great place to sleep! Let's get our stuff." She crawled out and dragged in her backpack and the Triple Goddess.

"We're going to stay here?" Rae did not sound impressed.

"It's a good place. It's fairly dry and protected from the rain, if we get any more. It's hidden from the bad guys and easily defensible."

Rae looked around. "Where are we going to have our fire?"

"We're not going to have a fire."

"We're camping. We have to have a fire."

"We're not camping. We're running away."

"How can we make s'mores?"

"We don't have graham crackers, chocolate or marshmallows. A lack of a fire is a moot point." Why was Kellen even saying this stuff? "We'll eat dinner—"

"*What* dinner?" Rae asked suspiciously.

Smart kid. "A breakfast cookie with peanut butter on it and some water."

"I like cookies! I want milk." Rae started to droop so suddenly, Kellen was caught unprepared. "I'm hungry. I want my daddy."

"And you're tired." Kellen helped her take off her boots.

"No. I'm not!"

"Okay. You aren't." Rae's shoes and socks were still wet. Kellen hung them on a branch and hoped they would dry by morning.

The light was disappearing.

Rae slapped at a leaf. "It's scratchy in here."

"It's our own secret hiding place." Kellen got out the breakfast cookie, spread it with a thick layer of peanut butter, divided it and gave half to Rae.

Rae scarfed it down and looked for more.

Kellen gave her a drink out of the canteen and the other half of the cookie, and went to work spreading out the all-weather blanket for protection from the cold ground and the sleeping bag on top.

Rae quit at three-quarters of a cookie and whimpered.

It was the first whimper Kellen had ever heard out of her cheerful, chatty daughter. Tears, yes. But never a whimper. "Come on, honey. This is an adventure. Remember?"

"I want my blankie." Her grubby yellow yarn blankie.

"Coming right up." Kellen kept her voice cheerful. "Let's get in there."

Rae hugged her blankie and climbed in the sleeping bag. "Mommy, I'm scared."

Kellen took a farewell look at the one-quarter of the breakfast cookie and slid it into a baggie. "Now I'll take off my shoes and socks and jacket and put them at the bottom of the bag—" and put the pistol, safety on, in its holster close at hand "—and climb in with you."

"We'll snuggle!"

"Right. We will." Rae slid into Kellen's arms, and Kellen awkwardly rubbed her head.

"My nose is cold."

"Mine, too." With the sun gone behind the mountains, the temperature dropped rapidly.

In a serious voice, Rae asked, "Mommy, have you ever seen a dead person?"

The smell of charred wood and burned flesh. A metal coil melted in the dirt and the knowledge of young lives ended too soon. A pain in the region of her heart, and a knowledge that she had done the wrong thing. Such a wrong thing. She knew death—but now, she had delivered victims into death's bony grip.

"Yes, I have. In Afghanistan. I was in the war. I saw… Yes, I've seen dead people." Kellen thought she ought to say something more, something bracing, so she continued, "Sometimes they were my people."

"Your friends?"

"Not always, but people who were on my side. Even if we didn't like each other, we defended each other. We stood back-to-back and we fought for each other. Because when you're fighting for the same cause, that's what you do."

"Like ThunderFlash and LightningBug!"

Hoo boy. "Exactly like that."

"I haven't put the Triple Goddess head in our book. When we stop, I'll draw the head."

"Are you going to draw all our adventures together? That's going to be quite a book. We've got to walk tomorrow—" and hope to hell none of the hunters found them "—and find a ranger station. You're up for all that, aren't you, Rae?"

No answer.

"Rae?"

No answer. Just like that, the kid was asleep.

Kellen sighed in relief, folded Rae's blankie and tucked it under Rae's head as a pillow. She didn't know how they were going to find a ranger station, exactly. Wilderness surrounded them, and they were avoiding the paths where the park signs offered guidance. They were avoiding other hikers who might be able to point them in the right direction. So in the morning, they'd head downhill, because the ranger stations had to be accessible to the most people and the higher and more difficult the path, the fewer people there would be.

Plan in place, she prepared to drift off…

Rae punched her in the ribs.

"Ow!" Kellen reached out. "Honey, don't—"

Rae kicked her in the thigh, dangerously close to her wounded hip. She was asleep, Kellen could tell, but clearly she did not rest peacefully. Kellen put her arms around Rae's body and turned her so she faced away. Rae relaxed.

Kellen started to drift off again.

Rae tried to turn sideways in the bag, head toward Kellen, knees scrunched up to her chest. Which wasn't comfortable for Kellen and couldn't be comfortable for Rae. And wasn't because Rae followed that by straightening her legs and hitting Kellen under the chin with a head-butt.

Kellen grunted and woke, rubbed her chin and figured what the hell and turned so her back was to Rae. At least this way, Rae could only take out her ribs and spine.

She slept.

Rae quieted.

Then Kellen was wide-awake, aware Rae was too quiet.

Something was very wrong.

Rae was gone.

15

Alarm slammed through Kellen. She groped all the way down in the narrow bag. Rae's clothes and shoes were there, but Rae was simply gone.

"Calm," Kellen muttered. Panic wouldn't help. Although right now, panic seemed like the right thing to do. "Think." No one had rustled through the bushes, so Rae had to be nearby. Kellen crawled out of the bag into the freezing mountain air and, still on her hands and knees, looked around.

The starlight was bright, bright enough to show the shrubs that surrounded and protected them and—that shivering rock hadn't been there before. Rae had wrangled her way out of the bag, probably punching and kicking all the way and, still asleep, was curled into a frozen little ball.

"Oh, sweetie." Kellen picked up her child and put her in the sleeping bag. She rubbed her cold toes and hands, hugged her close and cried terrified tears and tucked Rae's beloved blankie close around the child's head. What if she hadn't woken when she did? Rae would have died of exposure and it would be Kellen's fault.

One more big black mark on the bad mommy chart.

For the rest of the night, Kellen slept in short bursts, waking every few minutes to check on Rae and hoping against hope she hadn't done Max's child irreparable harm.

★ ★ ★

As the sun rose, Kellen finally fell into a deep sleep and woke awash in anxiety and guilt.

But Rae was right there, lying on her stomach, her blankie bunched under her arms, with her crayons, drawing in her ThunderFlash and LightningBug book.

Kellen watched her, noticing how much like her cousin Rae looked, how she frowned as she put all her energy into coloring, that she seemed healthy after her brush with freezing death… "How are you?" she whispered.

Rae turned to her, smiling as brightly as ever. "I'm fine, Mommy." She kissed Kellen on the mouth. "How are you? I woke up before you and I put on my shoes and socks and got my crayons and my book. See?" She showed Kellen a new page of superhero drawings in purple, red and yellow. "I got my own breakfast. I picked huckleberries and ate them."

That explained the smears of red and purple on her face.

"I came back to bed and colored until you woke up." Rae beamed. "I saved you some berries."

If the child wasn't okay, she was faking it well. Kellen looked at the squished blackish purple berries piled in the dirt, waiting for her.

She ate them.

Rae chatted. "What are we going to do today? Will there be bad men after us some more? Are we almost there? Will the park rangers take us for a pizza? I want pesto, cheese and chicken."

Absurd conversation. "No anchovies?"

Rae shrugged. "They aren't my favorite."

Another flash of maturity in a child obsessed with princesses and flashy sequins.

Kellen rolled to look at her backpack. The contents were strewn from one end of the hedge to another. "You put your shoes and socks on, and got out of the sleeping bag, and got back in."

Rae nodded, uninterested.

That explained the pine needles poking Kellen in the legs and the—

"Were your shoes and socks dry?"

"Yes. Lookee!" Rae showed Kellen the newest drawing. There was a stick figure, tall and dressed in red and black. Rae said that was ThunderFlash. There was a shorter stick figure, dressed in a cape of pink and yellow stars. That was LightningBug. And a hideous white head-like thing with too many eyes floated beside them. Solemnly, Rae said, "We have a talisman."

Where did this kid get her vocabulary? Kellen felt her shoes and socks. They *were* dry, thank heavens. "What talisman?"

"The head! The Triple Goddess will guard us. Look at how she took out that man when you hit him! And that guy from the van!"

"Actually—" Kellen couldn't believe she was indignant about this "—I'm the one who aimed the head well enough to take him down." She took a breath and tried to think how to explain this to a seven-year-old. "Faith in something unknown is a great thing, but you have to combine faith with action. So if you saw a bad guy sneaking up on us, would you pray to the Triple Goddess, or would you scream a warning?"

Rae screamed. Kellen jumped and grabbed her, ready to put her hand over Rae's mouth. Stopping herself, she listened as birds took flight in the trees above. With a sound so high-pitched, anyone within earshot would be looking up for a hawk or a cougar.

She relaxed. "Nice. But let's not scream again unless there's trouble. Now—what if the bad guy grabs you first?"

"Kick them?"

"Where?"

"Some place that hurts."

"Right. The best places to kick or hit are the head, the sternum and the groin."

Rae giggled. "Groin!"

Kellen pretended like she didn't hear. "It's easy to remember. You punch right down the middle of the body. Face—" she pointed at Rae's nose, mouth and throat "—sternum—" she pointed at Rae's breastbone "—and groin."

When she pointed at Rae's groin, Rae stopped laughing and her eyes got big. "I hit a tree one time on my bike and fell off the seat and landed on the bar. It hurt so bad."

"So you know what I'm talking about. It hurts men, too, worse than it hurts girls." Kellen reflected for a minute. "Although maybe that's not true, maybe men are more whiny about it."

"Groin..." Rae giggled again. "Groin. Groin. Groin."

The chanting was going to get old fast. Kellen dived to the bottom of the sleeping bag, retrieved her jacket and boots and socks and got dressed. She crawled out of the bag and started rolling, organizing and stuffing.

Rae stopped chanting and cocked her head. "What's that noise?"

She whispered, and her quietness got Kellen's attention. She froze and listened.

Footsteps. Someone was walking toward the thicket where they hid. Heavy footsteps. A man.

No, two men.

In a panic, Kellen looked toward Rae. Would the child be quiet?

Rae put her finger to her lips. She was shushing Kellen.

Kellen nodded slowly, subduing her terror.

"I would swear I heard someone scream," one of the men said.

"It was a bird." The other guy lit a match and puffed on a cigarette so hard the cloud of smoke drifted across them in a wave.

"Fine. It was a bird. Then where did they go?"

"Who cares about them? Where did the *head* go? That's where the value is."

Both men kept their voices low. Both men had Eastern European accents. In slow motion, Kellen slid down and looked at their shoes.

Shiny black leather, unsuited for hiking. That confirmed her suspicions; this was Group 1, the Greedy Bastards.

"We're supposed to be chasing them toward the ranger station, toward the other team. But if we find them first, I say we handle the matter ourselves."

The first guy said, "The boss could be a difficulty."

Mr. Cigarette grunted an agreement.

"And what about the kid? He didn't tell us about a kid."

"So he doesn't know everything." The cigarette dropped to the ground. The guy stubbed it out with his shoe. "A little girl, they said. I like little girls."

They walked on.

Kellen gestured to Rae to remain still and quiet.

Rae's eyes were big; she didn't even blink. She had heard the words, and while maybe she hadn't understood all his meaning, his tone revealed far too much of his sick pleasure at the idea of killing a woman and her child. And more.

They sat very still for long chilling minutes.

Finally, Rae stirred. She whispered, "Mommy, what are we going to do?"

Kellen finished packing the bag. "Change of plans. We're going to the Restorer as quickly as we can."

"Where's he?"

"Uphill."

"Okay!" Rae crawled under shrubs, reached out and nabbed the cigarette. She crawled back and handed it to her mother. "I don't like this man. He's gross. He *litters*. But I like the Restorer. Right?"

"Yes. He's one of the good guys." She hoped. Nils Brooks didn't necessarily associate with the good guys. She fieldstripped the cigarette, scattering the tobacco and shredding the paper. "Wait here." She crawled out and scanned the area.

The men's footsteps led away and downhill, and as far as she could see, they hadn't doubled back. "Come on, Rae, we've got to get going."

"Mommy, what are we having for breakfast?"

16

By the time Max had gathered his gear and hit the road in one of the tough old winery pickups, it was afternoon. The sun set about nine, he needed food and sleep, and he couldn't find anything in the dark, so he stopped for the night in Centralia. As soon as he got into the motel room with a greasy bag filled with a hamburger and large order of fries, he locked the door behind him and called Nils Brooks.

Brooks sounded rough, gravelly, as if Max had woken him from a sound sleep.

"Ah, I'm sorry." Max faked sympathy. "You're on Eastern Time. I guess it's late there, huh?" He took a large bite of the burger and chewed.

Without preamble, Brooks asked, "Did you find the head?"

Max stared at the mashed burger in his clenched fist. If he had Brooks here now, he'd rearrange his smug face. "You mean, did I find Kellen and our daughter? No. I got a late start, what with not being told the truth by *you*. Any word on their whereabouts?"

"No."

"Did you tell the Restorer? Is he going after them?"

"All he's got is a radio. I couldn't get him to pick up." Max heard a woman's sleepy voice say something, then Brooks sounded more awake and as if he was moving. A door shut, and he said quietly, "Which doesn't mean he wasn't there listening, just that he wouldn't reply."

A woman. Max was racing across Washington trying to find and save the only beings that gave his life value, and Brooks was screwing some woman. In disgust, Max dropped the burger back into the bag. "What do you mean?"

"Look. The Restorer is not exactly a helpful guy. He's a mystery and a hermit. He doesn't like people. Maybe he heard me, maybe he'll care enough about the head to search for Kellen and Rae, but I'm afraid—"

"You go to hell." Max hung up. What a prick. What an absolute prick. He could only hope Brooks was a limp prick who would leave that woman unsatisfied.

At dawn, he got a message from Brooks.

No word from the Restorer. No word from Kellen.

Max called his mother.

She hadn't heard from Kellen and Rae, but she sounded strong and once again assured him Kellen would keep Rae safe.

He headed into the Olympic Mountains to find his daughter and his...and the mother of his daughter.

The map Nils Brooks had sent directed him to President Roosevelt Road, a narrow gravel lane that wound up and down and around the mountains.

Kellen and Rae had been gone almost twenty-four hours, out of touch the whole time. Few people could face the challenges up here, making this isolated land one of the last true wildernesses on earth. If Kellen and Rae were on the run, how could he find them? Kellen's military training would serve to keep them safe, but would also prevent him from locating them. Logically, Kellen would make a run for the ranger station. There she and Rae would be safe. They'd have a way to communicate and a way to get away. So that's where he would go, too.

A tow truck rounded a corner, coming straight at him on the narrow road. He pulled as far over to the side and waited while the truck squeaked past him. Then he saw it. The burned and blackened van, the one that had picked up Kellen.

In a flash, he was honking the horn, yelling and getting the driver's attention. He rolled down his window.

The female driver rolled down her window. Dust boiled into both vehicles.

"Yeah?" The female wore a name tag that said, *Hi, my name is Dakota.*

"My girlfriend and daughter were in that vehicle." Cold sweat. He'd broken a cold sweat. "What happened?"

"It burned."

"No bodies inside?'

"No! Not unless you want to count a couple of princess doll casualties."

Relief and residual fear made him dizzy. "Were they found? My girlfriend and my daughter. My girlfriend—" not his girlfriend, but a lie told in a good cause "—she's about five foot six, shortish hair, kind of blond with dark ends, blue eyes. My daughter's seven, blond hair, brown eyes. They look a lot alike. Did you see them?"

"No, sorry." Dakota looked sorry, too. "One of the park rangers found the van and called me to come up and tow it. He didn't know what caused the fire or what happened to the driver or any passenger. We were both happy that whoever it was got out safely. We figured they'd been picked up by another hiker. I'm taking the van down to have the cops look it over and see if they can figure out who it belongs to."

"Can I look?"

He must have looked pretty sick, because she said, "I shouldn't, but yeah." She opened her door. "Come on."

He got out, too, and followed her back to the van.

Most women would have worried about being on a lonely mountain road with a man his size. Not her; she was six feet tall and if the sleeveless shirt was any indication, she lifted weights.

Heavy weights. She saw him looking. "You have to stay in shape to do my job."

"I'll bet."

Smoke had given the exterior paint a grayish patina. The fire's heat had broken the windows and warped the side panel door open. Flames had blackened the interior, melted the upholstery, and yet...under the back seat, he could see a flashing sprinkle of warped sequins.

His daughter had been there.

He must have looked ill, because Dakota asked, "You okay?"

"You're *sure* there's no bodies in there?"

"I swear. The ranger looked it over, and I looked it over, too. You can hop in if you want."

"I trust you." Time for the million-dollar question. "What caused the fire?"

"Something went wrong under the hood. You suspect bad doin's?"

"Yes."

"What were they doing up here?"

"My girlfriend had a job. My daughter tagged along. Not that she was supposed to."

"Sounds like a handful."

"She is so much trouble."

"And you love her to death."

"Yes." He turned away. "I'd better go find them." He stopped. "Where did this fire happen?"

"About three miles up the road. You can't miss it. The flames scorched the shit out of a couple of Douglas firs, could have started a forest fire, but a rainstorm in the afternoon put them out." She saluted him. "Good luck."

Something about the way she saluted made him ask, "You former military?"

"Army."

"So was my girlfriend. Captain Kellen Adams."

"I don't know her, but when I talk to the park rangers, I'll let them know your story, tell them about your family."

"Thank you." He handed her his business card. "Not that cell phones work up here, but leave a message and maybe I'll go high enough to catch a signal."

They headed to their vehicles and took off in opposite directions.

Max drove, not paying a bit of attention to the gravel washboards or watching the sides of the road, because he knew what he was looking for. Wherever that van had burned, that was the place to start looking for his little girl and his big girl.

He needed to remember—Kellen wasn't his yet.

But right now, when he was terrified, it was hard.

The burned spot was, as Dakota said, three miles up the road. Max pulled up at the spot the van had been parked and started searching the ground. He found pink glitter and a melted princess doll that made him want to cry and a glittery trail that led toward the creek that flowed under the road and up into the forest. Kellen's footsteps dug deep into the gravel, as if she'd been running, and joined smaller footsteps that pressed into the creek sides and then up toward a clearing surrounded by trees where—

Max had his head down, following the tracks, intent on knowing where his daughter and his woman (not his, not yet) had been.

When he looked up, he saw the man's body, bound to the tree, slumped against the trunk, throat cut, blood spilling down his chest…

With that one glance, Max identified him. This was the guy who had picked up Kellen in the white van and driven her and Rae away to an adventure that could very well be the death of them. And this guy, whatever his name was, was now dead in a brutal bloody murder.

Max had to get to Kellen and Rae before it was too late.

He backtracked to his truck and drove on to the parking

area fast enough to make his jaw snap when he hit a bump. He parked and consulted his map. He had already made his decision. He would make no attempt to report the murder. The guy was already dead and if Max had contacted the authorities, he would have been there for hours, possibly detained as a suspect. Weighed against the threat to Kellen and Rae, the legalities were unimportant.

Kellen had to know the danger she was in.

Would she try to get Rae to the ranger station?

Or would she head for the Restorer's home base?

If she headed for the ranger station, Max knew she and Rae would be safe with them.

Max put the map away, shouldered his backpack and started the rough climb up to Horizon Ridge and the Restorer. If for some reason, Kellen headed that way, their chances of survival lessened considerably. Maybe he was headed the wrong direction, but they would need him there.

17

At about an hour, Rae had apparently forgotten all about the guys who had stood outside their huckleberry thicket and talked with apparent pleasure about killing them.

Kellen wished she could forget. The way that man sounded—he wanted the head, and he wanted to hurt them even more.

Oh, Max, I'm so sorry. By now he knew Rae had stowed away. By now he'd spoken to Nils. He must be worried to death.

Rae was bored with hiking. She wanted to stop and play in the stream, build a dam, fall in again and get cold, wet and covered with dirt.

Kellen wanted to keep moving, avoid being captured and stay alive. Trying to explain *why* made no impression on Rae, and Kellen knew it behooved her to keep her child entertained and walking. After all, Kellen was the adult, the mature human being, the parent. She knew without a doubt Max could do it. How hard could it be? All she needed to do was talk to Rae about something that interested Rae, preferably something that wasn't loud enough to attract the attention of the headhunters or the Mercenaries. Even better, she wanted to talk about something that didn't involve chanting, "Groin, groin, groin," like a primitive song from an early Star Trek episode.

Cheerfully, Kellen asked, "What do you think you could find out here and use for a weapon?"

"A weapon?" Rae sat down on a log. "I don't want to wear my boots anymore."

"Okay. Take off your boots." Kellen already knew who was going to have to carry them. "If someone was hurting you, what could you grab real fast and use to hurt them back?"

One boot half off, Rae looked up at Kellen in dismay. "Everybody likes me!"

"That's true." Kellen took the first boot. "Everybody who knows you likes you. But maybe someone is on drugs and sees you as a threat. You know about people on drugs, right?"

"They taught us in school." Rae got very solemn. "Drugs make people do bad things."

"Right. Some people have problems in their minds, even without drugs, and they might be afraid of you and strike out."

Rae frowned at Kellen. "Like in baseball?"

"No, I mean hit you." Kellen accepted the second boot and used a nylon zip tie to fasten them to her backpack. "Grab you and try to take you somewhere you don't want to go. What could you do to get away?"

"Run?" Rae jumped to her feet.

"That is a great answer!" Kellen took Rae's athletic shoes out of the bag and knelt down beside her. She straightened Rae's socks, made sure her athletic shoes were tied tight, and while she did, she listened to the sounds of the forest. Birds chirped. Small creatures scurried. An occasional breeze made the high branches creak. To her, it sounded normal, without threat or ambush.

She knew better now.

Again she thought, *Oh, Max, I'm so sorry.* Max took responsibility for the safety of everyone in his family. She remembered when she had saved his niece from kidnapping, everyone in the Di Luca family had toasted her, but it was Max who swore his allegiance to her. Even if they had never become lovers, she still had no doubt he would have protected and cared for her.

What would he do to keep his daughter safe?

"Come on," she said to Rae. "Let's keep walkin' and talkin'."

Rae put her hand in Kellen's. "I like talking with you, Mommy."

"I like talking with you, too, Rae." Kellen looked at the little hand in hers. How did the child get so grubby so fast? "How about this? Let's say someone knocked you down and sat on you and you couldn't kick them. Do you see anything around here you could grab to poke in their eye?"

"A stick!" Rae yelled and broke away to grab a broken branch off the forest floor.

"Good girl."

"I'm going to use this as a walking stick. It's too long. I'm going to break it. Wait, Mommy." Rae swung the branch as hard as she could against the trunk of a tree, missed and whacked Kellen across the thighs.

"Ouch!" Kellen said.

Rae's eyes filled with mortified tears.

No. No crying. Kellen was proud of her calm when she said, "That didn't work too well to break the stick, but it would hurt an attacker." She rubbed her leg. She could feel the bruise rising. "Try again and hit the trunk this time."

Rae did. The end broke off. She said, "Mommy, I'm sorry."

"I know. You'll be more careful in the future. Now you have a great walking stick and you can hike even faster!"

"Yeah!" Rae ran about twenty feet up the path, Kellen hot on her heels, before she slowed again.

Kellen figured, *Keep up the conversation*. "What if you want to whack a bad guy in the mouth and break his teeth? Could you find something to use?"

"A rock!" Rae looked hard for a rock and finally scuffed one out of the hard-packed dirt.

"You're good at this! What if a man was running at you, going to hit you with his fist?"

With awesome calm and logic, Rae said, "If he was fat like Zio Placido, I'd climb a tree."

"If you're fast enough, that might work. If they manage to grab you, break off a branch and poke them in the eyes. Never stop fighting, Rae. Never give in to the bad guys."

Rae stopped in the middle of the path, turned and faced Kellen. "Mommy, why?"

"Why are we talking about this?"

"Yes. Aren't *you* going to take care of me?"

"For as long as I'm able, I promise." Kellen urged her to turn and walk up the path again. "But I won't always be where you are, so you need to learn to take care of yourself. Come on, let's go."

"And if you're hurt, I need to take care of you."

Uh-oh. That wasn't at all the conclusion Kellen wanted her to draw. "You're little, and what's really important is knowing there's no such thing as a fair fight." Kellen got to the heart of the message she wanted to convey. "There are only fights you win and fights you lose. Once a fight is started, if you lose it, you're going to get hurt."

"Daddy says instead of fighting, to use my words."

"Good advice, and I agree." Sometimes it even worked, and those were the times when the fight didn't start. "I don't think we can talk to these guys who are chasing us. There are more of them, they're men and so they're bigger and stronger than we are, and they have a lot of guns and mean fists."

"I want to take karate!"

Kellen imagined solemn children in white gis and white belts, lined up and listening to their master. "That's a good idea."

"Grandma says little girls don't take karate, and she says anyway I don't listen."

Kellen made a note to herself to have a talk about karate classes for Rae. "How will you learn to listen if you don't try?"

"Yeah!"

Kellen managed to carry the discussion for another half hour and an arduous uphill trek. Then the path straightened and conversation moved on to:

What are we having for lunch?

I'm tired of peanut butter.

Are we there yet?

I'm not tired.

What's for lunch?

I'm bored.

Why did we eat all the huckleberries?

What's for dinner?

Are we there yet?

By late afternoon, Kellen knew she needed to find someplace for them to stop, to rest, to be safe, because apparently the headhunters had decided to let Rae drive her crazy to make their jobs easier.

Things were working out for the Mercenaries.

18

Kellen found her a place to rest and be safe in a small flat spot cradled at the top of a cluster of boulders ten feet above the surrounding forest floor. Up here, the rainwater had drained away from the sandy soil, leaving it damp but not unpleasant. Up here, Rae couldn't ask if they were there yet, because obviously they weren't, and even if hoards of mercenaries attacked, Kellen could hold them off for quite a while before she ran out of ammunition.

But mostly, in an hour it would be dark and she could roll out the tarp and her one-person sleeping bag, hide with her kid for the night, eat and sleep and refresh. If they put in some hard hiking the next day, even with constant questions and conversation, they could reach the Restorer and…

She looked at her daughter, drooping against the trunk of a tree. "Come on. It's like we're birds, and I'll help you get up there to our own private nest."

"I don't need *help.* I'm not *tired.*" Rae sounded cranky.

"I know. Let's get up there and eat and sleep."

"I'm not tired!"

"But Mommy is." Kellen pushed Rae up the steep, narrow, slick path to the top. Then dragged herself and her bag and the head up after her. That head was really starting to creep her out. No matter which way she stashed it, eyes stared at her, either the maiden, the mother, or if she caught an unlucky glimpse, the goddess. She was going to be so glad to deliver that thing to the Restorer…

"Mommy?"

Kellen realized she had locked eyes with the goddess, and was hypnotized by that wild angry stare. Not good. Not now. She pulled the jar of peanut butter out of the duffel bag, opened it and stuck her finger in. She took a scoop, put it in her mouth, and passed the jar to Rae.

Rae giggled. "Mommy! We're not supposed to use our fingers!"

"In a minute, I'll cut up an apple and find the protein bars." Which were crumbs by now, but why worry about that technicality? "Right now, let's get some good stuff into us."

Rae giggled again and dipped into the peanut butter.

That giggle. Maybe the forest muffled the sound. Probably it carried for miles. "You know what would be a good idea? If we had some kind of alarm that would warn us if the bad guys were coming."

"I like sirens! Can we have a siren?"

"Did you bring one?"

"No, but I'm not the mommy!"

The kid had a point. The mommy should have come better prepared, and when the mommy got back to civilization, the mommy was going to personally undertake a trip to Washington, DC, to place her boot up Nils Brooks's uncaring ass. "Since we don't have a siren, I can only think of one thing that would surprise these guys and make them yell. What if we built a giant spider web and strung it on the bushes around our nest?"

Rae licked her fingers one by one, thoroughly removing the peanut butter. "How?" She looked around. "Are there giant spiders?"

"Better than that." Kellen slowly drew Rae's blankie out of the bag. "We have lots of yarn here. If we take this apart—"

Rae lunged and grabbed. "No!"

Kellen released the blankie. "Your grandma can put it back together for you afterward."

Rae hugged it to her chest. "No!"

"Your blankie wants to keep us safe. It has magic love woven into it to keep us safe."

"That is *bullshit*!" The kid was too smart.

"Rae. You don't say that." *My God.* Kellen sounded like... like a parent. Like her aunt. *Like my own mother.*

Rae stuck out her jaw and looked like that photo of sulky little Cecilia that always made her mother laugh. The memory caused such an uprush of emotion that, before she realized it, Kellen had tears on her cheeks.

"Mommy?" Rae sounded truly horrified. "I'm sorry. I won't say it again."

"It's okay, sweetie. I'm just tired." And scared to death. Not for herself, but for Rae. Kellen had never had a mission like this. Not in the stony depths of Afghanistan, not in the sandy deserts of Kuwait, not in the terrorist attack in Germany. She was home, in the US. Everything was supposed to be safe and easy. She wasn't supposed to be staring at a seven-year-old and feeling...feeling...*things.*

She didn't want to feel things. She didn't want to remember... *Afghanistan, a twist of metal, the smell of burned flesh.* She didn't want to know that if she failed, death would follow. Death...

"Mommy?"

"It's okay." Kellen wiped at her eyes. "Let's call it bull pucky from now on. About your blankie. Honey, we have to use it for protection. If I could figure out anything else to do, I swear I would. Your grandma can put your blankie back together. Please? Let's do this."

In slow motion, Rae offered the blanket to Kellen. *"You."*

"What?" Kellen was so confused.

"When we get home, *you* make it again."

And now horrified. "You want *me* to take the yarn and knit you a blanket?"

"Crochet."

"What? Crochet? I don't know how to crochet. Your grandma—"

Rae crossed her arms over her chest. "Grandma says any idiot can learn to crochet."

Remembering the events of the day, Kellen muttered, "I have the qualifications then." Louder, she said, "If I promise to crochet the yarn into a blankie again, you'll let me use it as a trap?"

"A cobweb! Promise!"

"Oh, pucky. I promise." Kellen began to unravel the stained yellow blankie. What had she got herself into now?

Rae doubled over with belated laughter. "Mommy, you said *pucky*!"

Kellen looked at her daughter sideways. "If you don't tell Grandma I said that, I won't tell Grandma you said *bullshit*."

"Deal."

Kellen wound the yarn around branches that hung over their rocky refuge and down around the perimeter, sure that if someone stumbled on their hiding place, the yarn would indeed act as a spider web and trap them long enough to give Kellen time to wake and defend them. When she got down to the last six-inch square of crocheted yarn, she tied off the thread, clipped it and handed the square to Rae. "Here. This is the heart of your blankie. It will keep you safe."

Rae snatched it and cuddled it to her cheek. "Oh, blankie, I love you," she whispered.

Kellen felt like a scumbag. When she was a soldier, she thought she was doing the hard job. No one ever told her being a mother was a wiggling wormy bag of guilt, worry and difficult decisions.

Well, except Max. He'd made it clear enough, and now Kellen knew—he hadn't exaggerated. If anything, he had toned it down. "Do you remember all the stuff we talked about today? About defending yourself with sticks and rocks?"

"Sure!"

"There's one more thing. If I tell you to drop or hide or be small, do you know what to do?"

"Hide?"

"Drop means get flat on the ground, right away. Hide means look for someplace like our huckleberry bushes. Be small means get low and wrap yourself into the smallest ball you can be."

Rae clutched her tiny square of blanket tighter. "Because those bad guys are all around?"

Okay, maybe Kellen shouldn't have mentioned this now, when dusk slipped through the trees and the forest rustled with the movement of owls and bats and… "Right! Let's take off your shoes and socks and put them way down at the bottom of the bag."

"I thought we hung them on the branch of a tree." Rae sounded suspicious, as if Kellen was arbitrarily changing the rules.

"No, because today you didn't get them wet."

"Why do we put them at the bottom of the bag?"

So snakes don't climb in them. "To keep them warm for in the morning." She helped Rae out of her clothes and into the sleeping bag. As they got ready to sleep at last, the sun disappeared behind the mountain. The cold descended to nip at their noses, and Kellen listened too hard for movements below.

Even Rae seemed to hear the quiet, for she whispered, "Mommy, it's dark out here." Rae shivered, pulled herself into a little ball and cuddled her tiny scrap of blankie.

"No, it's not. Look up. Have you ever seen so many stars? The sky is nothing but light from all over the universe, coming directly to us." There! That was comforting and motherlike. Wasn't it?

Rae didn't sound impressed. "Tell me a story."

Right off the top of her head, the stories Kellen remembered involved wolves, lost children and wicked stepmothers. Out here in the wilderness, those seemed wrong. So she said, "My cousin was the bravest, strongest person I ever met."

"What was her name?"

Kellen hesitated. "Kellen."

"The same as you?"

"Exactly the same as me. Only I wasn't like her. Not then. I was a big scaredy-cat. I married a mean man—"

"Like Bluebeard?"

"Yes. Like Bluebeard." Who had told her the old scary fairy tale about the serial wife-killer Bluebeard? "My husband wanted to hurt me, but Kellen stood up to him and I escaped."

"What happened to Kellen?"

"She died." Such a horrible memory, not one to recount to a child. "But in her dying, she taught me to be strong and brave, too."

"That's why you're ThunderFlash. I'm LightningBug, and I learned to be strong and brave from you." Rae snuggled closer.

"I… I guess you're right. Kellen lives on in both of us, and what goes around comes around, even in a good way."

19

The next morning, Kellen gathered the yarn that had made up Rae's blanket, rolled it into a ball and packed it at the bottom of her backpack. "The safest place," she told Rae. She packed their jar of peanut butter and their apple core, and was folding their tarp when she heard a great rustling down the path, a rumbling of something large rolling up the slope. She heard grunts. She heard a rattle and a spontaneous curse. She looked at Rae and put her finger to her lips.

Rae mimicked her.

Keeping her head low, Kellen peeked over the edge of the stones and saw the first of a group of mountain bikers laboring up the slope and into the flat at the base of their hideout.

One of the women called, "I've got to stop here. That last ledge punctured my tire."

The leader held up her hand. "Roberts needs a break. Looks like a good spot for a rest."

Everyone nodded, gasping deep breaths.

The bikes ground to a halt.

MOUNTAIN BIKING GROUP:
FOUR MALES, SIX FEMALES, IN GOOD SHAPE. HELMETS, GOOD EQUIPMENT. LEADER IS SOFT-SPOKEN, EMPHATIC, COMMANDS WITHOUT BEING BOSSY.

They leaned their bikes against trees, pulled out bags of granola, rolls of dried fruit and energy bars, complained about their knees, the upkeep of the trail and swore they would never take this route again. They were grinning and obviously enjoying themselves.

Kellen slid down to sit on her rear and look at Rae. In a soft voice, she said, "Kid, we've got it made." Standing, she called down to the bikers, "Hi. My daughter and I have been hiking this fabulous wilderness, and it's great to see other people enjoying it, too!"

Startled, the bikers looked up as one entity. Two of the men and two of the women reached for tools and held them like weapons. Everyone studied her, wary and hostile.

Then Rae bobbed up and smiled. "Hi. My mommy and I are bonding!"

The tension oozed out of the group, but not all at once and not completely. Not from everyone. *Uh-oh.* "Is something wrong?" Kellen asked.

One of the guys, the one who still held a tool in his hand, said, "Come down and we'll talk."

Kellen studied them again. She didn't think they were violent, but something was definitely going on. Yet she had committed when she spoke to them, so she said, "Let me finish packing and we'll be down in a sec."

"Can I go down now, Mommy? Can I? Can I?"

Max said Rae had never met a stranger; Kellen saw the truth of that, and the potential for trouble, right now. "Wait for me."

Rae looked longingly over the edge of the rocks. "They have food."

"Rae, I mean it." Kellen used her Army-command voice. At least, she thought she had, but this time it sounded a little different. Oh, hell. It was a mother-command voice. She didn't even know she had it in her. "I'm almost ready."

Rae put her back against the rock, slid down onto her bottom, crossed her arms and sulked.

Kellen wrapped the head in the sleeping bag and attached it to the backpack, and as she did, she said softly, "Rae, please remember we're secret superheroes and we don't want to tell any of the bikers what we're doing up here or what has happened to us. If Mommy says something that's not quite true, that's okay. Okay?"

Rae still sulked.

Kellen knelt down beside her and lifted her chin until Rae looked at her. "Okay?"

"Okay."

Kellen gave her a quick kiss, then stood and pulled on the backpack. To the bikers, she said, "I'm coming down now." Best not to make any unexpected moves around these folks. She jumped down into their midst. "Come on, honey."

Rae bobbed up, sulk forgotten, beaming with the joy at the prospect of meeting the bikers and cajoling her second breakfast out of them. Kellen lifted her arms and caught Rae when she jumped and staggered backward.

Rae focused right on the muscular guy with the wrench in his hand. "*He's* eating granola."

Subtle. Kellen brushed Rae's hair off her forehead. In her most cheerful voice, she said, "I know! But we had breakfast already. Remember?"

"I'm hungry!"

The guy stopped eating and, guilty and undecided, looked at his bag of granola.

Kellen turned to Roberts—

ROBERTS:
FEMALE, CAUCASIAN ANCESTRY (ASSUMED), LATE 30S, 5'3", 100 LBS. BROWN HAIR, HAZEL EYES, FAIR SKIN. COMPETENT, WATCHFUL, INTERESTED.

—who was stripping her tire from the rim and replacing it with an undamaged tire. "I can't believe she eats so much."

Roberts grinned. "I've got twins about her age. Some days they eat nothing, but most days… Growing kids need a lot of calories." She pulled a bag of dried apricots out of her pocket. "We do this every year. We always bring too much. Give her these."

Kellen called Rae over and handed her six apricots.

She was already eating the baggie of granola. Not even Mr. Tool-as-a-Weapon was proof against her wiles. "Thank you, Mommy. Mr. Durant gave me this. He wants me to call him Brad. Did this nice lady give these to us?"

"She did. Her name is Mrs. Roberts."

"Thank you, Mrs. Roberts! Can you change your tire all by yourself?"

Roberts grinned at her enthusiasm. "When you're mountain biking, you have to be able to do everything all by yourself."

"Can I watch you?" Rae settled down to eat and observe.

Kellen eased back a step.

"Where are you headed?" One of the guys squatted on his haunches against a tree and the way he acted, as if he had the right to know, raised her hackles.

But the general attitude here was suspicion, and she needed these people. She needed the protection of a large group, and if she could somehow wrangle transportation to safety…to the Restorer… She stuck out her hand. "I'm Kellen Adams. You are…?"

"Wade McNomara."

WADE MCNOMARA:
MALE, ASIAN ANCESTRY/IRISH SURNAME (INTERESTING), 50 YO, 5'8", SO SKINNY NO ONE WOULD USE HIS DRUMSTICKS TO MAKE SOUP. NOT THE LEADER. UNFRIENDLY.

He lifted his index finger and waved it in a circle. "I'm the founder of the Cyclomaniacs."

"Cute name. We're headed to the lookout on top of Horizon Ridge."

Wade moved from foot to foot. "You don't want to do that. That guy up there—Zone."

"Zone? His name is Zone?"

"That's the least of it. He's weird. He's crazy."

"That's reassuring." She needed the information, so she squatted against another tree. "What's wrong with him?"

"His family owned Horizon Ridge way back in the day. It's an extinct volcano, above the tree line, and you can see forever up there. Even standing on the ground, it's amazing, and I've heard in the tower the view is west to the ocean and south and east for miles. When World War II rolled around, the federal government wanted to build a lookout up there, and Zone's great-grandfather was a shrewd old bastard with good contacts. Somehow he made them agree that if he built the lookout, his family had the right to live there in perpetuity."

"What's wrong with this Zone person living there? Sounds okay, if he has the right."

"You know how it is. When you're in the mountains, everyone helps each other and if you visit one of the National Forest lookouts, you can go up and take photos. If there's a ranger they'll show you around, and sometimes you can rent the place for a night or a week."

Kellen didn't know that. Her previous experience with the mountains was of civil war in Afghanistan. And this experience, in the Olympics, had been unrelenting terror driven by the hope of escape. But she said, "Sure."

"Zone is hostile."

That's the pot calling the kettle black.

"A loner. Barricades himself in. Two years ago, I took the Cyclomaniacs there. He came out on the deck with a shotgun."

"That's not good." She had believed she was leading Rae to

the one place they would be safe. Now another worry—would she get Rae safely to the lookout and be denied access?

"He never lets anyone come up, never leaves." Wade shuffled his feet some more, stirring the carpet of pine needles, making aggressive eye contact.

"He has to leave," Kellen pointed out. "If he lives above the tree line, he hasn't got a garden. He needs supplies."

"No one's ever seen him out with the real people."

"Is Zone his last name?"

Wade shrugged. "I think so."

"What's his first name?"

"Never heard it."

If she was getting this right, Wade had led the group up the mountain, promising a spectacular view. Zone had ordered them away. Wade had looked like a fool, and everything about him spelled anger and resentment.

No wonder he wasn't the Cyclomaniacs' leader.

Still, he tried. "So don't go up there," Wade commanded.

She hesitated. Of course she did. Would she be wiser to take Rae and head back toward civilization?

No. The Greedy Bastards and the Mercenaries were back that direction. She assumed they were headed up the mountain now, searching for her and Rae. The Restorer was closer, and even if he was everything Wade said, he was better than the men who hunted them. "We've got an appointment with this Zone."

"An appointment? You didn't even know his name!"

"This is a business trip. He's an expert on restoration. I've been sent to take something to him."

"I thought you and your daughter were bonding."

"We are. I didn't know there was a problem with him. Apparently I wasn't given all the information I needed. I mean, obviously." Damn Nils Brooks. Someday she was going to kill that bastard. "Still, I've got to deliver."

Wade watched her as if he didn't quite believe her.

She wanted to consider the idea of sending Rae on with the bikers. That would be safer...probably. But Wade was still behaving like she was some kind of criminal. Maybe it was better to bring their hostility out into the open.

She looked around. Everyone was watching her, either surreptitiously or openly. "What's wrong? Everybody's acting as if we're...as if we're dangerous."

The leader had wandered close and was listening to the conversation, and at last she butted in. "You didn't hear what happened a couple of days ago?"

Kellen shook her head. "We haven't talked to anybody." Who wasn't a gun-toting assassin and headhunter. She extended her hand. "Kellen."

"Liz Angelacos." She shook but didn't kneel with Kellen and Wade. "On President Roosevelt Road, there was a van that caught on fire."

Kellen had to play this carefully. "Right. I saw that. But... I assumed it was an accident."

"Everybody thought that, but no one knew what happened to the people inside."

"You suspect foul play?"

"Right above the site, some guy was handcuffed to a tree."

So they had found Horst. "That's weird."

Wade jumped in as if he couldn't wait to spread the bad news. "He had his throat cut."

20

"What?" Kellen didn't have to fake shock. "Cut like...he's dead?"

"Real dead. Blood all over. Flies. Lots of footprints." Wade told his story with relish. "No knife, no evidence, lots of footprints."

Kellen had left Horst tethered to that tree. He'd been unconscious but most definitely alive. What happened? Who had murdered him? In a sudden panic, she looked around for her daughter.

Roberts was showing Rae how to attach the fixed wheel to the bike and inflate the tire.

Kellen turned back to Liz and Wade. "Who found him?"

Wade shrugged.

"They don't have any idea who did it?"

"Maybe Zone."

Liz sighed in exasperation. "Oh, Wade."

That was Wade's spite and irritation speaking—Nils Brooks wouldn't send her to be murdered. Would he? If that was his intention, he could easily have taken care of the matter last winter.

Liz continued, "Maybe it was those two guys who stopped us and tried to push us around." She turned to Kellen. "They wanted our bikes!"

The Greedy Bastards with the shiny shoes. They must be tired of walking. Kellen looked up at Liz. "Are you going toward Horizon Lookout?"

"After what I've told you," Wade said, "you're still going up there?"

"I really do have an appointment with Zone, and I know he has some form of communication that works. It's faster going forward than back. If it's possible to get there today—"

"It is, if we give you a lift," Liz said.

"That would be..." *Fabulous. Such a relief. The safest way to keep both Rae and the Triple Goddess safe.* "If you would do that, I'll call Rae's father and he'll come to get us."

"There's no easy way to get up there except by helicopter." Clearly, Liz wasn't trying to discourage Kellen; she was giving her the facts.

"Then he'll do that." Kellen felt comfortable making that promise.

"You're assuming Zone will let you call out," Wade said.

"I'm assuming if he's a craftsman and recluse, he'll do anything to get rid of Rae." Kellen chose her words delicately. "She, um, talks a lot."

Wade darted a look at the chattering Rae. "We do this trip to get *away* from our kids."

"I understand. You don't want us with you for the duration." With every moment that passed, Kellen felt as if she'd made the right decision. "But if you could get us to Horizon Lookout, or at least close, we'd be grateful."

"We'll do it," Liz said. "It's three hours to the end of the trail. That's where we turn around and come back. The path up to Horizon Ridge goes up from there. You'll have to walk."

Kellen glanced around. "How do we do this?"

"Wade?" Liz handed it over to him. "You're in charge of emergencies." She walked back toward her bike.

Wade got to his feet and began to stretch, and he said to Kellen, "Ellen and I will double up. You can take her bike and your kid can ride on the seat. It's hard riding, but you're in good shape."

She was. In good shape, with a recent injury. She was sleep deprived, undernourished and had no tolerance for these high elevations. Didn't matter. That would work. "Sounds great."

He observed the low-level tremble of her fingers. "Sorry. Didn't mean to scare you that much."

"No, it's good you did. I know there's always a chance of trouble, but a throat slashed—that's terrifying." She felt compelled to check on Rae again, make sure she was close and healthy.

The kid was eating a cheese stick.

Kellen's stomach growled.

Wade handed her one of the what appeared to be endless bags of granola the group shared. "Here. Carbs will take care of that shake."

The granola contained oatmeal, dried cranberries, walnuts and—oh, ick—coconut, but Kellen finished the bag at record speed. "Thanks. That was fabulous."

"I make it myself." He smirked. "In fact, I made all the granola for this trip. For everyone."

"Well done," Kellen said weakly.

"It's fixed!" Roberts called.

Wade announced, "Adams and her daughter are going with us to the Horizon trail cutoff. They have an appointment—" he used air quotes "—with Zone. Let's hope he's not the homicidal maniac running loose in the woods."

The group exchanged glances, variously amused and exasperated, and Kellen figured she was right—no one believed Zone was the villain Wade painted him to be.

Ellen moved to Wade's bike. Kellen settled Rae on Ellen's bike. Liz gave her some instructions about mountain-biking rules, primarily *don't ride too close.* The group gathered, they put Kellen and Rae in the middle, and they were off.

Immediately, the trail dropped off into a gulley, and Kellen found herself roaring downhill at a thousand miles an hour, across a trickling creek and heading back up the other side. By the grace of God she managed not to fall, not to hit any rocks and not to scream with terror. She imagined poor Rae, clinging to the seat in wide-eyed fear, and slowed down.

Immediately, behind her, Roberts called, “You’re going to have to speed it up or we won’t make it to the trailhead before dark.”

“Go, Mommy! Ride!” Kellen’s daughter didn’t sound scared. The little traitor sounded thrilled and excited.

Kellen rode.

21

Max was a Di Luca. His family roots were in Italy. He had relatives on the US East and West Coasts. While Max was in his teens, his father died and he'd been the head of his family ever since. He'd played football for Alabama and got a business degree, too. For a brief amazing few months, he'd climbed peaks in the Himalayas, lived in a monastery, traveled out of range of modern technology, concentrated on learning inner peace and began the long slow process to become a man of wisdom.

Immediately upon his return, his niece, Annabella, had been kidnapped by her father, a worthless scoundrel intent on siphoning off the family's money. When he'd found her, he'd also found a young vagrant woman protecting his niece with fierce reckless courage. When Max remembered that day, the way she attacked Ettore Fontina, faced pain and death to save a child she didn't even know… He had seen a goddess, and he had fallen in love.

In love. With a homeless woman with no name, too many scars and fears he could only imagine.

She called herself Ceecee, and he had taken her into his home and been all kinds of a fool over her. He had courted her, romanced her and in a rush of tragic events, he'd seen his lover shot. He'd been with her as, still in a coma, she bore his child. He became a single father, and when Ceecee woke unattended and walked out of the hospital, he found himself a forsaken lover.

The wisdom of the Far East meant nothing when compared with everyday events.

Except, he had to admit, climbing the Olympic Mountains was easier when one had trained one's mind to concentrate on inner peace. Or maybe concentrate putting one foot in front of the other and *not* thinking about that body tied to a tree and bathed in blood. His mother had faith in Kellen's survival skills for both Rae and herself. He did, too. If he continued at this pace, they could all make it to Horizon Ridge at about the same time…

If Kellen and Rae survived the trek…

He blocked the thought of death and fear. Whoever had slit that man's throat would not find them.

"Sir!" Two park rangers stepped from behind a massive red cedar onto the uphill side of his path. "May we see your ID?"

Max skidded to a stop.

According to their badges, the female was Ranger Holt and the male, Ranger Nicolson. Both looked grim. Both carried sidearms.

Ranger Holt repeated, "Excuse me, sir. May we see your identification?"

Max took a step back. "Sure." Slinging his backpack off his shoulder, he went for the side zipper pocket.

The sound of a safety being released made him freeze. He looked up to see Ranger Holt in a firing stance, her unwavering pistol pointed at him.

The rangers were jumpy, and that made him jumpy, too. Jumpy and suspicious.

"My wallet's in here." Max touched the zipper. "I'll let you get it out." He passed his backpack to Ranger Nicolson. "With all due respect, the outfits look authentic, but may I see *your* IDs?"

Ranger Nicolson pulled his badge from his pocket and passed it over. "Will one do? Ranger Holt seems unready to abandon her stance."

"I see that." Max examined the badge. It not only looked authentic, it looked worn, like a badge that had been carried in a pocket for many years. That, more than anything, convinced him he had the real thing. Well, that, and the fact that if they were killers rather than park rangers, they could have already shot him. "May I ask what's up?"

"There's been foul play." Ranger Holt still stood braced to fire.

"Must be bad." Max kept an eye on Ranger Nicolson as the ranger bought out his wallet, flipped through driver's license and credit cards, then rummaged a little deeper. "You can search the whole backpack," Max said. "I've got rope, food for a couple of days, a change of clothes, bladder of water, sleeping bag, one-man tent and a knife. Knife's in the left zipper pocket in a sheath."

Ranger Nicolson pulled it out and examined it.

"What's the knife for?" Ranger Holt asked.

"Sometimes I need to cut rope. Or salami, which I'm carrying. It's a camping knife. Doesn't every camper carry a knife?"

"Have you used it lately?" Ranger Holt asked.

"Not on this trip." Max planted his feet. It was time to act like an innocent hiker unfairly detained. "What's happened?"

Ranger Nicolson replaced the knife. "Two men were attacked and bound."

"*Two* men? My God." Max only knew about the one. "Badly hurt?"

"One was shot, not fatally. One was hit and knocked unconscious."

They weren't talking about the guy Max had found. This was two different men entirely. Had Kellen been involved?

"And there was a murder."

"A murder? What kind of murder?" Max hoped he didn't look guilty.

"Throat slashed." Ranger Holt adjusted her stance and somehow looked even more forceful. "Someone saw a man fitting your description fleeing the scene."

Max broke a sweat. Someone saw him. He was in trouble—and that meant Kellen and Rae were in trouble. "Look. You checked out the knife. It's clean. I'm Max Di Luca. I'm related to the Di Lucas at Yearning Sands Resort. I manage the Di Luca Winery in Oregon. I left Oregon yesterday. I got here this morning." Max *couldn't* be detained here.

"I know your name," Ranger Holt acknowledged. "That doesn't absolve you of possible murder."

Max had to be very careful now. "I'm on a mission. My daughter and my...my girlfriend are up here somewhere."

"Okay." Ranger Nicolson drew out the word. "What made you decide they are in danger?"

Be wary, Max. "I didn't think they were in danger. Not before I met you."

"Then why are you tracking them?" Ranger Holt asked.

"I'm not tracking them. I know where they're going—to Horizon Ridge."

"Why would they do that?" Ranger Nicolson asked.

They were hammering him with questions, trying to catch him in a lie. But playing football had taught him how to remain calm under pressure, and that inner peace thing he'd learned at the monastery helped now, too. His voice remained steady, warm, trustworthy. He hoped to hell. "My girlfriend is in security. She got a job transporting an antique to that guy that lives up there for verification."

"What guy?" Ranger Nicolson asked.

"The Restorer, they call him? Apparently he's...odd."

"He is." As Max revealed what he knew, and Ranger Holt realized he had his reasons to be here, she seemed to relax. "Why is your daughter with your girlfriend?"

"It was kind of a...not-planned outing."

Ranger Holt came to attention again. "Your girlfriend kidnapped your daughter?"

"No! The opposite. My—our daughter decided go along for an *ad vencher.*" He tried to say it the way Rae had written it. "Her note is in my backpack. Left pocket."

Ranger Nicolson pulled out the paper scrawled in crayon and showed Ranger Holt. They exchanged glances.

Ranger Holt lowered her pistol and click-released the safety. "Your daughter is your girlfriend's daughter, too?"

"Yes."

"Your daughter is how old?" Ranger Nicolson asked.

"She's seven. Rae Di Luca. She thinks she should run the world. I'm pretty sure by the time she's eleven, she will." Max smiled the way he always did when he talked about Rae.

The rangers did not return his smile.

Max continued, "I've done a bad job of saying this, but I'm trying to rescue my girlfriend from my daughter. I can't contact them. My girlfriend's cell phone is going to voice mail. Now you tell me they could be dead?" His voice rose. He wasn't acting out for drama's sake; Kellen had taken a dangerous job, Rae had stowed along and somehow the job had gone sour. This delay and the knowledge he'd gleaned from the rangers only made him more anxious. "I need to find them. Can you help me?"

"We don't have communication right now any more than you do," Ranger Holt told him.

"What about the Restorer? Can you reach him?"

Ranger Holt laughed, brief and bitter. "Zone—the Restorer—avoids contact with us."

"When we get to a place where we can send out an alert to the other rangers, we will," Ranger Nicolson said. "Can you give us a description of your girlfriend and daughter?"

"I've got photos," Max said. "Same pocket as the note."

Ranger Nicolson looked and passed the photos to Ranger

Holt, who ran a scan on the photos with her phone. Nicolson returned the photos and passed Max's backpack to him.

Max slung it over his shoulder. "Do you have transportation I can borrow?"

"We're on foot, and no motorized vehicles are allowed in this area." As if he'd uttered a blasphemy, Ranger Holt narrowed her eyes at him.

Ranger Nicolson seemed less inclined to judge him with every word he spoke. "You can rent a bicycle at the Northwest Mountain ranger station—"

"Where is it?" Max asked eagerly.

It turned out to be eight miles in the wrong direction.

"Then I'll hike." Max started past them. "I'll run. Because there's a killer on the loose."

22

Kellen pedaled across bridges made of a single flat log, up hairpin turns and down them and ignored her imaginings of crumpled bikes, broken bones and bloody gouges.

The group stopped every hour to rest, eat and compare bruises, and every time Rae danced from one to the other, spouting a constant burble of exclamations, questions and pure joy. By the time they reached the trailhead, she had charmed even Wade. He gave her a giant baggie of granola—the kid was never going to be constipated again—and promised to send her grandmother the recipe, and privately, he gave Kellen his phone number and told her to let them know if they made it out alive.

Reassuring guy. Kellen figured as long they didn't have to descend any more vertical slopes on a bike, their odds of surviving were good. After all, she'd fought off mercenaries before.

Although Horst hadn't had a chance, tethered to the tree as he was, and—what kind of killer did that? Slashed a helpless man's throat? Maybe someone inclined to random violence, but that would be a coincidence. More likely, it was one of his team. "When you get back to cell service, call Di Luca Winery. Ask for Verona. Tell her Rae is with me and unharmed."

He nodded. "Will do."

The Cyclomaniacs got to the end of the trail and slammed

to a stop. They flipped their bikes around to face back the way they'd come.

Liz dismounted, shook Kellen's hand briskly, accepted a hug from Rae and pointed up the narrow, steep, challenging path. "He's that way. Here's some goose jerky and dried fruit. Good luck."

The group mounted up and pedaled back the way they came.

"Bye!" Rae shouted after them. "Someday I'm going to have my own bike and I'm going to come and ride with you!"

She got a couple of waves in response before they disappeared so swiftly Kellen figured they'd attained light speed and vanished.

"Rae, let's not shout." Kellen touched the Triple Goddess's wrapped head. "The bad guys are out there."

"Yes, Mommy. I know. A bike!"

"Yes, Rae, I know," Kellen mimicked. "See that?" She pointed up the same path Liz had shown them. "We've got to get up that way as fast and quietly as possible. We want to dodge the headhunters and reach Horizon Lookout before dark." She adjusted the backpack and gave Rae a little shove.

Rae ran up the first slope. "Mommy, I want a mountain bike!"

Of course you do. "Let's speak quietly." *As if you could.* "I think a mountain bike for you is a good idea." *Max would have a fit.*

"We can go mountain biking with Daddy!"

"I can't." Kellen was firm. "Mommy's a chicken."

Rae stopped, incredulous. "Why?"

"Mommy doesn't like going down those mountains at that speed." Kellen gave her another little shove.

Rae remained stubbornly in place. "You're not afraid of anything!"

"I guess I am. You're braver than me."

Rae thought about that for a minute. "That's because I'm LightningBug and I can fly."

Kellen wouldn't have thought she could laugh. Not now. Not

here. But she did and spontaneously hugged Rae. "You are the bravest, smartest girl in the world."

"In the *universe*," Rae corrected.

"Right. Now. Let's walk to the lookout so we can get there before dark."

Rae ran up the next slope and waited for Kellen. "I want a purple mountain bike."

"Shhh," Kellen warned.

Rae lowered her voice. "Because purple is the color ThunderFlash and her sidekick LightningBug share."

Kellen didn't know why she kept talking. Maybe because she could keep her voice down and Rae would always talk, and she always got louder. "Are you sure ThunderFlash isn't the sidekick?"

"Don't be silly, Mommy. I'm little. I'm the sidekick. You're big and smart. You're the head superhero."

At least she had that, Kellen reflected. On a mountain bike, she might cluck like a chicken, but she was the head superhero. "Talk quietly," she reminded Rae.

It would be one of a hundred times she said it that day. She said it right up to that moment when she realized the old Army adage was true—when things were going too well, you were walking into an ambush.

23

The attack came at 5:05 p.m., as the forest that had surrounded them began to thin, the winds to die and clouds started their slow descent on the mountain, bringing a damp chill and the premonition of darkness.

The immense amount of food Rae had consumed this morning had vanished on the trek up the mountain, and she had been pleading for an hour. "Please, Mommy, can we stop and eat dinner? I'm starving."

"Have a breakfast cookie."

"I don't want a breakfast cookie. It's not breakfast time. My feet hurt. I want to stop and have a fire and a hot dog and a bun and steak on a stick and a s'more."

"You're killing me. That sounds so good." They'd had a rest every hour since leaving the Cyclomaniacs, and a snack every time, but they had climbed far enough, fast enough, high enough that ahead, Kellen could see the end of the tree line: barren earth, boulders that stuck out of the earth like splintered bones and a trail worn into the hard-packed dirt. The path funneled between two steep ten-foot cliffs and there was even a sign, battered by wind and rain and cold: Horizon Lookout, 1 Mile. "We're almost there. Wouldn't you like to go to the lookout, give Zone the Triple Goddess, get warm, know we're safe?"

"No, I want to eat dinner." Rae, who never whined, was in

power whine mode now. She stopped and said defiantly, "I'm not having fun anymore."

Kellen killed a smile. The child was serious. Through all the shooting, the terrors, the rough conditions, the lousy food, she had been more than simply stoic. She had been almost unrelentingly cheerful, making the best of everything. When she said she wasn't having fun anymore, that was a serious statement, and Kellen needed to treat it as such.

"Do you want me to carry you?" Despite the fact her hip had been protesting for the last three hours.

"No!"

Kellen walked on. "We have to keep going. I have an itch at the back of my neck."

Rae caught up. "A mosquito bite?"

Without looking, Kellen could tell she'd stuck out her bottom lip, and she decided to treat Rae's comment seriously. Because honestly, she didn't know if Rae was being sarcastic—which seemed a little advanced for a seven-year-old—or honestly didn't understand. "It's just a saying. I'm afraid we're being hunted. If we can get to the lookout, we'll be safe." She hoped.

"I thought you said riding the bicycle would put us ahead of the bad guys."

"That's what I hope. But they knew where we needed to take the goddess's head, and we know they split up. If some of them came this direction right away, they're already here...somewhere." The story of Horst and his slit throat scared Kellen. That casual violence raised the stakes; Rae's young life could not be a sacrifice on the altar of the Triple Goddess.

Yet Rae was blissfully unaware. She only knew she was hungry and tired and cross. She stopped again. "Mo-o-o-mmy!"

Kellen wheeled around, knelt in front of her and took her arms. "Look, Rae—"

A roar. Bark and wood chips blasted around them, and for

one stupefied moment, Kellen stared at the smoking hole in the tree where she had been standing.

The Mercenaries had found them, and they were shooting to kill.

She slammed Rae to the ground, pulled her behind that tree and held her close for one moment, long enough for Rae to catch her breath, long enough for Kellen to whisper, "Crawl. To that rock." She pointed and pulled her pistol. "Stay low."

Rae crawled.

Kellen peered around the tree.

From her right side, a rifle thundered, ninety degrees from the last one.

Crap. There was more than one of them.

She vaulted up the hill after Rae, picked her daughter up by the waist and sprinted zigzag toward a boulder, a clump of trees, another boulder.

Shots followed, some from below, some from the side, some from above the tree line.

Kellen's mind clicked off the possibilities. Three or four shooters. Trying to corner Kellen and Rae, maybe send them away from the Restorer, back down the mountain and into the arms of more mercenaries.

No. Kellen heaved Rae over the top of a four-foot high boulder, vaulted over it, knelt beside her daughter and waited for a shot from that side. If it came, they were surrounded.

Nothing. So one direction to go—first sideways along the tree line, then up the slope and into the fog.

For the moment, they were safe here. Kellen put down the backpack, found the defective computer tablet, pulled it out and turned it on. She looked up, ready to explain her tactic, and saw Rae, round-eyed and with a trembling lip. "Are you okay?"

"You hurt me." Rae hugged her ribs.

"I'm sorry." Kellen was, for all the reasons. "I'm going to create a diversion." The tablet was heating in her hand. "I need you to stay low and run as fast as you can. Can you do that?"

A shot hit the rock above their head.

Rae nodded, an exaggerated up-and-down movement.

Kellen leaned sideways and assessed the landscape. One shooter's likely cover: a once-tall hemlock laid flat, its roots ripped from the ground by last winter's wind. He was in a good position to nail them. "Rae, go that way." She pointed toward a stand of trees, stunted and warped from the high winds that blasted off the Pacific.

Rae ran.

Kellen skipped bullets along the top of the log—and flushed him out. She fired again, a barrage of six bullets, more than she could spare. But she nailed him. His leg spurted red, flailed beneath him. He screamed and went down. Lucky shot at this distance, but she didn't take the time to congratulate herself. She sprinted after Rae, zigzagged toward a windswept pile of downed branches and needles and flung the tablet in among them. With luck…

She raced behind a tree, then another tree, then another, then into a clump of shrubs.

Shots followed her every time.

One shooter down, two or three left. Stormtroopers who couldn't hit anything. Or Kellen would be dead already.

She sprinted to the clump of trees where Rae hid, heard the barrage of shots, felt the slam of a bullet against her left arm between her elbow and wrist. Like a baseball player, she slid through the low-hanging tangled branches and into shelter and scrambled onto her knees.

Rae gasped. "Blood, Mommy!"

"I know." Kellen had been shot before. It never got easier. This burned like hell and bled a river, and until she pulled back the torn material, she feared it had sliced through an artery. But no. The bullet had slipped through her flesh like a hot knife through butter, a clean slice of pain that bled too freely and needed stitches. "It's okay. I probably won't lose my arm." An Army joke, an offhand way to say it wasn't fatal.

Rae burst into tears.

Wrong thing to say, Kellen. Again. "It's just a scratch. I promise. And you can't cry. I need you to help me."

"I don't know how to shoot." The child was trembling. "But I can try."

"Not that. Darling, you don't have to shoot anyone." Kellen rolled up her sleeve.

"I can throw a rock."

"No rocks. We're not that desperate yet." Kellen realized the shooting had stopped, and she held up one finger. She heard the soft fast shuffle of light footsteps. In a whisper, she said, "Not this time…someone's sneaking toward us. Be small."

Rae hunched down, wrapped her arms around her knees and squeezed her eyes shut.

In her mind, Kellen reconstructed the terrain. These trees, the cliff, the entrance to the canyon…the rocks whose shelter they had left. Whoever stalked them had followed Kellen's trail. Very smart. How unfortunate. She didn't want smart trackers, especially one moving at that speed. She didn't have time for subterfuge. She had to get off a shot. On her belly, she crawled around a tree trunk, stuck her head out and ducked back.

The bullet hit so fast it ripped a chunk of hair from her head.

She didn't take time to absorb the shock but leaped to the opposite side of the trunk and aimed in the direction of the shooter and pulled the trigger.

A low-voiced furious curse.

She zeroed in and shot again.

A scream, long and loud and vicious. High-pitched. A pause. More screams, longer and louder.

Okay. Okay. Two shooters dealt with. It didn't even the odds, but it helped.

Kellen leaned her back against the tree trunk. She had to raise her voice above the shrieks. "Rae!"

Rae lifted her head. "Mommy?" She sounded calm, but her eyes were dark; the pupil almost swallowed the iris.

"I need you to help me stop the bleeding." Kellen scooted toward her. "Get one of my socks out of the side pocket of the backpack."

Rae wrestled with the zipper and found a sock.

"And something to use as a pad to absorb the blood." What? Kellen needed to figure that out. Rae couldn't—

Rae extracted the small remaining square of her blankie.

Kellen was surprised at the depth of her own shock. "Not that! That's your blankie!"

"Mommy. I know what it is." Rae's voice trembled. "Now what do I do?" She took Kellen's wrist and carefully pulled the arm toward her. She was still weeping, leaking tears, but she was ready to help.

Kellen almost choked on some emotion she didn't understand. But she couldn't cry, too. She was the adult. No, more than that, she was the mother. Rae looked to her to be strong. "Press the pad on the bleeding part."

Rae gingerly placed it. "Does it hurt?"

"You bet. When we get to safety, I'll blubber really loud." Kellen wanted to urge her to hurry, but she couldn't. Not when Rae was already trembling in fear. "Now tie the sock around the pad."

Rae didn't know how to wrap it, so Kellen showed her, held one side as Rae clumsily wrapped the first stage of a square knot, then helped her tighten it down.

Kellen touched Rae's cheek. "Thank you. That's perfect. It feels much better."

"I'm glad." Rae's little hands were balled into fists. "Mommy, I don't like the screaming."

"Better him than us." Callous and probably not what a good mother would say.

But Rae said, "Yes, and the other bad guys can't hear us while he screams."

Kellen looked at her daughter. Pine needles tangled in Rae's blond hair. She had dirt smeared on her face and packed under her fingernails. The sparkle and charm of her pink clothes was lost beneath the forest's grime. Despite Kellen's diligence, Rae's cheeks had lost their plump roundness and her eyes were too big in her face. Most of all, she now knew things no seven-year-old should know, like a wounded man's screaming can be used as a concealment.

As Kellen stared, Rae's features rearranged themselves, became that of a brown-skinned girl with big eyes too sad for her young face.

The Afghan mountains. A burned-out house. A melted coil of metal. The stench of desperation and death.

"Mommy." The child was Rae again. "It's getting dark."

"Yes." Fog was slipping its pale fingers down the mountain, into the gulleys, coming to rescue them. If they could hold out long enough for it to get here, they had a chance of making it up the mountain. "Good. Here. Put on my hoodie." Kellen pulled it off and wrapped Rae in it, rolled up the sleeves and zipped it up.

"It's long!" Rae stuck out first one foot, then the other.

"It'll keep you warm." More important, the camouflage would conceal her from watching eyes.

Rae peeked around the tree. "There's smoke!"

Kellen smiled with evil delight. "Your tablet."

"Uh-oh. Daddy's going to yell."

Kellen gave a spurt of startled laughter. "About so much."

The pile of branches smoldered.

Rae's short legs couldn't run fast enough; Kellen would have to carry her. Everything else had to stay. Everything.

That was it, then. The Triple Goddess was the sacrifice for

Rae's life. If Rae wasn't along, if it was only Kellen, she'd figure out somehow to save that head. But just as these days had changed Rae, they had changed Kellen, too. She knew why, but she didn't want to think it, to speak it.

The Triple Goddess would be the ultimate diversion.

The smoldering branches caught and blazed.

A shot came from above, scattering burning branches.

Below them, a man shouted, "McDonald, no!"

But now Kellen knew the shots had come from about halfway up one of the sandstone cliffs. She also had a fair idea of the guy below, his location and his position in the gang. He was the boss. She had wounded two of his men. McDonald and the boss were left.

If Kellen and Rae were going to make it up the mountain, she needed to eliminate the sniper above. He had shot at her diversion, so he was trigger-happy and maybe nervous. Good news. She peered through the brush and waited.

Rae watched her. "Mommy?"

Kellen cut the tie that held the head to her backpack. "One more down and we can make a run for it. Get the ball of yarn out of my backpack. We're leaving everything else behind."

"B-but…the Triple Goddess." Rae's voice got squeaky. "She's our talisman."

"The Triple Goddess has cared for herself for three thousand years. She can do it a little longer. In fact, she's going to help us." Ignoring the ancient staring eyes, Kellen picked up that head with her good hand, held it aloft and shouted at the man below. "The head is what you want. I'm leaving it. Look!" Keeping her own head down, she placed the Triple Goddess on the stone to the west. "It's yours. I don't know who you are. I can't identify you. You're safe, so take it!"

No shots. No answer.

"Now get the yarn." Kellen spoke calmly, clearly, although

her vision wavered. Blood loss and pain were compromising her abilities "I promised to crochet your blankie."

Rae dived for the backpack.

"Dump it out," Kellen instructed, "and take the yarn."

Rae did as she was told and the whole time watched Kellen anxiously, which told Kellen how bad she must look.

Had any of the shooters seen Rae? Would the thieves let them go? Kellen had seen too much of war; she had little faith in the decency of mercenaries.

"That fog is almost here." Rae pointed at the damp white spreading out like a delta from the shallow canyon of the path.

"Be ready to climb on my back." Kellen got into a crouch, almost fell over, steadied herself with a hand on the rock. She spotted movement on the cliff; with her shouting and holding the head aloft, McDonald had figured out where they were and scooted into a precarious position, twenty feet up on a rocky shelf. "Stay down. Plug your ears," she said, aimed and fired seven shots, fast and loud. Then nothing. She'd emptied her magazine.

Worse, her wavering vision had betrayed her; she missed McDonald, hitting below him, sending up a cloud of sand.

McDonald's rifle steadied. He leaned out—and her luck changed for the better. The sandstone shelf disintegrated, gave way. The rifle fell first, a Barrett M98B with a scope. It clattered as it tumbled, and fearing an accidental discharge, Kellen threw herself over the top of Rae's body. When no shots followed, she peered around and saw McDonald scrambling for a toehold.

The sand kept giving way. Like a skier taking a fall, McDonald fell, twenty feet down and onto the sandy slope below. He landed on his chest. The air left his body with an audible, "Oof!" He rolled, all arms and legs and ominous silence.

Probably not dead, but at least unconscious.

"Come on!" Kellen said.

Rae climbed onto her back.

Kellen leaned down and ran into the fog, doing her best to keep a low profile. She didn't believe that the boss meant to let them go.

But would the goddess head occupy him long enough for them to escape?

Or would he come after them and go back for the goddess head? A single well-placed rifle shot, a through and through with a powerful rifle, would kill them both.

What if he pursued them? Kellen was moving as fast as she could, but she was exhausted, bloodied, in pain from her hip, carrying a thin little girl who should weigh nothing to her—but she did.

The stony path narrowed and narrowed, nothing more than a canyon between two cliffs. The fog came in patches, pale wisps and blank cool white walls. Far above and to the west, the sun still shone, and Kellen was grateful; as she ran, she could see where to put her feet. And she was terrified; if someone was following, maybe they could see her. She strained to listen for footsteps—or worse.

Then it came. The crack of a rifle.

Kellen fell to the ground and rolled to put Rae beneath her. She couldn't protect her from a bullet fired from a high-powered rifle, but that didn't mean she wouldn't try.

"Mommy?" Rae whispered. "Ow."

Kellen lifted herself to give Rae some breathing room. She looked behind them but could see nothing but swirling white fog. She strained to listen, but could hear no sound of pursuit. "Climb on my back," she said to Rae. "We have to hurry."

When Rae was in position, Kellen found she couldn't get off her knees. She couldn't stand, not with Rae's weight on her back. She let Rae slide to her feet. "Mommy's kind of tired, so let's see if we can find a rock for you to use like a mounting block."

"Like a pony?"

"Exactly. I'm your own personal pony." Yet even without

Rae on her back, Kellen couldn't stand. Exhaustion, hunger, too much exertion, the altitude and maybe something much, much worse…

She got up on her hands and knees and waited for the earth to stop spinning. Ick, she'd put her left hand in a brownish pool of… "Oh, no." Her blood had soaked the pad and was dribbling through her fingers. She'd left a handprint…

"Mommy?" Not during this whole ordeal had Rae sounded as frightened as she did now. "Are you bleeding?"

Kellen looked up at her daughter.

Rae wavered in the fog.

No, she wasn't wavering. Kellen was losing consciousness. "Listen to me. You have to go on by yourself."

"I can't!" Rae wailed.

"You can. You're LightningBug. You're brave and strong. Follow the path. You'll get to the lookout. Get Mr. Zone to let you in." She hoped he would. "Stay safe inside."

"I don't want to leave you!" Rae tugged at Kellen's arms.

"You have to go on by yourself." Kellen was starting to sound like Bambi's father. "Please, baby. I need you to go be safe."

"I'm going to bring him back to save you!" Rae whirled and started running.

"No, don't think that. Don't…put pressure on yourself. Get him to let you in and—" Kellen stared into the fog.

Rae was gone.

"Okay," she said. "Okay." Her strength gave out. She collapsed onto her face to die.

24

"I told you *no*." The man in charge looked down at McDonald, crawling with his last breath toward that stupid marble head.

McDonald looked back, his eyes wide with pain and greed, his hand reaching up toward the goddess. "Please!" His voice was hoarse and broken with pain. "It's worth a fortune!"

The boss lifted his rifle and aimed it at McDonald's chest. "That's not what I've paid you to do." He fired.

McDonald's chest exploded.

More blood. Such a mess.

One mercenary dead. One to go. The body count was climbing, but by God, the woman was still alive—and she had a child with her. *A child.* What an unnecessary and aggravating inconvenience.

The man looked up at the fog bank, shouldered the rifle and followed Kellen and Rae into the canyon. It was easy enough to track them; someone was bleeding. Not a lot, but in this narrowed passage, he found a drop here and there, shiny against the rocks, and that led him on. Then the fog opened, and he saw her—Kellen Adams, facedown, unmoving, on the ground.

How many men, how much money had it taken to get to this point? More than he had ever expected. Who would have thought Gregory's terrified, broken wife would put up such a fight? Even now, he didn't trust she was dead. He took the rifle off his shoulder and walked toward her.

She didn't stir.

Using his foot, he turned her over.

Her head lolled loosely on her neck. Blood smeared her arm and hand. But her chest rose and fell, and she moaned softly.

"Time to finish this thing," he told her. He released the rifle's safety and lifted the butt to his shoulder—and paused. From down the path, he heard firm footsteps. Someone large, probably a man, moving fast.

Too many complications here. Too many bodies, too much attention.

He slid into the fog and waited until the footsteps had hurried past, then turned back to finish cleaning up the mess—and the bodies.

25

So many gunshots. Too many gunshots. Max had heard too many to count, drawing him onward, feeding the ugly taste of fear in his mouth.

Then the blast of one…final…rifle shot. A sharp, ugly percussion that spelled death for…who?

Driven by terror, Max ran, bounding up the slope. A bullet had already taken Kellen from him once. Now their baby girl was involved, too.

Four hours ago, he had met the bicycle club. They'd been cautious of him; apparently he had looked desperate, unshaven and disheveled. When he pulled out his wallet and showed them all the photos he kept of Rae during all the years of her life, and the meager few photos he had of Kellen, and begged for help, Wade had given him the message Kellen had directed to Verona. They'd sent him on with information, food and good wishes. He'd been tracking Kellen and Rae ever since.

As he ran, the trees thinned. The air thinned. Lack of oxygen made him slow—and he spotted a body sprawled by the root of an upended hemlock. A man, captured by death in the throes of agony.

But that guy, whoever he was, wasn't Kellen. He wasn't Rae.

Max picked up speed again and found the body of another

man, chest shattered by a gunshot, one waxy hand pointed the way toward the marble head perched on a rock…

Max stopped. He stopped and stared at that *thing*, that *head* that had caused all the trouble.

It stared back.

Had Kellen abandoned it, given it up to the men who would kill to claim it?

Yes. That made sense. Kellen had used it to create a diversion.

Then why was it still here?

He looked around, spotted another body tucked downhill and in the woods.

Three bodies. Had Kellen killed them all? Had someone else killed them and now waited to claim the head…after eliminating Kellen and Rae?

Max snatched up the head, stuffed it in his backpack and sped up the path into the canyon, into the fog, into the damp silence. For a man who didn't give a damn about priceless antiquities, he sure spent a lot of time dealing with them, and this one—he would ransom it for Kellen and Rae.

As the canyon narrowed, he slowed down. Out here, every little thing enveloped by the encroaching fog took on a menacing shape. Trees were men. Branches were rifles. Rocks were bombs. And there—there was something that glistened in the pale, eerie light. He knelt, touched it lightly. His fingers came away sticky and the liquid smelled like…blood. Droplets of blood on the rocks, fresh and wet.

Who had been hit?

Max wandered back and forth, from canyon wall to canyon wall, looking for signs of Kellen and Rae's passage, finding it in the occasional spatter and smear. When he got them back…*when* he got them back, they were never leaving again. He wasn't letting them out of his sight. He didn't give a damn whether Kellen needed a fulfilling job. He didn't care if Rae wanted to go to camp or to school. He was keeping them within the property line and— *What was that?*

A body, unmoving, prone on the ground. A woman's body.

"No. No, dear God, no, please." He dropped to his knees.

Kellen. Kellen was unconscious. But she was breathing. She was alive.

She'd been shot.

He'd been here before, in Philadelphia. She'd been shot in the head. She'd gone into a coma. She'd almost died. And then… she didn't. She'd had his baby.

He looked around. No sign of Rae. Dear God. Where was Rae?

A deeper, colder fear seized him. Had all his fears come true? Was he too late? Would he find Rae's body now?

No. She was in the lookout. Rae had to be in the lookout.

Kellen was chilled and growing colder.

He took off his coat, wrapped Kellen in the warmth, his warmth.

She moaned as he lifted her, moved her. Her head lolled on her neck.

"I'm sorry, darling. Please, darling, stay alive while I—" He picked her up with care and haste, put her over his shoulder and sprinted toward the lookout, keeping a pace that was smooth and swift.

He heard voices coming toward him.

A man's voice, deep and impatient.

And a little girl's voice, fierce, insistent.

Max stumbled a little, gasping for air, gasping in relief. He'd been so afraid, but Rae was alive.

The fog parted, and coming toward him he saw a tall hairy beast and a little girl.

The little girl shrieked, "Daddy!", ran toward him and wrapped her arms around his legs.

She was alive and well.

Max hugged her with one hand, so relieved and yet, still so afraid.

"Is Mommy okay?" Rae's face was stained with tears. She was on the verge of crying again.

"She's alive." Max viewed the man before him. Skinny. Black baseball cap. Black curly beard that covered his face and his neck. Thick black-rimmed glasses. A few changes, and Max wouldn't have been able to pick him out of a lineup. "You're Zone?"

"Yes. Who are you?" No mistaking that hostility. This Zone guy had issues, or maybe he didn't like gunshots so close to his lookout.

Max told him what he wanted to know. "I'm the man carrying the ugly marble head in my bag."

"Then let's go." Zone turned and stalked up the path.

26

Kellen woke when the stranger said, "She needs stitches."

She felt a tug on the skin on her arm. Consciousness flood her mind. She opened her eyes and sat up. "Rae!"

"Stupid woman!" the unknown man's voice said. "You don't move when I'm sticking a needle in your arm."

"Relax, Kellen. Rae is here." Max's voice was soothing.

A flash of impressions: a tall black-bearded guy sat on the bed with her, holding a needle and thread and scowling. Max, his hand on her elbow, held it steady. Rae sat on the floor, eating a bowl of popcorn and staring wide-eyed as the stranger put stitches in Kellen's arm.

Rae was warm, dry, safe.

Kellen was warm, dry, safe.

Max was here. He had found them.

She looked at the man with the needle. Only one person it could be. Must be Zone.

"Rae is fine," Max said. "She saved you."

In a scramble of memory, Kellen recalled sending Rae away. Rae had insisted she would save Kellen and—the kid had done it!

Kellen smiled at her daughter. "Good job. Thank you, LightningBug."

Rae grinned, all big teeth and well-fed cheer.

Kellen fell back on the bed.

Zone cursed her again. "If you're done trying to rip these stitches through your skin, I'll finish sewing you up."

"Go ahead." She waved her other hand and closed her eyes, then opened them again to look at Rae, then closed them again. The thread tugged at her skin, but she felt no pain. Zone must have numbed the whole area.

He stitched with competence, he bandaged the wound, he informed her when he gave her an antibiotic injection, and he told her to take in fluids. Lots and lots of fluids. "You're more trouble than you're worth." The mattress creaked as he stood.

It creaked again as Max sat. "Because of her, Zone, you have your marble head."

"Yeah!" Rae said.

"Yeah." Zone sounded disgusted.

Kellen grinned and opened her eyes.

Rae had abandoned the bowl of popcorn on the floor and leaned against the bed.

"I've got water mixed with orange juice." Max helped Kellen sit up and handed her a bottle.

She drank with all the pleasure of someone who thought she would never drink again. She reached up and cupped Max's cheek. "Thank you." *Thank you for coming for us, thank you for finding us, thank you for bringing us to safety.*

He cupped his hand over hers and nodded. She could feel his emotion, see the way his eyes glistened. He hadn't wasted time worrying; he had come for them at once—and because of him, she was safe.

The mattress jiggled. "Mommy!"

Kellen leaned back on the pillow, smiled at Rae and held out her arms.

Rae hopped up enthusiastically. She and Rae rested on a twin-size bed tucked into one corner. A large, thick, luxurious and oddly out-of-place antique rug rested in front of it.

Kellen winced as every joint in her body flinched. Didn't matter. She wrapped her arms around her daughter. *Her daughter.*

"Be careful of those stitches!" Zone snapped.

"I will," Rae snapped back and cuddled against Kellen's good side.

Kellen relaxed. All was right with the world.

From the vantage point of the bed, Horizon Lookout appeared to be constructed as one big square building. Somewhere above, on the roof, she could hear a generator running, creating their electricity, and water gurgled as the clarifier made it suitable for use. This room appeared to be half of the building, as well as the all-purpose room. The bathroom door was in one corner. Dark shutters covered all the windows; from the look of them they let out no light.

That not only gave her a sense of safety, but also the knowledge that Zone understood the dangers that could lurk out in a forest where the most savage beasts weren't bears and wolves, but men.

Wedged against the far wall was a bookcase stuffed with worn paperbacks and a battered plaid easy chair and ottoman. When she craned her neck, she could see an open folding door that led into an entirely different room; the Restorer's workshop, by the looks of the high table and scattered tools. A bare-bones kitchenette was in the opposite corner from the bed, with a two-person drop-leaf table.

Max gave Kellen and their little girl a moment of cuddling, then reached for Rae. "Rae, Mommy needs to go to sleep."

"Can't go to sleep. Need the bathroom." Kellen sat up slowly. "And a shower."

"No one can argue with that," Zone spoke from the kitchen in the other corner of the room. "Your sweet feminine odor could attract flies—if we had any at this elevation."

Kellen eyed him evilly. "You're a charmer."

"Bathroom, yes," Max said firmly. "A shower can wait. You can't get that bandage wet anyway."

Kellen smelled like three days of sweat, terror and effort. She needed a shower more than food, more than fluids, more than good sense. "I *said* I *want* a shower."

When Max protested again, Zone came over with a garbage bag and duct tape. "Why waste your breath?" he said to Max. "She's going to do what she wants." And he went to work protecting Kellen's arm from water. When he was satisfied she would keep the wound dry, he gave her the go-ahead.

"I'll need help," Kellen said.

Hands up, Zone backed away. "Don't look at me. I'm retired from sex, but I'm not dead." He turned to Max. "You two had the kid. You've seen her naked."

Max made the slight pained sound of a man under torture.

If Kellen had any strength left, she would have slugged them both.

"I'll help Mommy!" Rae hopped to her feet.

"Perfect," Kellen said. "Thank you, Rae."

"Mommy, it's the neatest bathroom ever. The toilet is like an airplane, and the faucet shuts off by itself, and the shower has a chain to pull when you want the water on. I'll pull your chain!"

Zone snorted.

"Sweetheart, I know you will." Kellen slid an arm around Rae's shoulders. "You keep me steady, okay?"

"Okay! Mommy, Zone has canned Spam. Grandma won't let me have Spam because it's fatty and disgusting, but Daddy fried slices in the skillet and I ate a Spam sandwich with mustard and kale."

Kellen's stomach growled.

"And yogurt with canned peaches and a Twinkie!"

Kellen shut the narrow bathroom door behind them.

The two men stared at it, hearing Rae's cheerful, chatting voice and Kellen's occasional quiet reply.

Zone turned to Max. "Start frying the Spam. I'll open the peaches. Fuck, women are a pain in the ass."

27

Kellen wore a clean pair of her own leggings and one of Max's oversize T-shirts, sat at the table and ate the Spam and kale sandwich and the peaches and yogurt, and to keep her company, Rae ate, too.

"Growth spurt on the way," Zone muttered, his gaze on Rae. When he saw Kellen watching him, he turned away.

Who was he? Kellen had had enough stitches to know these looked like a professional had done them. So he was a doctor? Medic? Nursing professional?

It sounded like he knew about children. So he was a father?

And he was the Restorer, a man whose reputation for verification was so stellar that Nils Brooks sent a valuable artifact on a dangerous countrywide trek to be authenticated by him. According to the bicyclists, he was a jerk. And of course, a recluse, hiding on top of a mountain apart from everyone, despising the world, its people and its frivolities.

Interesting. "I'm sorry about the goddess, Zone. I had to leave her out there."

"No problem," Zone said. "Di Luca brought it in."

"What?" Kellen whipped her head around and stared at Max. "How?"

"It was sitting on a rock and watching. I hadn't seen it before, but no mistaking what it was." Max shuddered slightly.

"The Triple Goddess," Rae announced with a grand gesture that made Kellen look through the double doors into Zone's workshop.

The marble head stared regally at her from a tall table covered with tools and papers.

Kellen put her hand to her chest. Her heartbeat stuttered and hurried.

Max continued, "No one else was around, so I picked up that thing and came here."

Kellen tried to make sense of this turn of events. "I yelled at them. Told them the head was theirs. Put it on the top of the rock where they could see it. I used that thing as a diversion to get us away. Why didn't they take it and run?"

"Three bodies, Max said. It sounds as if they killed each other over it," Zone said.

Max interrupted, "Rae, do you want something else to eat?"

"Can I have peanut butter and banana?" Rae asked.

Max plucked the last banana, overripe and bruised, off Zone's counter.

"Hey!" Zone said.

Max opened Zone's jar of peanut butter, smeared it on the banana and handed it to Rae.

"Peanut butter? Really?" Kellen felt almost ill. "If I never have another bite of peanut butter, it will be too soon."

Rae stopped, the food halfway to her mouth. "Why, Mommy? Why?"

"Because I said so." *Because I said so?* Really? As a kid, Kellen had heard that phrase from her mother and father, her aunt and uncle. She had hated hearing that, and she told herself she would never say that to a child. Now it slipped out without a thought. Had everything she said to Rae been passed down through countless generations of her family?

Abruptly, Kellen knew her arm hurt, her head hurt, and mystery of the head or no mystery of the head, she couldn't stay up any longer. She had no more reserves. She stood, her hips and back creaking, her thighs protesting. "I'm going to lie back down."

"Good idea." Max had a funny tone to his voice. "Maybe you should have listened to me and stayed down in the first place."

Rae said, "Uh-oh," and scrunched down in her chair.

Kellen turned back to snap at him and realized—a flush climbed Max's face from chin to forehead, and a red flame kindled deep in his brown eyes.

And Rae looked like someone who recognized the danger signs. She met Kellen's gaze and used her sticky banana-and-peanut-butter hand to indicate a mouth opening and closing.

Kellen's gaze flew back to Max's.

"Very funny, Rae." His voice rose. "What did you think you were doing stowing away in that van?"

"I wrote you a note!" But Rae looked guilty and concerned.

Max went to the sink, wet a paper towel and cleaned Rae's sticky fingers and face. "You wrote me a note. What did you think I was going to do when I found out you'd run away?"

"I didn't run away. I was with Mommy!"

Max turned to Kellen. "What were you thinking letting her come with you?"

Zone turned a kitchen chair backward, sat down and cradled his chin in his hands. He watched the action and grinned.

"I didn't let her come with me. I didn't find her until—"

"You couldn't have called me?"

"Horst stole my phone!"

Max mocked, "The big bad Army captain let some half-wit thieving security man steal her phone?"

Before Kellen could answer hotly, Rae asked, "Daddy, what does thieving mean?"

"It means he was a thief!"

"Then why are you surprised he stole her phone?"

That was when Max lost his precarious grip on his simmering temper and roared at Rae, "Child! You stay out of this!"

Rae looked serious but not afraid, and Kellen realized this was the daddy Rae had warned her about—he had been scared, and so he yelled.

Rae started to slide out of her chair and sneak toward the workshop.

Kellen caught her arm. "No, you don't. We're in this together." Also, if she had to be yelled at, she was going to do it while horizontal.

Rae dragged her feet as she followed Kellen toward the bed.

Kellen sat sideways on the mattress, a slow controlled movement until she reached a critical point and collapsed. She leaned her back against the wall. Rae hopped up and leaned against her. They watched as Max followed and paced the floor and raged.

"Of all the careless, thoughtless immature acts—"

"Daddy, I'm sorry."

Kellen nodded. "I'm sorry, too."

"Do you know how worried her grandmother has been? Her nerves! When I called her tonight—"

"That poor woman," Kellen said, and she was being sincere. "Max, I hope she can sleep well tonight knowing Rae is safe."

"Don't think because neither one of you was killed, you can do this again!"

"No, Daddy." Rae's voice slurred.

Kellen looked at her. Her eyes had closed and her jaw hung open. She had fallen asleep without talking about her princess dolls or her blankie or whether she had eaten enough peanut butter and Spam to fill her empty belly. Rae trusted Kellen to keep her safe. Kellen let her slide limply down onto the bed and flung the plaid wool throw over her.

Max kept pacing and raging.

She watched him affectionately.

She was exhausted, so maybe that was what opened her subconscious, but it seemed to her she could remember her first time with him more clearly. In that faraway time in Pennsylvania, he had been unendingly gentle, with never an unkind word. He must have had fears and frustrations he wished to share, but he never did, and she had felt like a cherished crystal he feared would break under any rough handling.

This yelling—this felt real. Like they had a relationship, with fights and misunderstandings and making up and… Like a cat around her kitten, she wrapped herself around Rae and listened to him rage without really hearing the words.

In midsentence, Max stopped shouting, stopped pacing and stared at the two females asleep on the bed.

Zone came to stand beside him. "You have those women terrorized."

"I know. What's a man to do?"

"Seems like you're doing okay. Tuck 'em in!"

"Right." Max dragged Kellen and Rae to the top of the bed, slid pillows under their heads, covered them and smoothed the hair over their foreheads.

He went back to the kitchen table where Zone had his weird spy mechanics spread out. "Can you see anything alive out there in those woods?"

"Nothing human. Only critters." His green eyes gleamed through the thick lens of his glasses. "That's a good thing. No one's going to attack tonight."

"Yeah. A good thing." Max allowed all his cynicism to leak into his voice. "Let's call the national park rangers and put them on the case. This is a crime scene!"

"Great idea. Which of us do you think they'll arrest first?"

Max remembered his encounter with the rangers, and his unease must have shown, for Zone said, "Exactly. They don't love me, either, and I have no desire to spend a month in custody trying to explain how some murdering sons-a-bitches climbed up my mountain and shot up the place and got offed by Kellen Adams, who is going to spend more than a month in custody, and God only knows what truthful thing your daughter would say that would send us all to prison."

"Never mind. We'll, um, handle it somehow." Max had never in his life been afraid of the officials and their calls, but he was afraid now.

"I handle everything alone. Learned that the hard way." Zone didn't look satisfied at Max's capitulation; he looked angry. "I can get right to work on figuring out whether that head is the real thing or a great forgery."

"You should do that."

"You can go sleep in the recliner. It's lumpy, but comfortable if you're tired enough."

"I'll do that."

Zone started to walk toward the double doors that led to his workshop. Halfway there, he stopped, turned and looked at Max. "You think something stinks about this whole operation."

Max hadn't moved. "Don't you?"

Zone asked the question that was haunting Max. "Why did they leave that potentially priceless piece of history sitting on a rock for you to pick up?"

"Exactly. Why?"

28

A punch to the ribs made Kellen grunt and wake. Her first thought was not *an attack!* Her first thought was *Rae*.

How times had changed.

She opened her eyes and found Rae asleep on the bed with her, one foot extended in kick position, the other twitching as if she was winding up for a kidney shot.

Everything was well. They were both alive.

Gently, she turned Rae so she faced into the room and looked across at Max and Zone. They stood in the kitchen and talked, their low voices a rumble as they leaned over a…a what? Something electronic. Kellen listened to them, picked out a few words, enough to rouse her interest and explain what they were doing—and seeing.

Raising herself on one elbow, she stroked Rae's head, swaddled her little girl in a blanket, pulled on the terry cloth robe that was at the foot of the bed and headed for the bathroom.

Both men stopped talking and watched her, maybe because they were concerned about her ability to stand. Maybe because they didn't want the little woman to hear what they were saying.

Too late for that. She shut the door behind her and used the facilities; her aunt and uncle's old camp trailer had a larger bathroom. She glanced in the mirror. She looked like hell.

Oh, well.

She came out and strolled over to the tiny old slump-shouldered white refrigerator. She looked inside. A slightly shriveled green apple sat on the top rack. She plucked it free, shut the door and bit into the apple.

Zone slammed his palms on the table. "Damn it! I figured that was disgusting enough I'd be the only one to eat it."

"Ever been to Afghanistan?"

"Yes."

"So have I."

He stared at her through those thick black glasses.

She stared at him.

He said, "Okay, then."

"Okay, then," she agreed. She glanced at Max.

Interesting. When she sparred with Nils Brooks, Max hated it. He hated everything about her and Nils. But with Zone, he watched them both with an affectionate half smile. Probably he thought Zone wasn't attractive?

ZONE (FIRST OR LAST NAME UNKNOWN):
MALE. ETHNICITY: BROWN (HISPANIC?) AND/OR CAUCASIAN/TANNED. 6'1", 160 LBS, SHAGGY BLACK HAIR HANGING BELOW THE BASEBALL HAT HE WORE EVEN INSIDE (BALDING?), LONG MASSIVE CURLY BLACK BEARD; RESEMBLES AN OLD TESTAMENT PROPHET. GREEN EYES, BLACK LASHES, DISTORTED BEHIND HEAVY-FRAMED BLACK GLASSES. FACIAL STRUCTURE UNKNOWN. DEDUCE SCARRING. HERMIT. AURA OF POWER, INTELLIGENCE, KNOWLEDGE. EASILY IRRITATED BY HUMAN CONTACT.

No, Zone was definitely attractive, if only for the mystery he exuded.

She asked, "What are you two looking at?"

"It's the radar for all submarines in the western Pacific," Zone said.

"No, it's not. It picks up life forms around the lookout." She met Zone's gaze again. "I heard you."

"It *used* to be a radar screen for… Oh, to hell with you." He stomped away and started rummaging through the cupboard over the miniature stove top and incongruously large dishwasher. He saw her watching him and said, "What are you looking at? I'm not going to wash dishes by hand."

"I didn't say a thing," Kellen pointed out.

Max chuckled, that nice low laughter that made her feel warm in all places south, then guilty for being so easily distracted from a very serious and deadly situation.

Zone got out three mugs. "Coffee?" He didn't wait for an answer but poured the mugs full, rinsed out the coffeepot and set it up again. He muttered, "Only thing I miss about civilization is espresso."

"Espresso machines aren't expensive." She finished the apple, tossed the core in the compost bin and accepted the coffee. She took a sip and amended that to, "Espresso machines aren't *terribly* expensive."

"Thanks for that!" Zone said.

She studied the screen. "When I look at this, I see a mile perimeter around the lookout, and I see life forms. Animals, right?"

Zone muttered something rude.

She figured she'd get used to that. She put the coffee cup down on the tiny countertop. "You must be Canadian," she said to Zone.

He grinned evilly. "How did you guess?"

"Because you don't look Turkish." To Max she said, "Only the Turks and the Canadians make coffee that strong."

"A few Venetians, too." Max sipped. "I've got an aunt who makes coffee that will keep you awake for days."

She pointed at the screen. "I can see creatures prowling around. Coyotes? Wildcats of some kind? Congregating around in the area where the battle took place."

"No living humans are out there," Max said.

She glanced at Rae, still sleeping hard. The child had been through enough hell. She didn't need to hear them talking about danger and death. Rae shouldn't know about death and pain at all.

But she did. She did.

"What happened to them? There were four shooters—three men and the man in charge. I shot two of them, wounded them badly and knocked one unconscious, but none of them were dead, and I left the goddess for them."

"As a diversion," Max said.

She nodded. "They were after us, Rae and me. I was carrying her. We got into the canyon, into the fog. I heard a rifle shot. I sent her away and passed out. Easy pickings for them." She dug her hands into the robe's wide pockets. "Where did they go? How did they not kill me? Why didn't they take the head?"

"Good questions," Zone said. "Nils called, wanted me to search for you. I said no."

"Who says gallantry is dead?" Kellen asked.

Obviously, Zone didn't give a crap about his lack of gallantry. "I heard a rifle shot, too, then a bunch of pistol shots, then more rifle shots. I was headed to the lookout to get in out of the firefight before I was a casualty." He made no apology for running away.

Kellen didn't blame him. "Not your battle," she said.

"No shit." Zone sighed mightily, and in a flat tone of resignation, he said, "Then I ran into the kid, and she dragged me to get you. She wouldn't take no for an answer."

"She never does." Kellen cleared her suddenly clogged throat.

Zone continued, "On the way, we met Di Luca and he had grabbed you."

"I sprinted up that mountain." Max leaned forward, gaze fixed on her, intense and grim. "I got into that place where the trees thinned and the path narrowed. Fog drifted like terrorized ghosts. I could see trees looming up, rocks. But I couldn't hear anything, anyone. Then someone shouted. And that rifle shot. Then no more shouting. I thought… I thought Rae was dead. You were dead. I ran toward the shot."

"Hero," Zone said.

Fiercely angry, Max jerked around. "If they're dead, I have no reason to be alive."

"Wasn't being sarcastic," Zone said.

Max closed his eyes, opened them and nodded.

"What happened, Max?" Kellen whispered.

"I saw a body. Then another. I found a trail of blood and *another* body, still warm, shot twice, once at close range."

Kellen broke a sweat. She wasn't out there anymore, in that wilderness of trees and stones looming out of the fog, but Max's words brought the anxiety, the fear, the desperation back to her. People had died for that head. *Rae* had almost died for that head.

She got up, went to the sink, poured herself a glass of water and sipped it. "Four shooters," she repeated. "None of them dead. Don't get me wrong, I would have killed them, but with a pistol I couldn't aim well enough, not at that distance. I killed no one."

"Then shooter number four offed them all." Zone was matter-of-fact.

She chewed her lip. "So one of the remaining mercenaries—the boss, I bet—must have killed the rest to keep the payment for himself."

"But he didn't take the head." Zone indicated his workshop; he'd covered the Triple Goddess with a cloth.

Kellen was glad. She got tired of locking eyes with that statue, and every way you turned there were eyes, if not the goddess's, then that relentless mercenary. "He was ruthless," she said. "He must be the one who slit Horst's throat. And killed his other men."

"Why isn't he out there?" Max tapped the radar screen. "We should have at least one human life showing on this screen. He should be watching for his chance to grab the head. When is he coming back for it?"

Kellen looked again at the Triple Goddess, and even though she was hidden beneath that cloth, Kellen could feel her gaze, critical, demanding that Kellen be all the things a woman must be—mother, warrior, protector. She looked toward Rae, toward that small face so sweet in repose and so vibrantly, irritatingly alive when awake. She whispered, "He wanted to eliminate the witnesses."

The events of the past few days rose in a tide of memory and overwhelmed her. She pulled the chair toward her, tried to sit, missed.

"Kellen!" Max lunged for her.

She thumped on the floor and burst into tears.

29

Max sat beside her, hovered as if he didn't know what he should do. "Kellen, what's wrong?"

"Rae… She used the last little square of her blankie to bandage my arm." Why that came out first, Kellen couldn't say. Why did that make her feel more guilty than all the other horrible things that had occurred on their journey?

Zone didn't care what her reasoning was. He said, "Fuck me a-runnin'," went into his workshop and shut the door. Hard.

Max gathered Kellen in his arms. "Shhh! Don't cry so loud. She'll hear you!"

Kellen totally agreed, but she couldn't stop. "It's all bloody and crusty and the rest of her blankie is nothing but a ball of yarn and I promised to crochet it again and I don't know how!" Kellen was wailing now, feeling absurd and trying to muffle her sobs in her robe.

Max pulled her toward the corner, behind the easy chair. "Rae is fine."

"Rae almost died!" Kellen turned on him, shouted in a whisper. "She almost died. She almost froze to death. She… They shot at her. She knows that the sound of a man screaming can muffle a retreat." She inhaled deeply and stared up at Max.

"It's unfortunate that all happened. I wish she could be the same child she was before she joined you in the hopes of bonding."

"I wish that, too." With all her heart.

He picked his words carefully, as if he desperately wanted to say the right thing. "She shouldn't have stowed away, but in all fairness to her, even if she had understood what true danger was, and she didn't, this trip shouldn't have been quite as harrowing as it turned out."

"No." Kellen sniveled, dug around in the pockets of the robe and finally dabbed her nose on a sleeve.

He didn't seem to be judging her, but then, it didn't matter.

She was judging herself.

He stood up and left her.

She didn't blame him.

But he came back with a roll of toilet paper, sat beside her again and handed it over. "How long's it been since you cried?"

She didn't want to tell him. He would despise her. He would see her as the irresponsible know-it-all that she was. He would realize she shouldn't be trusted with their daughter. Yet she couldn't stop the words, and they spilled out. "It was another life. In Afghanistan. When I killed a woman and her two daughters."

"Not on purpose." But he frowned, as if he couldn't imagine she might have made a mistake as a warrior.

"I didn't shoot them. It was worse than that. I was responsible." She unrolled a wad of toilet paper and blew her nose. Thankfully, there was a wastebasket beside the chair, and she tossed the wad into it and unrolled some more. And shredded it between her fingers, because she had to have something to do. Anything to take her attention off these horrible memories.

"In Afghanistan, in some of the rural areas, in the mountains, it's difficult to live. War. Constant war. Famine, all the time. For a woman, a widow with no relatives, it's not...good. Men control that world. More than this one. They're not always kind, and Ghazal had two children, two girl children."

"Ghazal was a friend?"

"Not a friend, no. She and the children lived on the edge of the poor village. A village filled with thin, pitiful people who paid both the government and the insurgents. In a hard, cold land, only the strong survive. Maybe. When our convoy went by, the eight-year-old stood out there and begged. Those big brown eyes, so sad and...old."

That face. Kellen needed to remember that face. She was the only person alive who did.

"Madeena said she had a mother and a little sister. I followed her home. That mother and her kids lived in a hovel. I've seen shacks in Wyoming that had been abandoned for a hundred years in better shape. It was freezing. The children were emaciated. The mother was skeletal." Kellen's heart still hurt as she remembered, and she shredded more toilet paper. "I gave them everything I had. Food. Blankets. I was cold and hungry that night, but—poor me." She had mocked her own hunger then. She mocked it now.

"Still you did help them." Max sounded strong, encouraging. "Did no one else take pity on them? Their own people?"

"Winter lasts for months. Crops fail. Food is scarce for everyone. No one could explain all the ins and outs to my satisfaction, but because men make the deals, and because Ghazal had no relatives, she couldn't remarry. Or wouldn't because of what would happen to her daughters in a family where they were not blood kin. She didn't conform, and in her part of the world, she and her girls were easy to forget."

He sighed. "I'm so sorry. But you *helped*."

"Stop using that word. It only makes it worse." She put down the toilet paper, straightened away from him, leaned against the wall, crossed her legs. She needed to be apart from him to tell this story. "I got them stuff online, went back a couple of times. Gave them picture books. A couple of toys. A Slinky, one of the good metal ones." She half laughed. "I've never seen children so fascinated and enthralled by one cheap little..." She caught her breath on a sob. "I did wrong."

"You shouldn't have...helped them?"

"The guys at the base, the ones who'd been there awhile, said, *Don't do this. Don't interfere. Never never. It won't turn out well.*" She saw her hands; she was wringing them, and it took an effort to stop. "I didn't listen. I told them I was sneaking in. I said no one would see me."

"You were risking your life."

"What would you have done?" She was fierce. "They were going to starve to death. I was afraid no matter what I did, that would be their fate." *Don't tell the story. It hurts too much.* "But they didn't starve."

"What happened?" Max put his hands over hers.

She had been wringing them again. Now she bunched them into fists. "I went to visit. Like I said, sneaking in. As soon as I got close I could smell that stench." She could smell it now, curling like bitter smoke through her memories. "I knew what it was. I recognized it from other missions. Char, desperation, death. The house was rubble and still smoldering."

"Did a mortar hit the house?" he asked calmly, as if by being composed he could make things better.

Never never. "That would have been too easy. No. *They* killed them." Looking back, Kellen didn't remember falling to her knees. She only remembered being on the cold barren ground, staring at the pyre where three innocent lives had ended.

A burned-out house. A melted coil of metal. The stench of desperation and death. Why was it always the innocents who paid?

Max slid his fingers between hers, loosened her fists. "Who's *they*?"

"I don't know." She looked up, racked by guilt. "Maybe the insurgents. But probably their neighbors."

"Why would they do that?" He didn't sound as calm now.

"They had reason. The insurgents would burn down a whole

village if one person was believed to be an American informant. So when the villagers killed a widow, an eight-year-old girl and a three-year-old girl for consorting with an American, they were protecting themselves and their families." Sometime in the telling of the story, she had stopped crying. Now the tears came again, fewer, hotter, more painful. She pulled her hands away from his and used toilet paper to keep the tears under control. "Ghazal and her children died because they were desperate enough to consort with...me."

Max watched her... Oh, he watched her kindly. But he knew now what she was. A fool and a butcher. "You didn't kill them."

"No. They would have probably died anyway or been forced into..." She shook her head. "There are so many sides there. There's no way to tell an enemy from a friend. I don't know who saw me, who told on me and Ghazal and her children. But when I saw Rae, and she said she was mine—" her own child, and she never knew "—all I could think of was that Slinky, stretched, melted, blackened, and the girls who, for one moment, had played with it and been happy." She looked Max right in the eye. "No matter where I went, no matter what I did, I never helped anyone again. I never looked at another child. I kept to my own kind, to my comrades who would fight and maybe die but not helplessly. Not hopelessly."

"That's why you were always running away from Rae." Max nodded. He got it now. "You were afraid you were going to love her, and disaster would follow."

"Disaster arrived. I came on this mission. She came along." Kellen leaned forward and in a voice that shook with intensity, she said, "I swear to you I didn't know she was there until it was too late."

"I know."

"Earlier you said that I—"

"I know she sneaked away to be with you. I know you would never have deliberately brought her along." He sounded disgusted—with himself. "I yelled because I wanted to blame someone besides myself."

"Why would you be to blame?"

"Because I'm her father and I know how that devious little brain works. I should have seen this coming. As soon as I read her note..." His voice rose again. "Do you know how scared I've been?"

She just didn't care. "Do you know how scared *I've* been? Those men murdered a helpless man for that head. They tried to kill us. What they would have done to a child—" Kellen's throat closed. Pure panic pumped through her veins. Everything she hadn't allowed herself to feel during the trek up the mountain, she felt now.

Max pulled her into himself as if he wanted to be part of her skin, her muscle, her bone. He hugged her, and he held her, and he must have done something special because slowly, ever so slowly, the terrible sense of being broken began to heal. After a long time, he whispered, "You brought her back to me. That's all that matters. You had a second chance to save a child, your child, and you did it."

"I never want to do anything like that again."

"Ha! Have you *met* Rae?"

She pulled away, incredulous at his lack of sympathy. "Could I spend *five minutes* basking in relief?"

"Sure. Bask." With finely tuned humor, he said, "She's still asleep."

Kellen wiped her face and blew her nose. "Thanks," she muttered. She looked up.

Max was smiling as if he saw something wonderful in her; in snotty, blubbering little ol' her.

She tossed the tissues into the wastebasket.

He took the roll of toilet paper out of her hand and put it to one side. "Done with that?"

"Um, sure." Her voice quavered a little.

He stroked her cheek, pushed her hair behind her ear, cupped his hand behind her neck.

Together, they leaned toward each other. Their lips almost touched, and—

The workroom door slammed open.

They jumped apart.

Zone couldn't see them, but he announced, "The Triple Goddess is real. She's real. This is the discovery of a lifetime!"

"Um. Great, Zone," Max said. "That's just dandy."

Kellen leaned around the back of the recliner and viewed Zone, standing there with his glasses in his hand, his eyes shining with excitement. "Whoop."

"Yes!" Zone punched the air, went back into the workshop and slammed the door.

"Where were we?" Max asked.

"I think we were going to, um, kiss. But the moment is gone. Right?"

"No, it's not. I could kiss you every moment of every day, no matter who stops us."

They leaned together again.

"Mommy! Daddy!" Rae's cranky sleepy voice halted their advance. "I want a drink of water."

Kellen looked deep into Max's eyes. "No matter who stops us?"

"Except her." Max stood. "I'll do it. My butt hurts from sitting on the floor anyway." He looked her over. "You need to go back to bed." Which was a tactful way of saying she'd been upset and crying, was tired and injured and in general looked like hell. He offered his hand.

She let him pull her to her feet. Come to think of it, her butt hurt, too.

Rae was sitting up, rubbing her eyes. "What were you doing back there?"

"Not kissing, that's for sure," Max muttered.

"I was telling your daddy about some little girls I used to know," Kellen said. "Some little girls I met from when I was a soldier."

"I'm not sleepy." Rae could hardly hold her head up. "Tell me."

"Someday I will. They deserve to be remembered."

30

The next morning, Zone scratched his chin through his beard. "That peckerhead Nils Brooks is having a fit over that goddess. That guy is a pain in the ass."

"You won't get an argument from me," Max replied.

The men were in grumpy moods, Zone because he was going to have to give up the Triple Goddess before he was done examining it, and Max because last night…well. Kellen slid a look toward him and caught him watching her. Because of last night's kissus interruptus.

She wasn't feeling grumpy at all. All that crying and gut-wrenching conversation followed by a good hard sleep and a decent breakfast had left her feeling positively cheerful. Getting dressed in the clean clothes Max had brought her and strapping her holster to her side returned her sense of accomplishment and reminded her of her own competence. It had been a difficult, dirty, murderous few days, but she and Rae had survived, and by the grace of God and Max, they had completed Kellen's mission.

She gave herself a mental high five, took her cup of Zone's killer coffee and went out on the lookout's porch, high on a ridge and twelve feet above the ground. A wind came up in the night, pushing the fog and clouds away, leaving a morning so pristine she saw the view Wade had spoken of—mountains and valleys, greens and browns and grays, blue sky fading to a pale horizon, and far, far in the distance, the ruffled deep blue Pacific. The cool air smelled like old gods in a new world, kissing her cheeks to give them color and bring her joy in this one moment when she still lived…and hoped. It was so peaceful—

Rae opened the door and dragged a kitchen chair out in a terrible scraping of wood and metal against wood. "Mommy, this is for you to sit down because Daddy says you shouldn't be standing all the time yet and Zone said you have a limp and they called Bills Brooks and he's on his way."

"Nils Brooks."

"Nils Brooks," Rae repeated. "He's on his way in a helicopter. Isn't that cool? Do you like my leggings? Daddy brought them. When I get to day camp, I'm going to do a show-and-tell and tell everyone about the Triple Goddess, but I can't show a photo because Zone won't let me. Did you know the Triple Goddess is valuable and priceless? It's going to be in a museum. I kissed her goodbye on all three mouths. Did you kiss her?"

Peace was overrated.

Kellen helped her daughter place the chair against the wall out of the worst of the breeze.

From inside the lookout, Zone shouted, "You born in a barn? Shut the door!"

Rae rolled her eyes at Kellen and slammed the door. "Sit down!" she commanded Kellen, and when Kellen did, she sat on her lap and was, miraculously, quiet. She leaned against Kellen and looked around and shivered because she hadn't bothered to wear more than a sparkly short-sleeved T-shirt, leggings and a tutu.

So Kellen put her arms around her and hugged her close.

Rae quickly decided there was such a thing as too much peace. "I like this place. Can we live here?"

"You can't have karate classes if you're up here."

"Karate!" Rae's fist shot out. "Hyah!"

"But maybe we could rent a lookout next summer."

"I'd need a cell phone."

Oh, this was going to be good. "Why?"

"How else could I call my friends?" Apparently, even before the words were out of her mouth, Rae realized that wasn't going to fly, so she added, "How can I call Daddy to come and save us if I don't have a cell phone?"

Kellen's temper rose fast and hot. "Daddy did not come and save us! I'm willing to give him credit for the last sprint, but *we*—"

"Listen!" Rae jumped to her feet. "Do you hear that?"

Kellen exhaled her frustration. "I do." She opened the door and called, "The helicopter is here."

Max glanced at the monitor on the kitchen table. "There's no one out there."

Zone strapped on his sidearm and handed Max a rifle. "Let's take every precaution." He looked at Kellen.

She patted the holster strapped to her side under her jacket. Because the helicopter should be carrying Nils Brooks, coming to pick up the Triple Goddess and carry it to safety. But by the time Kellen and Rae woke this morning, Max and Zone had been out to the battle site and located the bodies, mangled by the predators who nightly patrolled the woods: bear, coyotes, bobcats and hawks. The firearms had all disappeared. That left one man out there, a ruthless killer, unforgiving of failure, who if he could, left no evidence of his passing.

They would take no chances now.

Max came out on the deck and held the rifle at ready. "Go inside, Rae."

"I want to watch!"

"As soon as we recognize the guy inside the helicopter, we'll let you watch." Kellen put a gentle hand in Rae's back and pushed her into the lookout.

"This might be a bad guy?" Rae asked.

"Might be," Kellen agreed.

"I am really tired of bad guys," Rae said in disgust. "They make my life *very difficult.*" She went inside.

"Smart kid." Zone stood just inside the door with the well-wrapped Triple Goddess slung over one shoulder and Kellen's bag slung over the other.

Kellen watched the fast two-man helicopter hover over them, then drop slowly over the almost-flat bare gravel below the lookout.

The engine slowed. The door opened. Nils Brooks stepped out. He was the pilot. There was no one else.

"Perfect," she breathed.

Max lowered the steps from the deck to the ground. He started down, but Kellen caught his arm. "No. I get to do this."

He stepped back and allowed her to go down first.

She ran down the short slope to meet Nils. She opened her arms.

He was grinning. "It's real?" He opened his arms and prepared to hug her. "It's really real?"

She sucker punched him in the face.

He staggered backward, stumbled down the slope and fell on his rear.

She pulled her weapon and stood over him, pistol pointed at his bleeding nose. "That's for not giving me all the facts before I took the job!"

He pulled a handkerchief out of his pocket—of course, the American aristocrat Nils Brooks would have a handkerchief on him—and mopped at the bleeding. "I needed you, and what with having a kid and all, I was afraid you wouldn't do it."

"I ought to cut off your balls."

"You got up here alive!" He made it sound like she'd been skipping all the way.

"Barely! With my kid and all in tow!"

Nils sat up cautiously. "You can't blame me for your daughter stowing away."

"I can blame you for everything." Kellen heard the rattle of stones behind her as someone descended the path.

"Do I get to hit him now?" This time, Max wasn't yelling. This time, his voice was low and vibrant and oh so completely different from last night's meltdown. This time, he was ready to kill.

She stepped back and let Nils scramble to his feet. "Nils is a dirty fighter," she said.

"That's right. Defend your boyfriend from me." Nils balanced on the balls of his feet, ready to attack.

She looked him in the eyes. "He's an ex-football player with a reputation for foreign bar fights. Take him on if you want."

Nils hesitated. Exchanged a long hard stare with Max. Stood flat-footed again. "Where's the Triple Goddess?"

"Zone's got her. There were four mercenaries, and she was left behind." Max used a tough guy voice Kellen had never heard from him before. "I rescued her."

Diverted, Nils paid no attention to the tough voice. "The mercenaries didn't grab her when they had the chance?"

"Before anyone touched her, one mercenary killed the other three," Max said.

"He wanted the head for himself," Nils declared.

"Maybe. But he knows where the head is, the outlook isn't impervious to attack, and there's been no attempt to retrieve it."

While Kellen listened to the men rehash the events and try to make sense of them, the events of the past weeks flashed through her mind. Everything at the winery had been calm, normal, boring. Then Roderick Blake had shown up, climbed on the roof, knocked a tile onto the ground where it blasted into shrapnel, and everything since had been skewed by pain, fear and a sense of putting a puzzle together…while blindfolded.

She was missing a crucial piece. It was almost in her grasp, and if she had one moment of peace to think, she knew she could—

A great spattering of stones rattled down the trail, and Rae arrived at a run. "Hi, I'm Rae Di Luca. You must be Bills Brooks! We've been waiting for you. Daddy wants to shoot you. Mr. Zone said he'd watch. Mommy said you'd give me a ride in the helicopter. I've never ridden in a helicopter before!"

"Hi, Rae. I'm *Nils* Brooks." Nils knelt on one knee in front of her. "I can't take you for a helicopter ride right now, but—"

"You can." Kellen nudged Rae out of the way and knelt, her posture a mirror of his. "Max and I have to get down the mountain. There are killers out there hunting for…for the head. I am not subjecting my child to danger when the treacherous son of a bitch who put us in this situation is in front of us with a way to get her out and get her home."

"Mommy!" Rae was reproachful. "I thought you liked Bills Brooks?"

Kellen answered Rae, but she never took her gaze away from Nils. "I trust him to care for the head, and you. There's a difference."

Nils stared at Kellen. Looked up at Max, then at Zone who had silently arrived. Nils nodded, stood, brushed the dirt from his knee. "I guess you're going for a ride, Rae Di Luca."

"Cool! Where are we going?"

"You're going home," Kellen said. "To the winery. Your grandma will be excited to see you."

"Di Luca Winery in the Willamette Valley. You think you can find that, Brooks?" Max's voice still held that soft sibilant threat, like a snake giving warning of a strike.

"I can find it."

"Good," Max said. "You'll take our daughter there. You'll deliver her into the hands of her grandmother. Then you can fly with that head wherever the hell you want and do whatever the hell you want with it. Don't call us again. Ever. About anything."

Kellen watched Max out of the corners of her eyes. She had pegged him as a man who was kind and gentle, intelligent and businesslike, devoted to his family and friends. She hadn't realized that devotion included a threat and a promise of violence in defense of his loved ones.

Something to add to her mental dossier.

"Wait. I'm going home?" That hadn't occurred to Rae, and she backed up, eyes wide. "I don't want to go home! I want to stay here. I like it here!"

"Now, honey—" Max began.

Kellen interrupted. "Mommy and Daddy aren't staying here. We're going to hike down the mountain. You remember the mountain? Not enough food, no fire, no s'mores, no fun?"

"Bikes! Mountain bikes! We could get mountain bikes and—"

"Kid, there's no place to get mountain bikes within a day's walk of here." For Zone, that was incredibly patient.

Max put his arm around Rae's shoulders. "You'll be home in an hour. You can tell your grandma all about your adventures. You can play with your princesses. You can eat whatever you want—"

"Not Spam," Rae said sulkily. "Grandma won't let me have Spam."

"Kid, you ate all my Spam," Zone said.

"You can call your friends and tell them where you've been," Kellen coaxed.

"Why aren't you coming in the helicopter?" Rae asked.

"It's a Robinson R22. They aren't kidding when they call it a two-man helicopter. At this elevation, I'd never get it off the ground with that much weight," Nils said. "I need to get going. Are you coming for a ride in the helicopter, Rae? Or not? You're afraid, aren't you?"

Rae's skinny chest swelled with indignation. "I am not!" she yelled.

"Okay, then." Nils winked at Kellen and headed for the helicopter. "Let's go."

Rae ran after Nils.

Kellen and Max ran after Rae. They ducked below the slowly

rotating blades, hooked Rae into the seat, told her to be good, put her headphones on, kissed her and waved her off.

As the helicopter rose in the air, Max said, "Brooks is better with kids than I expected."

"If the pictures are to be believed, he's got a ton of family, nephews and nieces."

"I thought he was hatched." Max nudged her with his elbow. "I didn't have a reputation for foreign bar fights. When I was in football, I was clean as a whistle."

"He doesn't know that."

They turned to walk back to the Horizon Lookout.

Zone blocked the path.

Uh-oh.

"I'm headed down to pick up supplies—Spam!—report those guys and their deaths. Call me an accomplice, but I won't mention either of you. The trip will take me three days, down and back. You've got three days here to heal—" he glared at Kellen "—make sure your killers lose interest and get your stupid relationship figured out."

Kellen stared at him, her eyes so wide they felt stretched and dry.

Zone marched up the path to the lookout, picked up the large camping backpack leaning against the bottom step, hoisted it over his shoulders and said, "Be gone before I get back." He walked into the canyon, down the path, took a sudden right and disappeared from sight.

"Where did he go?" Kellen asked.

"When we were out searching for the bodies, I figured out pretty fast he knows this area way better than anyone else. He takes paths no one else could ever find."

"So he's going the back way?"

"Looks like it."

They were alone.

Awkward. Kellen tilted her head and watched Zone disappear into the canyon. "I get the feeling he doesn't like us in his space."

"He doesn't like anyone in his space. His instructions to me were to not get ourselves killed while he was gone." Max pressed his index finger into the middle of Kellen's back, urging her toward the lookout. "Standing out in the open makes me uneasy. Shall we go up?"

More awkward. "Of course." She was limping, damn it, undernourished and unready to make a hike of twenty-five miles over rough terrain, even if it was mostly downhill.

But she was also unprepared to be alone with Max, her former lover and the father of her child. Zone had not only told them to work out their relationship, he had shone a spotlight on their relationship so neither of them could ignore it. Now they were going to be alone for three days. Alone. Isolated from mankind and civilization alone. *We can't avoid discussing and deciding our relationship* alone.

She wasn't prepared. She would never be prepared.

Kellen hadn't seen the lookout from the outside before, what with being unconscious and flung over Max's shoulder when she arrived. Now she examined the twelve-foot-tall foundation of concrete block topped with a white-painted hut surrounded on all sides by a three-foot wide deck. She saw solar panels on the roof and a few crooked wires sticking up like Dr. Seuss reindeer antlers. "Interesting. How is he generating enough power to run the place?" Casual conversation with Max. Very good.

"I believe he's an inventor."

"As well as a doctor, and verifier and restorer of antiquities? And a master of disguise? Because I swear without the beard and the glasses, he would be a different person." She got to the top of the stairs and turned like a bobcat on the defensive. "Max, if you want, you can start down the mountain. You probably want to get back. I'll rest for a couple of days and—"

"Really? After what's happened?" He stood on the step below

her, exactly her height, too close, breathing her oxygen, looking in her eyes. "You think that I would leave you to walk down alone? That's what you think of me?"

"No, I just… I don't know what we're going to…" Frustrated, she burst out, "I wish I could remember more about us. I wish I could remember if we worked."

"If we worked?"

"If we could have made it together."

He smiled, a slow, wicked curl of amusement. "I can help with one aspect of whether we worked." Without touching her with his hands, he tilted his head, leaned in and kissed her.

31

Some men considered kissing nothing but a preliminary to the main event.

Some men considered kissing a coin to be repaid at the time and place of their choosing.

This man kissed for the bliss of sharing breath, sharing touch, sharing pleasure. Max tasted Kellen as if she was a glorious feast to be savored, one flavor at a time. The kiss intensified until she cupped her hands around his neck, held him in place and took control.

Then he climbed that last stair, crowded her against the look-out's wooden wall and kissed her in the sunlight, body to body. Heat built so fast she could hardly breathe. She tore her mouth away and thumped her head against the white-painted boards. "Look. Here's the thing. The same problems that stop me from walking down the hill make this, um…"

"Lovemaking?"

"That. Make it difficult for me to fully, sort of, participate—"

"In the *lovemaking*?"

"Yes. In that."

He moved back to the stairway, pulled it up and hooked it.

Kellen and Max were isolated and safe from the world.

"Eight years is a long time, and I promise I can take my time, work around your injuries, make the *lovemaking* good for you."

He irritated her with his emphasis and repetition of that word. "How will you do that?"

His brown eyes glinted with humor and promise. "I've practiced a lot when I was alone."

She gave a spurt of laughter and surprise, and grappled with the information he had so tactfully presented. "You didn't... You haven't..."

"No."

"But you thought I was dead."

"You weren't dead. You were gone. You were my woman. We had made promises. Not in a church, but with our bodies. I was always waiting for your return."

She blurted, "No wonder your mother doesn't like me!"

He threw back his head and laughed, all big grand amusement and beneath that, a simmering pool of waiting molten sensuality.

How did she feel about him waiting for her when he had no assurance she would ever return? Flattered and...and terrified. Because she wasn't anyone special. She had no exotic, erotic gifts. She cleared her throat. "I guess I should say that I never had any sexual relations while I was gone...either."

He caught his toe on a board on the deck and stumbled, righted himself and asked, "Why not?"

"I never trusted another man enough to open my body to him."

Max took a breath. "I should say that it doesn't matter, that however you lived your life was fine with me. But that would be a lie. Eight years ago, I won your trust. Won't you trust me again?" He held out his hand, palm up.

He had done that before, always leading, never coercing. "I have friends," she said. "After battles fought side by side, I trust them. They proved themselves to me and I proved myself to them. But you—you're different. I already do trust you. You are the one person I've always trusted. Maybe it's chemistry. I think it's an instinct in my mind and a wisdom in my soul." She put her hand in his.

He left the door open to the breeze and the birdsong and led her inside to the bed.

Max made good on his promise.

Long and slow and warm. Kisses on every bruise, care for every injury, words that cherished and enhanced.

This man not only loved to kiss for the pleasure of kissing. Each caress was a sensuous pleasure, the act of love was an act of worship that escalated into a steady deep rhythm: sweat and whimpers and groans and triumph.

And after…oh, after was a slow descent from the heights, cushioned by touch and breath and joy. Then sleep and waking, stretching to find her body felt better—sex as a cure-all?—and smiling as she watched him naked in the kitchen, stirring up something on the stove.

He saw she was awake and said, "I found hamburger in the freezer, a can of tomatoes in the pantry, some dried herbs and fresh garlic—apparently, Zone grows his own, which makes him a farmer, too. So I'm making my aunt Sarah's spaghetti sauce."

"Sounds good. Is there pasta?"

"No, but there's cornmeal, so we'll make polenta."

"Did I say good? That sounds wonderful." She was starving. "Shouldn't you put on an apron? It seems as if you're courting disaster."

"I hate to be putting clothes on just to take them off again."

"Aren't you—?"

"Cocky?"

"That's the word." A fully clothed Max Di Luca was a very nice-looking man. Naked, he was an inspiration. When he was cooking her dinner, he was… Well. She could never ever let another woman know about this. If word got out, he would be inundated with offers to star on a calendar as all twelve months of mouthwatering goodness.

He put the lid on the pot, turned the burner to low and came back to bed. He stretched out against her, and suddenly the single bed mattress was too narrow, especially when he propped his head on one hand and leaned on his elbow. "What do you want to ask me about?"

She had thought they were going to make love again. Which made her nervous and giddy at the same time. But talking—that made her nervous without the giddy.

She sat up and pushed the pillow against the wall and then didn't lean back. She had been avoiding so much, the questions and the answers about their relationship, about what exactly had happened that she could remember and what had happened she could never remember. She prided herself on her bravery, but she wasn't brave about this welter of emotions, joy and pain. She wet her lips. "I don't know how I had a baby. How was that possible? Tell me how I had a baby."

If she thought to disconcert him, she failed utterly. "I thought you would never ask."

32

Kellen plucked at the fraying hem of the wool blanket. "I figured…it was a birth like most births?"

"Like most births? Her mother was in a coma. *You* were in a coma." Max gestured widely. "Do you feel no curiosity about those months after the shooting?"

"It's not that I'm not curious. But for me… I feel as if I went crazy and woke up a different person. I feel guilty for being shot—"

"How could you feel guilty?"

"I was upset with you. I ran away rather than be mature and discuss our problems. Then *he* found me and shot me."

Max came to his feet. He ran hand over his face as if trying to create an expression of understanding. "That's ridiculous. I didn't know your whole story, but it was clear you'd been hurt in a relationship. Hurt…physically. Hurt in every way possible."

"Yes," she said faintly. "An abusive relationship…"

"I got that figured out. When we met, when you saved Annabella from that bastard who is her father, you had scars. Burn marks. There had been broken bones. You were still in the process of healing physically and mentally. So after we got together, you were jumpy. Something happened…" He trailed off.

She didn't fill in the blank. Even now, she was a little shocked, a little angry that he had snooped into her private papers. He read her cousin Kellen's résumé and believed it was hers.

He continued, "And you got scared and upset, and you ran. No guilt."

Shocked and angry didn't change the facts, and she took responsibility for her actions. "Running away was thoughtless and led to disaster."

"You might as well blame my sister for marrying the bastard who tried to kidnap their child." He shook his head. "There's too many threads here. I can't even begin to process the idea of your guilt."

Hostility rose in her. "Nevertheless, I feel guilt."

"Okay. Fine. My sisters say women are allowed to feel what they feel and men should shut up about how feeling that way is stupid because men are a bunch of insensitive beasts."

"That's what your sisters say?"

"When you strip away all the tact and rhetoric, yes."

Kellen relaxed, laughed again and held her stitches. "I feel guilty that I don't remember Rae's birth."

"All right. *All right.* Look. You were shot in the head at close range." He came to her side and lifted her bangs and smoothed the red ring of scar as if he'd done it many times before. "You were in the hospital. You weren't expected to live. No one could figure out how you were alive at all. But you were so strong. Annabella told me she could feel your spirit fighting to survive. I don't know. Probably she said that because I sat there for so many hours by your side because I—" he looked directly at her "—I felt guilty."

"Why?"

"I made you run away. I didn't run fast enough to save you before that bullet..." He faltered.

She took his hand. "You didn't make me run away. I ran because, when I was presented with a problem, that was what I did...then. It's different now. If there's one thing I learned in the Army, it's that no one can outrun a bullet."

"So I shouldn't feel guilty?"

"No, please continue. It's nice to have company in Guiltyville. When did you realize I was pregnant?"

He tensed again. "Not for a damned long time. You were being fed and given fluids intravenously, and your body was under huge stress as you went from trauma to a desperate bid to repair the damage. The doctors were amazed that, first, you lived, then that you seemed to be...not recovering, exactly, but that your brain seemed to be creating new circuits, going around the damaged areas. The medical team said they'd never seen anything like it. They were so focused on your head, and it never occurred to me it was possible for you to be pregnant. You had told me—"

"—that I couldn't have a baby. I didn't think I could. I lost a baby. My husband's child." She carefully phrased her next words. "The miscarriage occurred in difficult circumstances."

"What did your husband do to you?"

So it didn't matter how careful she was. Max understood that Gregory was at fault. "He pushed me down the stairs." Kellen said it without flinching or crying for the loss of her baby. Maybe she'd already cried all those tears. "The doctor told me I couldn't get pregnant again. But he was a small town doctor. He didn't do any tests, so I guess maybe—"

"He wasn't right? Obviously not. What did he say about your bruises and burns and broken bones?"

"Nothing to me. If he had the nerve to say anything to Gregory, I imagine he was told to mind his own business." She thought back. "In fact, that was the last time I saw that doctor."

Max watched her; just watched her.

"I'm fine now," she assured him. "I can take care of myself. No one's ever going to hurt me again."

Still, Max watched, as if he wanted to burrow into her mind and understand her past and all the moments that had formed her.

She prompted him, "How did you discover I was pregnant with Rae?"

"Oh. That. It took a cleaning lady to say, 'How come she hasn't had a period?'"

Kellen began to comprehend that chaos and emotional turmoil Max must have felt. "How many months along…?"

"Almost five months. Rae was tiny. She'd had a traumatic first few months in the womb. Once the cleaning lady said her piece, I saw the baby bump and it was like—how could I have been so blind?" He was angry, at himself, at the world. "I'd spent hours with you, days and weeks, and I hadn't noticed."

"How could the *doctors* have been so blind?"

"There is that."

The lid rattled on the pan on the stove.

He leaped up to give the pot a stir, then returned to bed. This time, he sat on the edge of the mattress as if he could no longer relax, as if this story required him to be alert. "They did all the tests, ultrasounds, everything, and at five months, Rae was racing to catch up developmentally. She was doing well, and the doctors…they theorized that the pregnancy hormones were so powerful that they were the agents that repaired the damage in your brain."

"So you knew I was going to wake up?"

"No! No. The monitors detected brain activity but it's a long way from a few sparks to walking and talking and…you're a miracle." Max had a way of looking at her as if she *was* a miracle, one he loved and appreciated.

He made her take deep breaths, feel the warmth. "What about Rae?"

"It was now a balancing act. We wanted to save Rae—"

"Of course." Kellen understood that. She was glad of that.

"The medical team wanted to keep her in the womb until

she was at least seven months along and had the best chance of survival. Then they would take her by C-section."

Kellen put her hand on her belly. She had no scar.

"The team kept telling me Rae was normal, and I could see in the ultrasound she was active and... I was hopeful and broken at the same time. Then." He shook off her hand and walked to the window and looked out.

"Then?"

"They had monitors on you all the time. Monitors all over. I didn't understand... I mean, maybe they told me, but they told me so many things and I was... They weren't monitoring you for labor. They didn't realize you were in labor until my mother was watching the fluctuations in your blood pressure and said, 'That's it!' By that time, they couldn't do a cesarean. Rae was in the birth canal." His voice grew thick with emotion. "I thought I was going to lose you both."

"I'm sorry." Kellen wasn't apologizing, but offering her sympathy.

"The doctor didn't get there in time to catch the baby. Your nurse delivered her. She handed Rae to me in a towel. You can't comprehend how tiny she was, and she opened her eyes and..." He turned to face Kellen and put his hand on his heart.

Kellen felt tears welling. He had been so alone.

Then, with Rae, he wasn't.

"The first time I held that baby, we bonded. The months after her birth were... My God. There weren't enough hours in the day, enough days in the week. Every minute was claimed. I should be with Rae, I should be with you. The court case against my sister's husband was ongoing. Then he committed suicide and the death made news. After realizing that the city hospital didn't have the resources to care for a comatose woman, not even to realize she was in labor, I had you moved to a private hospital. You had twenty-four-hour care. You were never alone...except that time when you woke up."

She nodded.

"Meanwhile, Rae was in an incubator for two and a half months. I was there every day for hours, holding her, feeding her, making sure she was cared for. When I wasn't there, my mother and sisters took turns. I was so afraid she would die, but she was a miracle baby. At last, she came home, and I discovered what being a single parent meant. My family helped so much, but a baby is a full-time job!" He looked helpless, as if the mere memory stripped him of strength. "She had to be fed all the time, then she got colic and cried for months. I wanted to bring her in to see you, to put her in your arms so you'd know, somehow, that you had given birth to a wonderful healthy baby girl."

Kellen didn't point out that a wakeful colicky baby didn't sound so wonderful to her.

Max paced toward her as if he couldn't stay away. "I feared to take her into the hospital. Private or not, infections and illnesses were rife."

"I understand."

"One day, you were gone. Security video showed you waking, struggling to your feet, getting dressed... You'd been showing signs of waking, and we were hopeful. But my God, to come out of a coma and leave? The medical establishment was amazed." His beautiful brown eyes grew dark and muddy. "I was livid."

She could believe it, looking at him now as he stood by her bed, his cheeks red and flushed, and his fists clenching. She put her hand over one of his. "I'm sorry. When I woke, I thought... I thought I was in an asylum." That she remembered all too clearly: her panic, her desperate need to escape.

"You should have had someone with you at all times. You were supposed to have someone with you." He turned his hand in hers, grasped her fingers. "If I hadn't seen the security footage that proved you were alone for less than fifteen minutes, I would have sued them... I should have sued them, but I didn't want to destroy that young woman's life."

"The nurses' aide?"

"Yes. She left you alone because she was in the corridor, receiving a marriage proposal. I couldn't. I just couldn't. But I still don't understand how the Army would take you. I searched… It never occurred to me to check the military." He was asking the questions now, wanting to know, to understand. "How could they let you in? You were too thin. You were weak. You had the scar of a gunshot on your forehead!"

"I faked it well. They liked my degrees. They loved my degrees." *They weren't really my degrees, but I presented them as if they were.* She hesitated.

My name is Kellen Adams, and that's half a lie.

She should tell him, but they were just now beginning to talk about the important things. Naked. After making love.

She wanted to tell him the truth. About her. About who she really was.

She *would* tell him the truth. "Max?"

He watched her with anticipation, as if he had been waiting for this moment. "Go on."

Across the room, Zone's communications panel came alive with two words.

"Mommy! Daddy!"

33

At the sound of Rae's excited voice, Max vaulted off the bed and flung a blanket over Kellen, dragged the comforter over his shoulders, then stood blinking. "Wait," he said. "There's no video."

"Right." Kellen pulled the blanket off the bed anyway.

Still wrapped in the comforter, he headed toward the satellite station and flipped the switch. "Hi, honey. Did you make it home okay?"

"Daddy! Daddy! Daddy!" Rae could hardly speak—for about two seconds. Then she was off and running. "Bills Brooks took me on a tour over the top of the winery and I saw everything from the air, and I waved at everybody, and Grandma clutched her chest, and Mr. Brooks put the helicopter down right in front of the winery, and he told me when I got out to wave like the Queen of England, and I did!"

"That's great, sweetheart." Max gestured Kellen over. "So now you're with your grandma?"

"I'm right here, Maximilian." Verona sounded more than a little stern. "It was a thrill I wasn't expecting to see my youngest granddaughter drop out of the sky with a stranger."

Max looked helplessly at Kellen.

Kellen stepped up to the microphone. "We should have called you, Mrs. Di Luca, but after Rae left Max had to help me back into the lookout… This trip hasn't been good on my hip and I don't know if Rae told you, but I was shot."

"Shot? She told me it was nothing but a scratch!"

"I did say that to her." Kellen didn't even have to work to put a chill in her voice. "Not long before I passed out."

Pause. "Oh."

"Mommy, are you okay now?" Rae asked.

Phooey. Kellen had wanted to scare Verona, not Rae. "After Zone sewed me up, I was fine. You saw him do it."

"I want to be a doctor," Rae announced.

"I thought blood made you sick." Verona sounded surprised.

"It used to," Rae said.

Before she'd seen a lot of it. Before Verona could connect the dots, Kellen asked, "Is Mr. Brooks still there?"

"He left before I could even thank him for bringing her home," Verona said.

"He had to take the Triple Goddess someplace safe." Rae sounded very serious. "Grandma, it's an *important historical artifact*."

Kellen and Max exchanged grins.

"I'm sure it is, whatever it is. And I'm sure your daddy is taking good care of your mommy." With an edge in her voice, Verona said, "Maximilian, remember what happened last time you took care of Kellen Adams, and this time, practice safety!"

How did she know they were standing here naked except for some bedclothes? *"Are you sure there's no video?"* Kellen mouthed silently at Max.

"Grandma, Mommy can't help if she was shot at while she was saving me!" Rae was squaring off with her grandmother. Over Kellen.

Kellen dived toward the microphone. "Did you show your grandma the yarn that was your poor blankie? Did you ask her if she would teach me to crochet so I can put it back together for you?"

"What happened to your blankie?" Verona sounded angry.

"We used it for a spider web to catch the bad guys. Let me show you!" They heard Rae's shoes clatter away at a run.

In a low voice, Verona asked, "She was in real danger, wasn't she?"

"I'm afraid so," Kellen said. "But she's home with you now, safe and sound, and I promise I'll never take her into danger again."

Verona took two slow, audible breaths. "It wasn't your fault. She's a feckless child, adventurous to a fault, and I...thank you for keeping her safe. I've just been so frightened. So frightened." Verona was making an excuse for herself, for her rudeness.

Kellen understood. "Of course. She *is* my daughter."

"She's very like you," Verona said. It was not a compliment. But it was a fact.

Max was looking at Kellen, frowning, as if they were speaking in code. Which Kellen supposed, to a guy, they were.

"Verona, would you do something for me?" Kellen asked. "Would you call Yearning Sands Resort and talk to Birdie Haynes, tell her that I'm safe, and I'll contact her as soon as I get off this mountain?"

"Of course. I'm glad to do that for you." Verona took a breath. "Be safe. Be safe. I know how to crochet. I can put her blanket back together. I can even teach you to do it. But I can't fix everything. So *take care*."

34

"So Rae's strategy worked. You're bonded." Max beamed at her, his brown eyes bright and triumphant.

"Yes." Kellen realized she sounded disgusted, possibly not the response he was looking for, and hastily she added, "I know it's a good thing. But I have so many regrets for what I've missed, and I can see so much pain ahead."

He waved away her concerns. "Don't worry about what you've missed. With a little prompting, my mother will give you the whole Rae-from-birth-to-first-grade-graduation slide show."

"How long will that take?"

"How many weeks do you have?"

Kellen narrowed her eyes at him. "It can't be that bad."

"Mom never deletes a picture," he informed her.

"Yippee."

"I wouldn't mind so much, but since I'm the tallest she always cuts off the top of my head."

Kellen chuckled.

"Do you remember my family in Pennsylvania at all?" He had a way of making her laugh, relax and then—wham! He slapped her with a question or a memory.

Kellen opened her mouth and shut it, squinted and tried to explain. "I remember some things very well. I remember being on the streets and seeing that man dragging that screaming, crying little girl."

"My niece, Annabella, in the hands of her father, Ettore Fontina. That worthless bastard." Max's mouth was set in an unusual cruel crescent. "Did I tell you he hung himself? When he found out that this time, not even his wealthy Italian mama could get him out of prison, he hung himself in his cell."

"Hung himself in prison? Good. That's good. I can never forgive him for that shot that stole—"

"Memory, love, a year of your life? More than we can even say?"

Max's anger hung on the air between them. In a placid tone, she said, "He taught me the value of time."

"I should have killed him when he tried to kidnap Annabella."

"You'd still be serving your sentence."

"I'd get off for good behavior." He dismissed that with a wave of his hand. "What else do you remember?"

"Your sister." Kellen had spoken with her once on the phone since regaining her memories, but there had been no family visits yet. Kellen suspected Max had insisted the new family have time alone. "She was so grateful to me for saving her daughter. She kissed me on both cheeks. I remember thinking she was a little nuts. Then I remember realizing everyone in your family thought I was more than crazy, or on drugs."

"I didn't think that."

"I know. You always believed I was just—"

"—hurt."

She swallowed and nodded. "I remember your mother. She liked me a lot more in Pennsylvania than she does now. I remember—" Kellen was squinting again, trying to see through the fog of amnesia to those winter days eight and a half years ago "—Christmas! Your family! So many of them. I don't know that I could have remembered them even if... Even that spring if I hadn't been shot in the head." She touched the round scar on her forehead and looked at him. "Mostly I remember you. I remember how kind you were to me, as if I was fragile."

"You were fragile. I was afraid at any moment you were going to break and run."

"I did break and run."

"Why didn't you talk to me?" he muttered.

He sounded so wretched she was at last able to say, "I panicked when I realized you snooped into my papers."

"Was that so awful?" Immediately, he answered his own question. "Okay, yes, I know it was. You had vigilantly not said your real name or confided your past. I had no right. I told myself it would help our relationship if I knew. I lied to myself. I apologize."

Nothing about this was easy. Everything was guilt and confusion. "I was a coward, and I guess I got what I deserved."

"You made a mistake. No one deserves to spend a year in a coma for a mistake." Max knew what he thought, what he believed. He slipped from the bed to a place on the floor. He knelt before her, naked and on one knee. "Kellen Adams, will you marry me?"

She stared in horror at him.

He said, "You just turned pale. You look like you're going to throw up. You're upset because there's no ring? No flowers?"

She shook her head. She couldn't speak.

Max had proposed to Kellen Adams.

My name is Kellen Adams—and that's only half the truth.

But that was the real problem. She could confess who she was, and Max would understand her evasions. Might understand. She hoped. But that revelation was only the beginning. "I can't. Max, I can't."

"There's no reason to be frightened." Slowly, he reached for her fingers. "I'm not going to hurt you."

"I know that. I would never think that you..." He was right.

She felt queasy and sweaty. "I trust you," she said, but she pulled her hand from his grasp.

"Can you tell me why you won't marry me?" he asked.

"I can't." *Not without telling you all my secrets.*

I've got the scar of a gunshot on my forehead.

35

He limped down the mountain to the lot where he'd parked his Lexus NX Hybrid.

He had disposed of the firearms. In a wretched, rugged, ridiculous wilderness like this, that was easier than he could have hoped.

But he'd had enough of hiking and tracking and waiting for these supposed professionals to do their jobs. He would make one more attempt to handle matters using the help, and if that didn't do it, he'd take over. He would get the job done, clean up the loose ends and be gone.

How hard could it be to kill one lone woman and her brat?

36

Three days later, late in the afternoon, the message from Zone arrived at Horizon Lookout.

I'm on the way back. Get out.

"Mr. Rogers he's not," Kellen observed as she helped Max pack his backpack full of whatever foodstuffs they were able to scrounge from Zone's pantry. It wasn't much; they had to get down the mountain quickly or they'd starve.

Max took one last look at the screen that scanned the area for life. "Nobody out there," he said. There had been no signs of humans since Zone had disappeared off the screen.

"That's good," she said.

"Sure is," he agreed.

They were both spooked.

And she was uncomfortable.

Max had proposed, naked and exposed.

She had rejected him and refused to tell him why.

He'd been mild, calm, conciliatory. For days. Hands off. A caretaker.

She was still waiting for the other shoe to fall. Because she'd come to know Max well, and the man wasn't mild and conciliatory. He had an agenda and he worked it until he got his way.

But she had too much at stake to abandon her stance.

I've got the scar of a gunshot on my forehead.

Max shouldered the backpack, stepped onto the deck, performed a visual survey of the Horizon Lookout surroundings and lowered the stairs. "If you feel weak or need help, you tell me, but the sooner we're off the mountain, the better."

She followed Max down the steps and into the canyon. "You don't believe we're safe."

"Do you?"

No. Of course she didn't. Someone had murdered those men, those thieves and assassins, and that person was still out there somewhere. Their days in Horizon Lookout had given them a respite, but whoever it was, he was still out there, waiting and watching.

She was not completely recovered; the stitches in her arm itched, her hip ached, she slept hard and ate with appetite. Having abandoned her backpack on the trek here, she now walked unencumbered, carrying her weapon in her holster and a sleeping bag strapped to her shoulder. Going downhill would be easy…until they passed through the canyon and into the site of the battle for the Triple Goddess head.

Everything about this place was haunted: the bloodstains, the ashes caused by the burning tablet, the few human remains that lingered after three days of predation… Kellen had visited and revisited battlefields, but this was different. In this one, she had feared not for herself, but for her daughter, and as she stood here and remembered, her heart pumped fear and desperation through her veins.

Max took her arm. "We can't linger."

"I don't even want to. Though somehow I think—"

"You could find a clue about the man who hired the hunters?"

"Yes."

"We looked. Zone and I searched separately and together."

Max herded her down the mountain. "Whoever was chasing you and the head had access to funds."

"Considering the value of the head, I suppose I shouldn't be surprised." It wasn't until they turned onto the bicycle path that she relaxed and walked with Max without looking over her shoulder. "It's beautiful up there on Horizon Ridge—and I don't ever want to go back."

"The farther away we get, the happier I am. I like this descent. I hear music in my head, the kind they play in the action movies to make your heart pound, but it's a good feeling. We're getting away. We're almost safe."

"Right. Almost safe." That sounded like something they said in those action movies right before everything went south. "What music did you hear when you were going uphill?"

"Uphill was different. The music was ominous, I was walking and running, terrified I would be too late. It was like one of those nightmares where you want to sprint, but your feet are too heavy." As he spoke and recalled, he moved faster and faster, into the evening's gathering dusk.

She was good with that. The forest surrounded them, the wilderness lands released their call and gathered in the people who knelt against the earth and listened to its call. The sun set, that impressive sudden slash as the mountain ripped the light away, and suddenly they were in darkness.

Kellen stopped walking. "Listen to the quiet. I can't hear the call of a night bird or the scamper of a squirrel. It's as if we were alone in the world."

For the first time in days, Max pulled her close. "We're not going to make it all the way down the mountain tonight. Not in this dark. What do you say we…linger…a few more hours?"

Their last night alone, without responsibility, feeling like teenagers and loving like adults, the two of them together again, understanding that each moment might be the last.

She cupped his face, seeing his dim outline in the starlight and recognizing it in her heart. "Look at the sky. I'll remember this for the rest of my—" A thin, bright red beam flashed across the clearing and into her eyes.

Max slammed into her, hard and fast, knocking her backward, slamming her head into a boulder and shoving her to the ground behind its shelter.

A rifle shot blasted the world to pieces.

She gasped for breath.

No air.

She struggled against a weight.

His weight, collapsed on her, two hundred pounds of muscle, bone and fury, bunching, preparing to—

He rolled off and disappeared.

She was alone.

Her head splintered with blinding pain. The black sky weighed on her like an iron sheet, pressing her into the dirt. She sank. The stars were holes poked through the iron, allowing those few hints of light from beyond.

She still couldn't breathe.

The pain in her head was blistering cold.

She still couldn't move.

She couldn't run.

The gray was coming for her from that place where it hovered, waiting to take her.

It pounced, and she traveled out of time, out of mind, to nowhere and nothing.

From far away, she heard another shot. So final, so fatal.

She was back. Sprawled on the ground. She could hear shouting. Men shouting. A series of thumps, hard and fast. But no more shooting.

Was Max alive?

He had to live.

She wanted to stand up, to see, to help. She couldn't move.

Nothing. She tried to wiggle her fingers, her toes. She was trapped in her own body, panicked, silently screaming.

The gray waited, always there.

No malice. No kindness. A hell of nothing. Blank months. Wasted years.

She cried without tears.

And was gone forever.

Again.

37

Something wet fell into Kellen's palm.

She flinched and opened her eyes.

Gray again. Gray sky, the beginnings of dawn in the mountains.

So not months and years. Hours only, wandering toward death.

Somehow, while she was gone, Max had wrapped her in blankets, placed her in the sleeping bag, protected her from the cold night.

He was alive. Whatever else had happened last night, he had lived through it.

Now he knelt beside her, eyes closed, cradling her hand and crying as if each silent sob was an agony, as if he had never cried before.

Maybe he hadn't.

He was afraid. For her. Afraid she had lapsed into a coma.

She lifted her hand and touched his cheek.

He opened his eyes, took a shuddering breath, kissed her fingers. "Eight years ago, I saw Fontina shoot you. I didn't get there in time to stop him."

She stroked his tears away. "I saw you running. Milliseconds, Max. I've seen men shot." So many men. Soldiers she knew, soldiers she didn't know, enemies and friends, in harsh foreign mountains and terrorist attacks in civilization's heart. "I know about milliseconds, about the tipping point between life and death, suffering and thankfulness. You can't blame yourself."

"I saw him shoot you," Max repeated. Apparently, he *could* blame himself. "I saw you fall. I hit him—I was already launched at him, I couldn't stop myself. I couldn't catch you in time." Roughly, he wiped his face on his sleeve. "You hit the ground so hard the world shuddered."

Her heart hurt for him. Slowly, so slowly, she lifted herself, leaned against the boulder. Her mind was stirring: that red light meant someone had aimed a sniper rifle at her.

Assassin...

"You saved me this time," she said.

"Yes. This time I did."

"What happened while I was unconscious? Did you kill the shooter?" She bumped the back of her head on the boulder and winced. "Head hurts," she muttered.

"Don't think about anything," he said. "Stay awake. Stay with me. We have to get off this mountain as quickly as possible."

She looked at him, kneeling beside her, wearing a black coat that didn't quite fit, with shoulders too tight and arms too long. "That's not your coat. Where did you get it?"

"It's Zone's."

"He's here?" She looked around.

"After he left to go down the hill, he didn't like the way the facts were adding up. So he was close when he messaged us. He followed us down the mountain. He got to the sniper before me."

She began the process of unwrapping herself from the blankets, exposing herself to the cold air, letting it clear any lingering gray mist from her brain. Zone had been here. Zone was weird, with an unsettling personality. "What did he *do* to the sniper?"

"He didn't do anything except detain him."

"The sniper got away unscathed?" She could hardly believe that.

Max pulled off his glove and showed her his knuckles, scraped, battered and bloody. "I promise you he did not."

She had grown used to thinking of herself as a warrior, trained by the US Army and honed by battle into a weapon. She handled things like snipers who hunted by night. Max was a civilian, and everything she knew about him made her think he was a particularly kind, conscientious and generous one. Yet… "Max, what did you do?"

"I beat the bastard to a pulp."

She wet her lips. "You don't fight. You said so. You said you were clean as a whistle."

"I said I didn't fight, not that I didn't know how." In the predawn light, his brow looked black with anger and frustration.

"But you don't kill people," she insisted.

"I would have. I wanted to. Zone stopped me." Max helped her hold the canteen to her lips and drink. "When Ettore Fontina kidnapped my niece, I didn't kill him, and he destroyed you. Us. I swore I would never allow someone to destroy us again."

This was not the Max she knew. He looked different, sounded stern, uncompromising, a man who had suffered through years of pain for his perceived sin—letting a man who hurt Kellen and his niece live to hurt again. He said, "Zone recognized the sniper. He was a professional, an assassin for hire. He said the assassin would never give up. He said he would handle matters, and he took the assassin away."

"Took him away, like to law enforcement?"

"I doubt it." Clearly Max expected Zone to handle the matter in a final way—and he was glad.

"Will we ever discover what happened to the body?"

"No."

"Okay. Someone is trying to kill me." Her brain clicked off the instances. "Roderick dropped a roof tile on me. If it had hit, that would have made my death look like a bizarre accident."

"But an accident nonetheless."

"Horst was after the Triple Goddess. So were his accomplices. But someone murdered Horst, and that's when the game changed."

Max helped her, solicitous and worried. "Those men chasing you up the mountain. They ignored the head when you offered it. Now they're dead. All of them."

"For failure? For knowing too much? Roderick is the first assassin. We need to talk to him." She used Max and the boulder to get to her feet. Her knees wobbled, but she could stand.

Max rolled the sleeping bag and stuffed it into his backpack. "What did Roderick say to you? At the hospital when they were wheeling him away? What did he say?"

"He said..." In her mind, she saw him again: bulging blue eyes, focused on her, hand outstretched to grab her throat. For one moment, she felt faint. Not unconscious, but fearful. "He said, 'Run, bitch.'"

Max looked up sharply. "You didn't think to tell me *that*?"

"You didn't think to ask? I thought he was a nutcase and an alcoholic. Climbing on the roof, throwing fit after fit, abusing everyone who tried to help him..." She pressed her bare palms to the cold, hard stone, letting the strength of the earth seep into her bones.

"He was warning you."

"Not much of an assassin then."

"You climbed up to him. You saved his life."

"So...repayment? Morals from an assassin?"

"Yes. Maybe." Max continued to pick up, clean up, delete the marks of their presence. "We have to get out of these mountains. I can carry you."

"Not easily. I weigh a ton." She punched at her ribs. "Solid muscle." She smiled at him, trying to lighten the atmosphere.

Didn't work. He was grim and intense. "You were unconscious for hours. You shouldn't be—"

"I'm conscious now." She put her hand on his arm. "Really,

Max. My head hurts—I hit pretty hard, but death hasn't come for me yet."

He took her hand and held it.

She gently stroked the scabs on his knuckles. "I can do this, Max. It will be faster if I do."

"All right. But you'll let me know if you need help."

"Yes. Anyway, this whole assassin thing doesn't make sense. Who would want to kill me?" She half laughed. "Wait a little and—" She stopped, but not soon enough. Guiltily, she looked up at Max.

Max stopped his hurried packing. He looked at her.

She looked at him.

That was it, then. Max knew. Kellen supposed she realized that had to be true, but when she tried to put that fact into the cluttered half memories and tragic events of eight years ago, she couldn't make it fit.

Max said, "Ettore failed. Somehow...somehow the bullet didn't do what it was supposed to do. It didn't kill you. You survived and recovered. You're a miracle. You have the scar on your forehead—" he brushed her bangs aside and touched the scar with gentle fingers "—and no exit wound. I was there. I know what the doctors said. I know what you're afraid to say. You have a bullet lodged in your brain."

38

Kellen woke when the vehicle bumped from the gravel onto the asphalt. The ride smoothed out and sped up—and Max's phone started squawking and pinging and making every noise of which it was capable. She crawled up off the bench seat and straightened up.

He handed her his phone. "You want to see what that's all about?"

She watched messages and texts scroll past. "Everybody has called you. Everybody has texted you. Everybody's concerned."

Without a bit of irony, he said, "It's good to be loved. Any word from my mother?"

"Rae is fine and back in day camp. Your mother is fine. She wants to know where we are right now and what's going on right now."

He grinned. "You want to call her?"

"Good God, no. I mean…there aren't enough bars on the phone for a clear call. I'll text." She sent a reassuring message with the promise to call later. "Birdie's pretty upset. We text all the time, and I told her I had a security job. Mind if I…?" Kellen didn't wait for permission, but texted her best friend, It's Kellen. I'm alive and well. Coming back to civilization.

The return text was funny and stern. When I see you, I'm going to kick your ass.

"What did she say?" Max asked.

"She said she loved me." Kellen looked around. The late-afternoon sun was in her eyes, and she knew this area. "We're going to Yearning Sands Resort?"

"Yes. It's a good idea." Max glanced at her. "How do you feel?"

"Better." She yawned. "That going into a brief coma thing is tiring."

Max didn't laugh.

All the way down the mountain, as they hiked along, he had worked at not being solicitous and worried. He wasn't very good at it; he took care of everyone, family and friends, and to hover over her after her bump on the head had been instinct. But she gave him points for trying. Their only real fight had occurred when she insisted on the detour to get Rae's bag.

"I promised," she said.

"She'll understand," he answered.

"Don't be silly. She would *never* understand."

He couldn't argue about that, so they got the bag, took it to the truck and headed out. The last she'd heard before she went to sleep was they were going to the Portland hospital where Roderick Blake had been recovering.

"Why the change?" she asked.

"We're not related to Roderick, so the hospital wouldn't and can't give us word about his condition."

She hadn't thought of that. "Right. Damn."

"But *I* have connections with the Virtue Falls sheriff's department."

She knew exactly who he meant. "Sheriff Kateri Kwinault. She can get us information relating to Roderick and his current whereabouts."

"Exactly. Also, we need to find out who wants you dead and why. Most obviously, you served time in the military."

"Yes. I was a soldier. I killed the enemy. I directed the transport of men and goods across enemy territory. In some places, I offended by the mere fact I am a woman."

"A woman who tried to help other women."

The hard cold mountains of Afghanistan. The smell of charred wood and burned flesh. A metal coil melted in the dirt and the knowledge of young lives ended too soon.

At the memory, she teared up. "Am I endangering Rae by the fact I'm her mother?"

"It's possible. That's why we have to find who is doing this and stop them." Max had taken over the hunt. "Are soldiers often tracked by old enemies into the US?"

"Not that I know of." A chilling thought. "But in many cultures, vengeance is a long tradition and a deadly act."

"Another reason to visit Yearning Sands Resort. We'll talk to your Army buddies, find out if any of them have suffered from accidents. What else?"

Her mind swerved to the dark times during the previous winter. "There's Mara Philippi."

"She's confined in a high security prison."

"I know. But she was so smart, so corrupt, so cruel, so good at manipulation and camouflage."

"Between you and me, we destroyed her operation and put her away. She would love to hurt us both."

Kellen confessed, "Sometimes I find myself looking over my shoulder for her. Then I think I'm being paranoid. But maybe not."

"A sociopath and a serial killer. Yes. Let's put Mara Philippi high on the list of suspects, and I'll use my connections to make sure she's still in custody and not extending her talons toward my family."

Kellen put her hand on his thigh. "You're brave and smart, and I love your connections."

He swerved a bit. "You're in no condition to have sex."

"I am, too. Anyway, I merely touched your thigh. That's not

hinting for sex." No one else drove along this narrow two-lane road, so she inched her fingers a little higher.

He put his hand over hers, pressed it briefly, removed it and placed it firmly in her lap. "We have to get you checked out by a doctor."

"We can't do that at Yearning Sands Resort."

"I also have connections with a Virtue Falls doctor."

She laughed. "Do you have connections everywhere?"

"If I don't, someone in my family does." He wasn't bragging; he was making a flat statement of fact.

But he worried for no reason. There was nothing he could do about her eventual fate, and it was fruitless to agonize. "Max, for the moment, I am well. I shouldn't probably bump my head again, that's all."

He nodded judiciously, his gaze fixed on the road. "Once you've had the doctor's okay, I'll make sure we don't move too close to the headboard."

"Where I would thump my head continuously?"

"Maybe not continuously. But frequently."

"You, sir, are obnoxiously sure of yourself." She would let him thump her against the headboard anytime.

"Obnoxiously?" He had a hint of a smile around his mouth.

"That's the word."

Abruptly, he was serious, watching the road while talking intently. "You know I'm Catholic. Fairly devout."

He was going to talk to her about raising Rae in the faith. "I know. I'm going to take classes so Rae won't be confused. I'm glad to do it—if there's one thing being in a war zone teaches, it's faith and prayer."

"That's great. But actually, I'm talking about this thing we Catholics do called marriage."

"What?" *What?*

"It's when two people—say, me and you—lust after each other... We do, don't we?"

She crossed her arms. "Yes, we do that."

"And love each other." Eyebrows raised, he shot a look at her.

"Yes. Yes, I love you." Way to finagle it out of her.

"Then we go in front of our friends and relatives, make vows and become one heart, one soul."

She should have known he wouldn't give up on the marriage thing.

He gave her about thirty seconds and a quarter of a mile. "You're speechless, aren't you?"

She might be speechless, but she could glare.

He seemed unworried. "For all the above mentioned reasons, shall we be married?"

"No!"

"Why not?" Now he pulled over onto the shoulder of the road, turned off the engine, unsnapped his seat belt and faced her, arm across the back of the bench seat.

"You know why not."

"The bullet thing?"

"Of course, the bullet thing." He'd seen her unconscious, lost to the world. How could he doubt it? "When I was wounded in a bomb blast, I was unconscious and the Army discovered the bullet. They said I was a walking time bomb and discharged me. Surgery to remove the bullet was unlikely to succeed. I would go into a coma and die. And that was the good part. The other was—I'd be unable to move, to speak, to think, to be. I'd have to be on a ventilator, fed intravenously. The Army said… I didn't have long." The clock was ticking. It had always been ticking, but in her mind, the sound grew louder and louder.

"I know."

"Then why do you want to marry me?"

"I love you. I'll live a lifetime every moment we're together."

"But with so little time—"

"No one lives forever, and I've already lived without you. It sucked."

She liked that. Blunt. Honest. Male.

He continued, "When happiness is offered, grab with both hands. If you marry me, all I can promise is an arm to hold when we walk together, one lifetime of love in each season that is given us, warm nights and long days, and a child—our child—to love you, too."

So much for blunt and honest. That was poetry, sentiment, yet still male and damned if he didn't make her see things his way. Maybe he was right. And really, wasn't she already up to her eyeballs in the quicksand of this relationship? She took a breath, let it out, took another and said, "If you really feel that way, then… I would be honored to marry you."

He hugged her, suddenly, fiercely, holding her close enough to absorb her skin, muscles, bones into his. He tilted her head up and looked into her eyes. "What exactly is the name of the person I am marrying?"

39

Max's audacity took Kellen's breath away. She shoved at him. "Damn you! You could have told me you knew I wasn't Kellen Adams!"

"I didn't know you weren't Kellen Adams. Not for sure." He didn't grin or gloat. "Not until this moment."

She would have had to tell him. It wasn't a secret to be kept between a husband and wife. She had wanted to tell him…but this confession would hurt. She eased away, out of his arms. "What do you know?"

"It's not a matter of knowing. I've suspected, surmised, done investigations. I would like to *know*, to hear it from you."

Kellen had been Kellen for so long, she didn't even know how to explain what had happened, why it happened, how it happened. Briefly, she supposed, was best, and without a display of grief and tragedy. "I was married. He beat me."

Max tried to put his arm around her again.

"No." She stopped him with a gesture. "You can't do that. You can't be nice to me. Not if you want me to tell the story." Because she would cry the old tears again.

He took his arm away.

She continued, "My cousin was Kellen."

"Kellen Rae."

"Yes. She came to visit. She realized what he was doing to me. She was determined to rescue me."

Max's focus never wavered. "Who were you? Tell me."

"I was—am—Cecilia. I was a coward, afraid to face him. My husband, Gregory Lykke, the only son of a proud and wealthy New England family. Crazy, all of them. Murderous and cruel." She reminded him, "You met his sister."

"She deserved that death."

"Yes." Kellen nodded. "Gregory suspected I was going to leave him. He tried to kill me and himself. He killed my cousin instead. And himself. I ran."

"And lived on the streets and eventually saved Annabella, met me and we fell in love."

"That's the whole story."

"And you kept Kellen's identification papers through your whole ordeal."

"I had to keep her papers. She was so practical, and those papers proved she had walked on this earth, gone to school, graduated with a degree, been on the verge of life!" She took a long breath. "I didn't mean for anyone to think I was Kellen. I mean, not forever. At first I was simply trying to get away from the Lykke family, from Gregory's horrible sister and his weak mother. Then I found you, and I began to feel safe."

"And I looked at the papers and assumed you were Kellen, and when you found out, you ran. Ettore shot you, and when you recovered consciousness, you used the papers to join the Army."

"That made me Kellen forever, because lying to the federal government and the US military would result in jail time."

"Yeah." He put the truck in first gear and pulled back onto the highway. "Let's think on that. Then let me check my connections and we'll see if we can make all this legal."

She gave a brief spurt of laughter. "Of course. Your connections!"

"One more question—there's no one else left alive in the Lykke family, right? After Gregory's sister died, that was it?"

"They're all dead. A scourge wiped from the earth. They can't hurt me now."

40

Kellen hung up the phone after talking to their daughter. "Rae sounds great. Happy and not missing us at all." She was surprised to feel vaguely hurt about that.

"Rae is a happy, well-adjusted child who has bounced back from every trauma in her young life." Max sounded comforting, as if he understood her feelings. Spooky, to be so well attuned after so brief an...acquaintance.

Kellen looked across the broad coastal plane to that place on the horizon where the resort rose like a fanciful medieval castle with towers and turrets and colorful waving flags. "There it is."

The golden stone glowed in the sunlight, and she smiled. She knew from her time as assistant manager that the shoreline swept either way from the resort's main building: on one side, a long beach with groomed paths making their way down to the sand, on the other, cliffs rising over the Pacific Ocean. Three long wings filled with guest rooms reached out from the central castle structure. The Di Luca family had built here in the fifties, laying out paths for bikes, for walking, for ATVs. On the grounds, guest cottages of various sizes clustered here and there, surrounded by privacy fences.

Now, in August, the resort hummed with people and activities. Buses carried hikers and amateur botanists toward the mountains where they would enjoy guided tours. Whale watching boats left the Yearning Sands dock once a day, weather permitting, and a stream of bicyclists passed their truck going the opposite direction, and all of them had numbers on their shirts.

"Maniacs," Kellen muttered.

That earned her a startled glance from Max.

"Bikers," she added for clarification.

Max looked even more confused.

"Never mind," she said. She was still mentally scarred by those steep downhill runs and narrow, rutted paths with the Cyclomaniacs.

"Where first?" Max asked.

She looked at him.

He laughed; he knew the answer. He headed toward the resort maintenance buildings and her best friends in the world, the people she'd served with in the military, the people she'd hired when she became Yearning Sands's assistant manager. He parked in front of the three-bay garage, and she was out of the truck before he'd come to a complete stop.

She slammed through the metal door and found herself surrounded by hydraulic lifts, air compressors, welders, tire storage and enough steel tool cabinets to supply Lockheed. She took a deep breath of tire-and grease-scented air and wandered back toward one of the resort's tour buses, where five legs protruded from beneath the chassis; Temo didn't have his prosthesis on.

"We'll be with you in a minute," he called.

She squatted down and put her hand on his ankle. "I can wait… Cuauhtemo."

At the sound of her voice and his real name, the three mechanics' creepers shot out from under the tour bus.

Temo grabbed her first, hugged her hard.

CUAUHTEMO (TEMO) IGLASIAS:
MALE. 5'7", 150 LBS, FIT. HISPANIC-AMERICAN/SECOND GENERATION. BLACK HAIR, BROWN EYES, SPANISH SPEAKER. MILITARY VETERAN.

PROSTHETIC LEG. MECHANIC, HANDYMAN. BROTHER TO YOUNGER SISTER, REGINA. LEADER. FRIEND.

He loosened his grip and asked, "Are you healed?" From last winter and her encounter with Mara Philippi, he meant.

"I'm fine." Except for the stitches in her arm and the bump on her head, but those weren't worth mentioning to a man who had lost his leg in action.

Birdie Haynes rolled over on her creeper and the two hugged, long and hard. Then she punched Kellen hard in the shoulder. "You scared me to death! You couldn't even text?"

"Somebody stole my phone."

"Stole your phone? That's funny!" Birdie wasn't laughing. Her brown eyes swam with tears.

The two women fell into each other's arms again.

"Are they crying?" Max had made it inside, and he was doing the smarmy superior man thing.

"Looks like it." Carson Lennex stood up off his creeper and wiped his hands on a grease rag, then shook hands with Max.

Birdie and Temo: Kellen had expected to see them in maintenance. But Carson Lennex?

CARSON LENNEX:
MALE, 65, IRISH/HISPANIC ANCESTRY, 6'3", 200 LBS, IRON GRAY HAIR, HAZEL EYES, TANNED, ACTOR, MOVIE STAR, FORMER ACTION-ADVENTURE HERO. LIVES ALONE IN ONE OF THE TOWER SUITES FOR MOST OF THE YEAR. RETIRED. ALOOF.

And one more thing—he was violently in love with Birdie.

"What are you doing under there?" Max asked.

"Every time they drive this old bus up a steep incline, there's a burning odor. We're trying to figure out where it's coming from. It makes the tourists nervous." Carson managed to make it sound like he knew what he was talking about. Did he? Or was he that good an actor?

"Have you checked the radiator overflow?" Max asked. "If

there's a leak in one spot in one hose onto a hot spot, it could cause the smell."

"That's a thought." Temo lay down on the creeper and disappeared underneath the bus.

Carson followed suit.

"May I?" Max offered his hand to Birdie.

She took it and let him help her stand.

He used her creeper to join the other guys, and the three men started thumping, clinking and consulting.

"I suggested the hose theory myself," Birdie said between clenched teeth. "No one listened."

"What do you know? You're merely the head mechanic." Kellen hugged her again. "Anyway, who cares? Let them fix it. Where's Adrian?"

Adrian was the last of the guys Kellen had hired at Yearning Sands, loudmouthed, obnoxious and a good guy.

"Temo's sister has started accompanying some of the Olympic tours as an assistant. The tour is winding up, and Adrian's gone to pick her up."

Kellen grinned. "He's a good mother."

"I'm starting to think so. He's such a screwup, but he really cares for that kid, and Regina is blossoming here at Yearning Sands."

"I never saw any of *that* coming."

"Me, neither." Birdie didn't take a breath. "What are you in trouble about now?"

"Nothing! Why would you think that? Well, a little something." Kellen headed for the little old slope-shouldered refrigerator. "I'd kill for an iced cappuccino."

"Get me one, too." Birdie sank onto a chair beside the battered kitchen table. "What's up?"

Kellen brought two bottles of cappuccino and seated herself opposite Birdie. "Have you or the guys had any suspicious incidents lately?"

"By suspicious you mean...?"

"Snipers shooting at you?"

"You have snipers shooting at you?"

"Among other things." Kellen rolled up her sleeve and showed Birdie the healing gunshot wound and the stitches. "Also a few more eccentric attempts on my life."

"What is it about you, Kellen Adams, that so many people try to kill you?" Birdie sounded as if she was joking, but she wasn't smiling.

"It's my charming personality." Kellen took a long swig of the drink. "It did occur to us—me and Max—to wonder if someone from the war zone had it out for veterans."

Birdie shook her head. "Since you left, it's been real quiet around here. The worst thing that happened was when that dumbass texting tourist drove over Russell and into the lobby. He broke Russell's pelvis and sent him to the hospital."

"Russell is better?"

"Better. Yes. But not good. Not like he was before. That texting limp prick is wandering around, still texting and killing people." Birdie had a moment when she realized this wasn't the subject. "Nothing happening around here to us veterans. It's been blessedly quiet."

"Well, hell. I mean—not that I want you all to be in danger—"

"Mighty good of you."

"—but it would be nice if we could figure out *why* someone was after me."

From under the bus, Temo shouted, "I've wanted to kill you many a time."

The two women exchanged glances.

Kellen shouted back, "You're going to feel pretty stupid when I hide your leg!"

"My prosthesis?"

"No, the leg that's sticking out from under the bus! Idiot."

Raucous male laughter echoed across the concrete floor and around the walls.

"Anything else?" Birdie asked.

How did Birdie know? Kellen reached across the table, took her hand. "I wanted to ask…if you would be my bridesmaid?"

41

At 5:30 p.m., Max pulled the truck up under Yearning Sands Resort's sweeping portico and the doorman, Russell Clark, rushed forward to open Kellen's door. When he saw her, his smile challenged the sun. "Miss Adams, you've come back to us."

RUSSELL CLARK:
MALE, SOUTH PACIFIC/ASIAN/EUROPEAN ANCESTRY, 47, 5'11", 220 LBS, AUTISTIC. YEARNING SANDS DOORMAN FOR 31 YEARS. LIKES/NEEDS ROUTINE.

Kellen slid out of the truck. "I'm not back forever. But it's good to see you. Are you recovered from your accident?"

The texting driver had caused an entire redesign of the entry, paid a massive fine—and Russell limped as if every step was painful, yet he beamed at her for her kindness. "I am fine, Miss Adams."

"Are you going to physical therapy?" Kellen asked.

He bent his head in shame. "I'm supposed to."

"Russell, I'm disappointed in you. You can't recover completely without physical therapy and you know Yearning Sands needs you for many more years to come." She shook a finger at him. "You go to PT or I will speak to Leo and Annie!"

"Yes, Miss Adams. I will do that." He grinned and looked abashed at the same time.

"Good." She put her arm around his shoulders and hugged him, then walked into the resort.

Max shook Russell's hand and she heard him say, "You know you'd never get away with not doing your therapy if Kellen was still the assistant manager."

"I know. We miss her." Russell sounded sad.

Kellen stood in the lobby and took one long breath of rarified resort air. Here at Yearning Sands, she had returned from overseas and taken her first nonmilitary job on US soil. In this resort, she had seen stunning beauty and plumbed the depths of black despair, found friends and found treachery, grown strong and almost been killed. Here in this place she had found a family and a home.

Now it was at the end of summer, the high season on the Washington coast, and incoming guests pulled wheeled suitcases and stood in the check-in line. Guests walked into the elevators and out. They stood by the giant exotic floral bouquet in the middle of the lobby and frowned at maps. They sat in the breakfast area enjoying a complimentary glass of Washington wine.

Sheri Jean Haggerty manned the concierge desk; she looked up from a consultation with a guest and smiled at Kellen. Typical of Sheri Jean, the smile looked as if her teeth hurt, but Kellen chose to feel honored.

Three of the staff at the reception desk were new. One Kellen knew, and he gave a broad wave, then returned to helping an incoming guest.

Kellen walked through the breakfast area and toward the long wide sweep of windows that faced west across the Pacific Ocean and north up Highway 1 into Olympic National Park. She put her hand to her heart and sighed.

Max's arm reached around her waist and pulled her close. "The best view in North America," he said.

"It's true. Every day I—" She caught herself.

"You miss it? I know. The winery location is pretty, but tame. This is wild and breathtaking—like you."

She faced him and put her hand to his cheek.

He leaned in to kiss her.

A man's voice called, "Max! Kellen! Welcome to Yearning Sands. What a fabulous surprise."

Max winked at Kellen, released her and stepped forward to embrace his uncle, then shake his hand.

NAPOLEONE (LEO) DI LUCA:
MALE, ELDERLY, 5'10", 190 LBS, A LITTLE MORE STOOPED THAN THE LAST TIME SHE HAD SEEN HIM. SHOULDER-LENGTH GRAY HAIR, GANDALF EYEBROWS. RESORT OWNER. AMERICAN-ITALIAN WHOM MAX STRONGLY RESEMBLED. GOOD MAN/GOOD EMPLOYER/GOOD HUSBAND TO ANNIE.

"Kellen!" Leo embraced her, looked into her face, embraced her again. "You've come back to us."

"Just for a day."

"We were delighted when Max texted to let us know you were coming."

Kellen looked sideways at Max. He must have done that while she was asleep.

Leo continued, "We have the room we save for honored guests. Up in the tower. Kellen, you know the one. I suppose you want to get cleaned up and change, then Annie and I would love you to be our guests for dinner in our suite. She's having her lie-down now, but she is champing at the bit to see you. Where are your bags?"

"We might need to do a little shopping at the boutique," Kellen told him. "We're back from the mountains and looking a little rustic."

Leo chuckled. "It's Washington state, dear. No one minds rustic."

"Cleanliness is an issue, too, Uncle," Max said.

"Ha! Yes! Go find something comfortable to wear and—" he looked searchingly at Kellen "—can you be ready in two hours?"

"I'm hungry. I can be ready faster than that." She had never meant anything so much in her life.

"Excellent. Sheriff Kwinault is on her way with Dr. Frownfelter. We'll have appetizers waiting for you. Annie and I cannot wait to hear this whole tantalizing story."

42

Max and Kellen hurried through their showers and dressed in their new casual resort wear that made them look, so Max said, like tennis-wear ads from the 1980s. He struck a pose with an invisible racket.

Kellen shoved at him, draped her sweater around her neck and told him to hurry and shave before the appetizers were all gone.

He chased her toward the window and scraped his stubbled chin across her cheek and went in to shave.

Seconds later, he was back, and she started to chide him for not shaving...then he leaned down and slid his face across hers. "Better?"

"Smooth as a baby's bottom," she assured him.

So he *had* shaved. But he couldn't have done it in the amount of time she thought he'd been gone.

Where had she been? Caught by the gray? Unconscious on her feet?

She mustn't let Max know. He didn't need to worry more than he was. Not about something he could do nothing about.

He offered his arm. "Still hungry?"

"Of course!" She wasn't. Not now.

"Are you sure? You look a little pale."

"Show me the crab cakes." She smiled at him and took his arm.

He led the way, but she knew he was back to feeling solicitous.

They arrived at Leo and Annie's suite, a spacious, homey collection of rooms on the third floor not far from Annie's office. Annie's thin face lit up, and she held up her arms. "Hug me, darlings!"

ANNIE DI LUCA:
FEMALE, WHITE, ELDERLY, HEIGHT UNDETERMINED. UNDERWEIGHT. CURLY WHITE HAIR, BROWN EYES. WHEELCHAIR USER. RHEUMATOID ARTHRITIS. SEASONED RESORT MANAGER. KIND, INTELLIGENT, FRAIL, DEDICATED TO LEO AND YEARNING SANDS.

Kellen knelt beside Annie and on impulse put her head on Annie's shoulder.

Annie pressed her hand to Kellen's cheek and kissed the top of her head. "Is all well?"

There were a lot of different ways Kellen could respond. *I've got a child and she's like me. I've got a suitor and he loves me. Someone's trying to kill me and I don't know why.* She chose the easiest. "Max and I are getting married."

Annie sighed deeply. "May you face all the years of joy and sorrow together."

Kellen wasn't sure if Annie had blessed their union or cursed it.

Annie kissed her head again, and her voice lightened. "I'm sorry, dear. That sounded less than enthusiastic. I'm thrilled. Leo is thrilled. But instead of thinking of my joy for you and Max, I was thinking about Leo and me."

"Problems?" God forbid they would have marital problems; they both laughed and declared they'd been married since the earth's crust cooled and always seemed dedicated to each other.

"You know how we feel about this place, and since I was sick last winter, I haven't recovered as well as we hoped and I can't do what I need to do."

Oh. Whew. Not marital problems exactly. Life problems, not

less dire but more comforting for a prospective bride to hear. "You're thinking about retirement?"

"Talking about it, which is even worse. I knew this day would come. Leo is more excited than I am, of course. He wants to travel. And we will!" Annie smiled, but with an effort. She turned to the men who were conversing quietly beside the bar. "Leo, we need champagne. We must toast Max and Kellen's upcoming nuptials!"

Leo clapped Max on the shoulder, opened the floor-to-ceiling wine cooler and pulled out a bottle of Di Luca's best sparkling wine.

"You told her!" Max looked equal parts dismayed and pleased.

Kellen got to her feet. "Should I not have?"

Annie's eyes widened in horror. "Haven't you two told Verona yet?"

Max shook his head.

"Then we'll have this champagne and pretend we don't know why we're celebrating." Leo popped the cork and poured the champagne flutes full. He handed them out and lifted his in a toast. "May your love light the way for all the worlds and all the times."

They clinked glasses.

Kellen blinked away unexpected tears.

The house phone rang, and Leo picked it up, listened and hung up. "Kateri is here with Dr. Frownfelter."

Kellen's tears dried and she drank her champagne in a rush. She took a breath, metaphorically girded her loins and waited, dreading the next few hours of conversations...and revelations.

Sheriff Kwinault came through the door first.

SHERIFF KATERI KWINAULT:
FEMALE, 30? YO, 5'9" 140 LBS, FIT, BEAUTIFUL, HALF NATIVE AMERICAN. FORMER COAST GUARD COMMANDER, SWEPT OUT TO SEA WHILE BATTLING A TSUNAMI, BARELY SURVIVED. CARRIES A WALKING STICK. A LEGEND AMONG HER TRIBE. RESPECTED BY LAW OFFICERS. FRIEND OF MAX.

Not many women made Kellen feel like an underachiever, but Kateri Kwinault could, if she tried. She never tried, and Kellen had developed a tentative friendship with her.

Max hugged Kateri and handed her a flute of sparkling water. "Thank you for coming to meet with us."

"It's not *you*, Max." Kateri accepted the water and sipped. "It's Kellen, and the opportunity to have a meal with Leo and Annie, created by their excellent chefs."

"Amen." The doctor stepped through the door. "Best food within a fifty-mile radius of Virtue Falls."

"What about Virtue Falls Resort?" Annie asked.

He chuckled. "Let's not start a war." He headed toward the bar where a variety of appetizers were laid out.

Kellen had never met Dr. Frownfelter before.

DR. WALTER FROWNFELTER:
MALE, 70? YO, 6'2", 240 LBS, ALBERT EINSTEIN HAIR, RUMPLED WHITE COAT, RESEMBLES A BASSET HOUND. BRIGHT BLUE EYES; TOO OBSERVANT. TREATED WITH RESPECT; OBVIOUSLY WELL LIKED BY THIS COMPANY. LONELY.

While speaking with him, Kellen reached the conclusion he was lonely; he talked to himself too much and looked at the past with too much longing. That was the reason why, after their pleasant dinner was over, she wandered out onto the deck with him.

They were fourteen stories up. It was dark. They could hear the beastly roar of the ocean waves, smell the salt, the seaweed, the damp sand and up here, feel the truth of all the days of the world.

"I'm the reliable old Virtue Falls physician. Everybody likes me." Dr. Frownfelter made fun of himself in a rough, gravelly voice. "But I suspect I was brought here for more reasons than to fill my belly. You've got quite a scar on your forehead."

Maybe he had been warned. Probably he had noticed. He'd

been brought here for her, and instinctively she trusted him, so she told him everything about the bullet, the scar, the gray.

When she was finished, he contemplated the great darkness at the edge of the world where the ocean roared and chewed at the land. "I'm not going to tell you what to do, but I would suggest that you've had one medical opinion, from Army doctors. They think that bullet's going to move, and you're going to die."

"That's right."

"With all due respect to my military colleagues, I think you'd be wise to seek a second opinion. Medical technology improves every day. And the military medical establishment has different priorities than civilian medical establishment has—triage if possible, but nothing fancy."

"Right." She had suspected that, but the Army had been in such a hurry to get rid of her, and had given her such bad odds for surgical extraction of the bullet, she hadn't been in a hurry to get that second opinion.

Dr. Frownfelter continued, "Here in the States, sometimes a doctor is such a good specialist, she can change your diagnosis and save your life."

"Sounds like you have someone in mind."

"I might. In Portland." He heaved a sigh that made his broad belly rise and fall. "It seems like, with a daughter and a husband, finding out exactly what could happen with the proper surgery is the right move."

"Instead of just dying?" She rubbed her arms. Up here, even in the summer, the wind off the ocean chilled her.

"We're all born with an expiration date, but God doesn't print it on the side of our milk cartons."

She shouldn't laugh, but it was funny. And true. "But if surgery doesn't work, if I go into a coma and don't come out...you doctors won't let me die in peace, and I'm not going to live the next forty years hooked to an IV and a breathing tube, without motion or mind, while the world goes on around me." That was her nightmare, to be trapped in a living death.

He patted her arm. "It's all in the paperwork. Let's get you checked out and see what the specialists think. Then you can make an informed decision."

"I won't be a burden on Max and Rae."

"But Max and Rae are who you're doing this for."

"Yes." *Yes.* "I'll think about it."

"Don't think too long, Kellen." He looked closely into her face. "The decision needs to be made soon."

She wanted to ask him what he saw, but Max opened the door. "Kellen." Just the one word, but he wanted her inside.

She walked past him into a room of grim faces. "What is it?"

"I finally spoke to the right person at the Portland hospital," Sheriff Kwinault said. "Roderick Blake is dead. Overdose of morphine."

"Tampering is suspected," Max added.

"Dead like those other men on the mountain." Kellen shivered, still chilled from the balcony. "Who is doing all this? And why? There has to be a reason."

The next morning, Max decided to drive the winding coastal highway toward Portland, a short distance with many turnouts and high views of the Pacific Ocean where the sun glinted on the eternally rolling waves. He said they needed some stress-free moments, although she noted that he kept an eye on the rearview mirror and observed every car and every driver. That last sniper shot had left them both wary and watchful.

Still, she relaxed and enjoyed watching him drive. After her years in the military, directing transport, she appreciated a man with driving skills. He took the turnouts when she asked, smiled at her when he thought she didn't notice, and best of all, he was easygoing enough that he only swore at one slow tourist.

The closer they got to Portland, the more he suggested they

stop in to see the specialist Dr. Frownfelter had recommended. He revealed that Dr. Frownfelter had called in favors and got her an appointment late that afternoon. She would have every kind of exam, every test, and before the morning, they'd know what her chances were to survive an operation to remove that bullet from her brain. To survive, and more important, to recover.

She didn't want to go. She wanted more time to think, to make a decision about whether to welcome the gray unconsciousness into her life.

Max put his hand on her thigh and shot her a quick smile.

He was so patient, so generous. Smart, kind...and he loved her. Through all the years and the trials, he loved her.

And she loved him. She was going to marry him. They were going to live together until the end of their days...

Kellen opened her eyes and stared into Max's frantic face. "What's wrong?" she whispered.

"You were gone. Just—" he snapped his fingers "—gone."

She looked around. He'd pulled the truck off the pavement and he had her stretched out in the sun on the rough grass beside the road. Just over the horizon, the Pacific Ocean roared and crashed, sending its salty scent high into the air.

It was the Pacific that had pulled her back through the membrane between the endless gray and consciousness; that blustering wind, that writhing beast, that womb that constantly produced life, took life and re-created it again.

Sitting up, she smoothed her hair back from her face. Slowly, she nodded at Max. "Okay. Let's go see the doctor. And when the time comes, I'll have the surgery."

43

Two days later, Max and Kellen drove into the Di Luca Winery in the old truck, right into the middle of what appeared to be a private party. A blue-and-white canopy lifted its twin peaks on the lawn between the tasting room door and the picnic tables. Beneath the canopy sat a grand piano and a bar selling glasses of wine, crusty bread and charcuterie and cheese plates.

The pianist, an older man with a sharply pointed beard, waxed mustache and upward-pointed eyebrows, was playing "The Music of the Night" from P*hantom of the Opera*. A handsome woman about his age was dropping a twenty into his tip jar. Under the broad white oak trees, smiling people sat around new, brightly painted picnic tables. Customers wandered out of the tasting room carrying wrapped wine bottles and gift shop bags.

The scene was so counter to the winery's usual quiet dignity Max came to a stop in the middle of the driveway and stared.

"Who are these people?" Kellen asked.

"I haven't got a—"

Behind them, a horn blared.

Max let up on the brake, drove into the lot and parked next to a silver Lexus NX Hybrid. "Right before I left for the mountains, I did hire a new winery manager and gave him free rein to do what he wished and hire, at least temporarily, who he wanted."

Kellen looked at Max across the seat. "I believe he may have taken you at your word."

"I believe you're right." He opened the door and hurried around to help her out.

She eased out of the seat and onto the running board, and stood looking down at him. "I'm perfectly capable."

"I know." He helped her step onto the ground, taking special care of the still-healing wound on her arm, hidden under a light long-sleeved T-shirt. "That makes me like to help you even more."

How could she argue with that? Especially when he held her hand and smiled into her eyes, and she felt the not-quite-familiar rise of warm passion. She leaned into him and kissed him. She loved his scent, his heat, his taste, the scrape of his dark beard across her chin.

A cry from the house interrupted them. "Max!"

Max waved one arm at his mother. "We're back safe and sound!"

Verona ran down the porch steps and across the gravel lot.

Kellen pulled back so Verona could hug Max.

Verona did, and hugged Kellen, too, although without the fervent joy of the first hug. Still, her voice was vehement when she said, "Thank heavens you two are back and all right! You gave us quite a scare."

"I promise that wasn't our intention. Where's Rae?" Max kept his voice casual, but Kellen heard the intense undercurrent of concern. The events of the last week had scarred him.

"I insisted she go to camp. We paid the money. She is underfoot all day when she's here. She has done nothing but talk about ThunderFlame and LightningBug and draw pictures and tell me about the bicycle ride and the giant cobweb and the… the shootings." Verona had been complaining about her granddaughter, until she mentioned the shootings. Then the color washed out of her face.

Kellen eased a hand under her arm. "LightningBug is home safe where she belongs."

"ThunderFlame had better stay here, too," Verona said severely. "We expected you yesterday."

"ThunderFlash. She's ThunderFlash. We took a detour to Yearning Sands to get a shower and then to the hospital to get Kellen's stitches removed." Max lifted Kellen's arm and showed his mother the slash the bullet had left behind. He mentioned nothing of the MRI and the specialists whom Dr. Frownfelter had called in.

Verona looked them up and down. "Where did you get those clothes? Don't tell me—at the resort. Dressed like that, you'll fit in with the tourists. I'll fix a special meal to welcome you home." Verona's expression grew deeply thoughtful. "Yes, I think a celebration dinner is called for!"

Max and Kellen watched her turn and hurry toward the house.

"It's only noon. What's going to take her six hours?" Kellen asked.

Max laughed deep in his chest. "Are you challenging my mother?"

"Not at all! It was more of a rhetorical question." She deliberately bumped her hip into his.

He deliberately bumped back. "Want to help me shower?"

"I don't know. When we tried sharing a shower at Zone's, we got stuck."

Max cackled. There was no other word for it. He cackled. Then he sighed. "Oh, hell. Here comes Arthur. Arthur Waldberg, the new winery manager."

ARTHUR WALDBERG:
MALE, 5'7", 140 LBS, DESCENT: MEDITERRANEAN? MIDDLE EASTERN?, DARK CURLY HAIR, BROWN EYES. DRESSED FOR BUSINESS IN NEW YORK CITY. MOOD: CONFIDENT, PLEASED WITH HIMSELF.

Huh.

"Sir! You're back!" Arthur hurried up and extended his hand.

"Call me Max."

"Of course, sir." Arthur offered his hand to Kellen. "You're Rae's mommy. Miss Adams, I've heard nothing but your praises sung since my arrival."

Kellen lifted her eyebrows at him.

"From Rae," he qualified. "The two of you have had quite an adventure."

"We're glad that it's over," Kellen replied.

"I'm not so sure Rae would agree," Arthur said.

Max and Kellen moaned in unison.

Arthur laughed. "My children aren't the least adventurous. Thank heavens they don't take after their father."

Kellen added a note to his dossier.

ARTHUR WALDBERG:
BELIEVES HIMSELF TO BE ADVENTUROUS. SEEMS OUT OF CHARACTER WITH APPEARANCE.

"What do you think of the changes?" Arthur waved at the winery. "I plunged right in, hired reliable help to replace the staff you lost to Whistling Winds Winery. Temporary staff, of course, pending your interview and approval. Your vintner agreed to take on a talented young person as his apprentice."

"You convinced Freeman Townsend to take on an apprentice?" Max was incredulous.

"Not me. The apprentice convinced him with a combination of talent, fresh ideas—and lavish admiration."

"Wow. I can't wait to meet him."

"Her. Jessie Glomen."

Max shook his head in disbelief. "A female convinced that old misogynist to... Now I really can't wait to meet her."

"Not a problem, sir." Arthur waved his hand toward the path that led around the winery building and toward the sheds that held the huge stainless steel and smaller oak casks. "We'll start the tour there."

"Perhaps on the grounds, first." Max really couldn't keep his eyes off the changes.

"Very good, sir. The staff and I can't wait another minute to show off our improvements. You've already seen what we've done with the outside. Here, let me introduce you to the splendid young designer who created this warm and welcoming atmosphere." Arthur led them toward:

WARREN GOLOKIN:
MALE, CAUCASIAN ANCESTRY, MIDTHIRTIES, 5'10", 150 LBS, BROWN HAIR (STIFF POMPADOUR), BLUE EYES, BLACK EYELINER. FLAMBOYANTLY GAY. ACCENT: NEW JERSEY. IMMACULATELY DRESSED. THRILLED AND NERVOUS.

Max complimented Warren on the layout.

Kellen asked where he had found the artistically painted picnic tables, and on discovering he'd done them himself, suggested they start a shop for his works.

Warren wrung her hand in an outpouring of thankfulness and confessed fabulously decorated, utilitarian furniture was his passion.

Kellen talked to him about the objets d'art she'd seen in Afghanistan, about the hidden libraries and the labyrinth of caves filled with wonders of a bygone age, and the two of them would have gone on for hours, but Arthur caught Warren's eye and Warren broke it off.

"Miss Adams, I hope in the future we can sit down and discuss what you saw—the colors, the designs, how they made you feel. But for now, I know you want to meet the rest of the staff."

Not really. But meeting staff and exchanging pleasantries was the duty of Max's wife. *Her* duties, now, and as an officer of the US Army, she understood the importance of showing unity to the troops.

Arthur escorted them to the bar. "Our outdoor manager, Claude McKeith."

CLAUDE MCKEITH:
MALE, NORTHERN EUROPEAN ANCESTRY, 50S, 6'4", 200 LBS, BLOND, SMILING, JAW CLENCHED, BLINDING WHITE TEETH. IMMACULATELY DRESSED. THRILLED AND NERVOUS.

Claude explained that many customers came out of the tasting room wanting another glass of wine and refreshments. He served simple and locally sourced platters of cheese, meat and fruit, and offered samples to Kellen and Max.

Max snacked and asked the daily monetary take.

Claude replied with an amount that raised Max's eyebrows.

Arthur beamed. "I expect this to be a highly profitable and popular addition to the winery."

"I wish I'd thought of it," Max said.

"I'm sure you would have, sir, given time."

Kellen wasn't so sure. Max seemed rather set in his ways, and his shaken response to the change made her smile.

He glanced at her. "Oh, shut up."

She faked a solemn face.

He kissed her hand.

Arthur observed with interest. "The sojourn in the mountains seem to have refreshed you both."

"It does seem that way." Max didn't release her hand.

Arthur gestured at the young woman peeking around the corner of the winery building.

She scurried forward and bowed.

"Let me introduce our new chef, Pearly Perry."

PEARLY PERRY:
FEMALE, ASIAN (TIBETAN?) ANCESTRY, 5', 100 LBS, 40 YO. STRAIGHT BLACK HAIR KNOTTED INTO A SEVERE BACKSWEEP. BROWN EYES. SKIN RIPPLES WITH BURN MARK FROM LEFT FOREHEAD TO LEFT CHIN; LOOKS LIKE MARKS FROM FLAMETHROWER, PROBABLY A KITCHEN ACCIDENT. FLUENT IN FOUR LANGUAGES. IMMACULATELY DRESSED. THRILLED AND NERVOUS.

"What happened to our old chef?" Max asked.

"One Foot in the Grape Winery stole him." Arthur viewed Pearly with obvious respect and delight. "Not to worry, sir. Pearly has experience in a number of international cuisines as well as European foods—German, French, Italian and the typical foods to accompany the wines."

"That seems overkill to have a chef who prepares cheese and charcuterie plates," Max said.

"She's proven herself able to adjust at a moment's notice to please our Japanese, Malaysian and Thai visitors. Of whom we have many. The tour buses come in, the biking clubs arrive…" Arthur sounded quite sure of himself.

Max nodded as if dazed.

"Also, sir, you have the guest suites and the small kitchen you use to prepare their breakfasts. I think it not inappropriate to imagine a future with an expansion to include a small distinguished restaurant and a use of the elevated patio as a dining area for weddings, anniversaries, birthdays, special occasions."

Kellen turned to Pearly. "I've seen reality television and those cooking shows. It seems difficult. Do you really want to be a chef in charge of a restaurant?"

Pearly looked down, veiling her eyes and her expression. "I have worked hard these last twenty years to find the peace within myself to embrace the confines of the kitchen and seek satisfaction in the small chores that enhance lives. I know how to create marvelous cuisine and I know how to direct a staff." She looked up, and her smile transformed her scarred face. "If I were to become a famous chef, called from my kitchen to the applause of my customers, I would not object."

Kellen nodded, waggling her head. "Okay." Being in charge of a kitchen didn't sound like fun to her, but Pearly clearly knew what she wanted.

Max and Arthur had walked on, and she hurried to catch up with them.

"Our waiters," Arthur said. "These two gentlemen, while serving wines and eatable accompaniments, have doubled the size of the Di Luca Willamette Valley Wine Club."

MATEO COURTEMANCHE:
MALE, SPANISH/FRENCH ANCESTRY (BASQUE?), LATE 30S. BROWN HAIR, BROWN EYES, SMOOTH BROWN SKIN. FLUENT IN THREE LANGUAGES. IMMACULATELY DRESSED. THRILLED AND NERVOUS.

TAKASHI TIBODO:
MALE, AFRICAN AND JAPANESE? KOREAN? VIETNAMESE ANCESTRY?, 50 YO, 6'2", 160 LBS. CURLY BLACK HAIR, LARGE BROWN EYES, LASHES AND MOUTH AND... HANDSOME MAN. FABULOUSLY HANDSOME MAN. FLUENT IN SEVEN LANGUAGES AND CAN STRUGGLE ALONG IN THREE MORE.

"Good Lord." Max shook the two men's hands. "That's extraordinary. About the wine club, I mean. How do you do it?"

"The wines speak for themselves, sir," Mateo said. "And when Takashi sings, he summons the money from their wallets."

Takashi smiled modestly.

"Takashi, you sing?" As handsome as he was, that seemed almost too many gifts to Kellen.

"Yes, Miss Adams. I was trained by one of the greatest teachers of all time, Maestro Emil Kinsie. He taught me everything, and I dedicate myself to preserving his heritage." Takashi glanced toward Arthur, straightened, then focused on Kellen once more. "I listened to his music online."

"Someday I would enjoy hearing you sing," she said.

He inclined his head. "I would love to sing for such a gracious lady."

At some unseen signal from Arthur, the two waiters removed themselves and returned to work.

ARTHUR WALDBERG:
EXTREMELY ORGANIZED. A MANIPULATOR OF HIGHEST SKILL, DIRECTOR OF A STAFF THAT DOES HIS BIDDING WITHOUT QUESTION.

Max viewed the whole operation and said mildly, "Your new employees seem well accomplished and I'll be interested to sit down with them and discuss the possibility of permanent employment."

"They would love that, sir."

"I did notice it's skewed toward the male gender."

Arthur hung his head. "Yes, sir, I'm sorry. I wanted to start out with people I knew without a doubt would be knowledgeable and reliable, and those people are mostly male. I was lucky with Pearly—she was free at exactly the right time and came at once. I'll do better in the future."

"Where are they all from?" More than once, Kellen had seen a band of compatriots like Arthur and his people. She had been a part of a band like this, in the Army, honed and gathered by battle. She recognized that somehow, under some heat and pressure, these people had been formed into a cohesive unit. They supported each other. They depended on each other. They had the same goals, and the same leader—Arthur Waldberg.

How interesting.

Arthur folded his hands at his waist. "When I hire them, I'm not allowed to ask that kind of personal question."

"But where did you find them?" Max asked. "The competition for good winery help is fierce, and in less than a week you've stocked the place with accomplished workers. Do you personally know these people?"

Arthur met his eyes. "I do. They're from all around the world. We're fortunate to have so many languages to tap into. The Japanese and European tour buses have already made us the top preferred stop in the Willamette Valley."

Kellen thought Arthur hadn't quite answered the question.

Like her, Max seemed a little uncertain, and he watched Arthur closely. "That's wonderful."

Arthur hesitated, then added, "Sir, I have connections in places you might not know."

"Should I be worried?" Max sounded casual. He wasn't.

Arthur met his gaze straight on. "No, sir. My people will be an asset to Di Luca Wines, I promise you that."

44

"Then let's meet the rest of your new hires," Max said.

"Of course." Arthur pulled his elaborately folded handkerchief from his pocket, dabbed his damp brow, refolded it and put it back into his pocket. "But before we do, sir, I must tell you—I had to fire an employee, one Rita Grapplee. She was caught on video helping herself to the contents of the gift shop, and when she was discovered selling those pieces to the guests, her excuse was that she wasn't paid enough to maintain her desired lifestyle. She seemed quite convinced that was adequate reason to pilfer."

Max sighed and looked at the ground. "Will we have a lawsuit?"

"We perhaps would have, but she hasn't reported to her parole officer. She's effectively disappeared, one supposes onto the streets. Sir, while I respect your desire to help a person in rehab, Miss Grapplee had drug paraphernalia strewn throughout her apartment." Arthur's accent was crisp and disdainful. "The police are investigating."

"That explains a lot." Kellen remembered Rita's behavior on the day Horst had picked her up from the winery. "She was so..." So out there, so bold, so sure she could do anything without repercussions. She had asked too many question, taken photos of the van. Now, here, after the trip to the mountains, Kellen suspected Rita Grapplee had been on someone's payroll, paid to watch and report Kellen's every movement. She should have seen it before—but before, she hadn't suspected she was being hunted. "Let me know if she turns up," Kellen told Arthur. "I'd like to talk to her."

"Of course, Miss Adams." Arthur led them toward the piano, and as he did, he said, "Let me introduce you to our newest outdoor arrival, our pianist and a talented musician, Dan Matyasovitch."

DAN MATYASOVITCH:
MALE, CAUCASIAN ANCESTRY, 60 YO, 5'10", 175 LBS. THICK DARK GLASSES (VISUALLY IMPAIRED?), ECCENTRIC FACIAL HAIR. ACCENT: HOLLYWOOD AMERICAN. DARK JEANS, WHITE T-SHIRT, UNLINED BLACK SILK JACKET, WHITE ATHLETIC SHOES, NO SOCKS. PLAYS WITHOUT SHEET MUSIC. TAKES REQUESTS. THRILLED AND NERVOUS.

Max listened for a moment, then asked, "How did a man of your obvious talents come to play at my family's winery?"

"I started out in New York City, acting on Broadway, then in the orchestra pit. Lately I've worked in the jazz clubs, but staying up all night—that's a young man's game." Dan's fingers continued to play softly as he spoke to them, as if he didn't even need to think about the music to know "My Favorite Things." "I came west on a mission, and I'm happy to have found this position."

"He applied to work in the serving room, and he's got the chops to do it, but I'd already filled those positions. When he heard Warren talking about the improvements he wanted to make to brighten the winery, he suggested a pianist and offered to play for us."

"We didn't have a piano in the winery," Max pointed out.

"Mrs. Di Luca offered to let me audition on her piano." Dan moved effortlessly from "My Favorite Things" to "Strangers in the Night."

"My mother let you use her piano?" Max was clearly dumbstruck. "This is her piano?"

"Mrs. Di Luca has been incredibly supportive about all we've accomplished," Arthur said. "If you would come this way, Mr. Di Luca, we can look inside the tasting room."

"First, I'd like to discuss security," Max said. "With so many new guests and employees, that is a concern."

"Indeed it is, sir, and I've hired Parliman Security to handle everything." Arthur was the most efficient anticipatory employee Kellen had ever seen. "Would you like to meet Mr. Parliman first?"

"Is that him?" Kellen indicated a man standing at the fringe of the action.

"Yes, how did you know?" Arthur asked.

MR. PARLIMAN:
MALE. EAST INDIAN ANCESTRY. MIDDLE-AGED. DELIBERATELY NONDESCRIPT IN DRESS AND GROOMING. WATCHFUL.

"I've met men like him before, in Afghanistan, officers and enlisted men who use their eyes and their minds to stave off disaster."

"There you have it." Max put his hand on her hip and let it rest there. "How big is Mr. Parliman's firm?"

Arthur looked pleased. "We'll talk to him."

"I'll stay here," Kellen said.

"You don't want to meet him?" Max asked.

She looked at Parliman again. He had zeroed in on a guest who had overindulged and had sent one of his men to offer free bottles of water and a complimentary plate of cheese and vegetables. "No. I trust Arthur's judgment, and yours."

Max laughed. "And your own."

"In this case," she agreed.

Max walked off with Arthur.

Kellen relaxed and leaned on the piano. She'd been thinking the same thing, that an assassin would find the winery an easy place to take her out, and Rae and Max and… She didn't want the winery to be a war zone.

She was happy standing here, under the tent, soaking in the summer heat, listening to the music and looking at Max as he wandered around his winery, viewing and assessing the changes.

He wasn't sure. These weren't his ideas. But he was a fair man, and Arthur's enthusiasm—and the profit—was winning him over. The two men disappeared into the tasting room.

Dan said, "Arthur has spoken highly of Max and of you, and I understand Rae is your daughter."

"That's right."

"She's quite the inquisitive child. Impetuous. I understand she went with you into the mountains."

"It was an adventure." The heat seemed to dissipate and a shiver ran up her spine, the way it used to in Afghanistan when some unseen signal told her the enemy held them in their sights. She looked around.

A lot of people were watching her, especially the new hires, who still gave off the *thrilled and nervous* vibes. And that was definitely odd.

Dan switched to "Tennessee Waltz." He still played without sheet music; what a memory he must have. "You look as if your adventure agreed with you."

She briefly touched the still tender knot on the back of her head. "I don't think we'll be doing it again soon. I'd be fine with a little peace and quiet. What kind of acting did you do, Dan?"

"Mostly dramatic. I don't have the voice for musicals, and I never wanted to be in the orchestra pit." He smiled. "I like the attention. I like to be the lead."

She understood. She'd been an officer. "The responsibility can be a burden, but there are undeniable privileges."

Max was wandering through the crowd, observing the new operation. He met her gaze.

She raised her eyebrows in question. "Excuse me."

Kellen and Max walked toward each other, and when they met under the shade of an oak, she quietly asked, "So what do we think of these changes?"

"I don't know."

"Is this what you asked Arthur to do when you hired him?"

"Not exactly. But it seems churlish to complain when in a week the operation has grown by leaps and bounds through innovation and good hiring practices. Doesn't it?"

"Right... We wouldn't be suspicious of any wrongdoing if we hadn't just been chased all over the mountains."

"And shot at."

They were muttering at each other, looking around, arms crossed, backs to the tree.

"I'm not getting an assassin vibe from any of the new hires," Kellen said.

"No, but—"

An old van stopped at the end of the driveway.

The door opened, and a small, bright, brilliantly pink figure hauling a dirty pink backpack darted up the driveway yelling, "Daddy! Mommy! Daddy! Mommy!"

45

Kellen and Max converged on their daughter.

Max picked her up and kissed her, then set her on her feet.

Rae hugged Kellen's hips, made kissing noises at Kellen's face and demanded, "Did you bring my bag?"

"I did. I told you I would." Rae's smile made Kellen *feel* like ThunderFlash, and in turn, her smug smile at Max made him roll his eyes.

Win-win.

Predictably, Rae started talking. "Today we had show-and-tell and I told them about the Triple Goddess and being chased around the mountains by bad guys and sleeping outside and getting shot at and my ride in a helicopter." She started toward the house.

Max stood, stunned.

Kellen followed Rae. "Sweetie, maybe you shouldn't have told them that. It was all sort of secret."

"It's okay. I don't think my teacher believed me. She said that was quite a story."

Max caught up. "That's good if your teacher doesn't believe you, right?"

Rae shrugged, and Kellen thought she wasn't quite as nonchalant as she appeared.

Rae continued, "Then we went to art to paint our pottery

and Martin said nobody shot at us and I was a liar and everybody knew it. So I used my words like you told me, Daddy."

"That's good," Max said cautiously.

"I told him he was wrong, that Mommy was shot and she had stitches and she passed out. He said his mommy said my mommy wasn't a soldier, she was a hooker, and nobody would come to my birthday party because I had a bad mommy."

Kellen got a sinking feeling. "What did you do?"

"I did like you told me to when someone is mean to a friend. I socked him right in the sternum. He fell down and hit his head on the ground and cried. He had a big smear of yellow paint on his shirt, too, because I was painting the sun. Wait." Rae put down her backpack and dug around, then handed a piece of paper to Max. "I have a note from the camp director."

Max opened it and read it, and winced.

At the same time, Verona walked out of the old-fashioned farmhouse, slammed the screen door behind her and shouted, "Rae Di Luca, I just got a call from Martin's mother!"

Max started doing what Max did; handling the situation. He shoved the note into his pocket, took Kellen's hand and Rae's hand, and together they climbed the stairs up onto the porch. "Now, Mother. Calm down. Kellen and I can deal with this."

"Do you know what they do to bullies? In camp and in school?" Verona opened the screen she'd just slammed and gestured at them to enter. "She'll be expelled!"

"No, no." Max had his soothing voice on. "I got a note from camp and they're asking her to apologize to Martin."

"I will not!" Rae pulled her hand out of his and stomped inside.

Max continued, "Kellen and I have to take a class on raising a child who knows how to negotiate rather than use violence."

"You're joking." Kellen couldn't believe it. "Because she punched the little snot? He was being a bully. Does his mother have to take the class, too?"

"Probably not," Max said. "Martin didn't *hit* anybody."

"Because he's a wimp." Kellen pulled her hand free and followed Rae into the living room.

Verona swung the door into Max's hand and followed them both, scolding, "Kellen Adams, I hope you're happy. Rae never got in trouble before. Now she'll be kicked out of camp. She's going to be chastised and watched by her teachers. She's going to be marked as a troublemaker—"

Kellen lost her temper. She just lost it. No excuse, it was stupid, but she turned and shouted, "I'm not ashamed! Maybe Rae will be marked as a troublemaker now, but she'll grow up to be a woman who allows no man to hurt her, to abuse her, verbally or physically. She's going to be strong. She's going to be the boss. She's got my back and I've got hers, and I taught her that. Maybe someday *she'll* save some other woman's granddaughter from kidnapping, like I saved Annabella."

Verona took a breath.

Kellen wasn't done yet. "Rae might be in trouble now, but in the future, she's going to be a strong and confident woman, one who will make you proud!"

Verona's indignation collapsed like last night's angel food cake. She fumbled for words. "Oh. I suppose..."

"Mommy, you shouldn't yell at Grandma." Rae stood by the stairs. "She's a delicate flower."

Kellen stared at her daughter, then at Verona, who was wide-eyed and shell-shocked, then at Max whose face was working as if he didn't know whether to laugh or intervene.

"Well!" Verona cleared her throat. "Kellen. I spoke hastily. What you say is true, and I am grateful. But Rae needs to recognize the difference between a real threat and an obnoxious little boy whose jealous mother made unwise comments. You're Rae's mother. Explaining that is up to you."

Kellen's anger faded fast. She looked between Verona and Rae again, and realized the task she had set herself. "You're right. I should be able to do that. I guess Rae and I need to have a talk."

"Maybe while Rae is taking her shower and changing for dinner?" Verona suggested.

"Right. Come on." Kellen put her hand on Rae's shoulder and headed up the stairs with her.

Max stayed behind, speaking with Verona.

As Kellen and Rae walked, Kellen tried to think how to explain to a seven-year-old the degrees of danger that stalked the world. It came down to one simple thing. She stopped Rae in the hallway outside her room and knelt in front of her. "Is it possible for Martin to kill you?"

"No." Rae crossed her arms over her chest. "He's nothing but a skinny sissy boy."

"Then you can't hit him."

"But he said bad things about you, and you said we have each other's backs."

"We do. If someone was threatening you and he could really hurt you, maybe kill you, I would do everything in my power to protect you. You know that."

"Yes. But Martin said you were a hooker!"

"Do you know what a hooker is?"

"No." Rae looked disgruntled.

"It's a mean word meant to hurt. Words *can* hurt, but only from people you care about. If Martin and his mother want to call me a hooker—" Kellen waved a hand "—*pft!* I don't care. I don't know them, and I don't care what they think."

"Some people care what they think," Rae muttered.

Translation: Rae cared. That was important, and Kellen didn't want to easily dismiss her feelings. "Are you afraid some of your friends will listen?"

"Not my friends."

Kellen considered that. "Your not-friends?"

"Roxy Birtle laughed."

"Roxy Birtle sounds mean."

"She is!" Rae had red in her cheeks and her eyes were too bright.

"That's too bad. There's always a mean girl and there's always a mean boy and I always feel sorry for them."

"Sorry for them?" Rae's voice rose. "Why? Mommy, why?"

"Because they like being mean. Would *you* want to be like that?"

"No. I like people to be happy!"

"I know!" Kellen hugged her. "The important thing is we don't care what mean people say. You and me. We're Thunder-Flash and LightningBug. We're secret superheroes together."

For the first time, Rae relaxed and leaned into Kellen and really listened.

Kellen had to be careful now, phrase her words perfectly. "We only take action when we know it's necessary, when someone is going to be hurt and we can save them. We have to think when we're in a difficult position, when the time to act is and when it's better to be quiet and safe."

"That's not always easy for me to figure out." Rae looked grave and thoughtful.

Kellen's heart swelled with pride. Her little girl was so smart! And yet so kind, and that could be her ruin. "Not easy for me, either. But remember how in the mountains, I asked you about how to fight off an attacker, and you were so smart and came up with so many ideas? You and me, we'll talk about possible dangerous situations and figure out the best way to handle them."

"Okay." Rae perked up. "That'll be fun! And karate? You're going to get me into karate?"

"Yes, but not right away. You already have a full schedule. Rae, I'm going to be here for you for as long as I can." Kellen couldn't promise more than that, not after the loss of consciousness on the mountain and the blackout on the road. "Sooner rather than later, I'll prove to everyone the kind of person I am, and no one's going to think I'm a hooker, and everyone's going to know I was a captain in the Army. It'll happen. You'll see. Give me a little time."

Rae got that rebellious *I can't wait* look on her face.

Kellen remembered being that age and how long a minute was, how long an hour was, how it seemed she would never grow up and get to do whatever she wanted to do. She knew, too, that Rae's thump wasn't fueled merely by altruism—Martin had called Rae a liar and her teacher hadn't believed her story, and that chafed when all she'd done was tell the truth. "I'll tell you what. You're probably going to have to apologize to Martin."

"I won't."

Kellen held up one finger to stop her. "If you'll do that, I'll go to your teacher and ask if I can give a demonstration aimed at teaching kids like you how and when to defend yourselves. Once I do that, my credentials will be established, you'll be my assistant and Martin will be afraid to ever tangle with you again."

Rae thought about it. "You'll have to go to the camp director."

"Okay, I'll go to the camp director. Tomorrow. Can I ride with you in the van?"

"Yeah!" Rae shouted.

Kellen almost told her, "Indoor voice," and changed her mind. After all, the child was enthused that Kellen would be with her, and Kellen was enthused about the chance to look around the camp and view the security measures that would keep the children safe. She hated the thought that her daughter, that any child, would be in danger at a summer camp. But if she wasn't satisfied, she would volunteer to work there, and the kids would be secure.

Or...not. If someone was after her, would she bring danger to the camp? She would talk to Max, suggest he instigate measures to keep Rae safe no matter where she was.

Kellen stood. "Let's get you in the shower." She opened the

door to Rae's room, glanced inside and realized why Verona had sent her up here to handle this.

Revenge.

All the dresser drawers were open, spitting socks, underwear, leggings and tutus onto the floor. The closet stood as a monument to empty hangers and mounds of wrinkled dresses. Naked princess dolls created stepping-stones toward the unmade stuffed-animal-covered bed.

Kellen's austere Army-trained soul was horrified. "How do you know which clothes are clean and which ones are dirty?"

"The clean ones are in the laundry baskets."

Which meant a hundred pounds of clothes were dirty. "We've got to get you organized."

"Why?" It was an honest question.

"Because your grandma is right. This is atrocious."

"Grandma says my cousin Sammy's room is atrocious. If Sammy can be atrocious, why can't I?"

"How old is Sammy?"

"Fourteen."

"When you're fourteen, you can have an atrocious room if you choose. Until then, it's going to be organized."

"But not right now, right?" Max stood in the door, smiling at his girls, "Later, right?"

"Sure. First thing is to give Rae a shower and find her some clean clothes to wear." Kellen smiled back at him. "I'll meet you at dinner."

He turned away, then turned back. "Good job back there explaining the difference between life and death."

"I may have a grip on that."

46

When Kellen exited Rae's room after assigning her one simple job—pick up her naked princess dolls and their clothes and stack them in the massive dollhouse—Max put his arm around her and led her toward the bedroom. *His* bedroom.

Kellen pulled back. "I can't go in there with you. Your mother will have a fit. She doesn't want you to sleep with me!"

"Are you kidding? When she finds out we're going to get married, she'll be thrilled. She'll be in her element, Rae is going to have a blast, and little Martin's mother is going to wish she kept her mouth shut, because they're not going to be invited to the most important wedding this town has ever seen." He sat down on the bed, smiled and patted his knee. "Come here and let's talk about what we're going to do after the ceremony. Maybe have a demonstration."

"I have a bullet in my brain. I'm not supposed to strain myself. Remember? No bumping the headboard?"

"I'll make sure you stay very, very still…using merely my hands."

She was tired: from hiking, from falling, from having an MRI, from hearing a dire verdict of pain and little hope. They had time; right now, the blows to her head had caused swelling around the site where the bullet rested. If she took care and didn't reinjure herself, a few months would allow the bruising to subside and the surgery would proceed with the optimum chance for success.

Yet somehow, Max Di Luca managed to make her feel alive as she had never felt before. And that was worth risking death, anytime. "As long as you're doing all the work... I suppose I could rest in your bed and take it easy."

He chuckled. "Yes, let's rest together."

Max's phone whimpered.

Max rolled over on the bed and reached toward the nightstand. "It's my mother."

"Your phone whimpers when your mother texts?"

"I always know who it is. Saves time." He read the words. "Dinner's almost ready. She advises us to clean up."

"I can almost see the indignation curling off the phone."

"It's Mom's specialty."

Kellen rolled off the bed. "I'm going to go shower and change out of these resort clothes and into something real. I'm tired of looking like a tennis player."

He watched her dress. "Have I mentioned how pretty you are?"

"Not often enough. Have I mentioned how pretty *you* are?"

He fluttered his lashes. "I have a mirror."

She laughed. "Hurry up. I am not going down there alone."

Max and Kellen met in the hallway, clean, dressed and guilty and giggly as only having sex in forbidden circumstances could make them. They descended the stairs and walked into the kitchen, a large old-fashioned room with colorful tiles, modern appliances, a round table in the middle and one very irritated cook preparing bubbling brown stew with root vegetables and cheese biscuits.

The smells of garlic, tomatoes and browned beef permeated the air, and Kellen thought that the promise of good food would cushion the blow of Verona's disapproval.

Verona banged the lid on a pot. "Maximilian, I do not think that the two of you sharing a bedroom while in the same house as your mother and your daughter is appropriate behavior." The steamy heat made her brown hair hang in ringlets across her forehead, but her words were icy and clear.

"Wait a minute, Mom. We've got something to tell you." Max went into the adjacent parlor and bellowed up the stairs. "Rae, come down here please!"

Rae bellowed back, "Coming, Daddy!" Her shoes clattered on the stairs and she appeared in the doorway, a vision in pink, glitter and glue, which she had smeared on her cheek.

The Di Lucas were the loudest people Kellen had ever heard. Her parents, what she remembered of them, had been busy, boisterous people, but when they had died and Kellen went to live with her aunt and uncle, the household had been ruled by her aunt's migraines and the most commonly used phrase was, *Use your indoor voice, please.*

Come to think of it, Kellen didn't mind the Di Luca noise.

"Wash your hands for dinner," Verona said.

"I did!" Rae rubbed her palms on her shirt.

Max put out his hands. "Let me see."

Rae sighed dramatically and headed into the bathroom by the back porch. She didn't shut the door, so they heard the scrape of the stool across the Spanish tile, the splashing and the humming, and when Rae walked out, her hands, her hair and the front of her shirt were dripping wet. Proudly, she proclaimed, "I washed my face, too!"

Kellen waited for Verona to fuss.

Instead, she said, "Good thinking, Rae."

The family was so casual and encouraging about the little stuff and kept their drama for the big life-changing events. Kellen liked that, too, except—oh man, there was about to be drama.

Max got a kitchen towel out of the drawer and used it to wipe

Rae down. "Why don't you and Grandma sit down? Mommy and I have something to tell you."

Verona looked from Max to Kellen and sank down in her chair as if her legs were too weak to hold her.

Rae pulled her chair out from the table—another long scrape across the tile—and perched on her heels, leaned over the table and fastened her gaze on her father.

Max took Kellen's hand. They faced Verona and Rae, and with the flare of an accomplished showman, Max announced, "Kellen has agreed to be my bride."

The reactions were exactly the opposite of what Kellen expected.

Verona shot to her feet. "A bride? You're going to get married?" She clasped her hands and shook them at the heavens. "My prayers have been answered!"

Rae said nothing, but her eyes were big and wary.

"I wonder if we can manage it by Christmas?" Verona walked to the calendar that hung on the wall. "To get the dress done and the family here—"

"Two weeks," Max declared.

Verona swung around. "You're kidding."

"Two weeks," Max repeated. "We're getting married in two weeks."

"Two weeks?" Verona squawked like the chicken who had swallowed the rubber band, and faced Kellen. "Wait. Are you pregnant again?"

"Mother." Max sounded excessively patient. "Even if she was, we wouldn't know yet and anyway, we have a seven-year-old daughter together. We can safely say the scandal ship has sailed!"

Kellen grinned. "Nice interception," she muttered to Max.

Verona promptly returned to her main complaint. Which was, "I can't get a wedding together in two weeks!"

"We don't have to have a wedding," Kellen said. "We can get married at the justice of the peace and have a reception later."

Max and Verona and even Rae stared at her as if she was speaking a foreign language.

Max and Verona turned back to each other.

"How can everyone in the family make arrangements so quickly?" Verona asked.

"Do you really think they won't?" Max seemed casually confident.

"It's going to be an inconvenience to at least some of them!"

"If it's too inconvenient for them to come, they can watch the video."

"Max! Your attitude!" Verona paced the kitchen and wrung her hands. "How can we get the dresses made?"

Kellen looked at the stew bubbling on the stove, at the cheese biscuits stacked in the warming oven. Her stomach growled.

"We'll get dresses off the rack," Max said with rock-solid assurance.

"We are Di Lucas! We have relatives who are famous designers and we're getting wedding dresses off the rack?" Verona had become completely and emphatically Old World Italian, tossing her hands in the air and her head from side to side. "Have you run mad?"

Max was unimpressed. "We'll use *their* rack dresses."

"We could have a small wedding," Kellen suggested.

She got the same blank look as before.

Okay. Never mind.

She went to the stove and ladled stew into broad bowls, added a cheese biscuit—they were burned on the bottom—and placed them on the table.

Which seemed to send Verona's mind in a new direction. "The food!"

"If you can't handle the food, at least we'll have good wine," Max answered.

Kellen had to appreciate his ability to manipulate his mother. She grinned at Rae.

Rae avoided her eyes.

"If...if I can't... I will handle the food!" Verona sputtered.

"We'd better get the invitations out tonight." Max pondered the date and time. "An evening wedding, I think. A ceremony at sunset, in the grove where the new staff put up all the tables."

"It's almost time to start picking the grapes. The predictions are for warm weather. It will be a madhouse around here anyway, and you want to add a wedding?" Verona sat down, snapped her napkin and put it in her lap. "Why don't we ask Annie and Leo to host at Yearning Sands Resort?"

Max followed suit, only without the snap. "Annie almost died last winter. Do you really think that's a good idea, to put that kind of pressure on her?"

Kellen looked at Rae, shell-shocked and unhappy, and somehow, Max and Verona were too involved in planning a wedding to pay attention.

Verona pounced on another objection. "We have new inexperienced staff."

"They don't seem inexperienced to me. Let them prove themselves."

While Verona and Max squabbled, Kellen pulled Rae's bowl close. She shredded the beef and cut the carrots, potatoes and parsnips into tiny bites. She cut the burned bottom off the cheese biscuit and slid it back in front of Rae. She knelt beside her. "Doesn't that look good?"

Rae nodded, her gaze fixed on the food.

Kellen rubbed her back. "Honey, what's wrong?"

Rae's eyes filled with tears. "Married? B-but Daddy is mine!"

47

In Rae's mind, Max was her exclusive parent and Kellen had no right to take over any part of him. In a way, the child was right.

Kellen looked up.

Max and Verona were staring. Rae had their attention now.

But this was between Kellen and Rae, and Kellen tried to think of the right answer. "Your daddy is your daddy. He has no other children but you."

Rae nodded and wiped her nose on her sleeve.

Kellen felt a little thrill; she'd taught Rae to wipe using the nearest sleeve. "I'll be your daddy's wife. And I'm your mother. We're going to be a family." Kellen rubbed Rae's back. "I thought you wanted that."

Rae nodded and played with her spoon. "I do. But we are!"

"A family." Kellen relaxed and smiled. "We are, aren't we? We're a good family together just like we are."

"Yeah!"

"Your daddy and I don't really have to get married, do we?"

Max made a muffled sound of protest.

Verona thumped her head onto her palm.

Rae exploded in indignation. "Yes! Yes, you do!"

Heh. Kellen felt the slightest bit smug. "Honey, if we can be a family without a wedding, and a wedding makes you unhappy, then we won't get married."

"I want to wear pink!"

Just like that, Kellen had no idea what Rae was talking about. "What? Pink? You wear it all the time."

"To the wedding. I want to be your bridesmaid, and I want to wear pink!"

Wait a minute… From some depths of forgotten girlhood, rebellion rose. "You can be my bridesmaid, but you can wear pink at *your* wedding. That's *your* color."

"What's *your* color?" Rae demanded.

What was Kellen's color? "Purple!"

Rae's eyes got big and shiny. "Like ThunderFlash and LightningBug!"

"Purple?" Verona muttered. "She wants purple?"

"Can I wear a purple sash and a purple ribbon in my hair?" Rae asked.

"And carry a purple bouquet," Kellen assured her.

"That's almost pink," Rae said and dug into her stew.

Kellen knelt there on the floor, feeling as if she'd been outsmarted by a seven-year-old. She looked up to see Max and Verona smirking at her. "Oh, shut up," she muttered and sat to eat while they returned to arguing about a wedding that would take place in exactly two weeks' time.

The old-fashioned avocado-green kitchen princess wall phone warbled uncertainly like an opera diva whose prime had passed. Verona slid out of her chair and said, "I shouldn't answer. It's probably another spam call," and answered. "Hello? Who? Why? Yes, I remember you. But why? Hmm." She took the phone away from her ear. "Rae, it's for you. It's Mr. Brooks."

Max and Kellen looked in consternation at each other.

"Yay!" Rae hopped off her chair and sprinted to the phone. "Hello, Mr. Brooks! What did you figure out?"

Verona sat back down.

Max and Kellen leaned forward to eavesdrop.

"Why does that bastard Nils Brooks want to talk to my daughter?" Max whispered.

"Our daughter," Kellen corrected.

Into the phone, Rae said, "That's pretty close. How soon?"

Verona looked between her son and his fiancée. "He said they were negotiating."

"Negotiating what?" Max's voice got louder.

Verona lifted her hands and her shoulders in a massive shrug.

"It sounds pretty. She would like it there." Rae frowned deeply. "How long can she stay?"

Pause.

"When can she come back?"

Pause.

"Why can't she stay there forever?"

Pause.

"That's *bullshit*!"

Verona turned in her chair. "Rae!" She turned back and glared at Kellen. "And you!"

Kellen wanted to protest she hadn't taught her that. But she had taught Rae to wipe her nose on her sleeve, so she kept quiet.

"No." Rae spoke into the phone, and her childish indignation was emphatic and massive. "She needs to be someplace high and pretty where she can see and at night when everybody's gone she can wander around!"

Kellen looked at Max, who looked at Verona, and they all shrugged, without a clue about what was being discussed.

"You can do that," Rae said into the phone, her voice a stern imitation of her grandmother's. "You should do that. Let me know—but I expect you to *do your best*. Bye-bye." She came back, sat down in her chair and, without a word to them, started eating again.

When Rae looked up, Kellen said, "So...what did Mr. Brooks want?"

"When we were in the helicopter, I wanted him to give me

the Triple Goddess. He said he couldn't, she's too important and someone mean would take her from me." Rae stuck out her lip, not pouting, but thoughtful. "So I told him about how the goddess is our talisman—" she pointed at Kellen and at herself "—and he said he would fix it so we could see her sometimes. But I want her to be able to see us, too. You know?" She went back to eating.

Kellen reflected that most of the time she didn't know what Rae was talking about; half that time was because Rae was being a seven-year-old, and the other half was because Rae was being a genius.

"The Triple Goddess can't see you because she's stone. You know that, right, Rae?" Max sounded honestly anxious, like he was worried Rae was confused.

"Really, Max? That's what's bothering you about all this?" Kellen rolled her eyes at him, then turned back to Rae. "I understand why we want to see the Triple Goddess. And Nils Brooks is arranging to put her into a museum somewhere close?"

Rae nodded and kept eating.

"Where's he going to put her that she can see us?"

Rae pointed up. "He says there's a big house in Portland on top of a hill and he'll arrange for guards and stuff. But he says she can't stay there forever. I said that was bull—" She pulled herself to a stop and looked up guiltily.

Three pairs of adult eyes scrutinized her.

Rae shrank down in her chair and bent back to her plate. In a tiny voice, she said, "Pucky."

"Rae!" Verona said.

"Sorry, Nonna." Rae slid a sideways conspiratorial glance at Kellen.

Kellen pretended not to see it.

In between bites, Rae said, "He said she has to be researched more. Then she goes to live in a museum with locks and alarms. She won't like that. She does get to go on tour. She'll like the tours. She likes people admiring her. I told him she wanted to stay close to Mommy and me, and she likes Mr. Zone, too. Mr. Brooks said probably the closest she'd be is in a museum in San Francisco. I told Mr. Brooks she'll arrange something else."

"She'll arrange..." Max was obviously confused. "Who will?"

"The goddess."

Max turned to Kellen. "I'm not happy that Nils Brooks is calling my daughter."

"If I had a cell phone, you wouldn't have to know about it." Obviously, Rae believed she'd hit a home run.

"The best reason I ever heard not to get you a cell phone," Max said roundly.

Rae's smirk disappeared. "But—"

Kellen shook her head ever so slightly.

"I don't never get to win." Rae flounced off her chair. "Can I be excused?"

"*May* I?" Verona said.

"*May* I be excused?

"Of course," Kellen said.

Rae ran out of the kitchen.

Verona said, "Ever since she got back from your trip, she has been cleaning her plate."

The other two nodded.

"Tell me again," Verona asked, "*what's* a Triple Goddess?"

48

A week later, Kellen found herself crawling through the shrubbery—again. She didn't mean to be here, among the three-foot-tall azalea bushes that had been trimmed to provide a lush leafy display on top with bare branches beneath. Last time she had crawled through the bushes outside the wine cellar, she'd almost been killed by a falling roof tile. Some might call this childish behavior, but right now, being childish seemed more sensible than dealing with table settings and groom's cake and gown fittings.

The Di Luca family was everywhere, talking loudly about the grape harvest and giving Max unwanted wine-producing advice. He was unfailingly pleasant, but they weren't all here yet. In fact, according to Max, the influx had barely begun.

They were arriving from Italy, from the eastern United States, from California's wine country. They were old, young, laughing, melancholy, but all were nosy and all loud. They kissed and hugged her, spoke in Italian and English, cooked flagrantly and with extensive arguments. They overwhelmed with their exuberance.

Kellen settled, cross-legged, near the far end of the hedge. Occasionally, a pair of feet would wander past on the lawn; someone using a shortcut from the winery to the house, to the bocce ball court, to the tables that had been placed under the cherry trees.

Kellen pressed her back against the winery wall, breathed in the warm scents of bark mulch and vegetation and tried to meditate. But inner peace was elusive. She thought longingly about the door that led into the cool wine cellars, but she didn't dare make the dash because even if she didn't get caught before she reached the door, she was sure some of the Di Luca family would be touring. She would be expected to join the tour or, God forbid, lead the tour. That was so not Captain Kellen Adams.

Sometimes it seemed as if she was losing herself, the self she had created out of the remnants of Cecilia and memories of Cousin Kellen, in this wedding onslaught.

She heard the patter of running feet coming across the lawn and tensed.

Rae dived under the shrubs and slid close to Kellen. "Mommy, that man pinched my cheek!"

Kellen found herself instantly ready to kill. "Where?"

"In the yard!"

"No, I mean—where on your cheek?"

"Here!" Rae showed her a red mark on her face.

Kellen relaxed. "Which relative?"

"I don't know. He had a funny accent."

"Not Italian then." Kellen wasn't joking; they'd both heard so many Italian accents they thought nothing of it.

"No, a *funny* accent! He said he was from *fah* away and asked when and where I was *bawn*."

"Sounds like he's from Boston. What did he look like?"

"Like a man. Hair." Rae ruffled her fingers over her head.

"Brown? Blond?"

"Brown. Dark brown. Brown eyes. He wanted to know my name and all about you and I told him some stuff, but he kept asking and finally I ran away." Rae cuddled close to Kellen's side. "Grandma said I can't punch any of these people in the sternum. Because they're relations."

"No, you can't." Kellen hugged her. "But we can think about it with great relish."

Bushes rustled at the far end of the row of shrubs, and to Kellen's left, along the winery wall, Arthur Waldberg appeared, crawling toward them. He wore a white shirt, a blue tie, black linen pants and his handkerchief had been folded with precision and placed in the pocket of his gray sports coat. Sweat beaded on his shiny forehead. "Miss Adams, Miss Di Luca, I need some answers from the bride and the young maid of honor."

Kellen moaned and thumped the back of her head against the wall—and tensed. Nothing happened, reality remained within reach, and she mentally cursed the stupid bullet for making the most innocent gesture a trial.

Arthur settled next to Rae, looked around at the well-trimmed branches around them and the dense foliage of leaves above and said, "This is quite pleasant. Rather like the tent I played in as a child. No wonder you hide here." He pulled out his handkerchief and dabbed at his forehead, then carefully folded the linen into an origami fan and arranged it back in his pocket.

"Yes. To be *alone*," Kellen said with emphasis.

"I know, Miss Adams, I sympathize with your desires, but we're on a truncated wedding schedule and I must know what the bride wants." He sounded sympathetic but ruthless.

"Why don't you ask Mrs. Verona Di Luca what I want?" Kellen snapped. She wasn't bitter, not really. Having Verona be so sure of each decision had made the planning onslaught easier to bear. The only matter in which they had clashed, and Kellen held firm, was—

"Mr. Federico Di Luca says he must have a decision on which wedding gown you will wear," Arthur said.

Rae whimpered.

He transferred his attention to Rae. "He also wishes to know the *real* color of the little maid of honor's gown."

"I am not wearing any of the frothy frilly lace-ridden gowns he brought on Verona's command." Kellen took a deep breath and finished her pronouncement. "Rae is wearing purple. Not lavender. Not blue with a hint of lavender. Purple. Purple, purple, purple!"

"Yeah!" Rae said. "Can my dress be lace-ridden, Mommy?"

"Of course it can." Kellen kissed her head and turned back to Arthur. "If Zio Federico can't manage that, Rae and I will run away from home, go to Portland, find a couple of dresses at Goodwill and wear those."

"Yeah!" Rae said again.

"As I thought." Arthur pulled out a small leather notebook held together with a single tiny silver ballpoint pen. He opened it and scribbled a note. "Two days ago, while out of Verona's hearing, I spoke with Mr. Federico Di Luca, explained the situation and asked that he acquire gowns more fitting to two females of, shall we say, superhero powers." He shared a smile with Rae. "His rush order has arrived from Milan. He's ready to do your fittings. Having viewed the gowns, I believe you'll both find these more to your satisfaction."

Kellen felt a marvelously warm thrill across her nerves, a thrill contrary to her declared lack of interest in this wedding. "Thank you, Arthur. I appreciate your assistance. But what will Verona say?"

"I spoke to her, Miss Adams. I believe you'll find no further opposition to your desires in this matter." Arthur's phone chirped. He looked at the text, typed a few words.

Kellen heard a rustle of bushes coming from beyond Arthur's shoulder.

Arthur scooted forward. "Dan Matyasovitch has submitted a list of suggested music for the ceremony and the reception afterward." He gestured to the right, and the musician was crawling toward her.

With his jeans and collarless button-up shirt and jacket, he looked more at home down here beneath the bushes than Arthur. But really? He was crawling and perspiring so much his sunglasses were sliding down his nose, and sweat dropped off his mustache, his goatee, and circled around his upswept eyebrows. All he needed was a cigar to look like Freud stuck in a sauna.

Kellen slapped at a beetle that crawled up her arm. "Do I have to care?"

Dan worked his way around the trunks of the azaleas to sit next to Kellen's left knee. "You'll find leaving the matter in the hands of your mother-in-law will result in an arcane selection of late seventies and early eighties pop rock."

"I *like* pop rocks," Rae said.

Arthur, Dan and Kellen looked at each other over the top of Rae's head. "Do they still have those?" Arthur asked.

"Apparently." Kellen made some decisions she didn't know she'd even considered. She quickly listed her choices, closing with "'At Last,' Etta James."

"Good. I can springboard off those for the rest of the playlist. I've hired a talented bass player and a guitarist and am negotiating with a trumpet player. If I can't get him, I may try for a clarinet. The instrument gives the music a '40s vibe, but in this case, that's not necessarily a bad thing." Dan Matyasovitch turned and crawled back the way he came.

"Dan is a talented actor and musician. You can trust him with this list. When he's done, you'll have a reception to remember." Arthur checked his phone, pushed buttons, made his next pronouncement. "Now, about the food for the reception—"

Kellen began to feel as if she'd been ambushed. "On that, Verona can have her way." From across the lawn, she heard the thump of footsteps running.

Pearly Perry slid under the shrubbery like a baseball player going in to third base. She was slender to a fault, short and dressed in chef's clothes so loose they hung on her. She beamed at Rae, glanced nervously at Kellen, looked to Arthur for guidance.

Arthur came through for her. "Pearly, Miss Adams says she

wants Mrs. Di Luca to have her way about the food at the reception."

Pearly's dark eyes widened in horror. "Yes, Miss Adams, she knows food very well. But her baking leaves much to be desired, and the wedding cake! You must have what you want for your wedding cake!"

"You want to speak to the bakery on my behalf?" Kellen asked.

"I want to *make* it. I studied for years under a master baker!" Pearly took Kellen's hands and clutched them earnestly. "I will make you a cake that will be the talk of your friends for years to come."

"My friends?" Kellen chuckled as she thought about the men and women she had served with in the military overseas and at home. They were coming, all of them arriving the day before, except Birdie who would be here tomorrow for fittings and female bonding. "As long as it's eatable, my friends will be happy."

"What about your enemies?" Arthur asked. "What do you want them saying about your cake?"

Kellen exploded in a flurry of irritation. "For sh…pete's sake, I don't care what my enemies say about my cake! Why should I care what anyone thinks about my wedding cake? That's just ridiculous!"

Arthur cut his eyes toward Pearly Perry, who sat there with her head drooping like a lovely flower on a broken stem.

An alert and sorrowful Rae asked, "But, Mommy, what about Martin's mother? Remember when you did the self-defense class and she was cranky because everybody in camp thought you were so cool? Even her little boy, skinny scaredy-cat Martin?"

Kellen viewed Rae's reproachful expression and the barely hidden flash of triumph in her brown eyes. This was a conspiracy, and even her daughter played a part. "All right, Pearly. Do what you do best. But I don't want to hear about it ahead of time. Surprise me. All I demand is purple frosting trim. Purple, not—"

"—blue with a lavender tint." Arthur scribbled on his list. "You can trust Pearly to amaze and astonish."

Pearly shook Kellen's hand, then shook it again, then bowed, then scooted back to allow Claude McKeith to take her place. Over one of his shoulders, Takashi Tibodo bobbed and smiled. Over the other, Mateo Courtemanche offered her a cold bottle of water and a small gift-wrapped box.

Kellen accepted the offerings and opened the box. Inside she found a specialty from the winery and a favorite of hers: Southern cheese straws.

She laughed. She couldn't help growing more and more amused; this whole under-the-shrubbery wedding conference had a humorous side she couldn't deny. Before Claude could speak, she held up one hand. "Hire whoever you need, as much staff as you need, for service and cleanup."

"No limits?" Claude asked.

"Make sure they're bonded and credible, run them past Mr. Parliman's security team to make sure their credentials are clean, and no reporters. We're going to have a lot of wealthy famous people here and the Di Luca family would like to avoid thieves and publicity." As she spoke, Kellen wasn't really thinking of the Di Luca family's privacy; she was considering how easy it would be for an assassin to slip in and take her out, and worse, if someone was so determined to kill her, a lot of people could get hurt or killed.

There had been enough of that already.

She thought she'd been tactful, but Claude winced as if she'd hit a nerve and drew back. "I'll do my best, Miss Adams."

Mateo said, "Everyone on Arthur's staff is equipped to observe, supervise and care for the guests during this special occasion." He looked at Arthur, who nodded silently, then looked at the ground.

A silence fell that was almost awkward, so Kellen asked, "Takashi, will you sing for us at the reception?"

"I would be honored. I'll consult with Dan and we'll come up with something to delight you and your guests."

Warren Golokin appeared from nowhere, smiling and anxious to please. He unrolled a stiff sheet of 24-by-36-inch drawing paper with a site plan that included tents, tables, decorations and parking.

Kellen rolled it back up, pressed it into his hand, and said, "Do you realize how much I trust you? After seeing your talent, I know you'll make this wedding a waltz without music."

Warren teared up. "I won't disappoint you."

Kellen realized how exhausted she was when she teared up in response, and had to hug him. "I know you won't." She hadn't been sleeping well; the worry about Rae's safety and the assassin, the wedding and most of all, about the gray coma that hovered at the periphery of her mind.

Warren backed away, and Kellen asked Arthur, "Are we done now?"

Arthur made a whisking motion with his fingertips, and his cohorts disappeared the way they came. "Thank you, Miss Adams, I promise you you'll have the wedding of your dreams, and everyone is so much happier knowing your desires in these matters."

"Everyone is happier except my future mother-in-law," Kellen said with some humor.

Rae said, "That's not true!"

"What do you mean?" Kellen asked Rae and turned to Arthur. "What does she mean?"

Arthur gave Kellen one stricken glance and tried to flee.

Just like that, Kellen figured it out. She grabbed his sleeve and brought him to a halt. "This intervention was done on Verona's behest."

Arthur sat up very straight. "Absolutely not. Mrs. Di Luca was simply—"

Rae interrupted. "Grandma cried because you didn't care about our wedding."

"But I *don't*..." Kellen came to a halt, dismayed and confused. "Cried? Why?"

With great precision, Arthur put his notebook and pen into the inner pocket of his jacket. "Mrs. Di Luca doesn't wish for you to look back on this grand event with regret because it was not to your liking."

"I won't! I honestly don't care!" Why wouldn't anyone believe her?

Large feet in size twelve white running shoes came to a halt just outside the shrubbery where Kellen had fruitlessly tried to hide. Max leaned over far enough to look at the small group beneath the leafed canopy. "Arthur! Rae! Go on, I'll talk to Kellen."

49

Arthur Waldberg didn't scramble away; he had too much dignity for that. But he crawled briskly back the way he came.

Rae lingered until her father gestured. Then she crawled out muttering, "Just when it's getting good."

Max knelt down, one knee on the grass, and looked at Kellen. "You look hot."

"I am."

"I know where we can be alone."

She smiled with a come-hither look. "I don't think going there is going to make me less hot."

He wiggled his finger in rebuke. "We're going to the blending shed."

She knew what the blending shed was—that place filled with different grape varietals in various stages of fermentation where the vintner mixed the flavors to create a wine that indulged the palate. But she'd never been there, and she didn't know if she wanted to go. "Why there?"

"I'm creating another wine."

She squinted at him.

"All right, so it probably will be lousy. But it's quiet and cool in there, and we can talk."

She crawled out. She slapped the leaves and bark off the front of her shirt and shorts.

He lovingly dusted the bark mulch off her bottom, taking care that not a speck remained.

"Are you done yet?"

"Almost." He ran his hands down her legs, then straightened and grinned.

"You're nothing but a great big boy."

"I know." He slid his arm around her waist. "I can't wait to show you how big."

She sighed as if he was a trial and smiled because she enjoyed him so much, and he cherished her so dearly. Maybe tomorrow she would die from the bullet in her brain or a new bullet from an assassin, but today, she was with Max.

He led her toward the far buildings that marked the boundary between the rows and rows of vines, heavy with grapes, and the expanse of lawn, house, tasting room and bed-and-breakfast. "Here and now, do you sense a threat? Anyone at the winery who seems…out of place? Someone we employ?"

She understood him perfectly. "You're talking about Arthur Waldberg and his cohorts."

"Yes." Max seemed relieved that they agreed on this. "Their credentials were impeccable, but they were all so desperately eager to please, so oddly obsequious."

"They really want these jobs. And why? They're fabulous at what they do. They could work anywhere. Anywhere in the world."

Isolated by their distance from the bustle and the clamor, only the barn, one hundred years old and painted a traditional red, and the blending shed, a metal-sided cellar dug into the ground then built up over two stories to accommodate great tall casks, remained apart from the wedding bustle. "Arthur keeps calling them young," Max said. "Young? The youngest is, I'd say, in his late thirties."

"When you're Arthur's age, people in their thirties are young." But she knew Max had a point.

Max used his key to open the door and ushered her down the steps and inside.

Kellen took a deep breath. The scent of fermenting wine, heady, musky, now familiar, perfumed the cool air.

Huge barrels lined either side of the tall space. A wooden sign hung on each metal spigot stating the grape varietal within. Two long narrow tables were placed end to end down the center of the space, and clean glasses rested upside down on a crowded plastic drying rack. Plastic buckets, blue, orange and white, sat beneath each spigot to catch any overflow.

The lights were off.

Max left them off, and his voice grew hushed. "Did Arthur ever answer my question about where these people were from?"

"No. Yes. Sort of. I think what you wanted to know was where *he* knew them from, because they all seem similar. They're from different countries, different backgrounds, yet they seem as if they've lived in the same place for a long time."

The blending shed was tranquil: no relatives, no winery guests, no staff, no children. No voices. Kellen could feel herself taking shape again, becoming comfortable in her own skin, content with the day and the company.

"They're so bright-eyed, as if they're seeing the world for the first time, and nervous, which isn't terribly unusual. When I meet new employees, they frequently need to be put at ease. They don't know what I'm like, whether they need to be worried for their livelihoods or if I'm one of those guys with wandering hands." He viewed her, his brown eyes serious and stern. "Just for the record, the only place my hands will wander is all over you."

"That works for me." She had never had a doubt. She had met enough of the sleazy guys in the military to recognize that Max was not one of them.

"Arthur's people feel more…desperate, I guess is the word. I couldn't figure them out." For all that Max didn't have her gift for analysis, he still worked to understand people. "In light of what happened to you up in those mountains, I find everything about them slightly disturbing."

"Then we're agreed. They feel off, out of place, as if they're hiding secrets we can't afford to ignore. It can't be Arthur himself. He wasn't in the woods with us. He couldn't have been and accomplished what he's accomplished here." She ran through the Rolodex of characters in her mind. "His people don't seem ruthless—maybe Mateo Courtemanche—but I think every one of them is willing to do anything that Arthur asks, no matter how heinous. If, in a few short weeks, Arthur can reorganize this entire winery and plan a wedding, he's capable of plotting an assassination."

"Damn it!" Max slapped the table with his palm. "I didn't want to suspect them. I like them. They're efficient. With Arthur and his people here I can take time to—" He caught himself like he didn't mean to say so much.

"Take time to what?" What was Max doing he didn't want her to know?

"Make love to my bride."

She checked out the sturdiness of the first long table, then lifted herself up on it. "That's not what you were going to say."

"Damn it," he said more softly. Then, "I thought with all the guests arriving, someone would try to slip into the winery with them and we'd have another attempt that would reveal—"

"Max!" She gathered her thoughts. "Are you saying you've been using our wedding to trap an assassin?"

"Unsuccessfully!"

"And me as an unsuspecting target?"

"I've been watching over you!"

She stared at him in astonishment. "I'm flabbergasted. That's so...so..."

"Diabolical and heartless?" He winced.

"Brilliant! I wish I'd thought of it." He made her breathless with his daring. "I also wish you'd told me what you were doing so I could watch, too."

He gathered her into his arms and laughed loudly enough that outside, four of the Di Luca relatives who were touring the grounds frowned and hurried away.

She leaned her forehead against his chest. "This is nice, being here with you, a little like being in the mountains, when the sun is coming up, the light kisses the air, and the trees talk among themselves."

"Talking trees?" Max rested his cheek against her head. "Have you been reading *Lord of the Rings* again?"

"When I need to relax, it's my go-to book."

"It always was, even before you were shot." Max let her go and wandered to the first steel vat. He took two glasses, opened the spigot to vent a small stream of fermenting wine into the bucket, then poured a little into the glasses and handed her one. "What do you taste?"

She sniffed the burgundy-colored liquid, took a small sip, sloshed it in her mouth and spit it into the spittoon. Diplomatically, she said, "It's not wine yet."

"That's the challenge, mixing it with the idea of what it will taste like in a year, two years..." He tasted and spit and sighed. "It's mine. It's going to be lousy, like all the rest."

She grinned at him. "You don't have to be good at everything, you know."

"But I'm Italian!"

"No. You're American." She pointed at the two giant oak casks closest to the door, and the two wooden buckets set under the spigots. "Those are quaint. What's with the wooden buckets?"

"They add atmosphere. When we bring tourists in on tour, they like the pretend ambience."

"I agree. I like pretend ambiance, too."

Out of the blue, he said, "I spoke with Nils Brooks."

Kellen sat up straight on the table. She hadn't seen that coming, not with the way Max felt about Nils. "About Rae and the head?"

"No, about you and the assassins."

"Oh. Good idea. He does have connections with the FBI and other agencies." So Max had overcome his distrust for Nils to delve for information to protect her. "What did you say?"

"I told him about the attempts on your life."

"And he said he wasn't surprised that someone wanted to kill me."

"No, he didn't say that at all. He seemed…displeased." Max looked like he did when he tasted his lousy wine. "He feels a connection with you."

"Max, he and I didn't have sex."

"I know. He would be less peeved if you had." Max came over and sat on the table next to her. "I asked him if he knew without a doubt that Mara Philippi was still in prison. He said yes, in isolation in a maximum security prison, and when I pressed him, he made arrangements to show me the live feed in her cell."

"She's there?"

"She's there. I saw her. She looked up at the camera and grinned, as if she saw me."

Kellen looked at him, horror still twined in the memory of Mara and her masquerade, her cruelties and her greed. "Do you think she knew that you were there?"

"She shouldn't. How could she? But she is a seriously disturbed woman and much too pleased with herself for someone who has been stripped of her power and is living behind bars."

"It could be her, trying to kill me using her sycophants." No use in thinking that because they had defeated Mara once, they could defeat her again. She was powerful, manipulative, with an IQ off the charts. More important, she had no conscience and a psychopath's disregard to any feelings but her own. If she wanted something and someone stood in her way, torture and murder were logical ways to remove that person. In the war zones, Kellen had met coldhearted killers, but none frightened her more than Mara Philippi. "She thinks she would be justified to kill me in the bloodiest and most painful way possible."

Max agreed. "I thought that, too, so I asked Brooks if there was any way she was directing her old smuggling operation and/or a vengeful attack on you from within the prison."

"And?"

"He said emphatically *no.* Then even without my insistence, he said he'd look into the possibility. You know what that means, right?"

"What?"

"She disturbed him enough to get him off his ass." Max had that tone in his voice, that curl in his lip that he reserved for Nils Brooks. "Right before I came and got you out of the bushes where you were holding a pre-wedding conference—"

"Not on purpose."

"—Nils broke into the prison computer and phoned with another *no.* To all intents and purposes, she's been effectively neutered."

"That leaves us with nothing. Not that it matters." Kellen tried to smile. "Since our return from the mountains we've been busy, everything's been peaceful and— Can't we be hopeful that maybe the violence was about stealing the Triple Goddess?"

"Hopeful. But let's not stand on the track and wonder what that bright light is."

"No," Kellen said slowly. "But in truth, my attention has been directed elsewhere."

"I know. You've been intent on pleasuring me."

She slid him a sideways glance. "Yes. Of course. That's it."

"Or you've been worried about what the doctors told you."

Damn the man. He was perceptive and when he used that voice, that warm deep caring voice, she wanted to tell him all her problems. She wouldn't; right now they ranged from *I'm going to die* to *Why do I have to worry about the number of flowers in the arrangements on the table?* "I'm not worried, exactly. But thinking. I don't want to spend what remains of my life fighting about how many ruffles are on my train."

"I know you don't. My mother, however, doesn't know we have concerns about our timeline and we need to make every moment count."

Kellen laughed at his delicate phrasing. "I don't suppose she does. I hope we got everything straightened out in our shrubbery symposium."

"I hope so, too." He turned his head and looked at her straight on. "You have a very logical way of analyzing the people around you."

"I, um, after I woke from the coma, my brain worked differently. I analyze..."

"Everything?"

"No. And I'm not always right in my analysis. But when I meet people, I do catalog them. Very Rolodex-y, if you know what I mean." She watched him, waiting for his reaction. Would he be creeped out?

"That explains a lot." He scooted closer on the table, close enough for her to catch his scent and feel his warmth. "What does *my* Rolodex card say? 'Handsome, sexy, irresistible father of adorable daughter who fulfills all my needs?'"

"That's exactly what it says." Add *kind* and *caring*, and that was pretty close.

"You're very perceptive," he said smugly. "Dear one, you are unique among women and I would like to—"

"Me, too." How could she not? He was powerful, muscled and a pleasure to the eye. He was intelligent, loud and boisterous, a caring father and a thoughtful lover. Right now, in the dim light, when they talked, put their heads together, became one mind, one heart... If they could grow old together, they would be like that always.

But that was a trouble for later. For now—she attacked him. Kissed him openmouthed and with enough force to push him down on the table.

Not that he fought.

She tugged his shirt out of his jeans, stripped his belt away, stood on the floor and wrestled him out of everything he wore below the waist in a truly ungraceful and desperate move. She did the same for herself, hopping around on one sandaled foot until she got her shorts off. The T-shirt was easy, just a fast pull over the head, and as she unsnapped her bra, a thought made her pause. "Did you lock the door?"

"Of course. But you're moving a little fast!"

She sat back on her heels and looked at him, sprawled the length of the table, wearing only his shirt. She smiled with anticipatory heat. "You look ready to me."

"I mean—" he took her hand and pulled her close "—I like to be slow and careful with you."

"Today—" she twined their fingers together and climbed onto the table, and him "—try to keep up."

Max stretched and rolled with Kellen off the table.

She was humming as she found her underpants near the door, her bra hanging on the spigot of a wine barrel. She didn't care if that did invite the gray to overtake her; it was worth every millisecond.

Max looked pretty pleased with himself, too. As he fished his running shoe out of the wooden wine bucket, he said, "One other thing about Nils Brooks."

"What?"

"He's coming to the wedding, and he's bringing the head."

"As if assassins aren't enough trouble, we're going to invite the thieves, too?"

Max rumbled a laugh. "Someone needs to watch over Rae during the wedding. I don't trust Brooks in general, but I do trust him to do that. I've also talked to Temo and Adrian, explained the situation. They're coming early on the day of the wedding. They'll keep an eye on proceedings. Not that I don't have faith in Parliman's team, but I like having a couple of experienced fighters close who would kill for you. I thought you might talk to Birdie, brief her, too? Since she's your bridesmaid she'll be with you all the time and that adds another layer of security to the whole—"

Kellen smiled at him with all her joy and amusement.

"What?"

"You really are the best man I ever met."

He dropped his shoe back in the wine bucket. "Take off your clothes. This time I'm going to show you how much I love you."

50

The day of the wedding dawned bright and hot. Parliman's security men guarded the closed winery's gate, turned away tourists and welcomed wedding guests by checking their IDs and directing them toward the parking lots. Parking attendants waved the cars into place, then directed the company toward the new circus-size blue canopy. Hired bartenders stood behind the bars, pouring selected Di Luca wines, waters, juices and soft drinks. New servers circulated with hors d'oeuvres created by Pearly Perry and her staff. Claude McKeith supervised and directed every movement, and Takashi Tibodo and Mateo Courtemanche worked and watched and handled each crisis before it happened. At one point, a whole line of bicyclists rode in and were welcomed with screams of ecstasy from that loudmouthed little Di Luca girl.

As the killer stood on the front lawn, he thought it was like watching generals direct a battlefield, not realizing how futile their preparations would be, for the enemy was among them.

Beyond the blue canopy, the farmhouse and the winery with its bed-and-breakfast were stuffed with relatives and close family friends, preparing for the big event by shouting at each other to get out of the bathroom and taking turns at the mirrors.

The winery staff was everywhere, moving between kitchen to bed-and-breakfast to wedding venue, directing guests to the small buildings that had been randomly set up among the tall cherry trees and assuring them these were not so much portable potties as luxury temporary restrooms.

On the broad lawn behind the winery, a white canopy lifted its peaks toward the sky. Chairs sat in lines, a length of stiff white cloth defined the aisle, and an altar had been constructed at the front and decorated in exquisite silks, heavy laces and lofty white candles.

Meanwhile, where the vines began and the winery ended, workers picked the grapes, working hard to get them in before the heat grew intense and lowered the Brix. The crushing shed roared and gnashed, the resulting grape juice slid into stainless steel containers, the wine master, Freeman Townsend, and his apprentice, Jessie Glomen, tasted, urged, thanked, and most of all, they rushed.

Wedding or not, this was a working winery and the harvest was on.

Not far away, Kellen Adams paced the front porch, using her extraordinary powers of observation to inspect the new arrivals, to find anyone who showed surreptitious signs of being a killer.

He waved.

She waved back.

His disguise and his manner were perfect; she barely noticed him.

Her friends drove up, two men he recognized from the guest list. She'd served with them in the Army. She ran out to meet them. They all embraced, and laughed, and the men patted their suit jackets over the spot where a holster might hold a pistol.

What a clever girl she thought she was! She'd brought in extra personal security.

Good to know. He would have to handle that.

Ah, Kellen. She was no match for his guile. Wedding or not, *today* he would finish this job.

51

Bisnonna Benedetta stuck her crooked finger in Kellen's face and in a pronounced Italian accent, said, "It is good luck to be married as the first grapes of a new year are harvested."

Zia Giorgia said, "It portends a fertile union."

Zio Salvatore said, "They already have proved that they're fertile!"

The cluster of elderly Italian relatives seated around the kitchen table fell all over themselves cackling.

Sarah Di Luca from California sighed. "Salvatore. Hush. You'll embarrass her."

Kellen wasn't exactly embarrassed. Or at least not embarrassed for the reasons the relatives thought. Verona had stuck her in here until Max had been hustled to his room in the bed-and-breakfast, knowing full well the elderly relatives would keep them apart. As she'd been told multiple times today, it was bad luck for the groom to see the bride on the day of the wedding. To which she had finally said, "Then we should have been married in the morning and avoided all these machinations."

All she got for that were blank stares. The relatives were greatly enjoying themselves.

"They can have more children." Bisnonna Benedetta took Kellen's hand, turned it palm up and traced her fingers over the skin. "Look at her lines!"

"Show them to Bisnonna Debora," Leo said. "You know she reads palms better than anyone."

"Leo!" Annie turned her wheelchair toward him. "What is wrong with you?"

"What? Just because you don't believe doesn't mean I don't." Leo waved his hands at Kellen. "Go on. Let's see what Bisnonna Debora says."

"Verona won't like it," Annie warned, but she moved closer.

At age seventy-two, Bisnonna Debora wasn't the oldest here, not by a long shot, but when she was three she'd fallen ill of polio, leaving her with a twisted spine and a limp. Recently, as her overstrained breathing muscles had rebelled, she'd had to go on oxygen, and now it seemed as if her vitality was fading. But the life spark still glowed in her eyes and everyone in the family accorded her a special place of honor at the head of the table. Now, as Kellen presented her hands, she took them and smiled into the palms. "What a life! You're right-handed?"

Kellen nodded.

"So rare to see a palm marked like this. So many lines. Rare lines. Two marriages? One when you were very young." Her brown eyes sharpened. "It ended in flame and horror."

"Yes." Cynical Kellen supposed Bisnonna Debora might have heard that story from Max or Verona.

"I am sorry. But here's our Max." Bisnonna Debora pointed at the side of Kellen's hand. "Such a good solid dependable line, like Max himself."

Kellen found herself nodding along with everyone else.

"Here is Rae. What a healthy happy girl. So smart. We adore her." Bisnonna Debora patted Kellen's palm. "Other children are here. Two more. Maybe…no, two more."

"Only two," Zio Salvatore said mournfully.

"Not everyone wants to have so many children they can't remember their names!" Zia Giorgia said.

"Shut up, woman!" Zio Salvatore gestured vigorously. "I

remember their names eventually. I start at the top and shout. Sooner or later I hit the right one."

More laughter and nodding heads.

Bisnonna Benedetta said, "Shhh! Bisnonna Debora is *seeing*."

A hush fell over the room.

"Seeing what?" Kellen asked, then realized they meant precognition. She didn't like that; she'd seen some scary examples overseas.

Bisnonna Debora smoothed Kellen's palm, smoothed it again, leaned her ear close as if to hear it speak, ran her finger from Kellen's wrist to her middle finger. "War in your past. Strife. Struggle and mistakes. Still. You aren't whole in yourself. Divided into two. And this—" she tapped the line under Kellen's thumb "—this is—" She caught her breath, looked around, looked down and lied. Everyone knew it, especially Kellen. "This is good luck. It's good luck. You have good luck and happiness in your future. I see it. A sleep, a rest and a new dawn."

The back porch door slammed. Verona walked into the kitchen, took in the scene with one glance and spoke Italian, fast and angry. The older people jumped guiltily and cleared their throats and smiled with as much false gaiety as Kellen had ever witnessed.

Bisnonna Debora listened without expression, then traced a cross on Kellen's palm and kissed the spot where the lines intersected. In a low voice, she said, "God has graced you so far. He will not abandon you now."

"Thank you, Bisnonna Debora." Kellen cupped Bisnonna Debora's hand in both her own. "We'll trust in Him."

Verona grabbed Kellen's wrist and pulled her away. "The bride needs to put on her wedding dress. It's time! The makeup! The hair. You know!"

The relatives clucked and shooed at them, and when Verona and Kellen had exited the house, they burst into loud voluble exclamations of…something. Protest or horror, Kellen didn't know which.

"Bisnonna Debora is a lovely person, no? But old. All of the family from the Old Country is superstitious." Verona dismissed superstition with a wave of her hand.

"And Leo."

"That man!"

"I like him." They were headed toward the large three-story building that housed the tasting room, the wine cellars and the bed-and-breakfast.

"I do, too. But to encourage their silliness. We give the old relatives respect, of course. It's kind of them to come so far for Max's wedding, and yours. But the belief in the evil eye and the palm reading—that's ignorant Italian peasant. Not that the family isn't peasant stock and proud of it, but *we* don't believe in the supernatural." Verona sounded as if she was trying to convince herself. "Right?"

"I don't fear what's to come." Kellen knew what Bisnonna Debora had seen—and lied about. "It's been waiting for me for a long time."

"What do you mean?"

No reason to worry Verona. "The wedding. Max has been waiting for me for a long time."

A smile broke across Verona's face. "He has." She patted Kellen's hand. "He has."

They went in the side entry to avoid the tasting room.

"You're in a small suite now." Verona led her up the stairs. "We intended to put you in the wedding suite, as would be fitting, but at the last minute, Aurora Di Luca brought her whole family, children and grandchildren and third husband, after RSVP'ing for only her and her oldest daughter, and we had to put them *somewhere*. If she wasn't providing all the fruit for the wedding from her own orchard, I would…would…"

"That's fine. With so many long-distance relatives and guests, I'm happy not to be in a closet," Kellen assured her.

"We put the relatives we don't like in the closets."

Kellen looked at Verona. Was she kidding? Maybe...

On the second-story landing, they walked right into Rae—and Nils Brooks.

"My God, you made it!" Kellen couldn't believe he was here.

He held out his arms, then backed away. "You're not going to hit me again, are you?"

She remembered how she had sucker punched him up at Zone's, and laughed. It was a good memory. "I don't know why, but I'm glad to see you."

He opened his arms.

They hugged each other.

"He's here, and he brought the goddess!" Rae was in full Di Luca loud mode.

"Shhh." Nils grinned at her. "We're supposed to be quiet, remember?"

Rae whispered loud enough to wake the dead, "Daddy's going to show Mr. Brooks a secret place to hide her where no one can see her." She patted the bulging backpack slung over Nils's shoulder.

"That's great, Rae. As long as I don't have to carry her up another mountain." On that thought, Kellen grabbed Nils's shoulder. "I don't, do I?"

"No. No way." He put his hand on his heart to indicate truthfulness. "I brought the goddess for Rae before delivering her to Portland."

The hand on the heart thing made Kellen remember why she didn't trust him. For all his good looks and smarts, he was a user, and she wondered what he was up to now.

She found out fast enough.

"Are you sure you want to marry Max Di Luca?" Nils stepped

close to Kellen and looked deep in her eyes. "You and I would be good together. We could fix the problems of the world."

"Sir, I cannot believe you have the guts to show up on my son's wedding day and try to take his bride." In one moment, Verona became the scary female no one dared offend.

"I can't, either, Grandma. *I'll* sucker punch him!" Rae slammed her fist into his groin.

52

Groin, groin, groin, groin. As Nils collapsed, the memory of Rae's piping voice echoed in Kellen's mind. "Honey, you shouldn't—"

"That's my girl." Verona patted Rae's head.

"You're sending her mixed messages," Kellen said in exasperation.

"We'll have to deal with that later." Verona stood over his writhing body. "Kellen, your room is 345. Take Rae and go on up."

Kellen took Rae's hand and headed up to the third floor, and as they climbed, they heard Verona scolding in the kind of low-pitched menacing voice that would have brought Nils low, if Rae hadn't already done that.

Halfway up, they came face-to-face with Max. "Hey," Kellen said, because today, with him, she was full of witty conversation.

"Hey." He was equally eloquent. "You, um, need to get ready soon."

"Headed up there now. Not too much longer..." They moved toward each other.

"Daddy, you are not supposed to see Mommy!" Rae flushed with indignation.

Max glanced at his daughter and seemed to realize she was there. "Did you hurt your hand?" he asked her.

"A little." Rae cradled her fist. "When you punch 'em in the *groin*, it's sort of soft. It doesn't hurt like the *sternum*."

"Who did you punch in the groin?" Max asked, then started to laugh. "Nils Brooks? You punched the fabulous fighter, Nils Brooks?"

"Like mother, like daughter," Kellen said.

"I'm torn between wild amusement and worry. Will he be able to perform his duties?" Max asked with a nod to Rae.

"I'm sure he's staggering to his feet as we speak," Kellen said.

"Probably. I'd hate to admit a seven-year-old had brought me low, especially one I was supposed to be guarding." He slid his arm around Kellen's waist and brought her close. "You are so fabulous."

Rae interrupted impatiently. "I *know* I am. Daddy, wait until you see my dress. I get to have stars on my sash and on my hair thingie!"

"That's great, honey. Does that make you happy?" He was half listening to Rae, half wanting to kiss Kellen.

Verona appeared behind them. "Max! I am at the end of my rope. You're not supposed to be seeing Kellen, much less speaking to her. It's bad luck."

"I thought you weren't superstitious," Kellen said.

Verona gave Kellen the kind of look that reminded Kellen she had been an elementary school teacher and must have put the fear of God into her students. "Go get your stupid treacherous friend and take that pagan godless head and put it somewhere no one will see it! Now!" She pointed down the stairs.

"Mom, remember what I told you. Nils Brooks is going to keep an eye on Rae, just to make sure she's okay today."

"Yes, yes. I don't know why you're worried, but he can stand guard if you want him to." Verona shook her finger at Max. "But he'd better remember to show respect to me and my family!"

"I'm sure between you and Rae, he knows that now." Keeping close to the wall, Max slid around them, but he and Kellen never broke their gazes.

Verona gave Kellen a push between the shoulder blades. "Up the stairs."

"Wait." Kellen stepped close to Max again. "Did you put that special package in my room?" Her stash of emergency weapons: her smallest pistol, her most discreet knife and the weapons Birdie had brought.

"In the safe in the closet. You know the code to open it."

"My usual code?"

He nodded and leaned in to kiss her.

Verona gripped Kellen's upper arm and yanked her away. "Come on! Let your friend Birdie dress you. I'll get Rae ready."

Kellen had quickly figured out her official part in the wedding was wear the dress, speak the words, smile. Everything else was part of the Di Luca family steamroller. "You can bring Rae to my room to dress."

"Absolutely not!" Verona was still angry about Nils putting the moves on her. Or Max seeing her. Or...whatever. "My mother always told me the challenge to getting a child ready was whether to dress yourself first, then dress them and ruin your outfit in the process, or dress them first, then dress yourself and discover while you were busy they had made a mess of themselves."

Kellen glanced down at Rae, who was looking up at her. "Which of us do you think will make ourselves a mess, Rae or me?"

"I never know. You are both trouble."

Verona led Kellen up the stairs to the third floor. "Your room is here." She indicated door 345, then pointed at the far end of the corridor. "Rae will go to room 323 and wait for me there. Or she had better."

"Yes, Grandma." Rae scurried down the hall.

Kellen went back to the stairwell and yelled, "Nils will be hanging around out here, too, to keep an extra eye on Rae."

A groan from below answered her and, "I'm on my feet now."

"What an awful man! I don't know why we need him. I'll dress Rae and meet you at this spot—" Verona pointed at the flowered carpet at her feet "—in forty minutes. We'll go down to the tasting room, out the door and down the aisle at exactly six o'clock. Then you will be married."

"Yes, ma'am." Kellen risked a grin. "I'm looking forward to that."

"As am I. Why do I think something will go wrong?" Verona flung open the door to Kellen's suite and gestured her inside. If Verona knew about the weapons in the safe, and the reason for them, her current worry would escalate to a frenzy. Better that Kellen keep that information to herself.

She reached for her best diplomacy. "Max wants Nils to make sure Rae doesn't disappear again, so let's cooperate, okay?"

Reminded of all that had occurred the last time Rae disappeared, Verona took a forbearing breath and nodded.

Birdie was waiting, clothed in her bridesmaid's dress, dark eyes shining with joy and excitement. She gestured at the clothes spread out on the bed. "I never thought to see this day, Captain."

"No. But then I never expected to discover I have a seven-year-old, either." They both laughed, Kellen put her forehead against Birdie's, and they smiled at each other, two women who had survived war, survived grief and loss and now had found joy in the changes life had brought them.

"Anyone tried to kill you today?" Birdie had been thoroughly briefed on her role as bridesmaid and bodyguard, and intended to take both duties seriously.

"Not yet."

Birdie pushed Kellen away. "Good. With everything else we've got to do, we don't have time for any merry mayhem. We've got to get you dressed because your mother-in-law has given me strict instructions about the schedule and where you have to be when."

"I got that, too." Kellen headed into the bathroom. "Let me shower. Then you can shove me into all that underwear." She glanced at the bed and halted. "Tell me that's not a corset!"

Birdie put on her cockney accent. "Can't do that, luv. Zio Federico gave me explicit instructions on how to lace you in."

"I am not going to let you lace me in."

"I don't think he realizes how slender you are."

Kellen took another step and stopped again. "*Pantyhose?* Are those *pantyhose*?"

Birdie gave her a shove. "Go on, take your shower and be glad we don't have to contend with a hairdresser and makeup artist."

"I refused!"

"So I heard. Go on."

Kellen hadn't been in the Army for six years without learning how to take an efficiency shower. She was in and out in less than five minutes, shampooed and every inch of her skin scrubbed. She knew how to do efficiency hair, too: spray with texturizer, which she figured was a fancy term for hair spray, blow-dry, fluff and spray again. Makeup took a little longer than normal; she was great with foundation, concealer, blush, but add eyeliner and exotic eye shadows, and by the time she was done, Birdie was banging on the door shouting, "Come on! Come on! Come on!"

Kellen slipped into her lacy white panties and push-up bra—Max was going to greatly enjoy removing them, and she was going to enjoy his enjoyment—wrapped a towel around herself, jerked open the door and stepped out of the bathroom. "They can't start without me."

Birdie paused, her fist raised, ready for the next door-knocking. "I forgot. You clean up well."

"Thank you." Kellen thought she'd managed to make herself look good, and with only one terrible mascara blunder. "Is the hair okay?"

Birdie was suddenly all business. "We'll worry about that after we get you into that dress. With that corset and those petticoats, it ain't gonna be easy."

Birdie wasn't kidding.

The pantyhose had to go on first, then the corset, then the deceptively simple dress—heavy crepe with a formfitting bodice, natural waist wrapped by a fabric belt, and full skirt—which created its shape with boning and three weighty petticoats. The skirt had pockets hidden in the side seams, deep pockets for Kellen to hide her phone, her tissues, her lipstick. The final touch was the elastic lace garter that wrapped around Kellen's thigh so tightly she complained it was cutting off the circulation to her foot.

"Wait until you put on these shoes. You won't even notice the garter." Birdie put the stiletto heels on the floor and Kellen pushed her left foot into one.

"Damn Zio Federico. I wasn't going to wear them, then during that last fitting, he laid it on with the flattery, saying I was absolutely right about what I should wear, he agreed that I didn't need an expert to do my makeup because I'm beautiful enough without it, that my hair was perfect as it is and indicated to the discerning man that a tigress lived within my soul…" She took a breath, put her weight on the foot with the shoe, lifted herself and slid the right foot in. "He said that I had a great sense of personal style, that I was the most beautiful bride he'd ever dressed…"

"Are you saying Zio Federico flattered you into wearing heels?" Birdie laughed hard enough that Kellen was disgusted with herself.

"Yes." The pointed toes pinched and the heels threw her forward until she figured out how to lean her shoulders back and her hips forward. Her whole body was a counterbalance obeying the command of those damned heels. "All Italian women wear these. They climb mountains in them. What I want to know is how?"

"I don't know. *I'm* not wearing them. *I* didn't fall for the flattery."

Slowly, painfully, Kellen stepped toward the full-length mirror.

"But looking at you, I'm not so sure I made the right decision." Birdie adjusted Kellen's skirt.

Kellen gazed into the mirror. The movement of the crepe was fluid, flowing, rippling into a short train that looked like a pale silk stream. Zio Federico's cap sleeves and her own sculpted arms and shoulders made her appear… "Wow. I look like one of Rae's dolls with all the princess clothes on."

Birdie grinned. "You do."

"Like ThunderFlash."

Birdie smiled affectionately. "That, too."

Kellen noticed Birdie standing beside her, tall, thin and uniquely beautiful. "You're pretty fine yourself."

"Thank you. Zio Federico told me in Italy, with my facial structure, I could be a model."

Kellen scrutinized her friend. "You really could. Carson knows it, too."

Birdie waggled her head. "Carson wants to marry me."

"Will you?"

"No. I don't know. Maybe. He's a lot older, he's been married three times, I was widowed less than a year ago. We've got a good relationship as it is."

"All good reasons to put the brakes on." Kellen played the wise adviser.

"But sometimes when he looks at me…" Birdie pressed her hand to her chest. "I can hardly breathe for the joy of being with him."

"I know. I know what you mean. Max makes me feel as if…"

"As if you were in love?"

Together they laughed and hugged. They had faced battle, treachery, trucks that wouldn't start and ammunitions that blew too soon, death and joy. Through it all, their friendship had endured and grown.

The closer Kellen got to the wedding, the more her heart tugged and tore at the thought of having a daughter, a family, a home. The knowledge that someone had tried to kill her weighed on her more and more, and not for noble reasons. Not because Max might be hurt, or Rae or Verona, but because Kellen wanted time with these people who had come to mean everything to her. She wanted to be where they were, love them with all the fervency of someone who had died and was now coming back to life. She wanted that for herself...and in every way, that seemed impossible.

"Don't look so sad," Birdie said.

"I'm not. I'm just—"

At a knock, they separated.

"Is it time?" Kellen asked.

Birdie looked at the clock. "Not quite." She walked toward the door.

"It's probably Max again," Kellen said. "He was not happy about the can't-see-the-bride rule."

Before Birdie got there, the door slammed opened. Verona stormed in and waved a crumpled paper at Kellen. "Your child is pushing my buttons."

Kellen didn't grin, but she wanted to. "My child, huh?"

"I told her to stay in the room. I said I'd be back in ten minutes. I warned her not to do anything to mess up her dress."

"You left a seven-year-old alone in a hotel room dressed and ready for a wedding?" Birdie put her hand over her heart as if to contain its beating.

Verona swung on her. "Yes! Yes! I'm a bad grandmother! But Rae saw Max sneaking down the corridor toward your room.

She yelled at him and I chased him back to his room. The man has no respect for *tradition*." She emphasized the word *tradition*. Kellen's comment about superstition must have stung.

"Surely that didn't take ten minutes," Birdie said.

Exactly what Kellen had been thinking, and unease curled through her belly.

"You weren't really gone ten whole minutes?" Birdie prepared to abandon her role as bridesmaid and take up her duties as bodyguard.

"Maybe a little longer. It's his fault!" Verona continued to rant, "As soon as I turned my back, he was out again. I caught him and marched him right down to the kitchen where all the good old-fashioned Italian relatives were and told them to keep an eye on him!"

"So where's Rae?" Kellen demanded.

"I don't know!" Verona was clearly furious. "I got back to the room and she was nowhere to be found."

53

Birdie pulled out her phone. "I'm calling Temo and Adrian. Giving them a heads-up we have a possible abduction."

Kellen gestured slightly, wanting Birdie to be silent. Verona didn't know about the ongoing threats to Kellen, and Rae could so easily be led astray...by someone familiar. Someone she trusted. And that someone, whoever he was (or maybe she), could use Rae as bait to catch and kill Kellen.

What would happen to Rae then?

She would be killed, too, eliminated as a witness.

"Abduction?" Verona looked between Birdie and Kellen in alarm and then dismissal. "Don't be silly. Anyone who abducted Rae would bring her back fast enough."

"Temo's phone is going to voice mail." Birdie dialed again. "So's Adrian's. This cannot be good!"

"Where's Nils Brooks?" Kellen asked Verona.

"I don't know. He was hanging around outside our room, looking pained. I gave him a glass of water and a couple of aspirin. Now he's disappeared. Rae left a drawing on the desk." Verona snapped the paper at Kellen.

Kellen took it.

Birdie tapped at her phone. "Brooks isn't answering. They've all gone missing."

"I think it's supposed to tell us what she's doing. There's

something about Mommy and the head. But her handwriting is disgraceful. The schools simply don't emphasize penmanship anymore. I've worked with her, but she has no interest in learning how to… I love her. She's my granddaughter. But she needs two parents and—"

Maybe Kellen made a noise. Maybe Verona saw something in her face. Her tone changed from irritation to horror. *"What's wrong?"*

Kellen stared at the drawing, stared so hard her eyeballs hurt. Rae had drawn herself—LightningBug—going to find the Triple Goddess. Kellen knew it was the Triple Goddess because it was a floating head with yellow lightning bolts for eyes. A man walked behind her; the crude drawing gave no hint of his identity, but Rae had drawn a bulbous five-fingered hand on one side, and that hand held a black crook that was pointed at Rae.

A gun. Kellen was almost positive it was a pistol.

The crayon writing was sloppier than normal, as if she'd been in a hurry. Or scared. Brave little Rae…had she been scared?

"Rae didn't leave on her own," Kellen said. "Someone forced her to."

"But she wrote the note!" Verona didn't want to believe.

"That someone forced her to write the note." Kellen looked again at the note part of the drawing. "She wrote to me. 'Dear Mommy.' 'Hed.' 'Back.'"

Verona grabbed Kellen's arm. "What does that mean?"

"Something about the goddess head and—she has my back, and I have hers." Kellen headed toward the closet and the safe. She used her usual code, 3252.

The safe didn't open.

She took a breath, slowly punched in the number, 3,2,5,2.

The safe didn't open.

"No!" She slammed the flat of her hand on the safe. "Why? Why now?"

"Let me." Verona gave Kellen a gentle shove. "Do you know

how many guests forget their own code? Of course everyone of responsibility at the winery has to know how to open a safe." She typed in a special code.

The safe sang a little song, the door swung open— "There's nothing here," Verona said.

"No," Kellen said hoarsely. "No!" She swept the lighted interior with her arm, as if she was a magician with an empty hat. "Max was supposed to put my bag in here. My bag packed with arms and ammunition. Why didn't he? What happened?" Stricken, she looked at Verona. "Does Max know I changed rooms?"

Verona shook her head. "No, he doesn't know. The groom needs to stay far away from your bedroom. What do you mean, arms? What do you mean, ammunition?"

"He must have put my backpack in the bridal suite. How could such a thing happen?" Kellen answered herself, "Well, easily enough, with everything that's going on today. I should have carried my sidearm with me, but I was thinking of…corsets and ruffles and stiletto heels, and it never occurred to me—"

Verona got it at last. "There are guns in the suite with Aurora's grandchildren?" Her voice squeaked in horror.

"The safe is locked," Kellen assured her.

Verona dived for the phone and called the winery switchboard. She held out the phone as if begging Kellen to hear. "The line is busy. I have to leave a message!"

"Then leave the message in your sternest teacher voice," Kellen said. "You know whoever hears it will immediately do as you say."

"Right. They will." Kellen's trust in her abilities seemed to calm Verona, and Verona spoke into the phone, asking that someone be sent to the wedding suite to open the safe, secure the bag inside and bring it to room 345. She hung up and in despair said, "But today they're so busy. Who knows when they'll listen?"

"True. At the best, how quickly can they get it here?" Birdie asked.

"Not quickly enough. We need to move now." Kellen began to settle into that deadly calm before battle. "If whoever took Rae is already on the property—"

"What do you think has happened to my granddaughter?" Verona demanded in a high voice.

"She's been taken by someone who wants me dead."

"I'll call 9-1-1." Verona pulled her cell phone out of her belt pocket and waved it at Kellen.

Kellen clasped her wrist. "No."

Verona tried to jerk away. "Why?"

"I'll handle it." She indicated Birdie. "We'll handle it."

Birdie, tall, calm and intent, gowned beautifully and ready to fight.

Verona's gaze flicked between them both. "How can you—?"

"The police would make this a hostage situation. Rae might die. I didn't take Rae up that mountain and bring her back alive to lose her now. You can trust me." Kellen stared into Verona's eyes. "Do you trust me?"

Verona nodded.

"All right," Kellen said. *First crisis averted.*

Birdie said, "When I arrived, security seemed efficient."

"Yes. I thought it was. I think it is."

"But." Birdie nodded and went into the bathroom, searching for weapons.

Kellen turned to Verona. "Would you call Max?"

"He's in the kitchen! He won't hear!" Verona was all exclamation points and panic.

"Let's give him a try," Kellen said.

Verona started punching her fingers at her screen and cursing in a low voice.

Kellen retrieved her phone and called the security firm. "Mr. Parliman, this is Miss Adams. You're familiar with Max Di Luca's daughter, and mine? Yes. Rae." She nodded, although the man on the other end of the call couldn't see her. "Rae has been kidnapped by someone. A man, that's all I can tell you, probably white, possibly with brown hair." In the picture anyway. "Can you and your men make sure Rae and her kidnapper don't leave the property?"

"Of course. We have procedures in place for exactly this kind of emergency. We'll tighten the perimeter starting now." Mr. Parliman's response reassured Kellen, making her believe Rae would be found here, somewhere on the site.

Kellen's job was to make sure Rae was found alive.

"I need a weapon," Kellen told Mr. Parliman. "A pistol."

"Miss Adams, I can't loan you a pistol."

"Any kind of firearm. My daughter has been kidnapped, and I know whoever did this is a killer. I need to find her."

"I'm sorry, Miss Adams, I understand, but we cannot loan our weapons to anyone. I don't know what your weapons knowledge is—"

"I was in the military."

His voice was soothing and firm, as if she were nothing but a civilian, and a female civilian at that. "But if you accidentally hurt or killed someone while wielding one of our weapons—"

"I'm Captain Kellen Adams of the United States Army. I survived two campaigns in Afghanistan and a terrorist attack in Kuwait. If I hurt or killed someone with a weapon, it would not be an accident."

"Miss Adams, your hysteria proves my point."

For one moment, Kellen was blind with rage.

"Now." Parliman's patronizing tone eased. "I have with me two gentleman who claim—"

"Mr. Parliman, don't let Rae and this man get away, or you'll be nothing but a head on my wall." Done wasting time, Kellen hung up. Her child had been kidnapped. Kellen needed to go hunting. She required a firearm *now*, and he was worried about legalities.

Verona took Kellen's arm again. "I called Max on the house

phone and on his cell. No answer. He's in there with the Di Lucas. You know how loud they are." Verona was getting loud herself.

"All right. It's all right." Kellen grasped Verona's hand.

"Max isn't hurt, isn't he?" the anxious mother asked.

"Did you escort him back to the house and see him go into the kitchen?"

"I took him *into* the kitchen and delivered him into the hands of the relatives!"

"Then he's fine. He had no reason to believe we would have a problem." But Kellen needed help. "Are there any weapons available on this floor?"

"No," Verona said.

"In this building?"

"No! We try to keep weapons out of guests' hands, and that's the best way to do it."

"That makes sense." It did. Damn it.

"Why? Why?" Verona had grasped a measure of calm, and now let it slip beyond her grasp. "Why would anyone want to kill you? Why would they take Rae?"

"I don't know," Kellen said.

"Military assassin?" Birdie asked.

"That's my best guess."

Birdie used her phone to call again, and again said, "No answer from Temo and Adrian."

"Very bad." Kellen's teeth ached from clenching them.

"Is it that man?" Verona asked. "That Brooks? Did he take Rae?"

"No. Max doesn't like him, but with my approval, he trusted Rae to his care."

"Nils Brooks made a pass at you on your wedding day!"

Kellen thought of the writhing figure they had stepped over on the way up the stairs. "I didn't say he was a good man. I said he was dependable and a fighter, one of the best." And he was

MIA. Which only made Kellen more concerned about who had taken Rae.

"We've got to find him!" Verona was frantic. "And Max. We've got to get Max."

"Yes. But whoever this is—" she pointed at the man in Rae's drawing "—should be scared, but isn't. That child is not helpless."

Verona calmed, mesmerized by Kellen's certainty. "Wait. I know what to do. I'll call Arthur. He can handle anything!"

Kellen grabbed both Verona's wrists. "No. You must not involve Arthur or any of his people."

"You think Arthur Waldberg— No! No, he's so charming. So efficient. So polite and gentlemanly. He's not at all like all the other winery managers who are young and unruly and..." Verona's voice trailed off and her eyes got wide. She looked at Kellen. "You can let me go now. I'm never a fool twice."

Birdie came out of the bathroom with a rattail comb, a can of hair spray, and picked up the lighter by the fireplace.

Kellen continued, "Max and I talked about who we thought might be a problem." *Arthur and his people.* "Verona, go to the house, find Max and tell him what's happened. Tell him to bring the bag out of the gun safe in my room. The code is 3252."

Verona turned and fled, leaving the door open.

"This is pitiful." Birdie showed Kellen her stash. "If this guy's got a gun, we're going to die."

"We've got to find Nils. He brought the head. He'll have weaponry to protect it." Kellen thought through this logically. "Verona left Rae in the room alone. Nils was on guard duty. Rae begged to see the head. Nils wanted to make her happy, so they went to the Triple Goddess and were ambushed. That's how this guy and Rae got the head. It's the only thing that makes sense."

"So maybe Nils will have weapons, and maybe not, and maybe he's dead."

Kellen called his number. In the distance, they heard a ringing and walked out into the corridor. The door across from Rae's room was half-open, and she pushed it the rest of the way.

Nils Brooks lay sprawled on the floor. Blood oozed from the back of his head. "Not good!" Kellen knelt beside him and checked his pulse. "He's alive, but he'll have a headache."

Birdie flung herself at Nils's luggage. "You find Rae. I'll see what weapons I can collect."

Kellen ran to Rae's room. It was empty. "Who was he?" she muttered. "Where did he take her? Today, there aren't that many places where people...aren't. Wine cellar. Mixing shed. Storage." She stood in the middle of the tiny suite and looked around, trying to see anything out of place. Crayons were scattered across the desk. One naked princess doll had been tossed beside her pile of glittering clothes. Graham cracker crumbs festooned the rumpled comforter.

Rae's voice echoed in her head. *I've got stars on my sash and on my hair thingie.*

There. A star on the floor.

What a child she and Max had produced! She started out the door.

Birdie met her. "Whoever got Brooks cleaned him out of weapons." She offered the rattail comb.

"That's okay." Kellen picked two sharpened colored pencils off the floor. They weren't worth a damn at a distance, but they were deadly in close quarters.

Kellen and Birdie stalked down the corridor, two women gowned in wedding finery.

"Look." Kellen pointed to a star at the top of the stairs. "That's off Rae's sash."

"Hansel and Gretel. She knows her fairy tales." Birdie was impressed.

"She knows her superhero tales better." Kellen moved with deliberate haste down the stairs. "She's LightningBug, I'm ThunderFlash, and between us, we're going to make someone sorry."

54

Verona rushed into the kitchen where Max was pouring wine for the guests and laughing at wedding jokes, and signaled him to come with her.

"It looks as if I might be in trouble again." He put the bottle on the counter. "Help yourselves, and no fighting!"

He and Verona left on a wave of wine-fueled good humor, and as soon as they set foot onto the empty porch, his mother grabbed his sleeve. "Rae is missing!"

"Again?"

"Max, she's really missing. A man took her."

"What?" All his joy in the day fell away. "When?"

"A few minutes ago. Kellen said you knew who it was."

Of course. On his wedding day, like a fool, he had put all the safeguards in place and believed he could take a moment to be happy. He should have known. He should have learned from the past. He should have been more vigilant. "Kellen knows Rae is gone?"

"She sent me."

"Why didn't you call?" He should have never smiled. He should have been the man who understood there was no place for joy, not today, not ever.

"We tried. You didn't answer your phone!"

He pulled his phone out of his pocket. "My God." Four attempts to reach him.

"I was running here, and I kept calling you. I kept hoping you'd pick up."

His mother put him on a rack, broke his bones and his heart.

"Kellen's searching for Rae right now," Verona said. "She said for you to get the bag out of the gun safe in her closet. The code is—"

"I know what the code is. Stay here and keep watch." He sprinted around the house to avoid the mob in the kitchen, slipped in the utility room and up the stairs to Kellen's room and was back in less than three minutes, holding the bag and with a pistol tucked into his pocket. He found his mother telling Bisnonna Benedetta to return to the house. "Did you see anything?"

"No. The poor dear gets confused and— Max, why don't we tell everyone to search for Rae?"

"Because this person, whoever he is, is a killer. What good does it do us to find Rae and find her dead and the guests with her?"

Verona staggered. "A mass shooting."

Max caught her by the shoulders and steadied her. "Kellen said that I knew who had taken Rae?"

"It's Nils Brooks, right?"

"No. Not him. Do you have your scheduler on you?"

"Of course. Why? Who…?"

In a hard certain voice, Max asked, "Where's Arthur Waldberg supposed to be right now?"

"Arthur?" Verona paused in the act of retrieving her phone from her belt. "You think it's Arthur, too?"

"I'll find out fast enough. Where is he supposed to be?"

"Um." Verona pulled up the schedule on her phone. "He's in the wine cellar bringing up the first round of wines for the reception."

"Wouldn't the cellar be a good place to hide Rae?" Max went out the screen door. "I'll let you know as soon as I find something out."

"I'm coming, too." Verona ran after him.

He didn't wait. He touched the small revolver in his pocket, checked to make sure the safety was still latched. If he found Arthur fast enough, he'd stop the entire plot dead in its tracks. He came at the wine cellar from the back door, close to the shrubs where Kellen liked to lurk. He used his key, opened it quietly. When his mother would have gone in ahead of him, he held her back. He stepped into the cellar and listened.

From deep in the red wines, he heard the clink of bottles being moved. He pulled the revolver.

Verona nodded in approval.

Wow, Mom. With a gesture, he held her in place and moved silently toward the sound. He rounded the corner into the row where they kept the good cabernets and found Arthur removing the bottles, wiping them clean and placing them in a twelve-pack box. Even in this dusty place, Arthur looked immaculate, his suit and tie fitting for the festive occasion. Max pointed the pistol. "Arthur?"

Arthur glanced up and saw Max and the gun. His eyes widened, and he lifted his hands over his head. He still held one of the 2004 vintage bottles. "Sir?"

"Where's my daughter?"

"Rae?" Arthur looked from side to side. "Is she lost?"

"She's been kidnapped."

"Kidnapped?" Arthur faked confusion well. "Sir, I'd like to put the bottle down." He moved very slowly, slid the bottle into its slot and just as slowly stood straight. "I don't know where Rae is. Are you sure—?"

"Very sure. Tell me, Arthur, how much of a fool have I been? Who are you really?"

"I… I'm Arthur Waldberg…" But his gaze fell away.

Max moved with the speed of the linebacker he had been. He grabbed Arthur by the front of his starched white shirt, pulled him up on his toes and said, "Try again, asshole."

With impeccable dignity, Arthur said, "I am who I say I am, sir. You know, you've seen my efficiency in directing staff and I do know my wines."

"Where did you learn?"

Arthur took a big breath. "In prison."

"Arthur!" Verona had arrived, and she was appalled.

Max released him. *Now they were getting somewhere.*

"I'm sorry, Mrs. Di Luca. I didn't want to lie." Arthur straightened his shirt and tie. "In my job, I had previously worked alone, but while in prison, I found myself working in... The prison was in Texas. There are a lot of start-up wineries in Texas. Many of the wines are marginal, but as Mr. Di Luca has discovered, I have a good nose. The warden also discovered that, and by the time my term was over, I was in charge of the prison winery, creating wines and managing the staff."

"That's absurd," Max said.

"You'd think. But the warden made a fortune off Barbed Wire Wines." Arthur smiled almost imperceptibly. "I trust you've heard of them?"

Max had, and he stared at Arthur in disbelief.

"What were you in for?" Verona knew the right question to ask.

"I traveled around the world, masquerading as a gentleman of leisure, as an English lord, as old and noble Russian aristocracy. They welcomed me. They loved me." Arthur looked sideways at Verona. "I romanced the women and stole the family heirlooms. If I had chosen to steal from you, you would have never known who had taken your finest jewels. But I didn't. I wouldn't. I am now as honest as a man can be."

"That's not saying much," Verona said tartly.

"I collected a good staff at the prison winery, and I knew if

I could bring them together in one place, we could be the best. We could own the world of wines." Arthur's voice was clear and cold; he stated his past and his wishes for the future without knowing how Max and Verona would react. "I'd like to own the world of wines from this very estate."

Max glanced at his mother. She was not reacting well at all; her face was mottled with rage and…humiliation?

Arthur was a handsome man who looked every inch the nobleman. He spoke well, he managed people deftly…he had romanced Verona, and she now realized why he had directed his attentions at her. To get his way in all things concerning the winery—and it had worked.

"Which one of your people took Rae?" Verona asked. "Which one kidnaps children?"

"None of them."

"Is one of them a pedophile? Is one of them an assassin?" Verona was shaking with anxiety and anger.

Arthur tried to take her hand.

She slapped him away.

"No. I won't work with pedophiles or killers. I have counterfeiters, horse-race fixers, thieves like me. But I don't blindly trust everyone I've hired. I'm telling you, I watch them all. We meet nightly, we talk, I make clear how fast their lives will take a turn for the worse if they try anything illegal here. I'm not going to ruin my one chance to live a life doing what I love because someone wants to put a counterfeit Di Luca Wines label on an inferior bottle of wine." Arthur smiled with chilling menace.

"It doesn't matter what you think you know." Verona's voice rose. "Rae is gone."

"I hired one man with whom I haven't served time." Arthur pulled out his phone and punched in a number.

"The pianist," Verona said immediately. "Dan Matyasovitch."

"He was my latest hire." Arthur listened and hung up. "His phone is going to voice mail. I worried about him at first. He was friendly with Rita Grapplee. Then he pointed out her thefts and I got rid of her. That reassured me about him, but, sir—Rita Grapplee had no morals. She would do anything for money, and if she was working for Matyasovitch…" He punched another button. "Conference call with my people. They'll know where Matyasovitch is supposed to be, and they'll know where he was last seen. Mr. Di Luca, Mrs. Di Luca, we will find him, and Rae."

Verona's voice wavered. "But will we find them in time?"

55

Kellen and Birdie followed the star path down the back stairs and outside into blinding sunshine, startling heat and the heady smell of grapes from the crushing shed. Not surprisingly, Rae's stars headed away from the tents and the masses of people congregating for the wedding and toward the edge of the lawn, where the vines began their orderly march. There wasn't much out there, just the old red barn and the wine blending shed.

A gang of Di Luca teenagers were running across the lawn, laughing. Annabella and her cousins stopped and stared at Kellen and Birdie.

Kellen and Birdie waved vigorously. "Thirty minutes!" Kellen yelled and pointed at her arm, at the watch she wasn't wearing.

The kids waved back, smiled and went on their way, chattering about their early glimpse of the bride.

"Thirty minutes until the ceremony?" Birdie moaned. "We haven't got much time to wrap this up and get you married."

"The wedding is the least of our worries."

"Don't tell the three hundred waiting people."

"It might have been better if I wasn't the only woman dressed in bridal white." Kellen's stiletto heels sank into the grass, and she stopped, yanked them off and hooked them into her belt.

"You do stand out." Birdie lifted Kellen's train. "We've got to be careful of grass stains."

"Focus!" But Kellen understood Birdie. She was trying to keep things real, make sure Kellen was calm and prepped for battle. She pulled out her phone and kept walking. "I'll call Temo. You call Adrian. We need them."

One ring, and Temo picked up. Kellen heard a speed and volume of Spanish she had never imagined from the even-tempered Temo.

Birdie heard him, too, because she disconnected and stared.

"Stop, Temo. Stop!" Kellen spoke a little Spanish, but not like this. "What happened? Where are you?"

In painstaking English, Temo said, "This puke of a security man has detained Adrian and me. He has taken our weapons, and he is all puffed up with indignation and disbelief that you would bring in a couple of ringers, as he calls us. Like we are bells!"

"That dumb son of a bitch. Put him on." Kellen barely waited for Parliman to say hello. "You don't realize who you're messing with. Release my friends at once."

Her tone must have penetrated Mr. Parliman's thick skull, for he said loftily, "This is most irregular. I will speak with Mr. Waldberg and Mr. Di Luca about you. I was told these two criminals were carrying firearms by that man who—"

Kellen heard a thump. Abruptly, Mr. Parliman stopped speaking.

Somewhere near, a man shouted.

Another thump.

Temo picked up his phone and spoke to Kellen in a cold clear voice. "Two dumbass security men down. We'll retrieve our weapons and be there ASAP."

"Come to the edge of the property," Kellen instructed and hung up. She turned off the sound and put the phone on vibrate.

As they passed under one of the massive cherry trees, they heard a worried old voice call, "Kellen, *il mio cara*, you're not running away from Max again, are you?"

It was Bisnonna Debora, leaning against the trunk, and Kellen whirled to face her. "No. I won't do that."

"Marry him today," she said. "It won't be as bad as you fear."

Kellen believed her. But…she looked around. No one was near. "Bisnonna, what are you doing here so far away from everyone?"

"I was looking for the restroom." She dabbed at the sweat on her cheek, and her hands were shaking. "One should always go before a wedding. But it's very far and I'm afraid I'm confused."

"There's no one to take charge of her," Birdie said in a low voice.

The kids had disappeared, probably doing exactly what Bisnonna wanted to do—visit the restroom before the wedding ceremony began.

"We can't call security to come and get her," Kellen said.

Bisnonna Debora moaned and slid down the tree trunk.

Birdie caught her arm.

"Would you take her…?" Kellen asked.

"Okay." She slid her arm around Bisnonna Debora's waist. "We don't trust any of the staff now?"

"I don't know. Anyone Arthur hired—"

Birdie fumbled for her phone. "I'll call Carson. He'll meet me and take her."

"Perfect."

"We can do this. We'll get Bisnonna Debora cared for, and we'll be back as quickly as we can." Which was as quickly as Bisnonna Debora could walk. "As soon as you know your destination, let me know!"

"I will." Kellen moved on, moving quickly, holding her skirts off the grass, watching ahead of her, following the star path—which disappeared halfway between the barn and the wine blending shed. "No!"

Rae must have run out of stars. Kellen looked between the two buildings.

The barn was too open, with too many ways to get in. But the shed had one way in, the door.

The shed it was.

The door should be locked, but a pick set could open it. All the windows were up at the second-story roofline, a long line of old-fashioned warehouse-type awning windows. In there, a kidnapper could contain Rae and pick Kellen off as she breached the door—Kellen, and whoever came in with her.

Obviously, she wasn't going in the front door. She had to get to one of the windows. The cherry fruit pickers were finished for the summer, so no ladders were available, but there was a lean-to built onto the shed, a place to store lawn mowers and, oh gee, clippers. Kellen smiled. Nice shiny long sharp clippers, much better for defense than colored pencils.

When she tried the door to the lean-to, it creaked open into a shadowy interior. Inside, gardening equipment was neatly arranged on hooks around the walls, and the pink handles on the hand tools made Kellen think this was Verona's domain. So many of these tools meant to pierce and turn the earth qualified as weapons; Kellen chose a thin pointy set of pruning shears, light and easy to carry. She smiled at the eight-foot ladder; it would get her onto the lean-to roof and from there, up to the windows.

Climbing a ladder in petticoats and pantyhose was a special hell reserved for, well, her, but she did a good job of it. Dragging the ladder up onto the lean-to roof while trying to maintain silence made her strain and puff—whoever had invented corsets with their cursed plastic stays should be damned—and Kellen was glad that none of the windows were open. Of course, that might present a problem all its own…

She placed the ladder on the lean-to roof, leaned it against the shed's wall and wedged it into place with her colored pencils. With her heels tucked in her belt and the clippers in one hand, she got to the top of the ladder, to the last step that warned, "Danger! Do not step on me!" And she stepped on it. That got her chest height to a window. She dug her fingernails under the bottom seal and tugged. The hinge moved; the glass shifted a reluctant inch.

Yes! Yes! Why lock a window up so high? Using a deliberate motion, she opened it as wide as it would go, stuck her head in and listened.

There. She could hear Rae's voice saying, "My mommy and daddy are going to come for me, and you're going to be *sorry*." She gave the word a loud, whiny emphasis.

Kellen loved it. Her little girl was alive and defiant.

She pulled out her phone and to Max and Birdie, she texted, Wine blending shed. Then she waited, wanting to tell them who they were facing. She had expected to hear Arthur's voice. But while this voice was familiar, it was definitely not Arthur.

A man spoke. "The only part I'm sorry about is—" He stopped in the middle of his sentence, as if he was trying not to be goaded.

Kellen froze.

Who was he?

No matter. Rae was alive, and it wasn't going to be easy, but Kellen could get herself inside.

She texted, Not Arthur, slid her phone back into her pocket, hung her pruning shears on the wall, one handle on either side and out of her way. She placed both her hands on the sill, and using all of her upper body strength, she raised herself to the full extension of her arms. Now. This was the tricky part. She maneuvered herself sideways, crooked one knee and never mind the damned heavy skirt, got her leg inside. After that, everything else was easy. The turn, the rotate, the slow drop onto the top of the giant oak wine cask…

It was like killer Olympic gymnastics, only in slow motion and with death as the punishment for failure.

Her toes touched, barely, and she lowered herself to stand flat-footed. She took a moment to balance herself on the sloped oak.

"What was that?" The man's voice echoed up to the high ceiling and around the bare metal walls.

Kellen held herself carefully still and released her grip on the window. The wood was rough; it snagged her hose.

"I didn't hear anything." Rae's voice was blasé, then rose with excitement. "Wait, I did, too. That rustling noise?"

The sound of Kellen's skirts.

"Yes."

"That's a *mouse*."

"A what?" He sounded horrified.

Big tough man, killer of women and children, scared of a mouse.

Rae sensed his weakness. "Maybe a lot of mice. Or a rat!"

"You little brat." Loathing filled his voice. His familiar, almost recognizable voice...

Kellen took the pruning shears in one hand, slid to her knees and crawled, first hand, one knee, then the other hand, other knee, to the front edge of the cask. Her voluminous skirt made every movement an ordeal. The silk rustled and whispered.

In extravagant Di Luca–voice volume, Rae said, "I like mice. And rats. My science teacher says rodents carry fleas and disease, like the Black Plague. All these people dying of pimples exploding all over their skin. Gross! Don't you think it's gross?"

Rae was making life difficult for the man, working on his nerves, and doing a good job of it, too, while she waited for her mommy to arrive and rescue her. She had learned so much on their trek through the mountains...or perhaps she had a knack for annoyance.

Kellen grinned. That was her kid.

When Kellen got to the front of the cask, she found herself at the middle aisle that cut through the blending shed, high over the long table where she and Max had talked and made love. Directly below was the tap and the wooden bucket placed to impress the tourists. Facing the door were two figures, a balding brown-haired man dressed in a white suit and white shoes with no socks—okay, that was weird—and her daughter in her too-ruffly gown with the purple accents, holding her plastic princess doll case. Pink, of course.

The Triple Goddess sat on the table, her eyes facing forward, facing backward…and facing up, watching Kellen, demanding action.

"I'm not afraid of mice. Are you?" Rae's voice was now innocent.

"No!" The man tightened his grip on Rae's arm.

"I bet you are," Rae said. "I bet if I dropped one in your lap, you'd run and scream like Martin."

Kellen loved her daughter so much.

"There are no mice!" But he turned to look behind him.

He had no goatee, no mustache, no pointy eyebrows. His dark glasses had disappeared.

But it didn't matter how much he had changed his appearance, Kellen should have recognized this man; she was staring into the face of her first husband, Gregory Lykke.

Gregory. He had cut her, humiliated her, broken her bones, taken the child he had conceived with her and killed it.

Poor baby. Never a moment of life, of breath, all chance taken from her from the man who should have loved her most.

Then the man on the floor turned back toward the door, and the illusion vanished.

Not Gregory. Similar in bone structure, eyes, lips, brows, sure. But with thinning hair and eyelids that sagged over cool brown eyes.

Not Gregory—then who? A Lykke relative, obviously. She'd never met any of the male relatives; Gregory had been too jealous to introduce her to another man, but she did remember the family talking about Daniel, a cousin they scorned as a parasite, a musician and…an actor.

An actor.

Kellen took her mental identification card labeled Dan Matyasovitch, tore it up and threw it away.

He held Rae's upper arm tightly, so tightly that Rae squirmed and tugged and said, "My mommy's coming!"

"I hope so. That's the plan. That's why I let you scatter your stars." Rae must have stared at him in horror, for he laughed. "Did you think I didn't know what you were doing? Stupid kid."

"I'm not stupid!"

"Yeah? Think about this. Your stars will bring your mommy, and then I'll shoot her." He showed Rae the Glock he held in his free hand. "I'll kill her."

"You're mean. You're weird. Why would you want to kill my mommy?"

Yes, why?

"Because I'm a Lykke."

That Kellen had figured out. She placed the pruning shears carefully, where they would not topple to the floor.

"A like?" Rae was truly confused. "Like on social media?"

"No. A *Lykke.* Part of your mommy's first husband's family."

Using the balance she'd developed from years of yoga, Kellen stood on the sloped oak surface of the giant cask, lifted one stockinged foot and slid the blue garter off her thigh.

"Gregory was my cousin. The Lykke family is a noble, wealthy family from New England, and everybody's dead except me...and her."

There it was. Kellen's mind clicked all the pieces into place.

With everybody dead, the Lykke family fortune hung out there, waiting to be claimed. Kellen was really Cecilia. Cecilia had been Gregory's wife...and was of course next in line for the inheritance.

Money. Of course. Dear cousin Daniel wanted to kill her to secure the fortune.

56

Kellen hadn't thought of the Lykke fortune and her claim on it. Why should she? In the nine years since she'd escaped Gregory, her life had been in turns despairing, terrifying, adventurous and laced with the kind of surprises that would shatter most people.

Yet the money…*my God*. When she married Gregory, it had been in the tens of millions. On his death, his sister Erin had taken up the reins of the industry; she had been a brilliant businessperson, and fully as crazy as her brother.

Kellen's mind clicked through the facts: Gregory had lived long enough to tell Erin that Cecilia still lived. Last winter, Erin had hunted her down, tried to kill her, and killed herself instead. Cousin Dan must have been thrilled to think he was the sole heir and the fortune was his, but Erin had left information letting him know that Cecilia lived. And true to the family's mad creed, he had come after her—and her daughter—intending murder. Not for vengeance, but because by now, the fortune must be worth…

Wowza. A lot.

Kellen wanted to jump on him and kick him into next week. Maybe she could have, if she wasn't wearing this wedding dress and all its petticoats and the corset and…

Damn Zio Federico. And praise him, too. Right now, these spike heels were the best throwing weapon in her arsenal.

First, she needed Daniel to face her. She stretched the garter between her hands like a giant lacy rubber band and shot.

The stupid thing didn't so much fly as wobble, catching unseen air currents and doing no more than ruffling Dan's thinning hair. He half turned to look behind.

Rae spotted her and shouted, "Mommy!"

Kellen pulled one spiked heel out of her belt and flung the stiletto heel as hard as she could.

It bumped Dan's chest with enough impact to make him exhale with an "oof!"

She threw the second heel.

He leaned forward, into the arc of the next heel, and the stiletto lived up to its name—it took a divot out of his cheek.

He let go of Rae and grabbed his face.

Blood dripped.

"You bitch," Daniel shouted.

Kellen heard the hint of a Boston accent. *He* had been the one pinching Rae's cheek and questioning her.

With the pruning shears in one hand, she slid down the curve of the barrel and dropped six feet to the cold concrete floor. Her feet slipped out from under her—damn slick silk hose!—and she landed in an ungraceful heap. Pain shot through her hip. She struggled to right herself and move into the fight.

He lifted his Glock and took aim, his brown eyes cold and intent.

Kellen was about to die, and her daughter would die with her.

Instead, her daughter—*her daughter*—yelled, "Watch this, Mommy!" and swung the pink princess doll case at the side of his knee.

Rae couldn't do any real damage. She didn't have the muscle mass. But she used all her strength.

He stumbled sideways.

The shot went wild.

In a stunning follow-up, Rae opened the case and flung five naked princess dolls under his feet.

He stepped on one, then another, off-balance, arms outstretched, weaving madly.

"Rae, run!" Kellen shouted.

Rae whacked him, a good princess-case blow to the groin—*groin, groin, groin, groin*—and took off toward the back, toward the barrels, where she could hide.

Kellen didn't take the time to stop and laugh. She laughed as she charged, pruning shears extended. She laughed as the points hit him in the belly right above the waistline.

Daniel screamed. Red stained his white suit jacket, but the material must have been patented for superheroes, for the shears bounced back and out of her hands. They clattered away on the concrete floor.

Daniel put his hand over the wound, lifted his palm and stared at the blood. He looked up, she gazed into his eyes and she saw his soul. She saw the evil cruelty that permeated the Lykke family. The differences she saw settled the debate of nature versus nurture; viciousness was bred into their bones and had corrupted their hearts.

Kellen whirled and ran back toward the oak cask, grabbed the wooden bucket and, when she turned back toward him, he was once again lifting the pistol in his bloody hand. She ran forward and swung the bucket by the handle, up and around in a wide circle. Discarded red wine blasted her, the floor, the walls. The heavy oak hit his wrist with a resounding thunk, not enough to crunch bones, but his hand flapped out and up, and he lost his grip on the pistol, it flew through the air and smacked the side of the stainless steel barrel.

Kellen ducked reflexively, fearing the unsecured gun would discharge.

But the Glock skidded away to hide under a cask.

There. She felt a bone-deep satisfaction. That made things a little more even.

He grabbed his wrist, staggered backward, stepped on another princess doll, did a clumsy dance to keep his balance. Then, before she could blink, he pulled a thin knife out of his sleeve.

The son of a bitch had come prepared to fight, and like Gregory, Daniel was tall and long-armed.

Damn men. They always had the unfair advantage, and took it, too.

He lunged at her, blade outstretched.

She retreated. The hose on her feet was beginning to shred. She had traction again. Thank God, because this gown dragged her down and the only way to fight this guy was—lifting her skirts high, she kicked at the hand holding the knife.

The weight of the gown slowed her.

Daniel anticipated the kick, moved aside and slashed.

She swung in a circle and stumbled. Agony slithered up her leg. Blood, sticky and warm, slithered down from the gash in her ankle. She gasped, unsure how badly she was hurt, unsure if she could stand.

"I've had to keep up my fighting skills to get parts," the actor told her, and lunged with the point of the knife.

He was right on target; Kellen thought she was dead, pierced through the heart by a knife wielded by the greedy pig who wore her dead husband's face.

The point of the knife stuck in the plastic stays of her corset. Stuck—and remained. Daniel couldn't jerk it loose.

His eyes bulged, disbelieving. He lost his grip on the hilt.

Kellen lifted her skirts again, ready to kick.

As she swung around, Daniel grabbed her train and spun her faster, farther, then jerked and pulled her feet out from under her.

She fell hard, hitting the smooth concrete with a slam that jarred her from jaw to knee. Pain brought tears to her eyes, but she bent her elbow, slammed it up and blocked him as he leaped on her.

He reached for her throat.

From out of nowhere, an empty blank wine bottle appeared, swung, slammed into the side of his head.

His eyes rolled back and he fell sideways, off Kellen and onto the floor.

Rae. Rae held the bottle in one hand—and the Glock in the other. "Mommy, here!" She offered the pistol.

Before Kellen could react, Dan came to life and lunged for it. He slapped Rae's face, fast and furious, and ripped the pistol out of her hand. He moved so quickly she couldn't react, this little girl who had never been deliberately hurt in her life. He turned the pistol on her, on Kellen's daughter, cocked it and—

Rae threw herself on the floor.

Kellen pulled the knife out of the corset and stabbed him in a swift upward motion between the ribs.

The point entered his heart. He jerked in surprise. He opened his mouth to speak.

And as he died, the pistol shot blasted and echoed, back and forth across the blending shed.

57

The world went still, motionless, cool, dim, blank, gray. The only sound was the ringing in Kellen's ears and the thunder of fear in her veins.

Rae. Did Daniel kill Rae?

"Mommy?" Rae's voice was tiny. Her hand groped for Kellen's shoulder. "Are you okay?"

The world resumed spinning.

The metal door to the shed slammed open, smacked the wall.

A crowd of people stood silhouetted against the sun. Max, Arthur Waldberg, Birdie and Verona…

Kellen yanked her hand off the hilt of the knife and shoved Dan's inert weight off her.

A moment of terrifying silence followed.

Rae flung herself at Kellen. "Mommy, you saved my life!"

Kellen wanted to laugh. Rae was so dramatic, making sure everyone understood exactly what had happened. At the same time…her little girl had almost died.

If she had, Kellen would have died, too, of heartbreak and guilt.

She hugged Rae, hugged her hard and burst into tears.

"Mommy!" Rae touched her cheeks. "Why are you crying?" The child didn't understand how close it had been.

Kellen cried harder.

Temo and Adrian came through the door at a run and skidded to a halt at the sight of a bride, a child, a corpse and an active messy fight scene. "Trust the captain to put the *ding* in *wedding*," Temo said aloud.

Arthur flung a canvas over Daniel's body.

Kellen looked up at Max, at Verona. "I never meant to kill someone in front of Rae!" The least of today's dramas, but the most immediate.

"He was a bad man. He hurt me!" Rae indignation radiated like heat from her little body. "He hit me!" She pointed at her bruised cheek.

Max knelt beside them and oh so carefully, pulled them into his arms. "Kellen, I left you alone to save Rae and fight off a killer. So leave off the blame!"

Still weeping, Kellen nodded.

"We're a family," Max said softly to Kellen and Rae. "We stand together."

Verona Di Luca came to kneel on the ground by Rae and cradle her.

Birdie knelt beside Kellen to hug and cry. In a moment, Temo and Adrian joined them. They were all here, together, her friends and her family. The groups melded and became one, crying, hugging, murmuring words of love and admiration. Somehow, Max, Kellen and Rae came together in the middle, and the emotions grew and swelled…

As they at last subsided, Arthur Waldberg clapped his hands. "If we are to salvage this wedding, we must do it now."

People straightened up, wiped their noses, laughed a little, exclaimed a little more.

Kellen stood and winced. That cut on her ankle was long and painful.

"If I may?" Arthur examined it. "This isn't deep. I can fix it."

"Are you a doctor now, too?" Verona asked tartly. "Or a seamstress?"

Arthur pulled a tube out of the inner pocket of his suit coat. "In prison, for those accidental slices with a blade, we used superglue."

"Good idea to carry it with you for emergencies." Birdie knelt beside Kellen and pulled the skin together while Arthur dabbed superglue on the wound.

"How do you know these things?" Verona wrung her hands.

"It will need real medical attention," Arthur said, "but this officially qualifies as an emergency."

"That's right." Kellen winced as they worked on her. "I'm not letting this little injury stop my wedding. Not after all this fuss!"

"But her pain. The possible infection!" Verona said.

"Mother, there are doctors among the guests," Max said. "We'll have her checked out as soon as we've completed the vows."

"What about—?" Verona pointed at the canvas covered body.

With an awesome calm, Arthur Waldberg said, "Don't worry. I'll take care of him."

"And of the Triple Goddess!" Rae said.

"And of the Triple Goddess. In the meantime, you are currently—" he checked his watch "—eight minutes and fifty-two seconds late for your wedding, and your guests will be getting restless. So if I may?" He offered his hand to Kellen.

In a daze, she took it. He pulled her to her feet—she was surprised to realize her knees were trembling—and led her to the sink. He turned on the water, held her hand under the faucet and used soap to wash it as if she was a child, incapable of taking care of herself.

He might have had reason—she hadn't noticed the blood that stained her skin and nails until it disappeared in a pink swirl down the drain.

He took a small clean white towel from the waiting pile, wet it and carefully wiped her face clean. "There's no saving your makeup," he explained. "No problem. You're beautiful without it. Still..." He looked around at the others, still immobile and staring. "Does anyone have lipstick?"

Birdie jumped as if stung. "I do! I've got lipstick! Zio Federico gave it to me with strict instructions I was to keep it on me to refresh Kellen's look." She pulled the tube out of her pocket and with a shaking hand, offered it to Arthur.

He took some on his fingertips and blotted it on Kellen's cheekbones, then skillfully blended it. "There. You don't look quite so white. A pale bride is always lovely, of course, but you had taken the aspect to stricken." He looked around. "Now you, Miss Rae."

"What am I thinking?" Verona stood, shooed Rae to her feet and over to the sink. "Come, Rae, we've got to clean you up. Quickly, now!"

The scene, which had been quiet and weighed with intense emotions, changed, became one of bustle and haste.

Verona scrubbed Rae's hands and face, except where Daniel had hit her. There the swelling had turned dark red and was starting to bruise, and the look on Verona's face boded ill for Daniel Lykke, should she ever meet him in the afterlife.

Kellen supposed she wouldn't; Verona wasn't going the same place Daniel had gone.

Arthur lifted Rae's chin and examined her face. "As soon as we get close to the ceremony, we'll get her a cold pack," he told Verona. "She'll be sore, but it will be gone in a week. You'll see."

Rae was far less concerned than the adults and asked, "Can I have lipstick on my cheeks?"

Using a light touch, Arthur accommodated her.

"And on my lips?" Rae asked.

Arthur fought a smile and took care of Rae.

Max splashed water on his face, straightened his cuffs, ran his fingers through his hair and muttered about running in the heat and smelling manly at his own wedding.

No one had a comb.

Arthur apologized for that. "I do have kits assembled for any bridal emergency, but sadly I didn't think to put one in the blending shed."

Birdie worked on Kellen's hair, then burst out, "The veil! The ring! I left everything in the room!"

In a soothing tone, Arthur said, "It's being handled as we speak. All will be waiting for us at the back of the white tent—where we must arrive as soon as possible."

"But first..." Max knelt in front of his daughter who had been wiped and tweaked by her grandmother. "You look lovely. No one would ever know you were a superhero."

"I'm LightningBug!"

"No one must ever know. No show-and-tell about this." He gestured at the covered corpse.

Rae didn't even bother to look at it. "No one would believe me anyway." She sounded annoyed about that.

"Superhero pinkie promise." Kellen held out her finger.

Rae wrapped her pinkie around Kellen's. "I promise."

Kellen smiled at Rae, at her daughter. The child was the best daughter ever, perfect, agreeable, kind, accepting, a fighter for good...

Kellen's consciousness faded, then she focused again. "We are one," she whispered.

"Are we ready?" Arthur opened the door, held it wide and made a shooing gesture.

Max picked up Rae and ran into the bright sunlight and toward the wedding canopy.

Kellen and Birdie followed. Temo and Adrian brought up the rear. Kellen glanced around to find Verona and saw her waiting while Arthur spoke to Mateo Courtemanche.

Mateo Courtemanche, who had been waiting outside for them. He looked quite unlike the pleasant young man who waited tables and sold wines and instead appeared narrow-eyed and coldly efficient. Apparently Arthur had sent for him to deal with the body. Mateo's résumé must include skills Kellen hadn't imagined.

But she wasn't going to worry about that. She had other, more pressing matters. Like getting married.

At the back of the tent where the wedding would take place, the side panels had been lowered to shield the wedding party from the waiting guests and to allow them to prepare in private.

Inside the canopy, Kellen could hear the guests buzzing with speculation.

Max put Rae on her feet. Arthur handed him a chemical cold pack, and Max pressed it to her cheek. "Are you going to be okay?"

"Sure!" Rae was remarkably unconcerned about her trauma and her bruise and intent on enjoying her role in the wedding.

Verona caught up with them. "Arthur's people found Takashi Tibodo."

"Takashi Tibodo!" Kellen hadn't realized anyone else had been victimized. "What happened to him?"

"When we realized who was really responsible for the kidnapping," Verona said, "Arthur had a conference call with his people. Takashi didn't answer his phone. Apparently, he had figured out Dan Matyasovitch was not what he claimed to be, so Dan knocked him unconscious and locked him in the supply closet behind the tasting room."

"Is Takashi going to be all right?" Birdie asked.

"He's apparently quite angry and insists he will be able to sing at the reception. He also says he can step into that dreadful man's place and handle the music direction."

That dreadful man being Daniel Lykke, Kellen surmised.

"Has somebody checked on Nils?" Kellen asked.

"Oh, yeah. Nils." Birdie mashed the antique veil on Kellen's head.

Verona stiffened and her expression became that of a stiff-necked schoolmarm. "He's alive, which is more than he deserves."

"Concussion?" Kellen asked.

"I really couldn't say," Verona answered. "One hopes."

Birdie stuck pins in the veil. "I hope these hold long enough to get you down the aisle. I'm a mechanic, not a hairdresser."

With smug assurance, Rae said, "None of this would have happened if I'd had a cell phone to call for help."

Something clicked in Kellen, some sense that this cell phone issue needed to be handled, and it needed to be handled now. She said, "That's true. I was thinking of getting you a puppy as a friend and protector. But if you'd rather have a cell phone..." She let the sentence trail off and rearranged two hairpins that were sticking right into her scalp.

"A puppy?" Rae froze. "I can have a puppy?"

"No, no, no." Kellen waved a dismissive hand. "You're going to get a cell phone."

"What kind of puppy?" Rae moved like a robot to stand in front of her mother.

"I thought we could go to the animal shelter and you could pick one out," Kellen said casually. "But a cell phone is a good idea, too."

Rae wet her lips. "I'd rather have a puppy for...for companionship and to take care of me."

"A cell phone is a better idea. A puppy is a lot of work." Kellen shook her head solemnly. "They have to be trained—"

"I can train her!"

"And fed and washed—"

"I can feed and wash!"

"And they're always wanting to be loved and petted and played with."

"I can love and pet and—" Rae stopped, and Kellen could almost see her mind working. "Wait a minute. I'm being manipulated."

The switch from eager little girl to smart almost adolescent was dizzying and carried a clear warning of the future. But Kellen told her the truth. "Yes, you are. Puppy or cell phone, those are your choices."

"Puppy!" Rae threw her arms in the air. "I get to have a puppy! I get a puppy!"

Verona watched her granddaughter jump up and down and chant, and said sourly, "The only person who is going to wash this dog's flea-bitten carcass is Grandma."

Kellen patted Verona's arm. "It rains a lot here and it's muddy. I'm sure I'll get my chances."

Max pulled Kellen close. "My mother would never even discuss a dog for Rae. How did you pull that off?"

"It's a good idea. A dog will protect Rae and alert us of danger, and as for your mother—before, she didn't realize there would ever come an occasion that Rae would need protection. Three weeks ago, it hadn't occurred to *us*!"

Max smiled at Kellen, smiled into her face as if she was the smartest, most beautiful woman in the world.

"Go on!" Verona gave him a push. "There's time for that later."

Max left, walking backward, still smiling at Kellen.

Verona yanked and tweaked Kellen's skirt. "I know you wanted purple and I resisted, but really. To go to these lengths to get purple on your white gown!"

"What?" Kellen glanced down.

Wine stains splattered her skirt in random patterns that started at the hem and faded as the material moved toward the waist. Here and there, a brown stain…blood. She craned her neck; her train looked as if it had been dragged through the wine—and in fact, it had. She laughed. "The bucket. I hit Daniel with the bucket and the wine sprayed everywhere!"

"I'm sure it was all a ploy to make sure you got your way."

Verona's mouth was pinched like a prune, as if she didn't want to laugh.

Kellen realized—Verona was trying to be funny. She wasn't good at it, but she was trying.

Then Verona frowned for real. "Why do you have a tear in your bodice?"

"That's where he stabbed her!" Rae said fiercely.

Verona grabbed Kellen's arm and held her up as if she would faint. "Are you hurt?"

"No." Not quite true—the knifepoint had not pierced her skin, but the violence of his attempt had left a sore spot and a bruise. "The bracing on the corset caught the point and I'm fine." Still, Kellen was vain enough to ask, "Does it look terrible? The wine and the tear and the wrinkles?"

Verona stepped back and scrutinized Kellen from head to toe. "Actually, it's oddly striking. It makes you look wild and untamed."

Birdie handed Kellen the bouquet. "You look beautiful." Her voice wavered with sentiment.

"Have you got the ring?" Verona asked Birdie.

Birdie patted her pocket.

Arthur arrived, not a hair out of place. "Are we ready?"

At Kellen's nod, he signaled Temo and Adrian, who escorted Verona to the front row. The music started, and Birdie walked down the aisle to the front where Max and his groomsman waited.

Arthur handed Rae and Kellen their bouquets of purple roses and asters with baby's breath and tendrils of ribbon.

Kellen took her daughter's hand.

Together they stepped through the entrance to face the guests, who stood on cue, then gaped as Kellen and Rae walked down the aisle together.

Rae smiled and greeted people as she walked.

Kellen saw no one except Max, still smiling, still watching her.

When asked who gave this woman, Birdie, Temo and Adrian answered, "We do."

Rae got the most laughs and the most tears when she announced, "And I give my daddy to my mommy!"

It was the perfect wedding, especially for the surprised winery guests who dropped in and discovered a celebration in progress.

No one stopped them or requested their invitations; Parliman Security had left in a huff.

58

For three hours, the music played, the food and wine arrived in waves and the guests grew louder and louder and more and more convivial. When Pearly Perry wheeled out the wedding cake, guests gasped and cooed.

The main edifice had been shaped and frosted to look like a three-foot-tall oak barrel. Frozen sugared grapes hung in bunches around the rim. A long slice from top to bottom displayed an ombre of colors from pale yellow to lavender to an intense, Syrah dark purple. All around the cake, purple or pale yellow cake filled crystal wineglasses; the frosting was contrasting buttercream.

Behind the scenes, Dr. Frownfelter and Dr. Brundage had worked on Kellen's ankle, approved Arthur's work, given her pain relief and an antibiotic and told her sternly not to indulge in any of the fine wines served at her wedding feast.

Kellen sighed and complied, circulating on Max's arm to visit the guest tables and thank them for their attendance. When they reached the table Annie and Leo were hosting, she collapsed into a chair and smiled at two of her favorite people in the world. Almost everyone here belonged to Max, but Annie and Leo—they belonged to her, too.

Verona joined them, looking flushed and out of breath. She had had a dance with Arthur.

"We're so excited, dear girl, to welcome you into the Di Luca family." Annie handed Kellen a small rectangular box. "This is for the two of you, if you wish to have it."

The box felt oddly heavy for its size and had been tied with a lush purple silk ribbon.

Kellen looked up at Max.

"Go ahead," he said. "Open it!"

She did, and inside was a giant old-fashioned iron key. "What does it open?" she asked.

"It's the original key to Yearning Sands Resort," Leo said.

Kellen shook her head. "I don't understand."

"It's for you and Max. We know how much you love Yearning Sands, and with my current lousy health, we have to retire." Annie was clearly disgusted with herself. "But I know my darling home will be in loving hands if you and Max take it over."

Kellen handed the box to Max. "But the winery—"

"Someone else in the family can take it over," Max assured her.

"Someone who can blend a good wine," Leo suggested.

Max glared at his uncle.

Leo cackled.

"Did you know about this?" Kellen asked Max.

"No, I didn't see this coming. But it does make sense, except for—" Max stopped short.

Kellen understood his train of thought, and he was right. She knew he was. Taking Annie's fragile hand, Kellen held it. "I would love to come to Yearning Sands and take it over as managers, but we can't. Rae is our first priority, and the school system in Cape Charade isn't good." She realized what she'd said and winced. When she decided to own motherhood, she went all the way.

Max got it, too, damn him, for he murmured, "The keys to a minivan are within your reach."

"Shut up," she said.

Verona leaned into the conversation. "But the resort is an ideal place to raise a child. Isn't it?"

"In the summer when there's no school, yes," Kellen agreed. "To be out there on the coast, running free... Yes. It would be good for Rae."

"I have a thought." Kellen's new mother-in-law looked bright-eyed and enthusiastic. "I was a grade school schoolteacher before I retired. I can move with you to Yearning Sands and home-school Rae."

Kellen felt faint, and not with joy. They were just married, and already Verona wanted to *live* with them? *Permanently?*

Verona pulled her chair close to Kellen, excluding Max, excluding Annie and Leo, and in a low voice, she said, "Look. I know we haven't gotten along. I didn't trust you. I didn't believe you. I didn't like that you...that you saw Rae and didn't instantly love her. But the way you did it was better. You got to know her, then you loved her."

"Yes. Yes, I did. We bonded." Kellen wanted to laugh as she remembered Rae's Monster MegaBond speech. But now was not the time.

Verona continued, "I've been with Rae since she was born. I love her, and she loves me. You're going to be working. It's a big resort. I can stay out of your way and still be close to Rae. And I am, if you'll excuse my confidence, a damned good schoolteacher."

Kellen took a breath. Everything Verona said about Rae was true; she loved her grandmother, Verona loved her, and most important, when Kellen had been unconscious and then missing, Verona had been there for Rae and Max every minute, and that could happen again. In fact, it might be necessary. "Then I think that's a great solution," she told Verona. "I think that's exactly, *exactly*, what we need to do."

"It won't work forever. Sooner or later Rae will need higher education, more than I can give her, and we'll have to move."

Verona had clearly decided she would be part of the household forever. "But she'll have the best educational foundation any child could ever have."

"She already has an amazing vocabulary." *Which sometimes isn't comforting.*

Verona smiled smugly. "She tests at the top of her class in every subject."

Kellen offered her hand. "Well, then. It's a deal."

Verona shook her hand, then pulled her into a fierce embrace. "In the Di Luca family, we hug."

Kellen stiffened, hesitated, then relaxed and hugged her in return.

Verona pushed her chair back, whisked tears from the corners of her eyes, looked around and announced, "It's settled, then. We're moving to Yearning Sands."

Annie and Leo and the other guests at the table, Di Lucas and otherwise, clapped in appreciation and congratulations.

Max slid the key into his inner suit pocket and helped Kellen to her feet. "Although this is, of course, our favorite table, we should visit our other guests."

They exchanged cheek kisses with all the relatives, and as they moved on, he said, "That was a good thing you did."

"Your mother's right. It is the best solution."

"You didn't have to go for it." He turned Kellen to face him. "You do know you didn't, right?"

"I know. I just… The resort *will* be a great place to raise Rae, and I'll have a job, and you'll have a job."

"No doubt. We'll be working all the time." He sounded satisfied.

"If she can get a quality education there—and I know your mother will see to it—then we have everything we need."

"Except time." The bitter words slipped from him.

"Then we shouldn't waste what we've got." She joined their

hands, leaned her body close, matched their lips and whispered, "Shall we leave on our honeymoon?"

Someone whistled in appreciation.

"Right now?" Max's lips moved against hers. "We haven't cut the cake."

"To *hell* with the cake."

"I knew it from the first moment I met you. You are the woman of my dreams." He kissed her, long and slow, ready to take up his husbandly duties the moment they were alone.

Max didn't realize that Daniel Lykke hadn't lived to complete his dream of taking control of Lykke Industries, but he had fulfilled his desire to harm her; he had slammed her to the floor one too many times. Something was wrong with her. She suspected he had moved the bullet in her brain, for the edges of reality had become fuzzy and gray, like a camera with Vaseline rubbed around the edge of the lens.

But how did she tell Max that, on this day when he had married her and their daughter was safe from threat?

"Look!" he said. "The dead arises!"

At the fringe of the crowd, Nils Brooks stood, head bandaged, eyes bloodshot, looking as if...as if he'd been racked and beaten all in one day.

"He's not having a good time," Kellen observed.

"I know!" Max sounded fierce. "He deserves every ache and pain. I trusted him to guard Rae, and he screwed up."

"He really is a good fighter." She watched as one of the tiny Di Luca boys toddled over and embraced Nils's leg with sticky hands. Nils picked up the child and grinned at him, then relinquished him to his laughing mother. "He likes kids, Rae bosses him around, and he took his eye off the ball."

"You're too forgiving."

Kellen met Nils's gaze.

For the first time since she'd known him, he looked sorry and embarrassed. He dipped his head in apology.

"I am too forgiving. But I keep thinking... I will never let him live this down."

"I'll never let him near you again."

"Check. No more jobs for Nils Brooks."

"We should probably have our first dance before we leave. For Rae's sake." Max knew what his little daughter liked, and he knew, too, she would miss them while they were vacationing in Italy.

"That sounds like a lovely plan," Kellen agreed.

In deference to her injuries, Max and Kellen's first dance was a slow waltz, a wonderful spinning tribute to love that made the guests sigh with pleasure.

Then Zio Federico stepped onto the floor with Rae, and the old man and the child danced in circles around them. Max waved his arm at the family and friends who were watching, and soon dozens of couples waltzed in a burst of rhythmic joy.

Carson and Birdie.

Verona and Arthur.

Temo and Adrian.

Max said, "Zio Federico approves of the splatters on your dress. He wants to know how you created it."

"What did you tell him?'

"That it was a spontaneous demonstration of creative sophistication."

She chuckled. "You're a genius."

"I know. I've got you."

That fuzziness advanced, the edges of her vision diminished. She slowed. "I've begun to think that's not such a smart thing."

Max's smile faded. His face became watchful. "Why?"

Kellen had to tell him. Warn him. She looked around, avoiding his gaze, and— Rae had disappeared from the dance floor.

"Where is she?" Kellen searched the wedding party.

"Who?"

"Rae. Where is—?" Kellen caught her breath.

There, at the edge of the dance floor, she saw them. Rae, her charming trusting lovely daughter, smiling and talking to… to a…

FEMALE, WHITE, TANNED, HEALTHY, 5'6", 130 LBS. AGGRESSIVELY PHYSICALLY FIT. DARK HAIR. BRILLIANT BLUE EYES.

She looks older than the last time I saw her…

Mara Philippi, smuggler and serial killer, the woman who had almost murdered Kellen. The woman Max and Kellen had captured and sent to prison.

In slow motion, Mara knelt before Rae and listened to Rae's enthusiastic babble, then turned her head and smiled directly at Kellen, taunting her with her helplessness.

"She's here." Kellen stopped dancing and dug her fingernails into Max's arm.

"Who's here?" He looked around, alarmed.

"Mara Philippi. She's here. She's with Rae. She has Rae." The gray mist moved like an ocean fog over Kellen's mind, invincible, blinding her, binding her.

"Where?" He held Kellen up by her elbows and helped her circle in slow motion.

"There." Kellen tried to point, but when she stared at the place where Mara Philippi and Rae had been, they were gone. "Rae. Where is Rae?"

"I can see her. She's with my mother and Arthur, talking and dancing. She's safe, Kellen, she's safe."

Kellen looked up into his eyes. "No. I wasn't hallucinating, Max. Mara Philippi is back, and she wants to kill everything I love. Save Rae. Take care of yourself. I love you forever." She collapsed in his arms.

I have three confessions:

1. My name is Max Di Luca.

2. I'm a father and a husband, and I'll do what I must to save my daughter and my wife from harm.

3. I will kill to protect my family. Make no mistake about that.

★ ★ ★ ★ ★

Find out Kellen's fate in
the next book of Christina Dodd's
pulse-pounding Cape Charade series,
Strangers She Knows,
coming soon from HQN Books.

Acknowledgments

Nothing was as important to the writing of *What Doesn't Kill Her* as my daughters, Shannon and Arwen, who taught their amazed mommy how smart, how annoying and how funny little girls can be. The terror a parent feels about the safety of their children is universal; translating that terror and the incredible bond that grows between parent and child was a challenge I hope I captured in some small part, and communicated to my dear reader. Thanks, my dear girls, for making me a better person.

When it comes to positioning the books, sales navigates the increasingly challenging and constantly changing platforms that are book placement. In the case of *What Doesn't Kill Her,* the HQN Books sales team was also the guiding light behind the name change and the cover redesign. Thank you so much, Fritz Servatius and the team. I'm so excited about the changes.

To Allison Carroll—so many brilliants insights and ideas wrapped up as horrible queries! Keep up the good work!

Thank you to the whole trade and hardcover art team, led by Erin Craig, and to Sean Kapitain for the *What Doesn't Kill Her* cover and the formatting of Kellen's mental Rolodex files.

Thanks to Lisa Wray, manager, publicity and events. Despite bad weather and broken planes, what an entertaining publishing year we created! I look forward to working with you on many more fabulous and unique publishing events.

Thank you to Craig Swinwood, publisher and CEO, Loriana Sacilotto, executive vice president, and to Susan Swinwood, HQN editorial director, for the opportunities you've given the Cape Charade series.

Dianne Moggy, vice president of editorial, thank you. After so many years of anticipation, working with the HQN team and seeing the care with which you publish is a privilege. You used the word "stellar," about *What Doesn't Kill Her*; what a treasure for me to enjoy!

Mount Laurel Library
100 Walt Whitman Avenue
Mount Laurel, NJ 08054-9539
856-234-7319
www.mountlaurellibrary.org